MARLYN SPAAIJ

SISTERS OF THE MIST

FLYING EYE BOOKS

LONDON – LOS ANGELES

For my sisters Meike, Tessa, and Carlijn

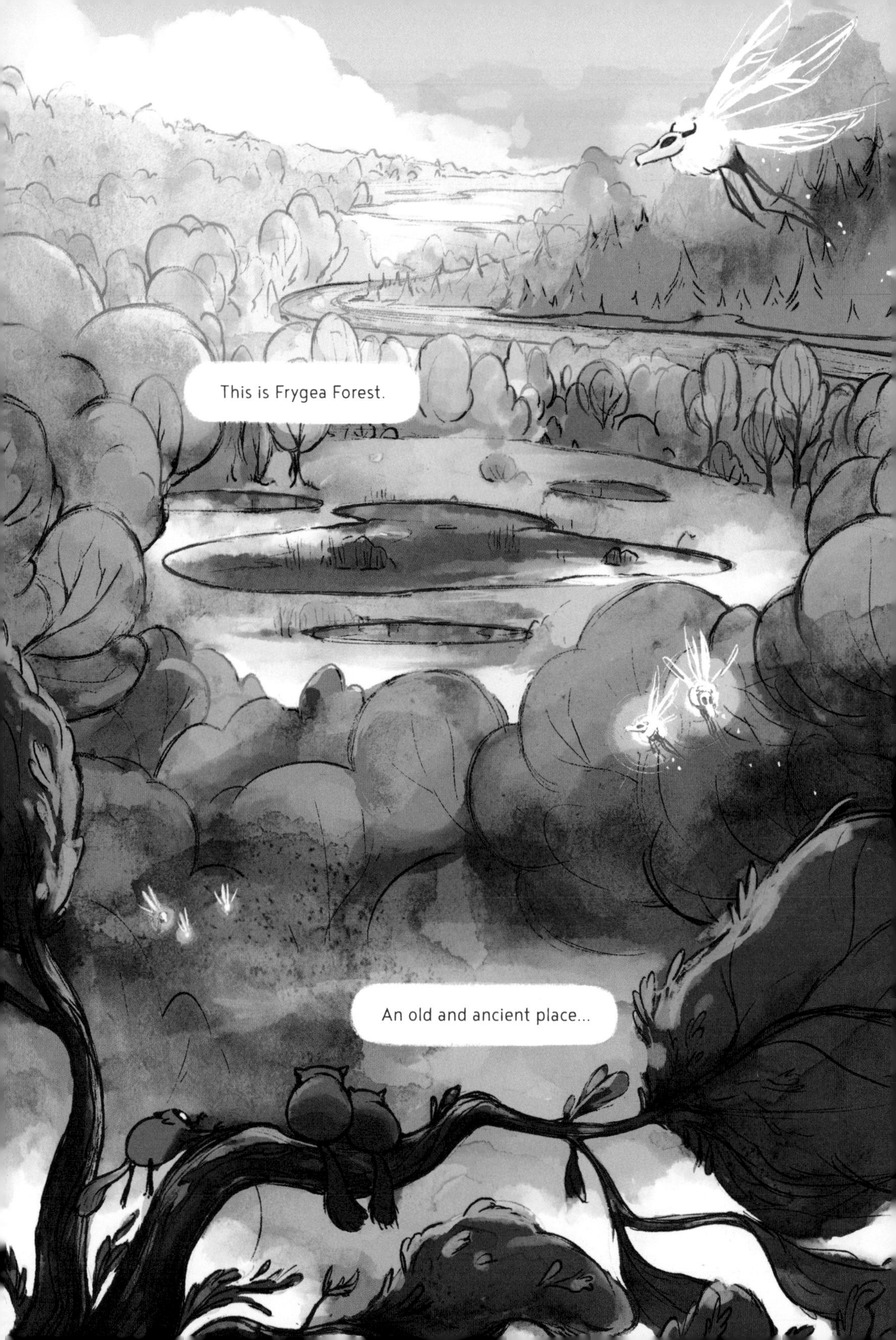
This is Frygea Forest.
An old and ancient place...

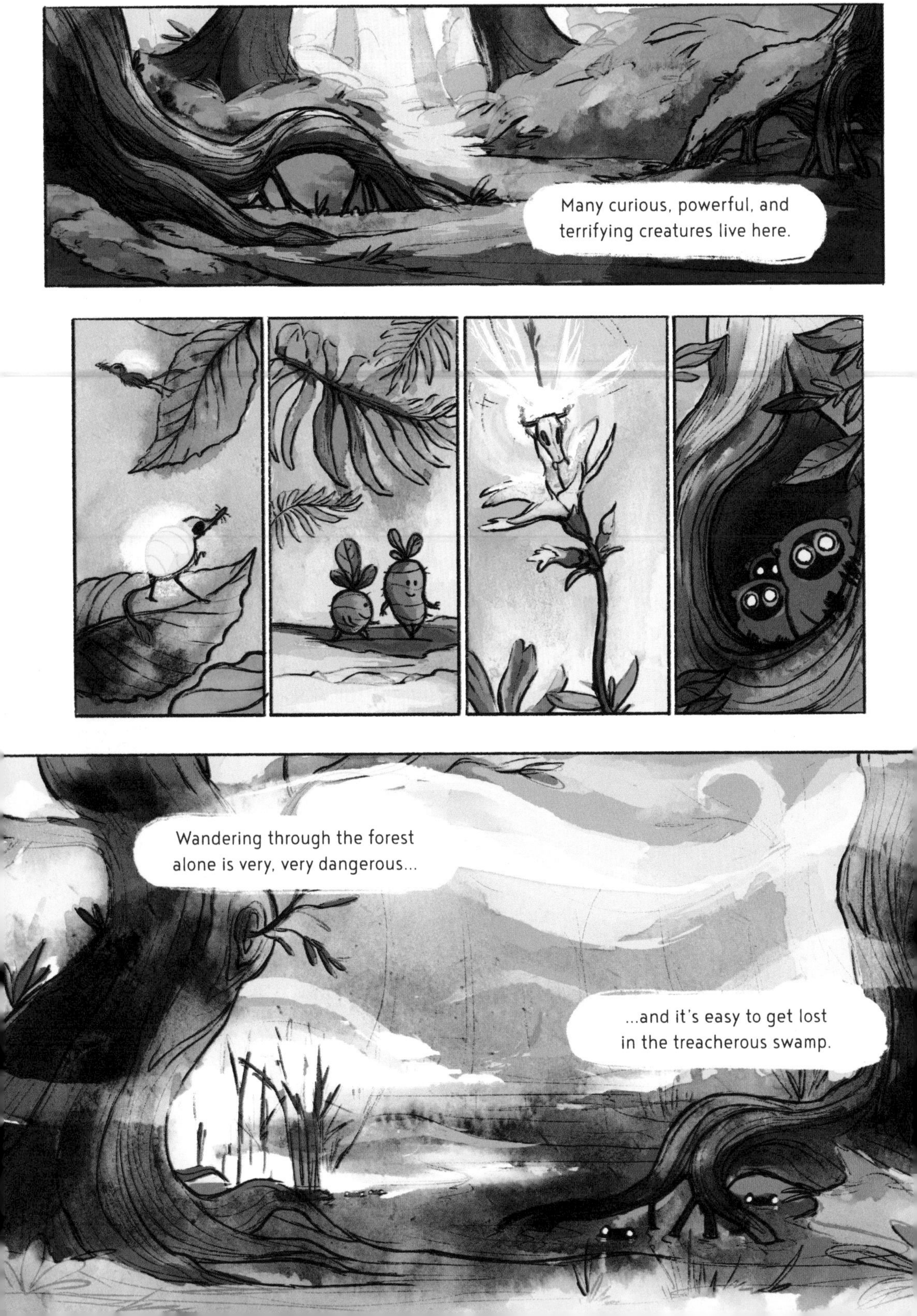
Many curious, powerful, and terrifying creatures live here.
Wandering through the forest alone is very, very dangerous...
...and it's easy to get lost in the treacherous swamp.

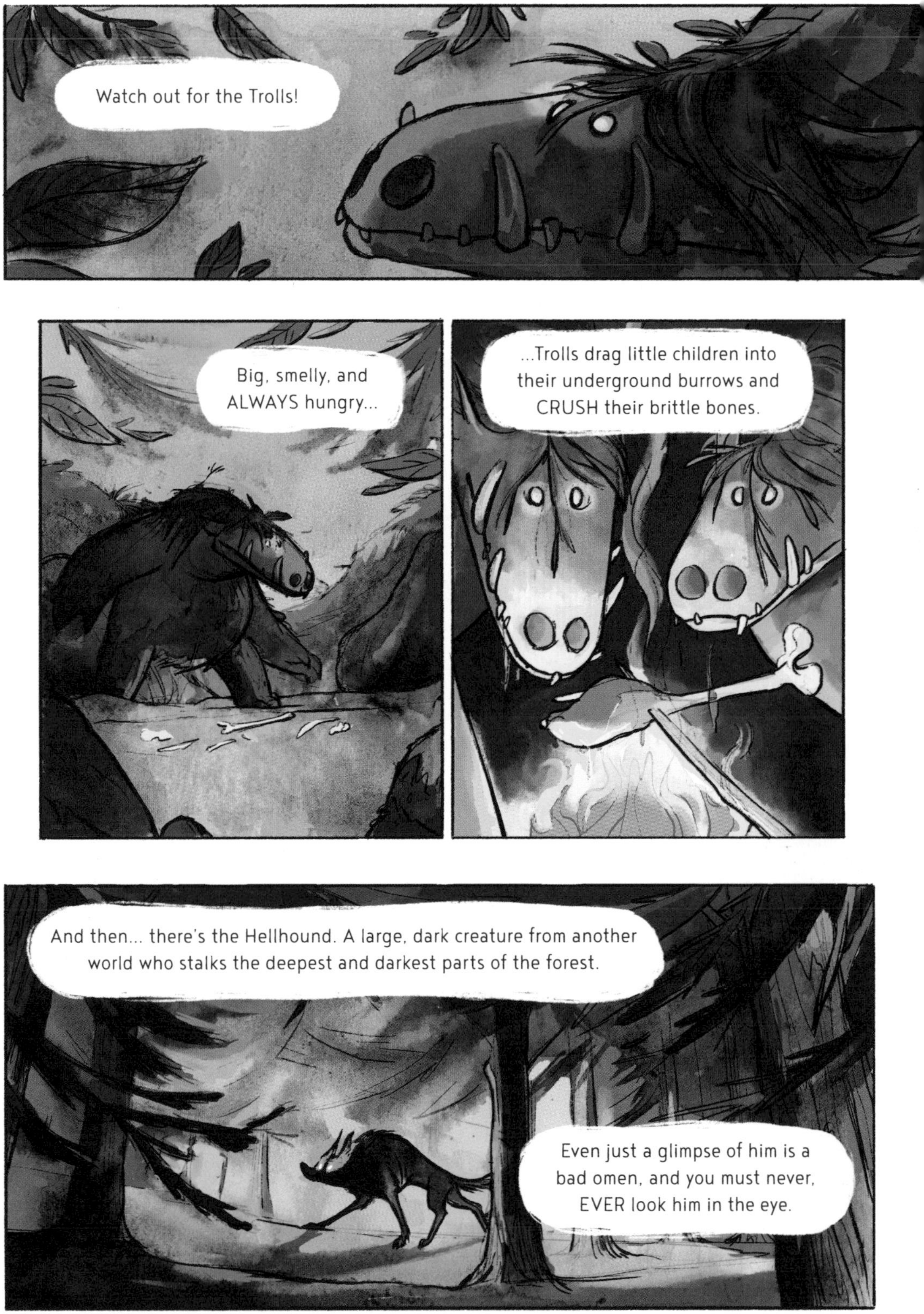
Watch out for the Trolls!
Big, smelly, and ALWAYS hungry...
...Trolls drag little children into their underground burrows and CRUSH their brittle bones.
And then... there's the Hellhound. A large, dark creature from another world who stalks the deepest and darkest parts of the forest.
Even just a glimpse of him is a bad omen, and you must never, EVER look him in the eye.

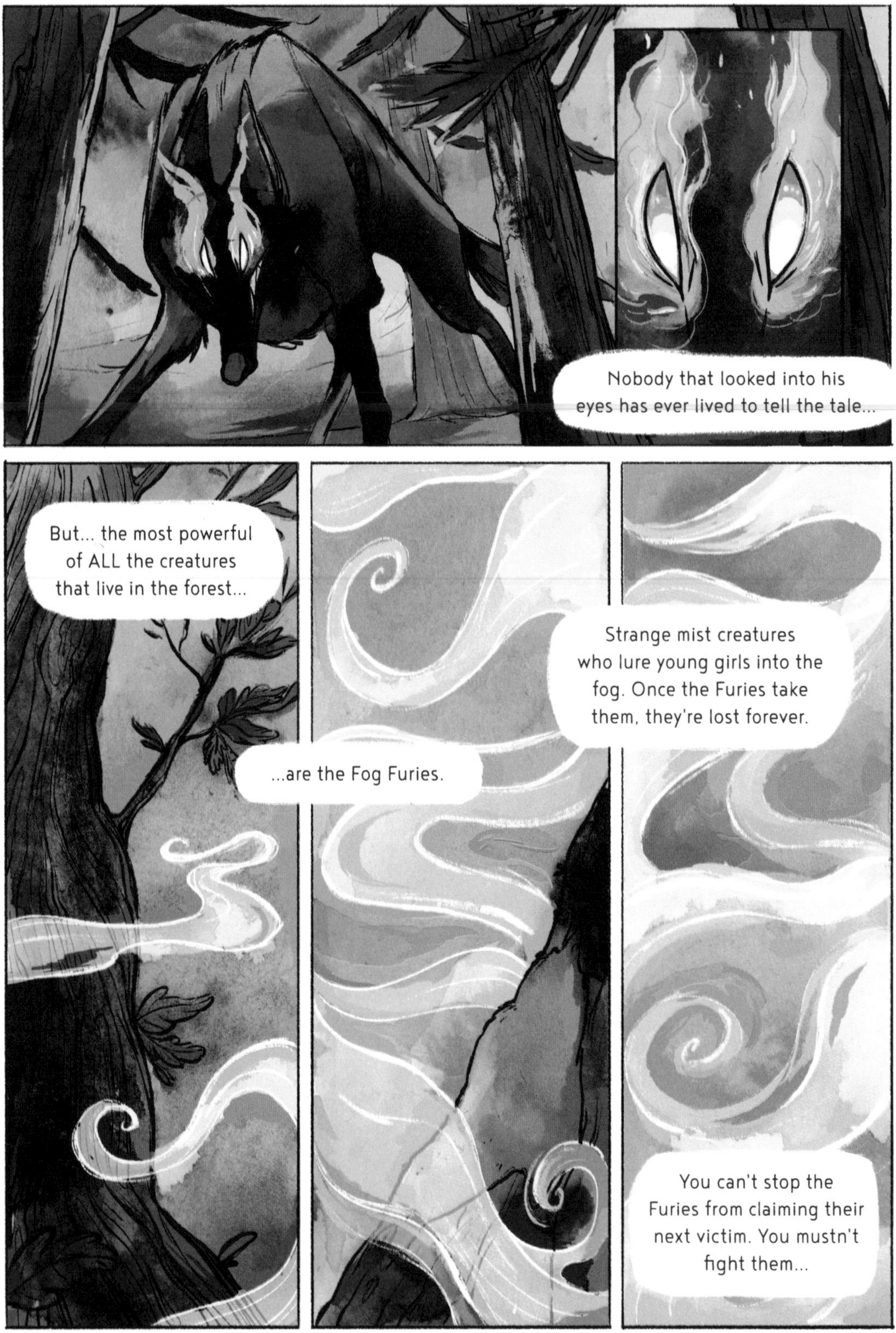
Nobody that looked into his eyes has ever lived to tell the tale...
But... the most powerful of ALL the creatures that live in the forest...
...are the Fog Furies.
Strange mist creatures who lure young girls into the fog. Once the Furies take them, they're lost forever.
You can't stop the Furies from claiming their next victim. You mustn't fight them...

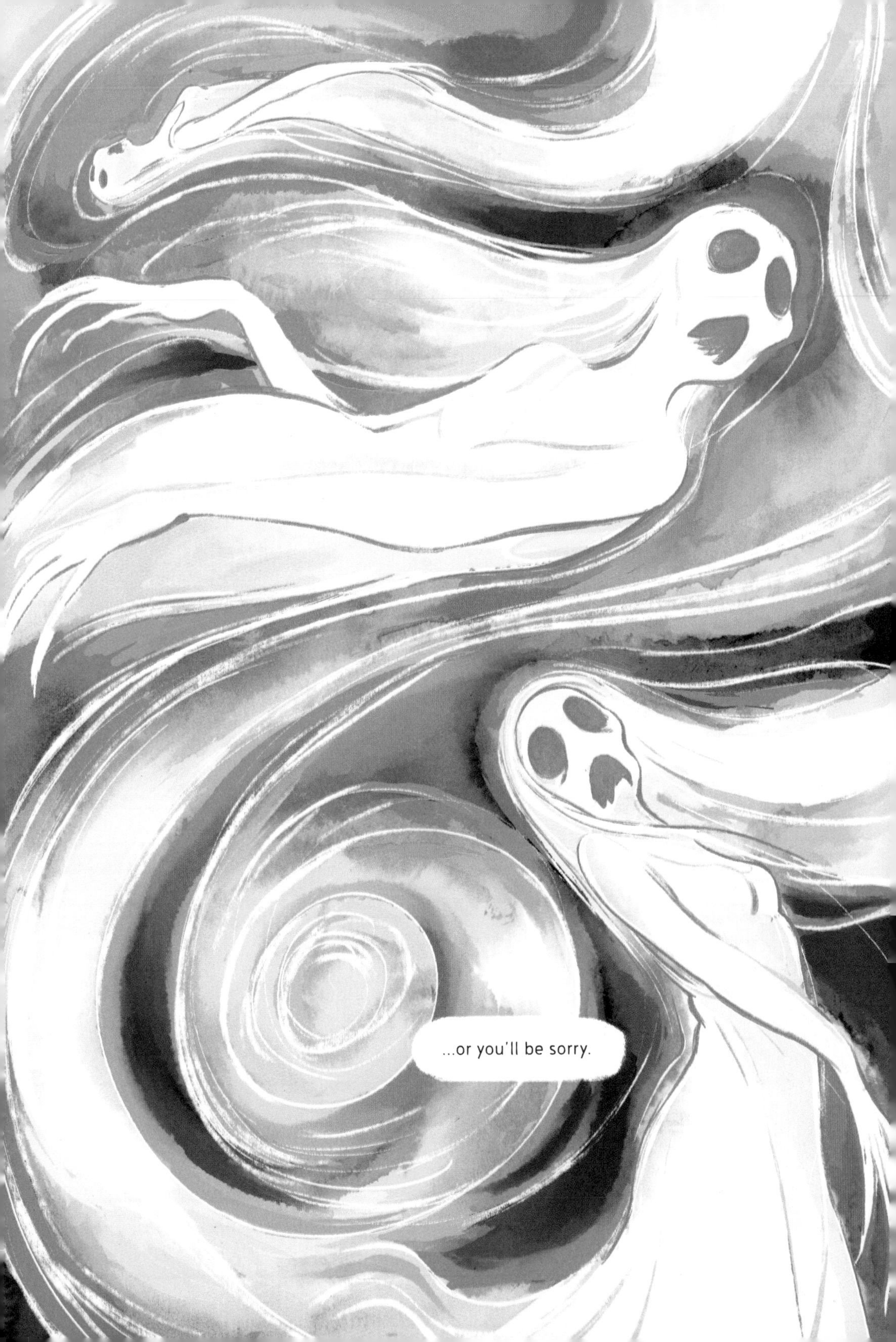
...or you'll be sorry.

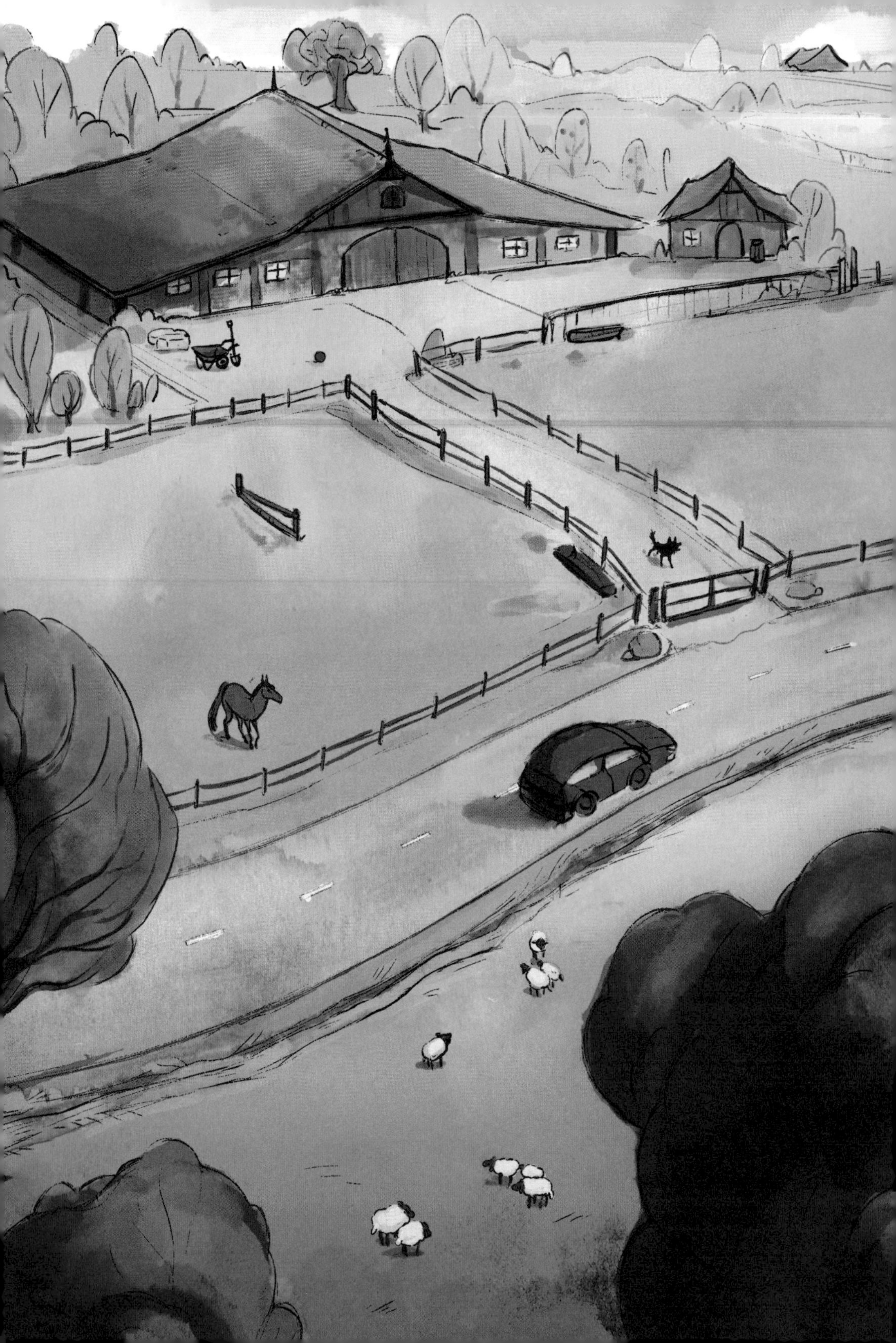

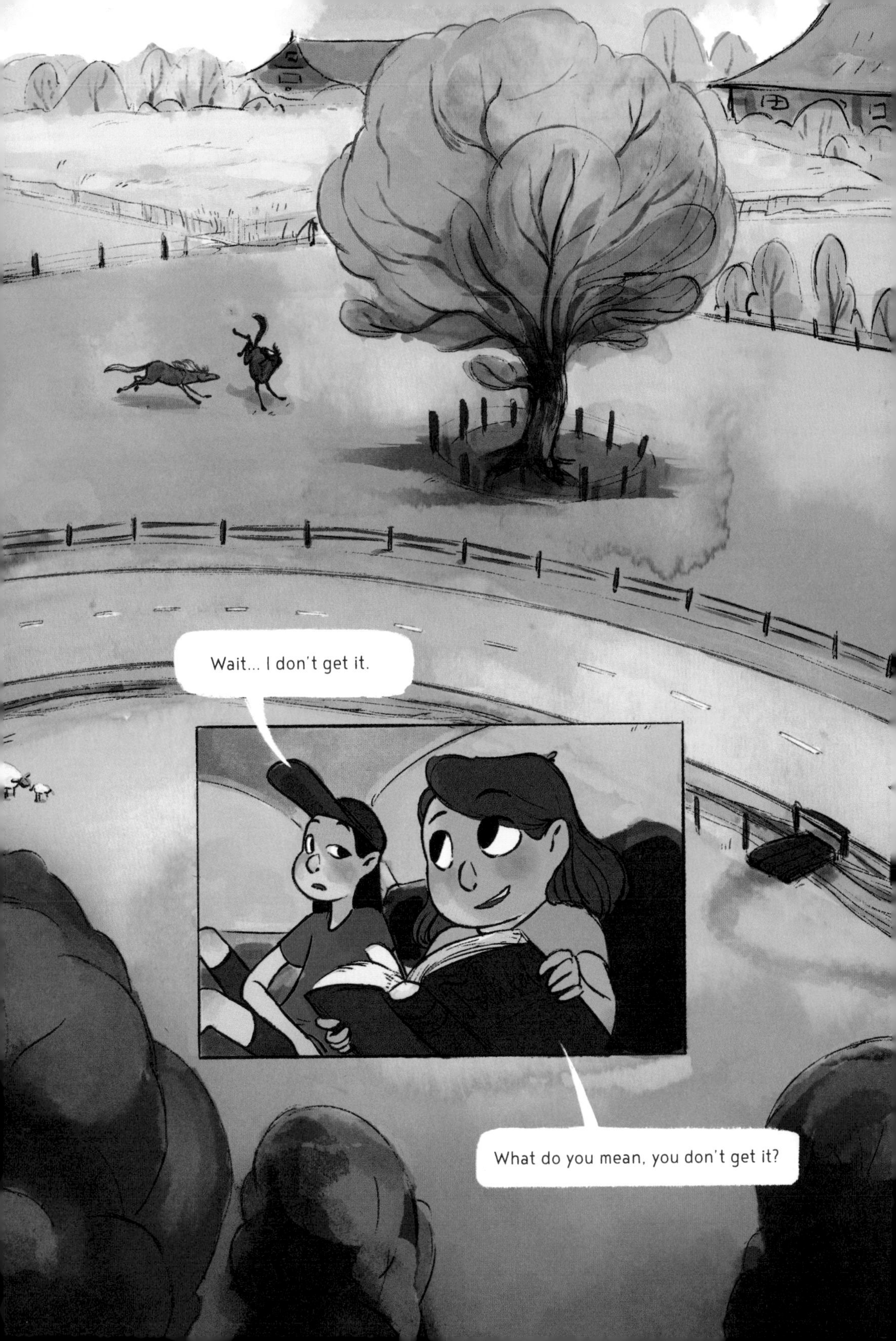
Wait... I don't get it.
What do you mean, you don't get it?

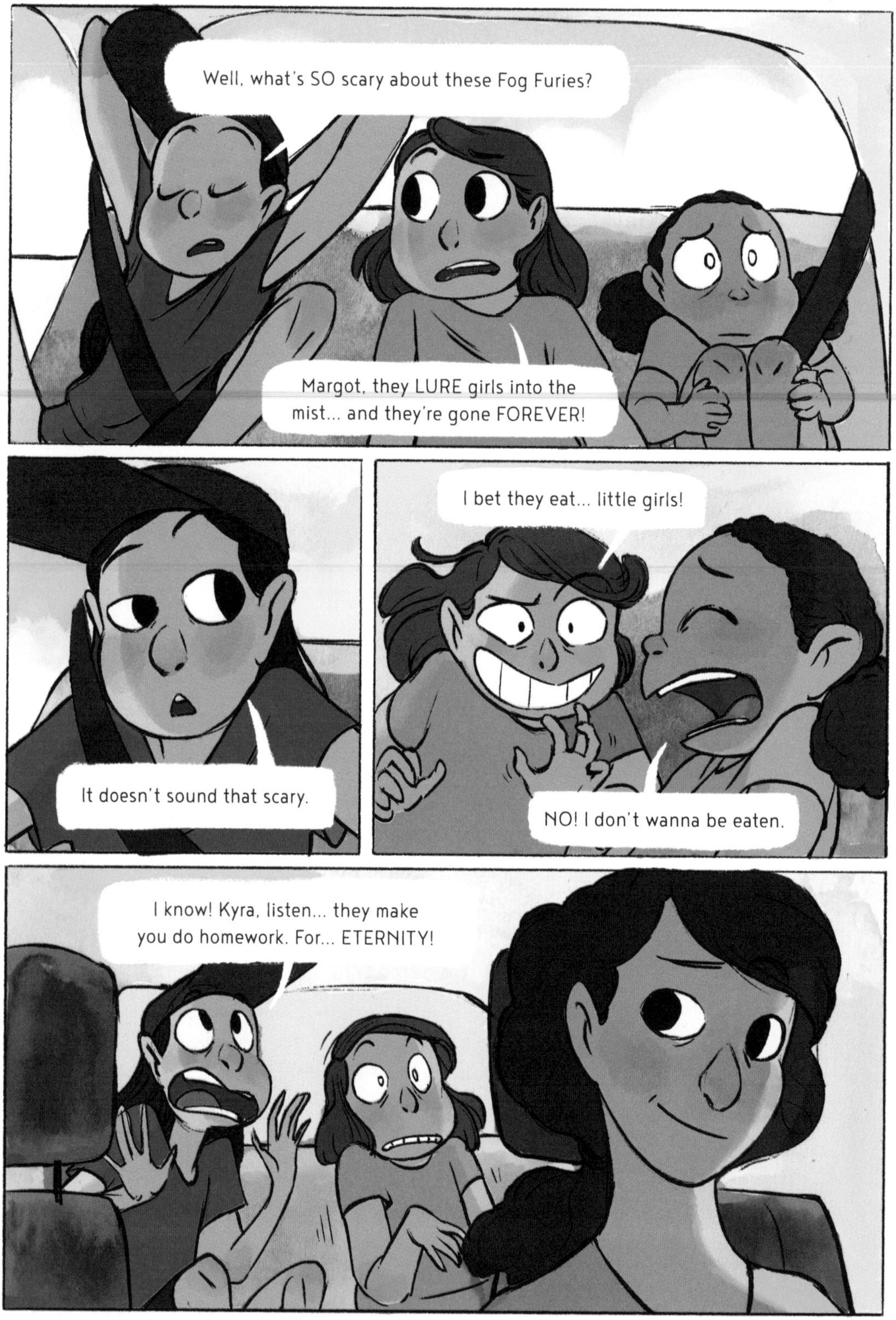
Well, what's SO scary about these Fog Furies?
Margot, they LURE girls into the mist... and they're gone FOREVER!
It doesn't sound that scary.
I bet they eat... little girls!
NO! I don't wanna be eaten.
I know! Kyra, listen... they make you do homework. For... ETERNITY!

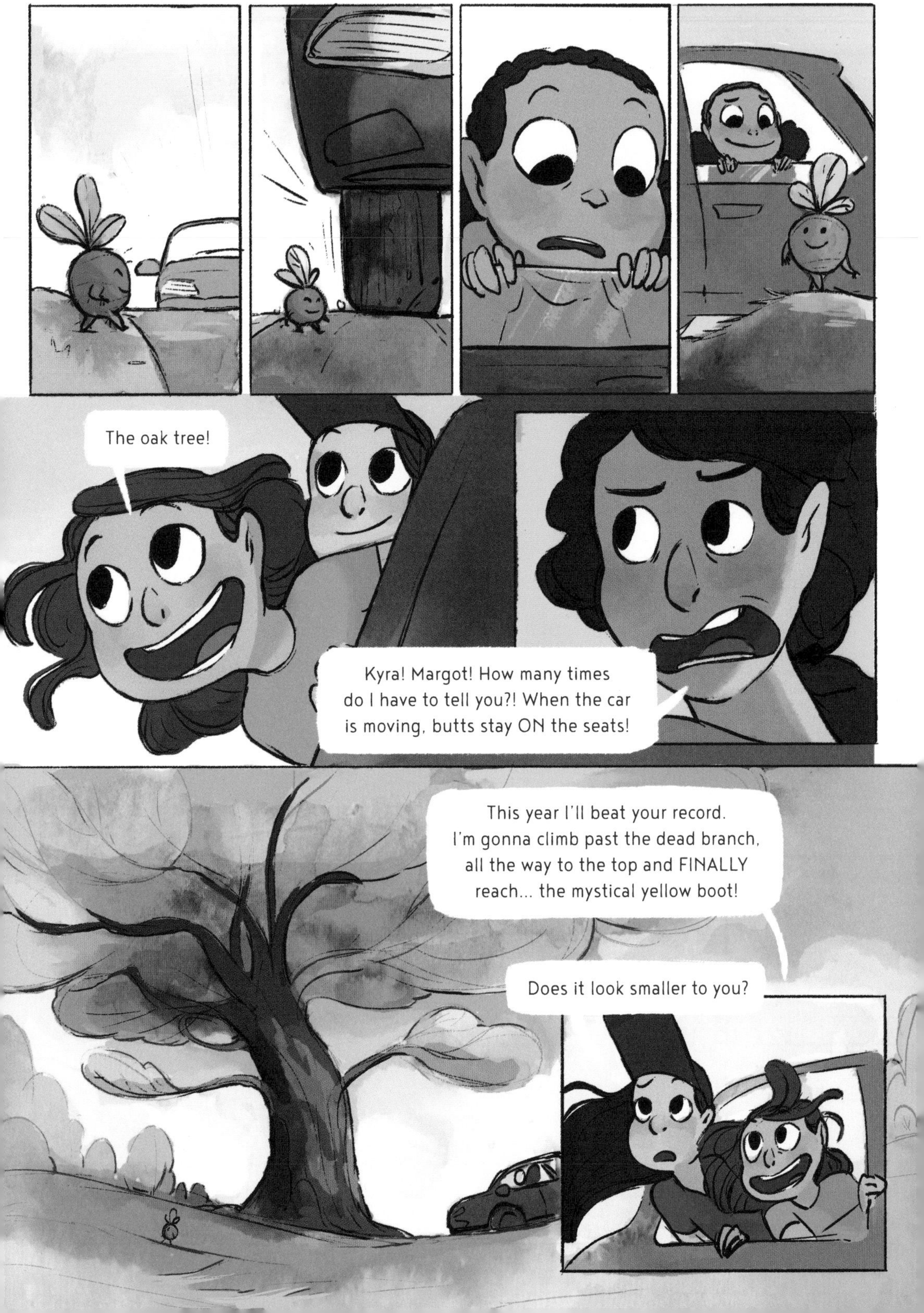
The oak tree!
Kyra! Margot! How many times do I have to tell you?! When the car is moving, butts stay ON the seats!
This year I'll beat your record. I'm gonna climb past the dead branch, all the way to the top and FINALLY reach... the mystical yellow boot!
Does it look smaller to you?

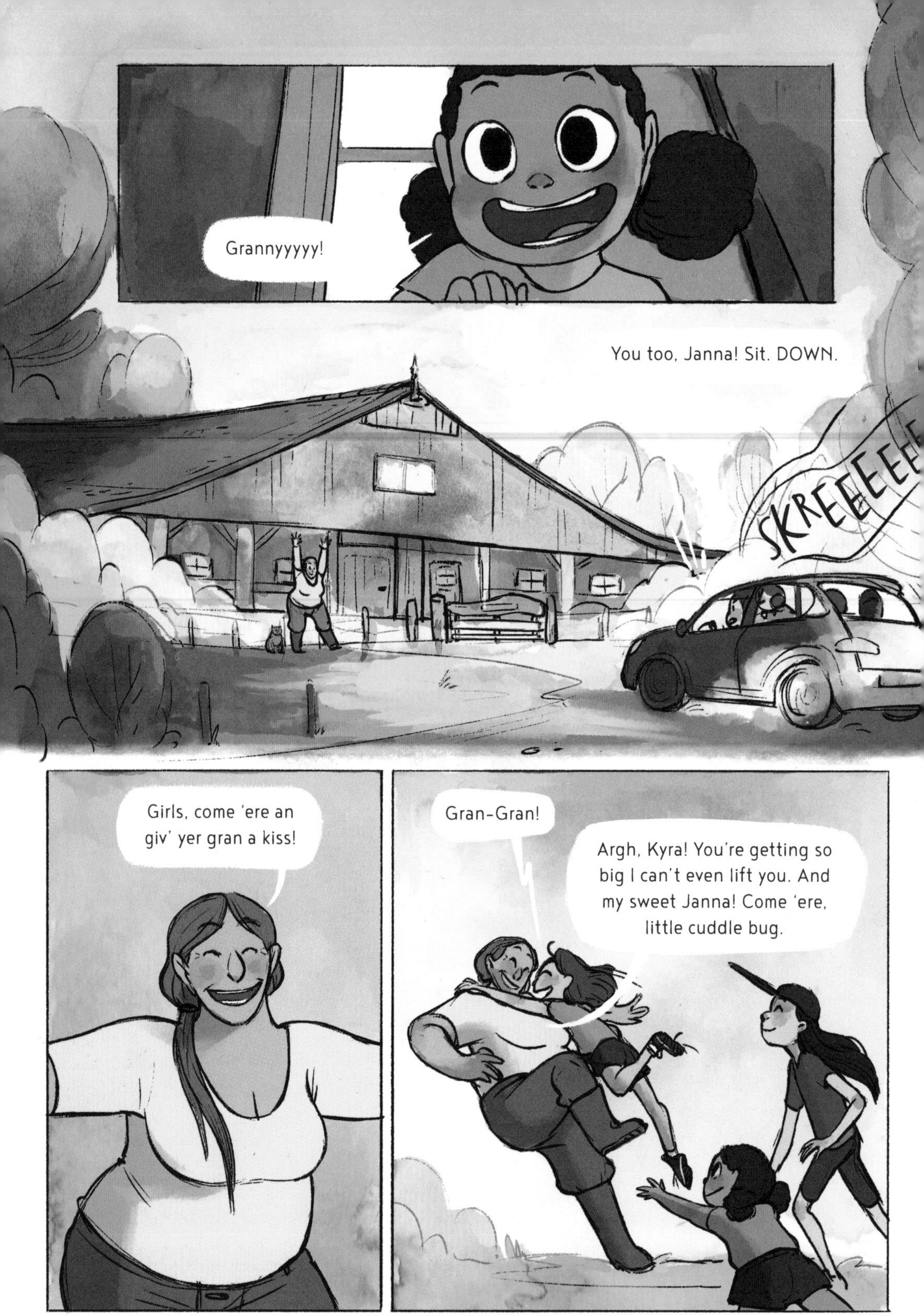
Grannyyyyy!
You too, Janna! Sit. DOWN.
SKREEEEEE
Girls, come 'ere an giv' yer gran a kiss!
Gran-Gran!
Argh, Kyra! You're getting so big I can't even lift you. And my sweet Janna! Come 'ere, little cuddle bug.

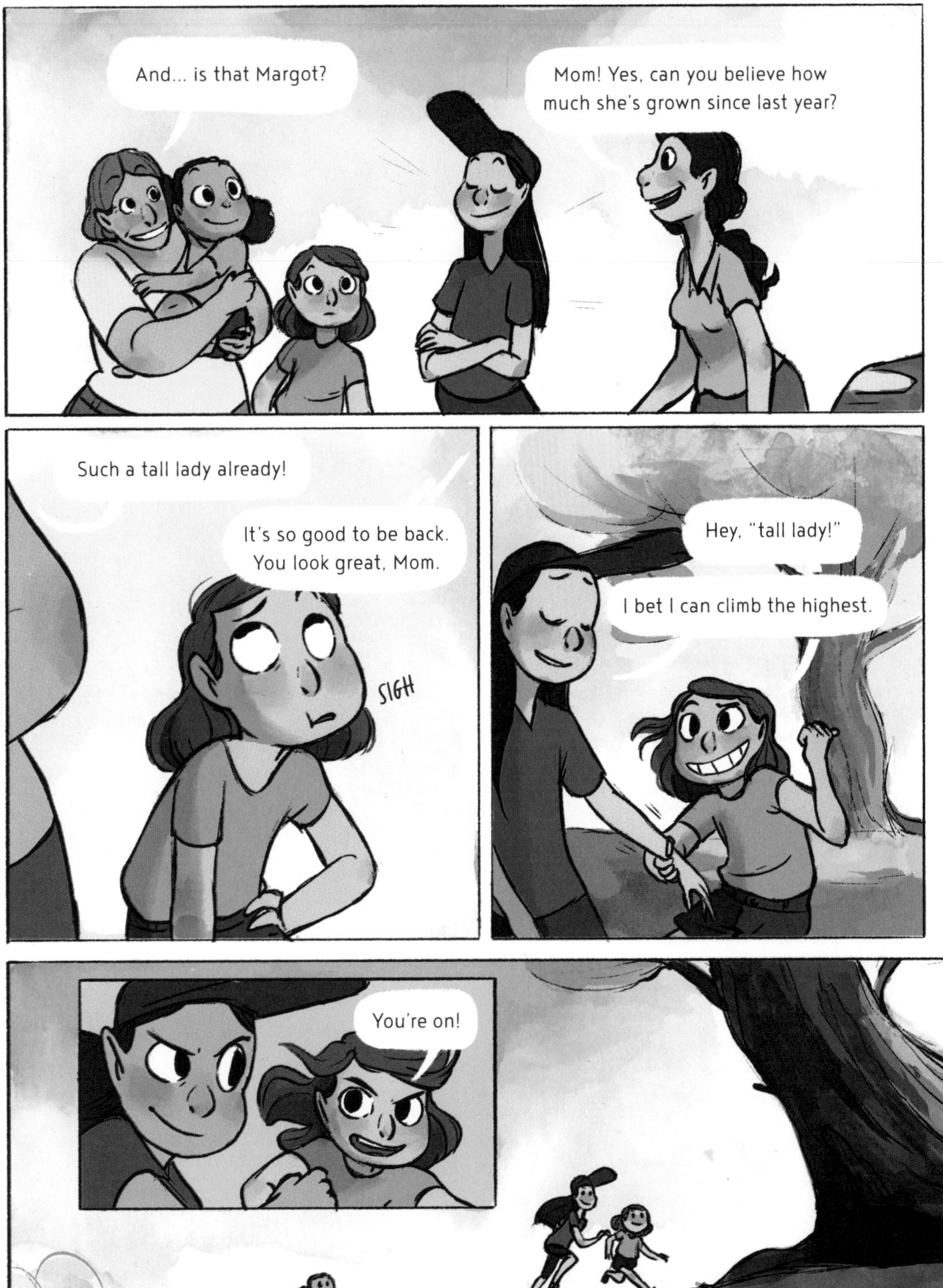
And... is that Margot?
Mom! Yes, can you believe how much she's grown since last year?
Such a tall lady already!
It's so good to be back. You look great, Mom.
SIGH
Hey, "tall lady!"
I bet I can climb the highest.
You're on!

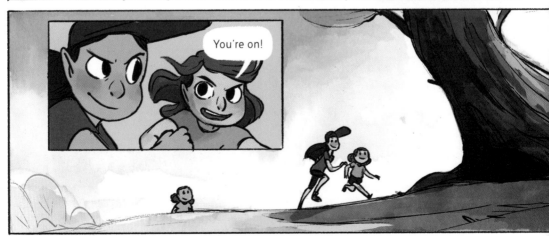

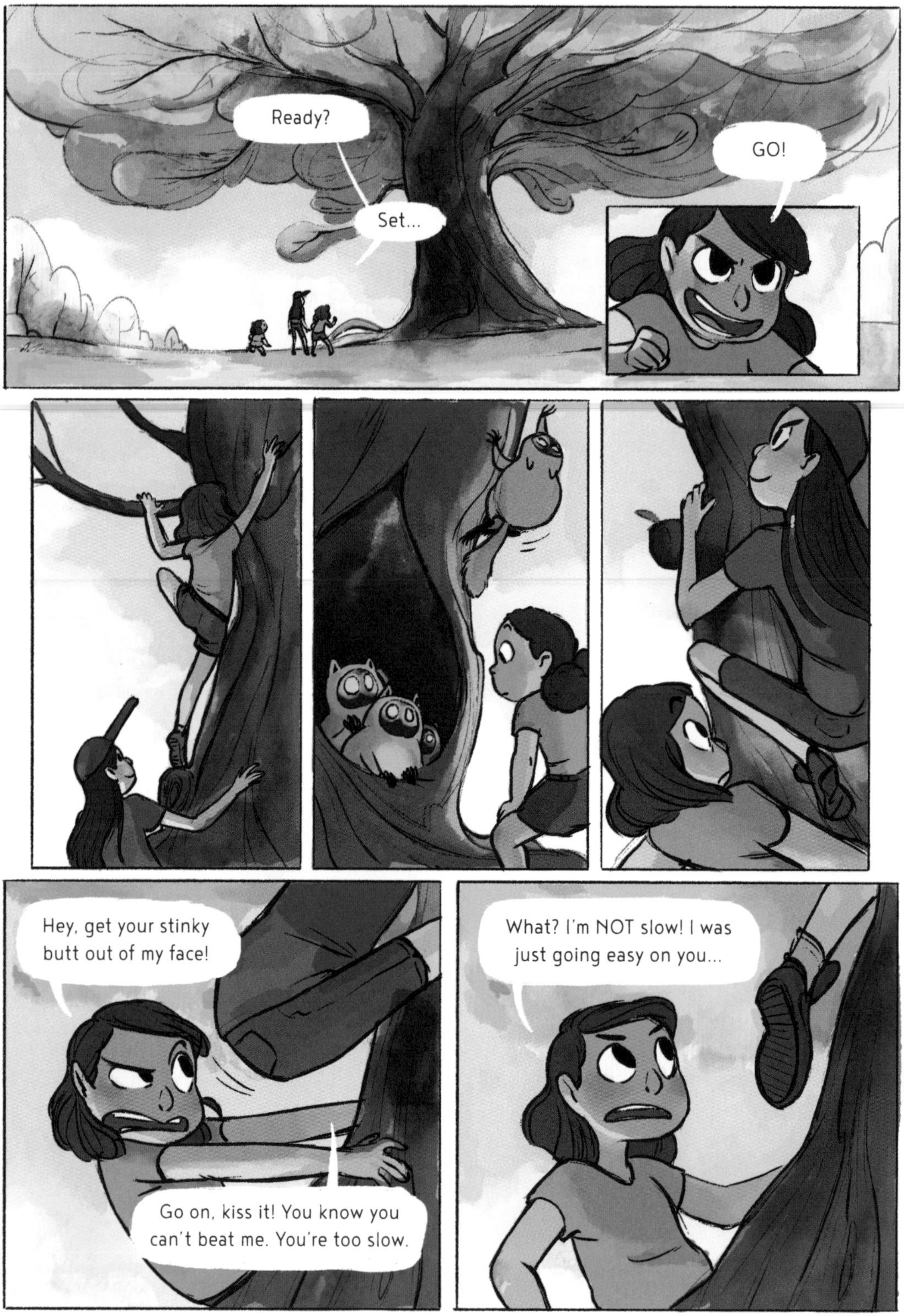
Ready?
Set...
GO!
Hey, get your stinky butt out of my face!
Go on, kiss it! You know you can't beat me. You're too slow.
What? I'm NOT slow! I was just going easy on you...

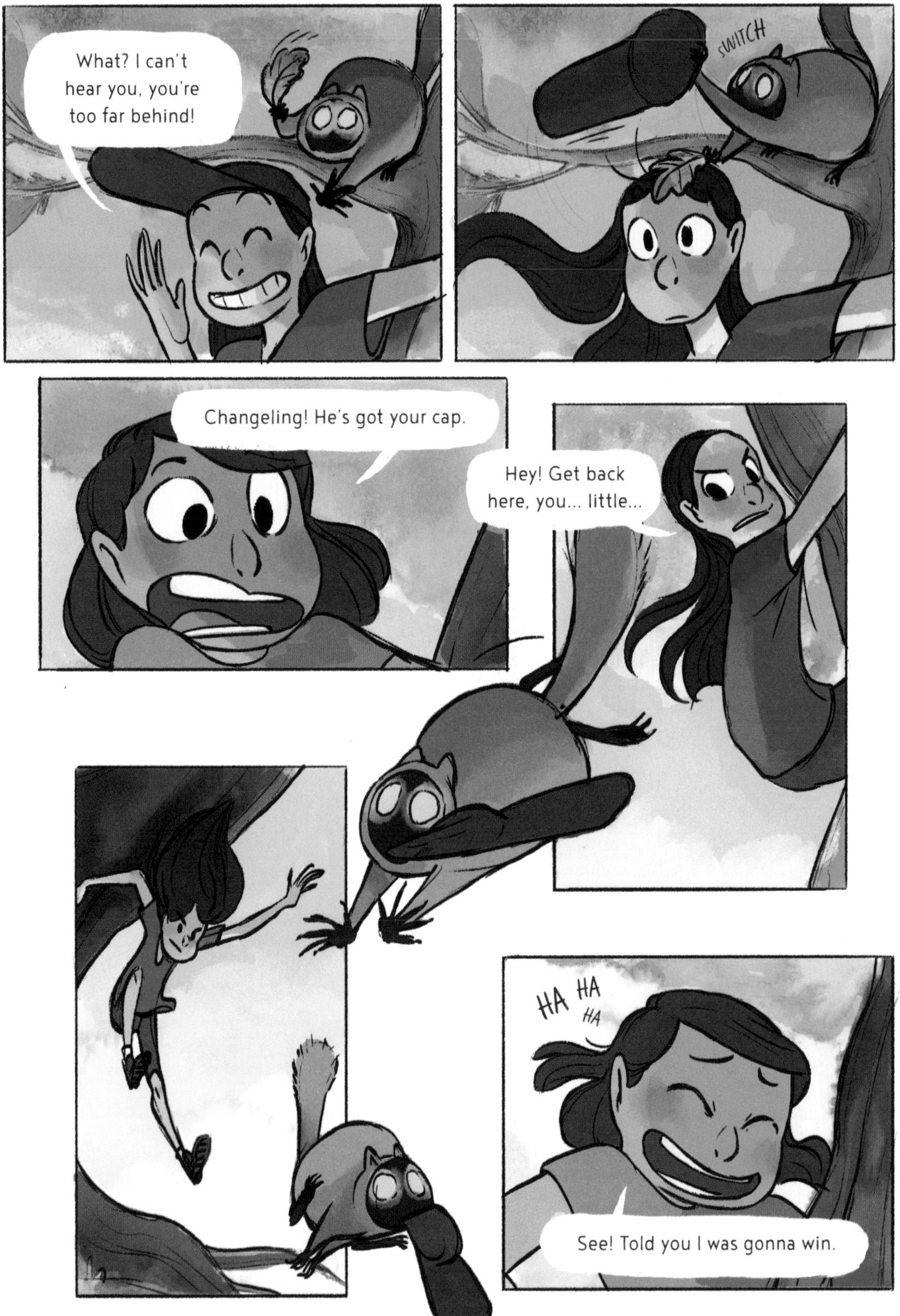
What? I can't hear you, you're too far behind!
SWITCH
Changeling! He's got your cap.
Hey! Get back here, you... little...
HA HA HA
See! Told you I was gonna win.

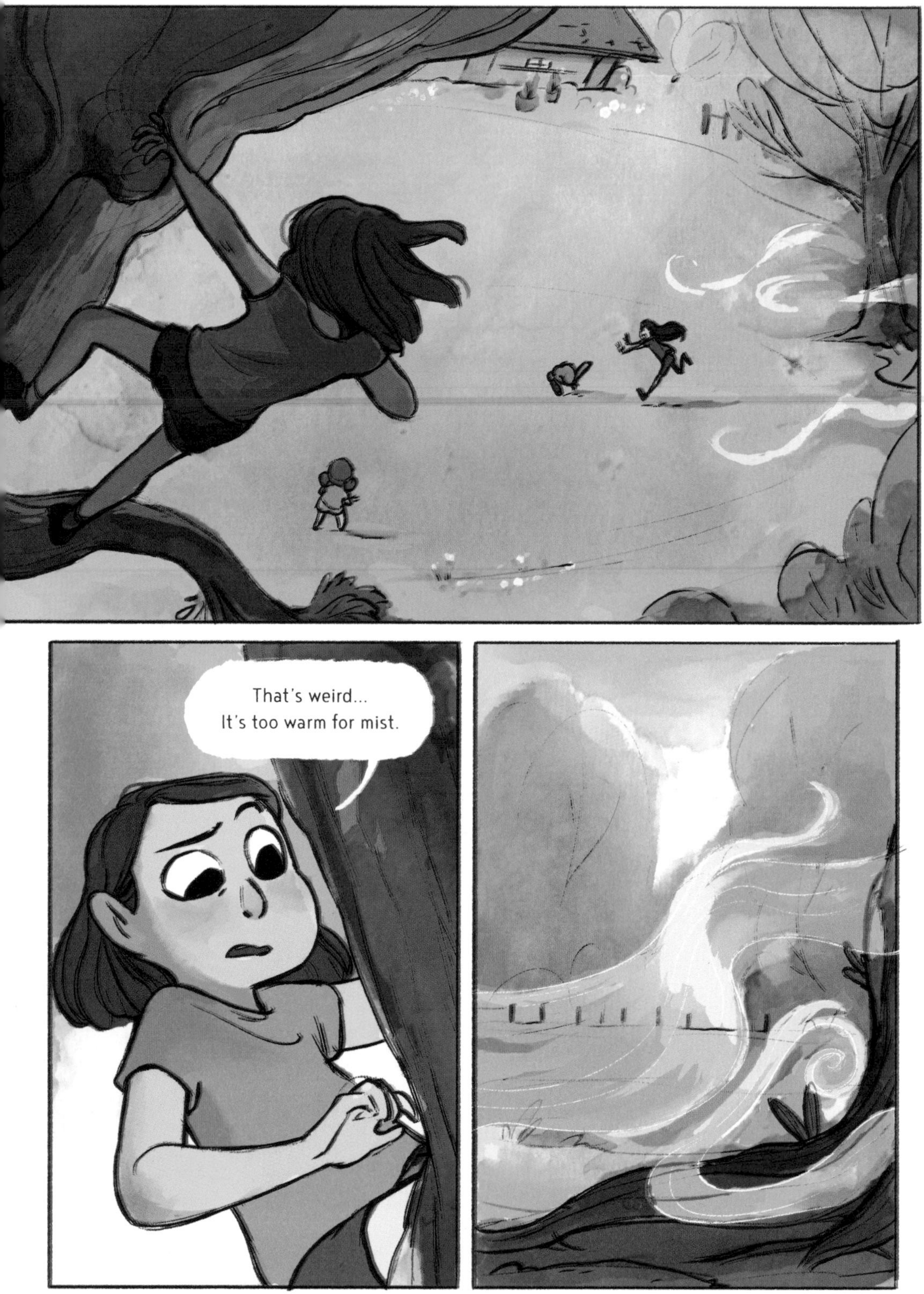
That's weird...
It's too warm for mist.

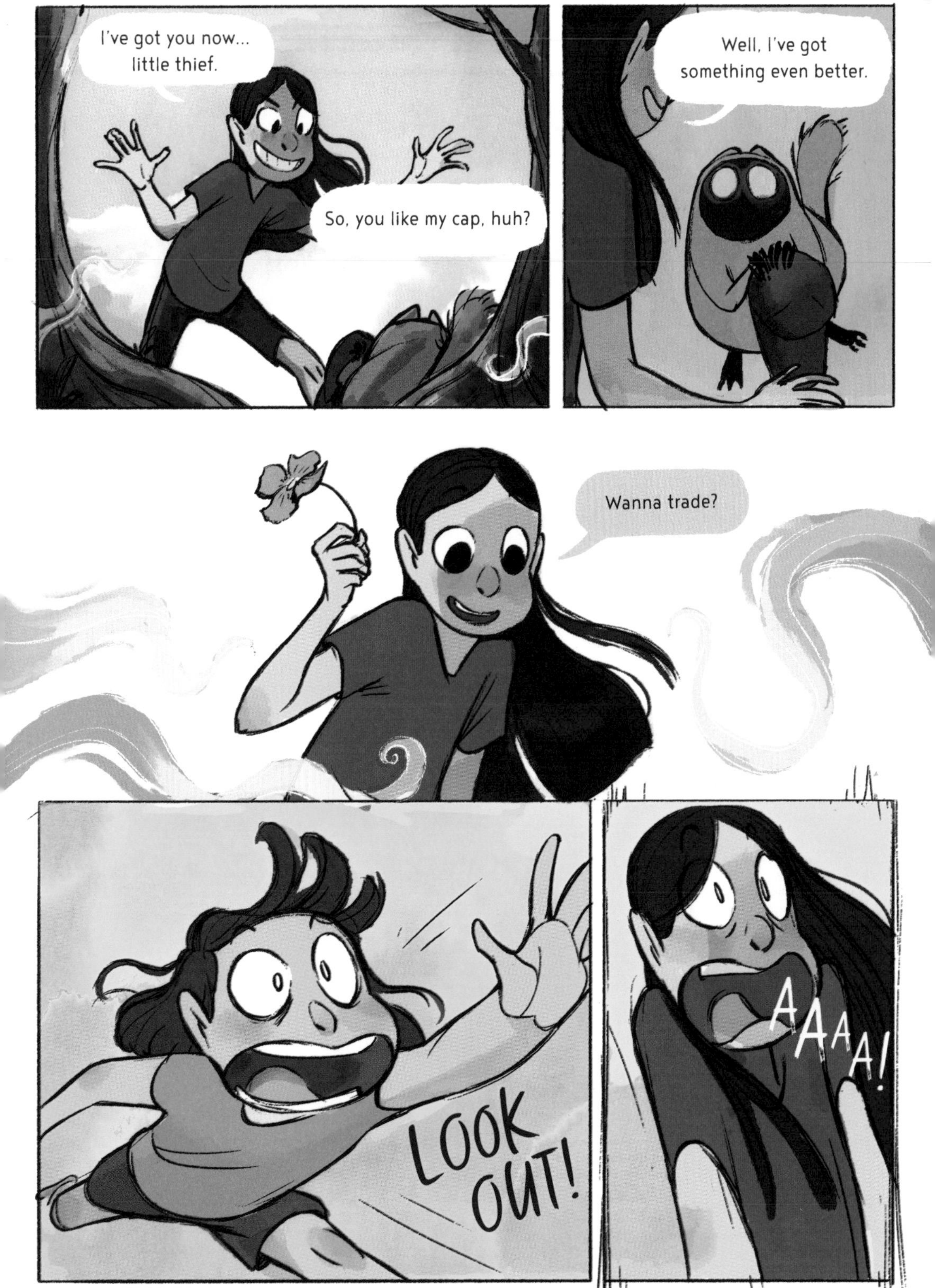
I've got you now... little thief.
So, you like my cap, huh?
Well, I've got something even better.
Wanna trade?
LOOK OUT!
AAAA!

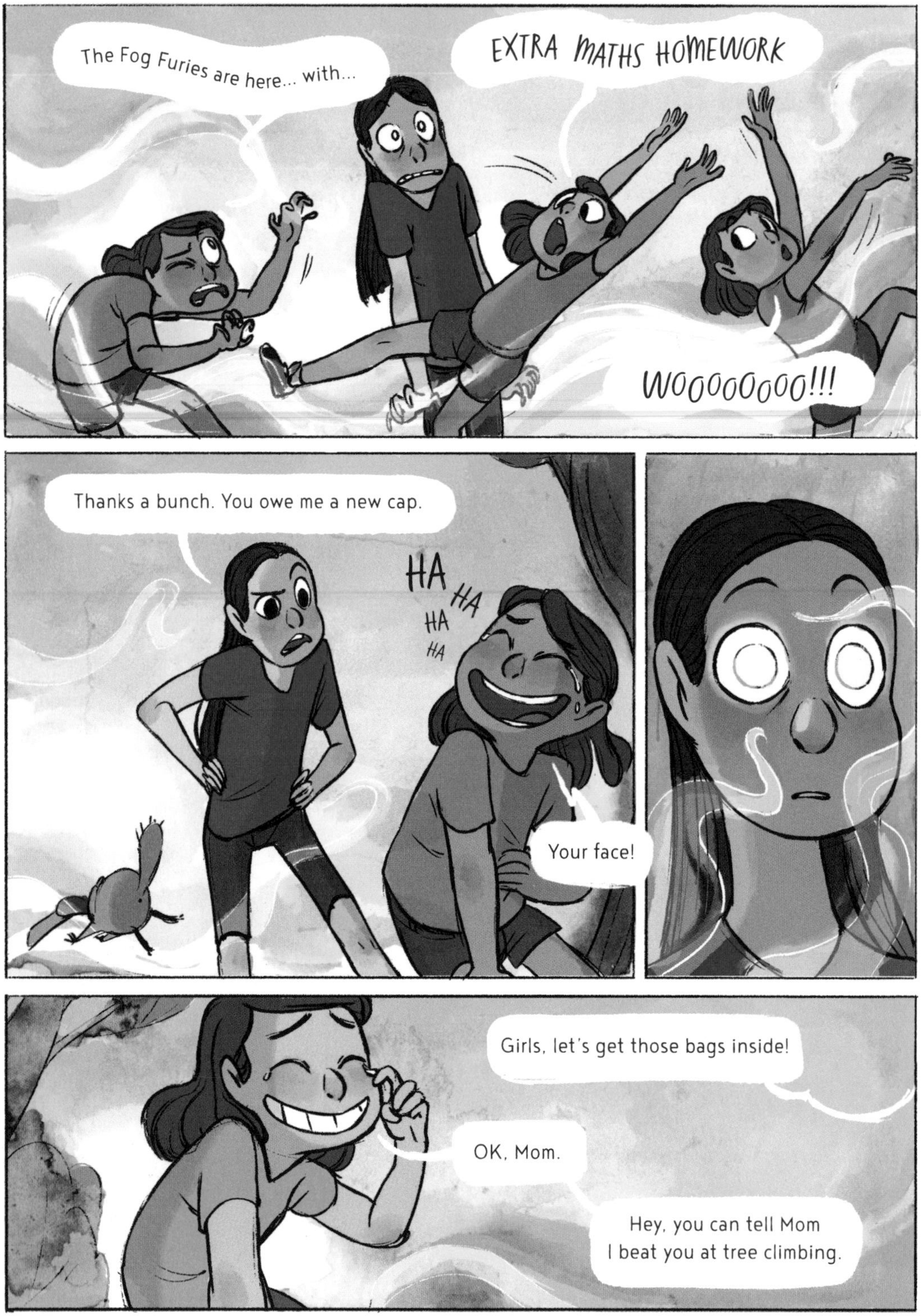
The Fog Furies are here... with...
EXTRA MATHS HOMEWORK
WOOOOOOOO!!!
Thanks a bunch. You owe me a new cap.
HA HA HA HA
Your face!
Girls, let's get those bags inside!
OK, Mom.
Hey, you can tell Mom
I beat you at tree climbing.

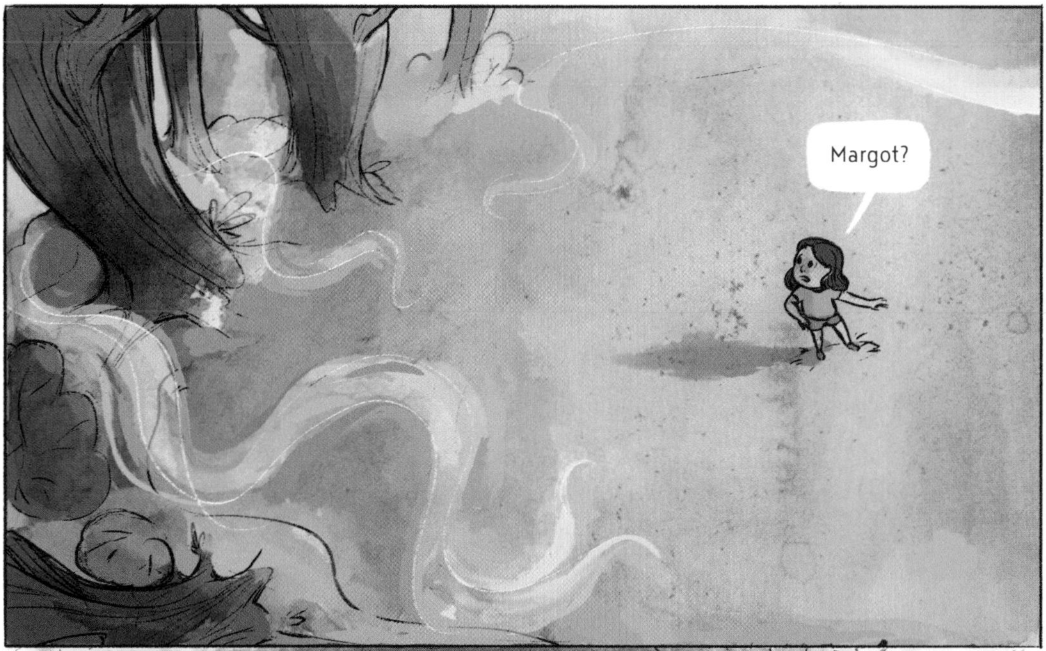
Margot?

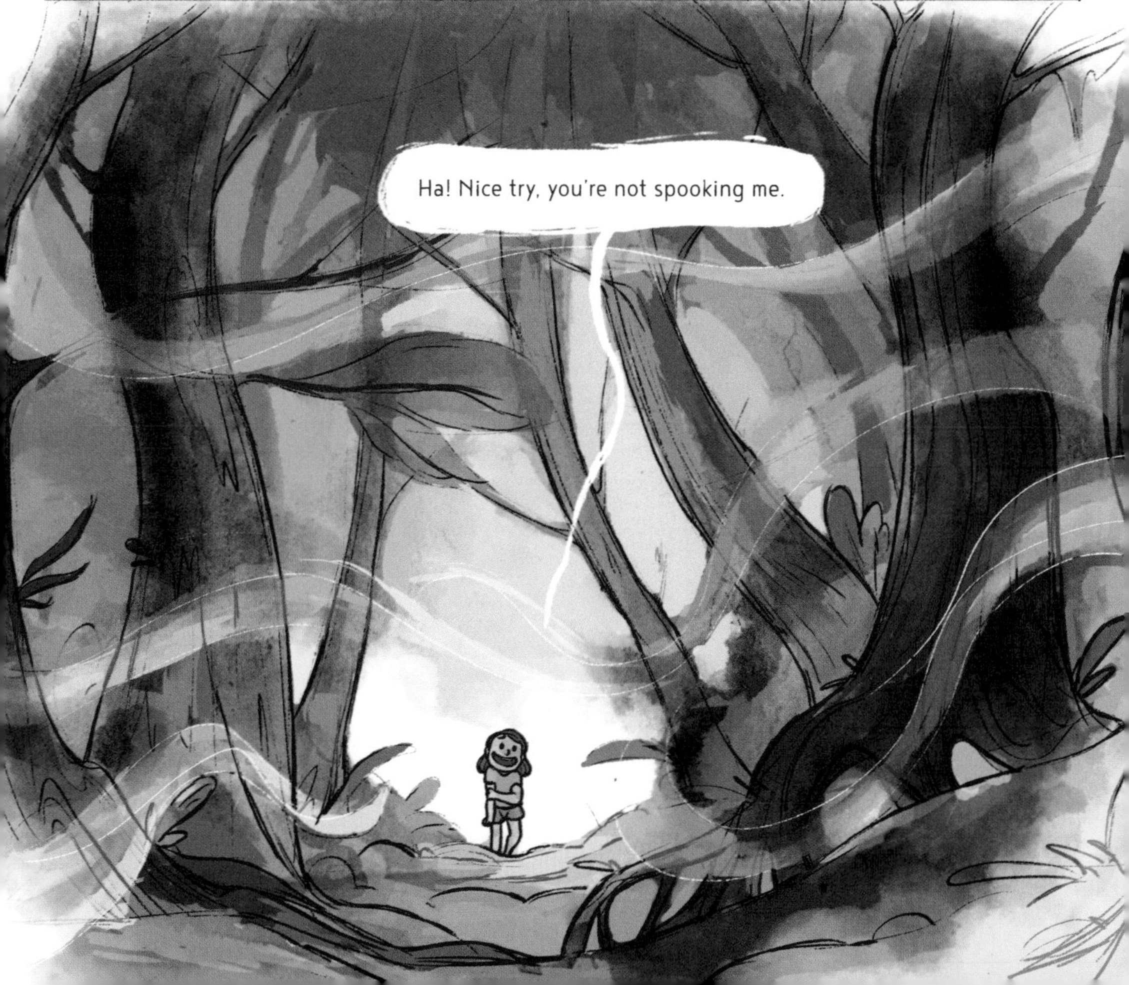
Ha! Nice try, you're not spooking me.

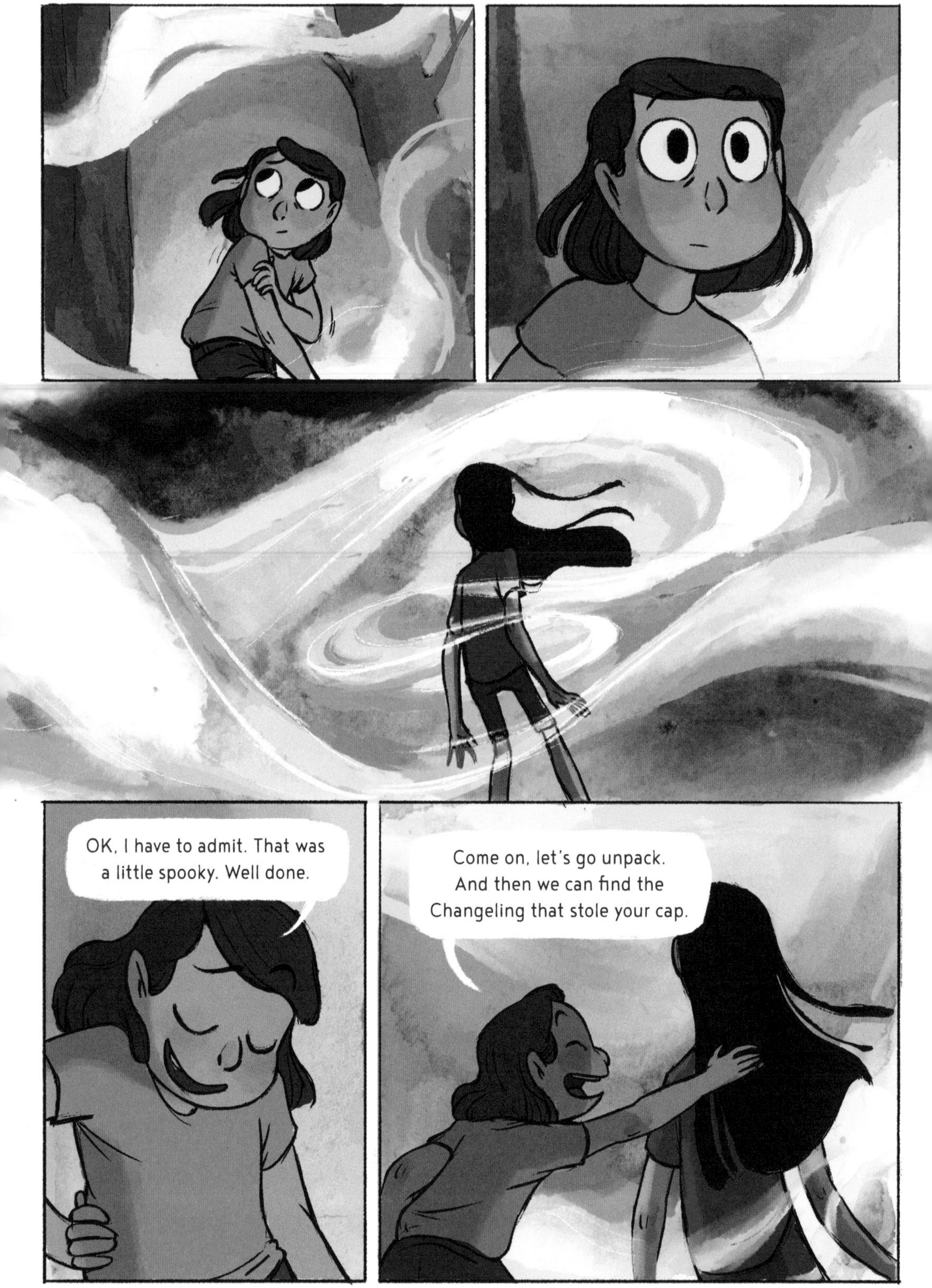
OK, I have to admit. That was a little spooky. Well done.
Come on, let's go unpack. And then we can find the Changeling that stole your cap.

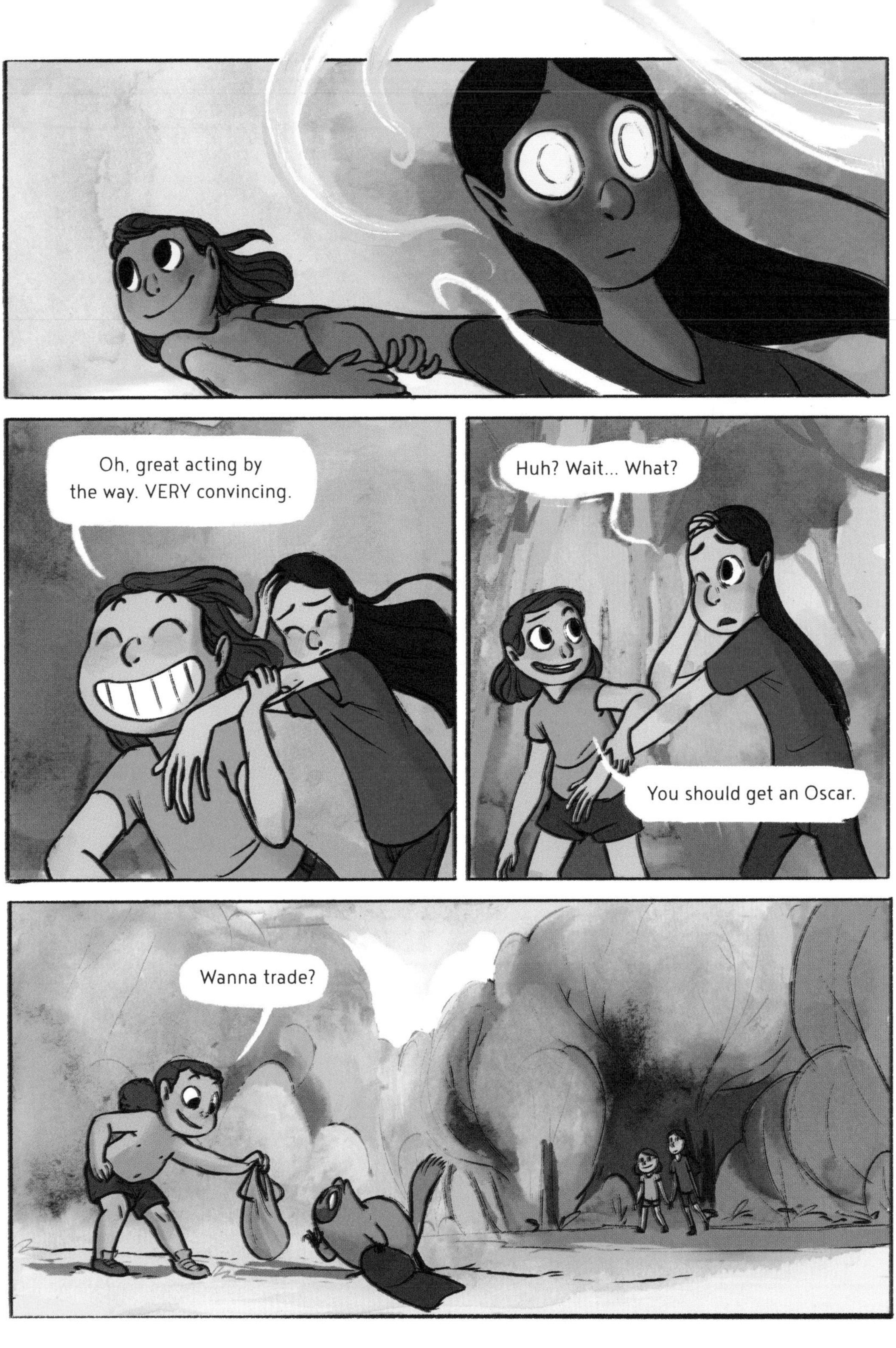
Oh, great acting by the way. VERY convincing.
Huh? Wait... What?
You should get an Oscar.
Wanna trade?

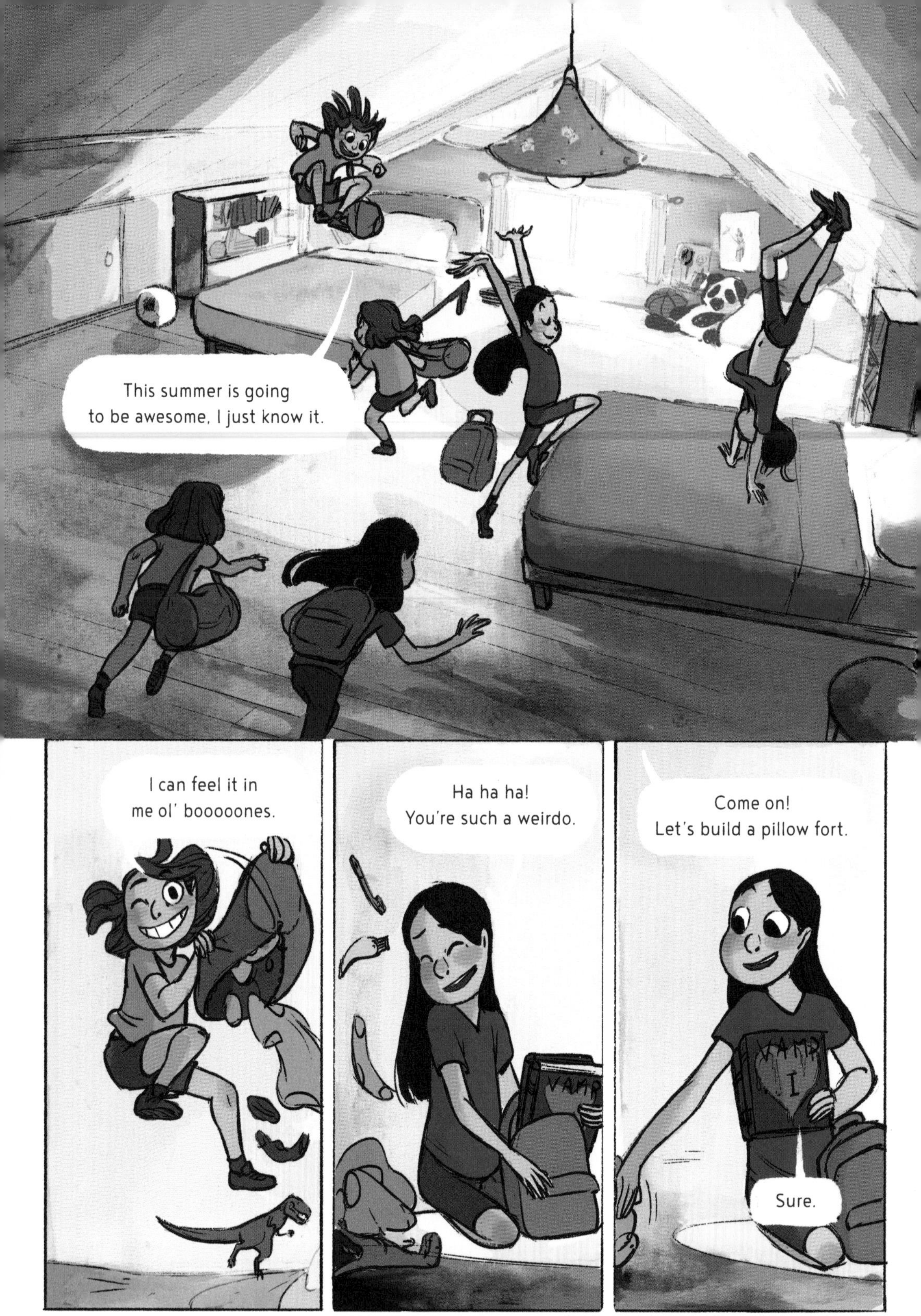
This summer is going to be awesome, I just know it.
I can feel it in me ol' booooones.
Ha ha ha! You're such a weirdo.
Come on! Let's build a pillow fort.
Sure.

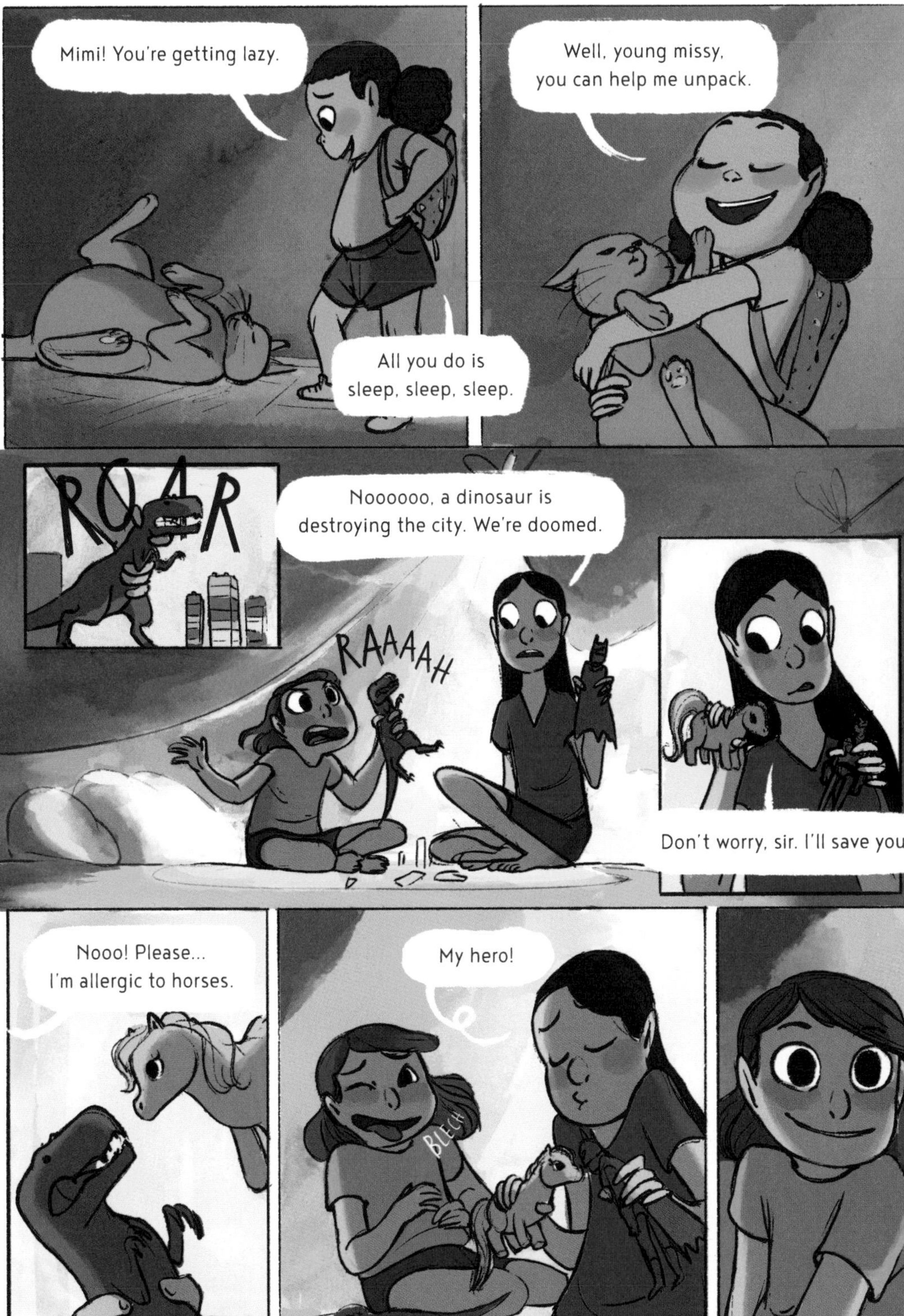

Mimi! You're getting lazy.
All you do is sleep, sleep, sleep.
Well, young missy, you can help me unpack.
ROAR
Noooooo, a dinosaur is destroying the city. We're doomed.
RAAAAH
Don't worry, sir. I'll save you!
Nooo! Please... I'm allergic to horses.
My hero!
BLECH

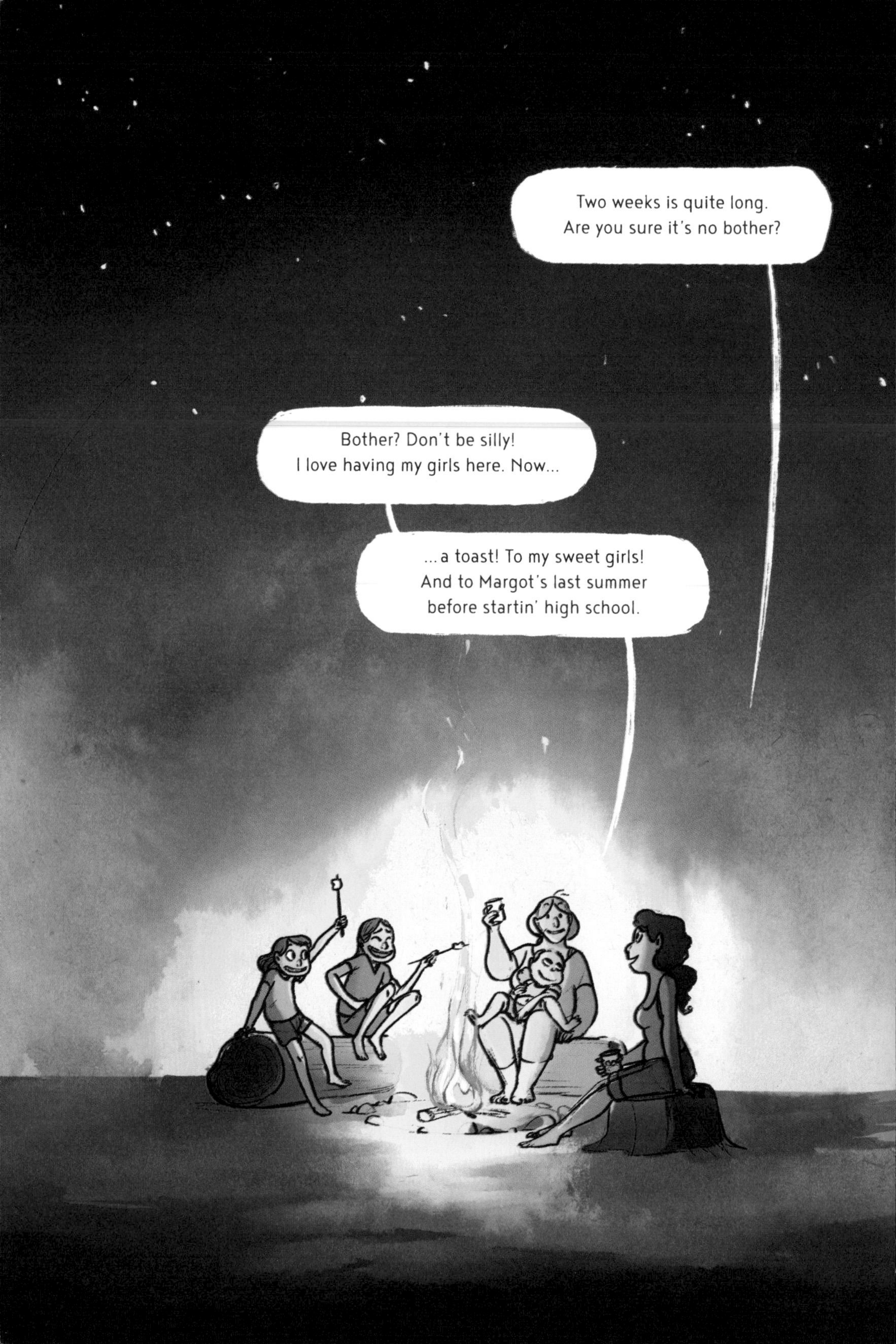
Two weeks is quite long. Are you sure it's no bother?
Bother? Don't be silly! I love having my girls here. Now...
...a toast! To my sweet girls! And to Margot's last summer before startin' high school.

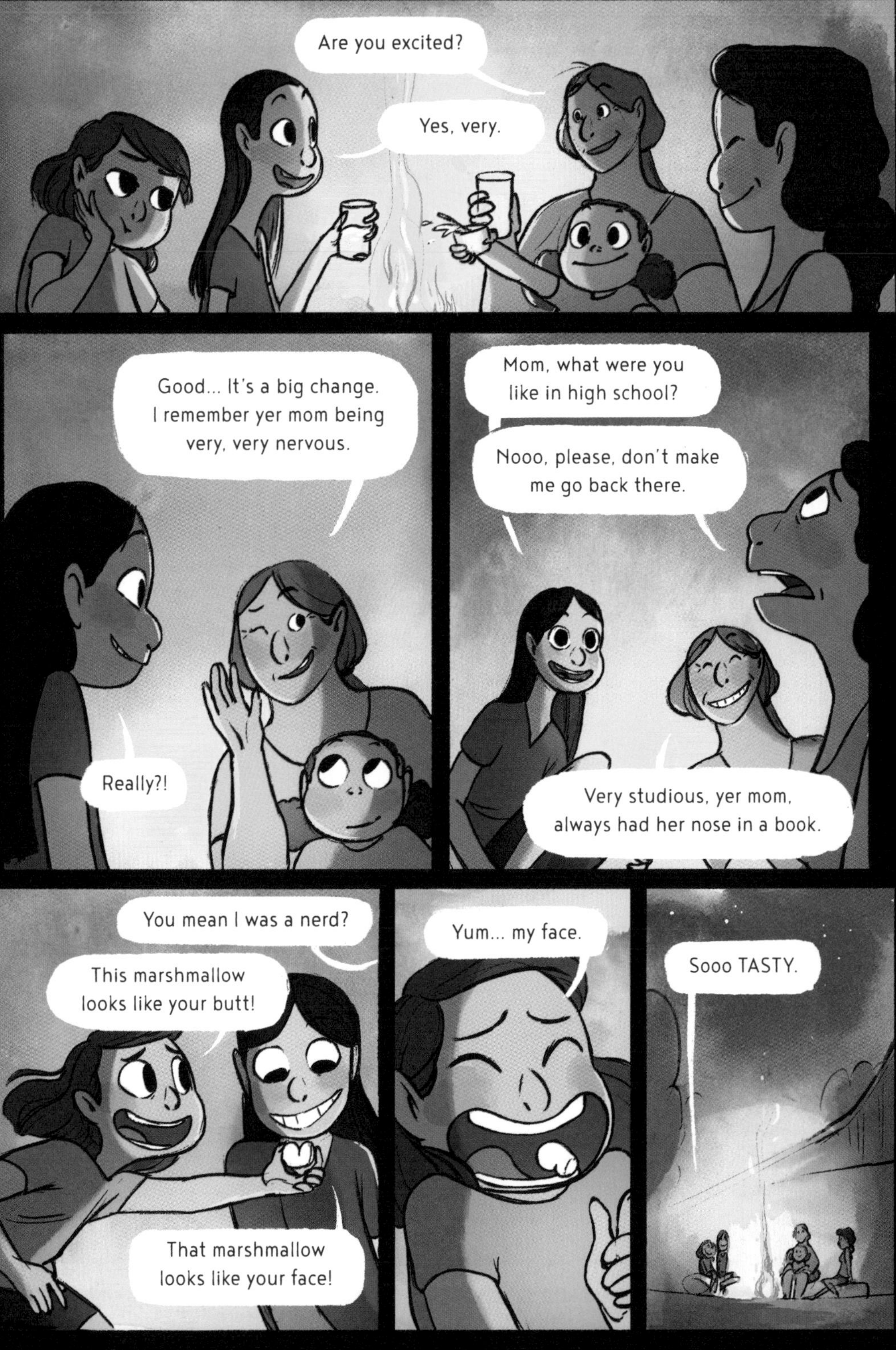
Are you excited?
Yes, very.
Good... It's a big change. I remember yer mom being very, very nervous.
Really?!
Mom, what were you like in high school?
Nooo, please, don't make me go back there.
Very studious, yer mom, always had her nose in a book.
You mean I was a nerd?
This marshmallow looks like your butt!
That marshmallow looks like your face!
Yum... my face.
Sooo TASTY.

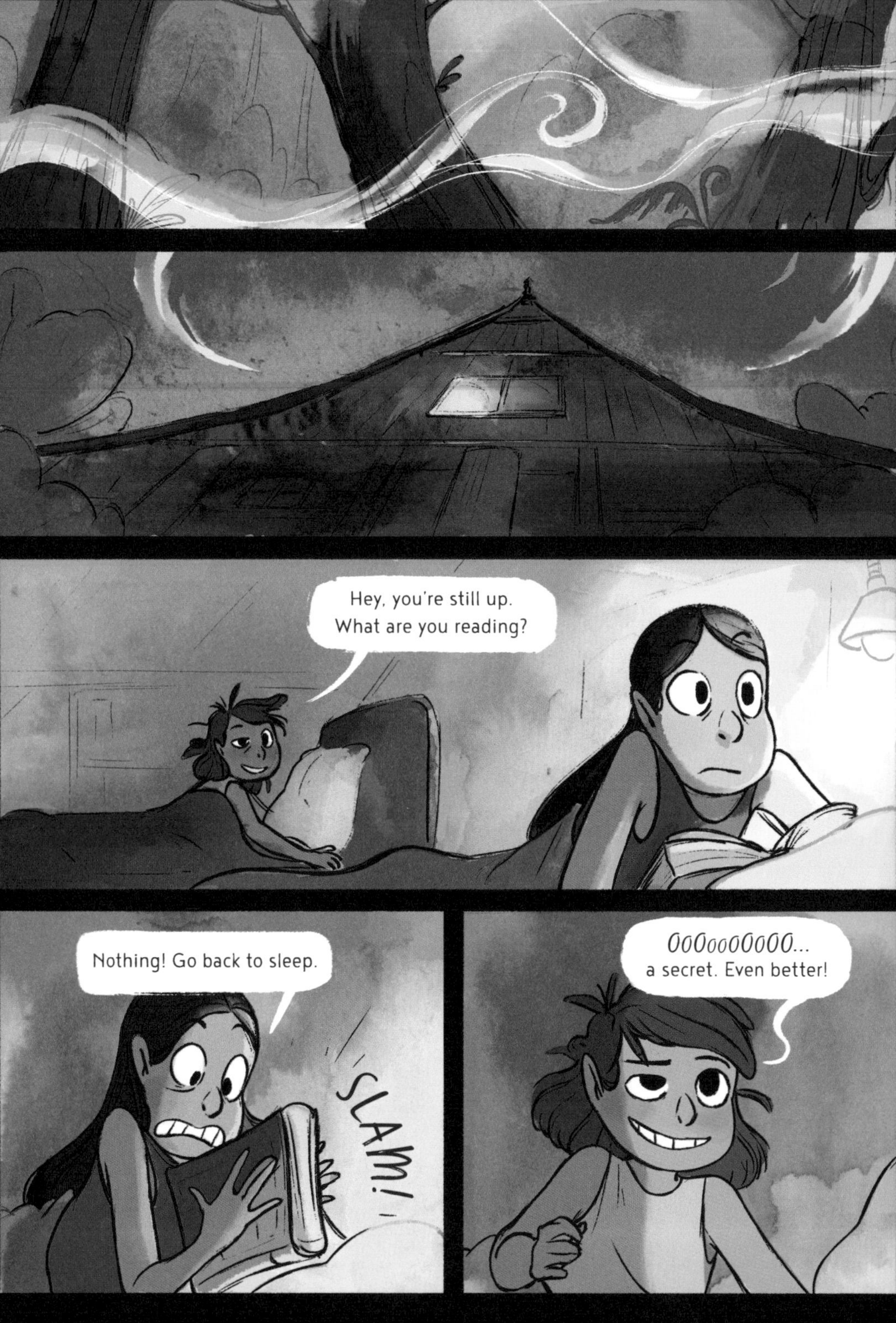
Hey, you're still up.
What are you reading?
Nothing! Go back to sleep.
SLAM!
OOOooOOOO...
a secret. Even better!

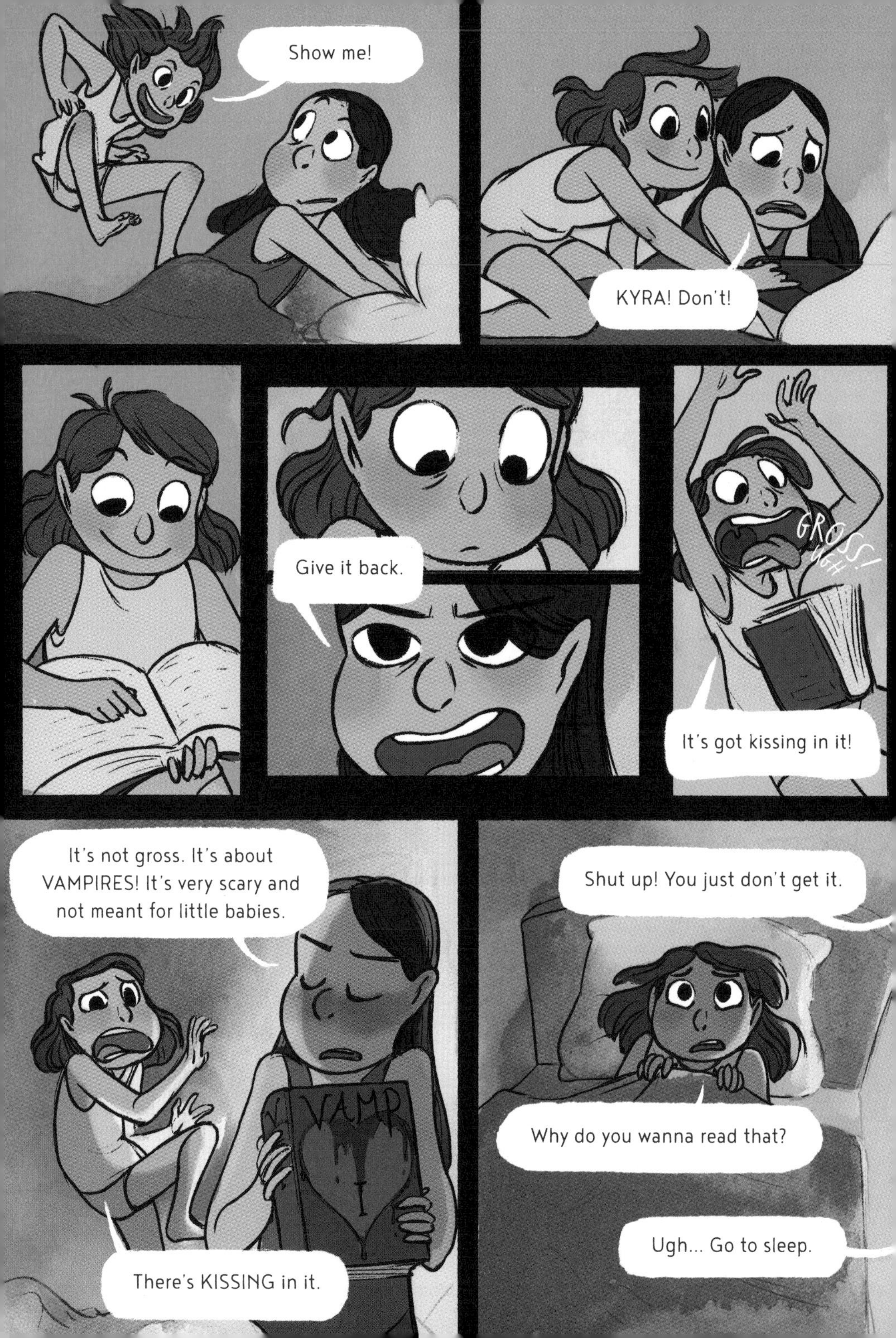
Show me!
KYRA! Don't!
Give it back.
GROSS!
UGH
It's got kissing in it!
It's not gross. It's about VAMPIRES! It's very scary and not meant for little babies.
There's KISSING in it.
VAMP
Shut up! You just don't get it.
Why do you wanna read that?
Ugh... Go to sleep.

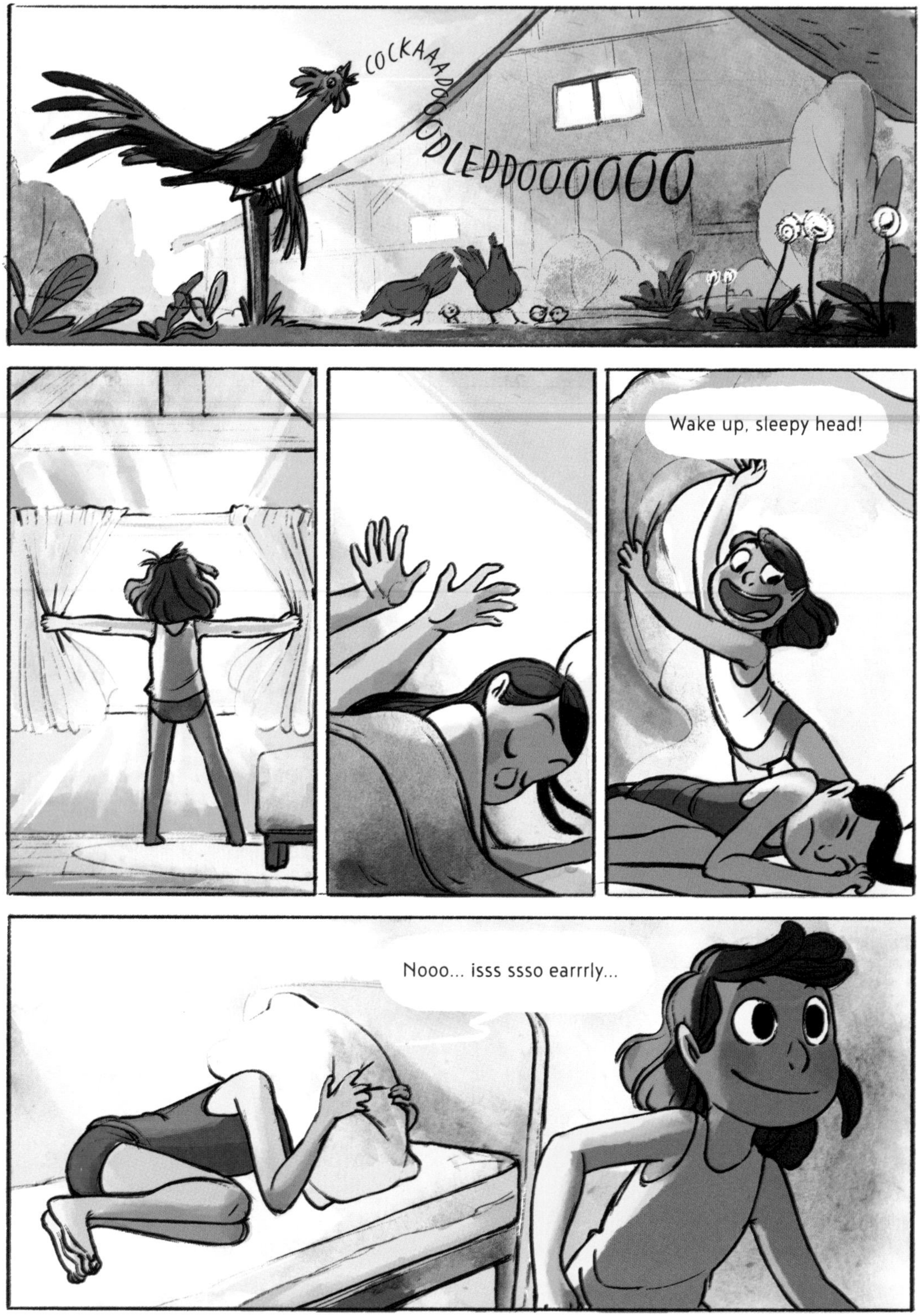
COCKAAADOOODLEDDOOOOOOO
Wake up, sleepy head!
Nooo... isss ssso earrrly...

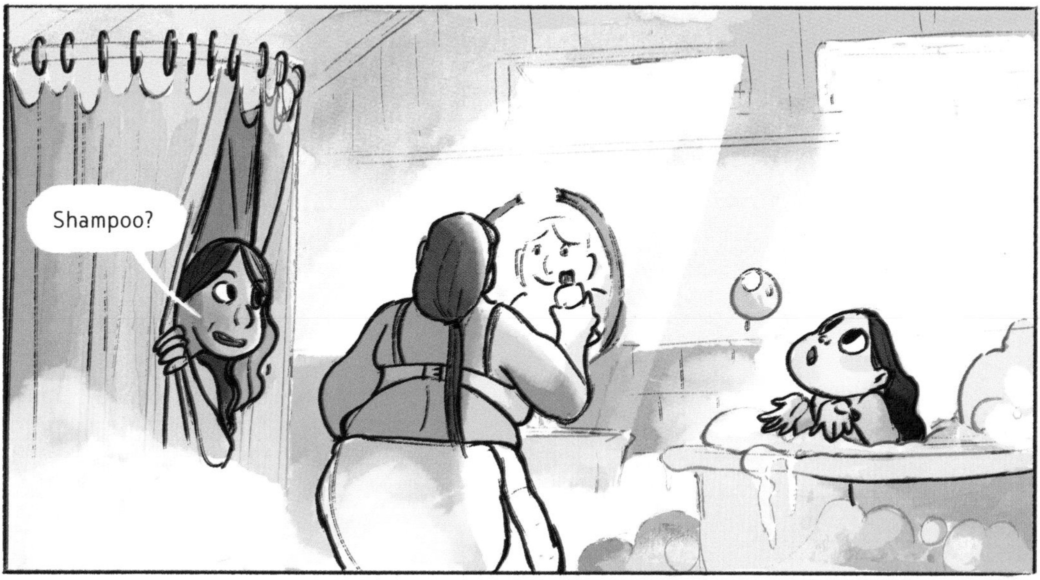
Shampoo?

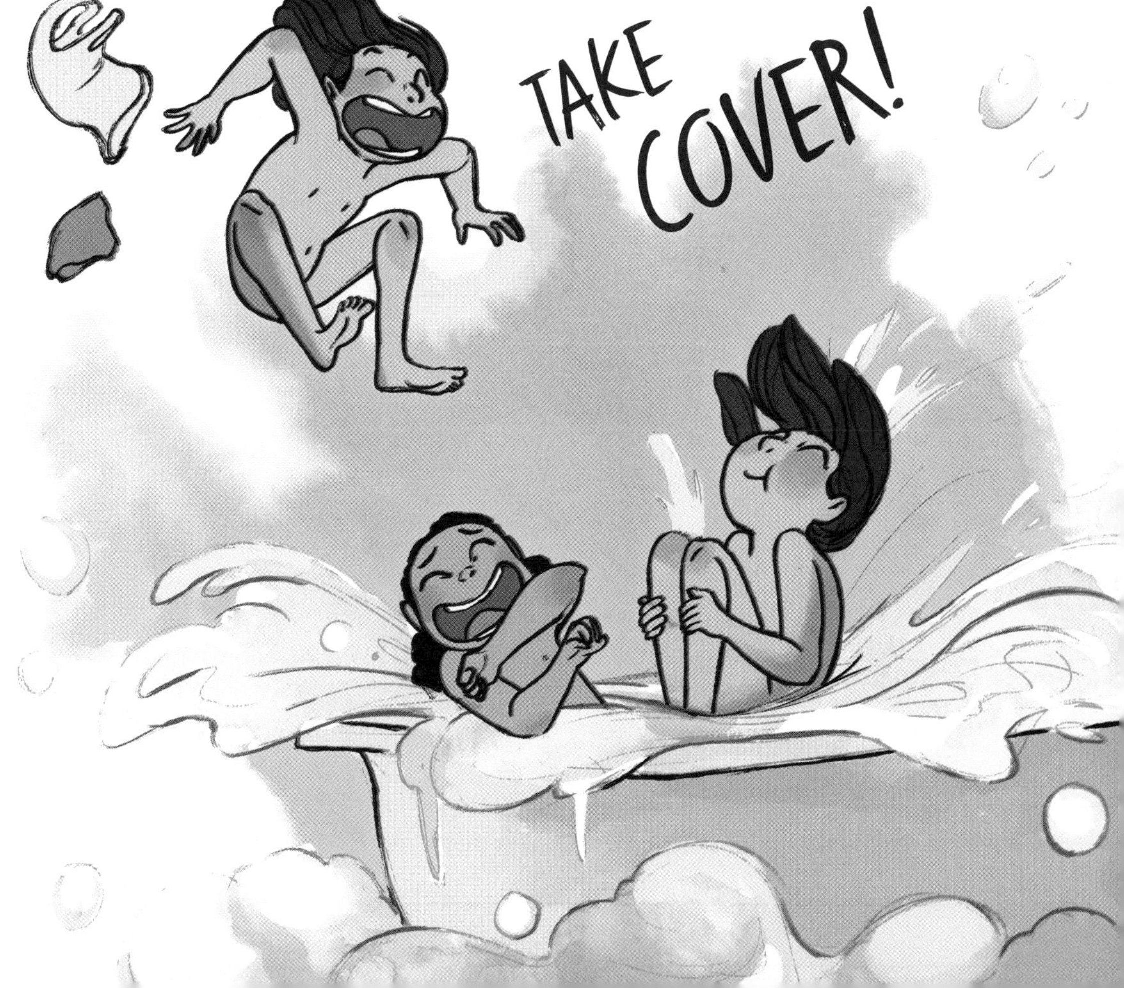
TAKE COVER!

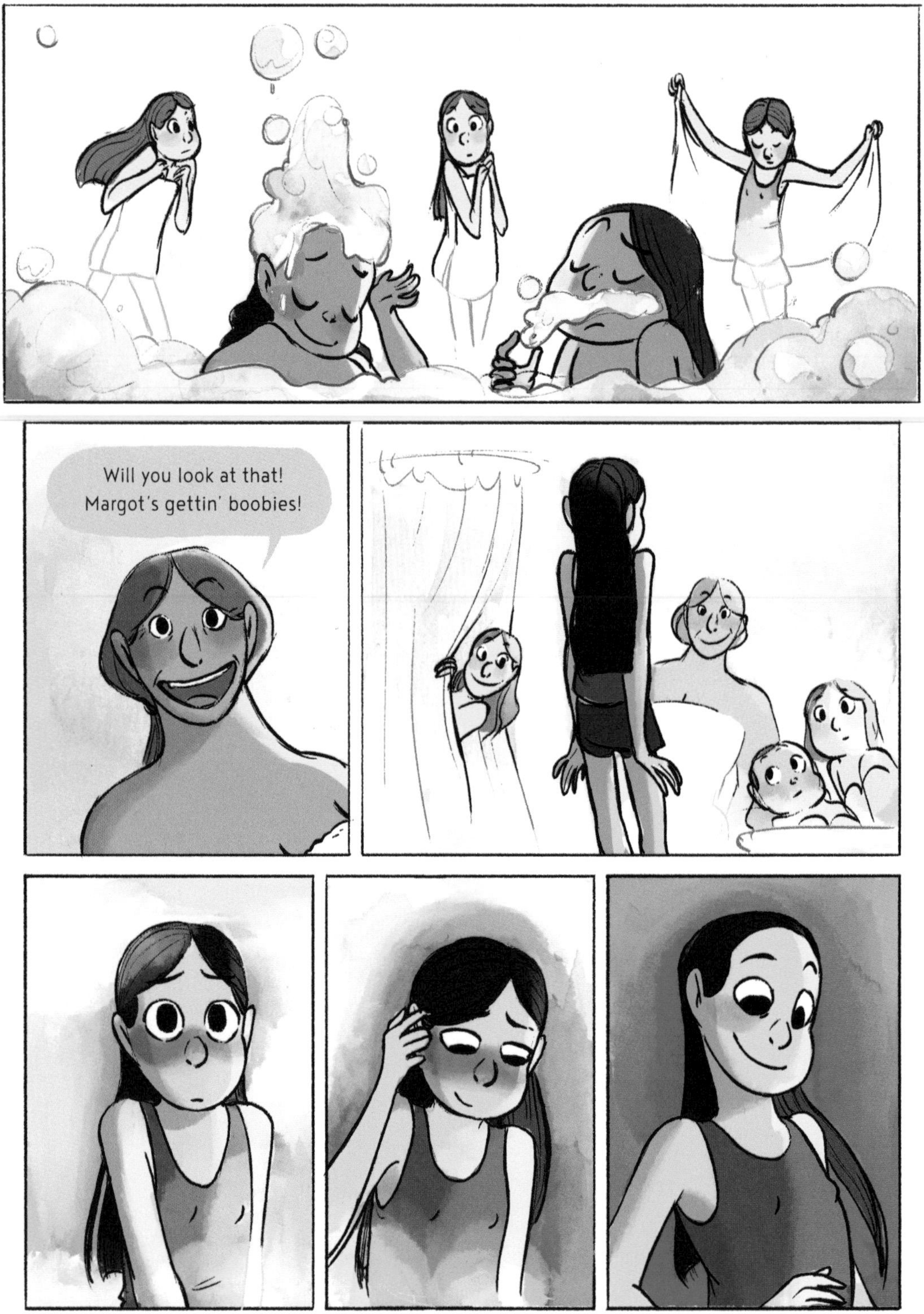
Will you look at that!
Margot's gettin' boobies!

Gran-Gran, you must be getting old. No boobies here, only tiny...

Teeeeensy weeensy... tiny, tiny, tiny titties.

Just wait, they'll be just as big as Mom's.

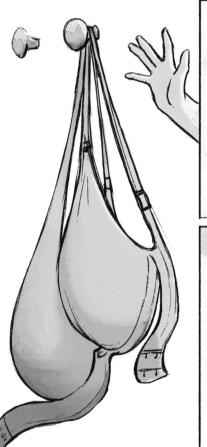

Or they'll be as big as Gran-Grans...

HA HA HA HA

And what's wrong with that?!

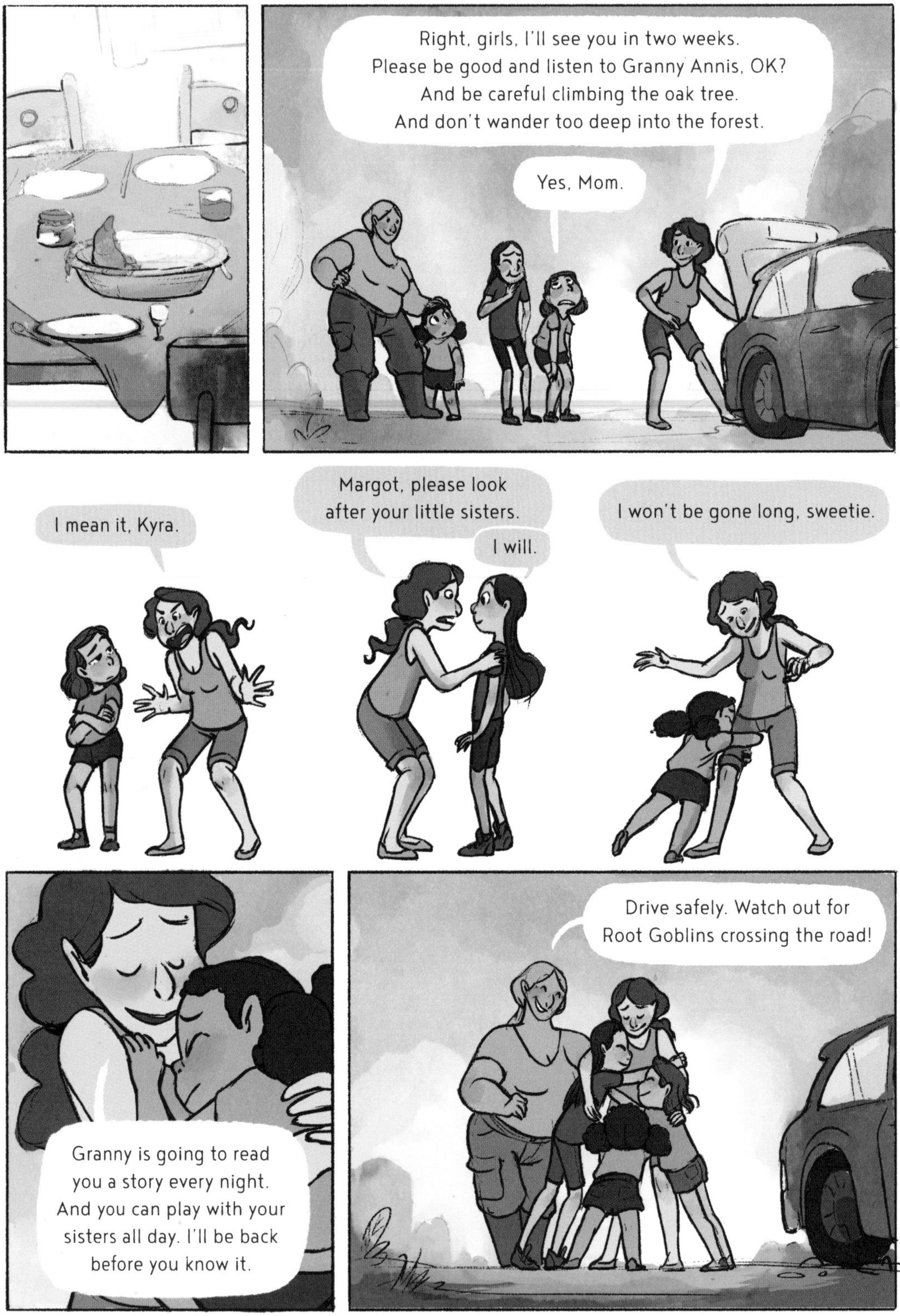
Right, girls, I'll see you in two weeks.
Please be good and listen to Granny Annis, OK?
And be careful climbing the oak tree.
And don't wander too deep into the forest.
Yes, Mom.
I mean it, Kyra.
Margot, please look after your little sisters.
I will.
I won't be gone long, sweetie.
Granny is going to read you a story every night. And you can play with your sisters all day. I'll be back before you know it.
Drive safely. Watch out for Root Goblins crossing the road!

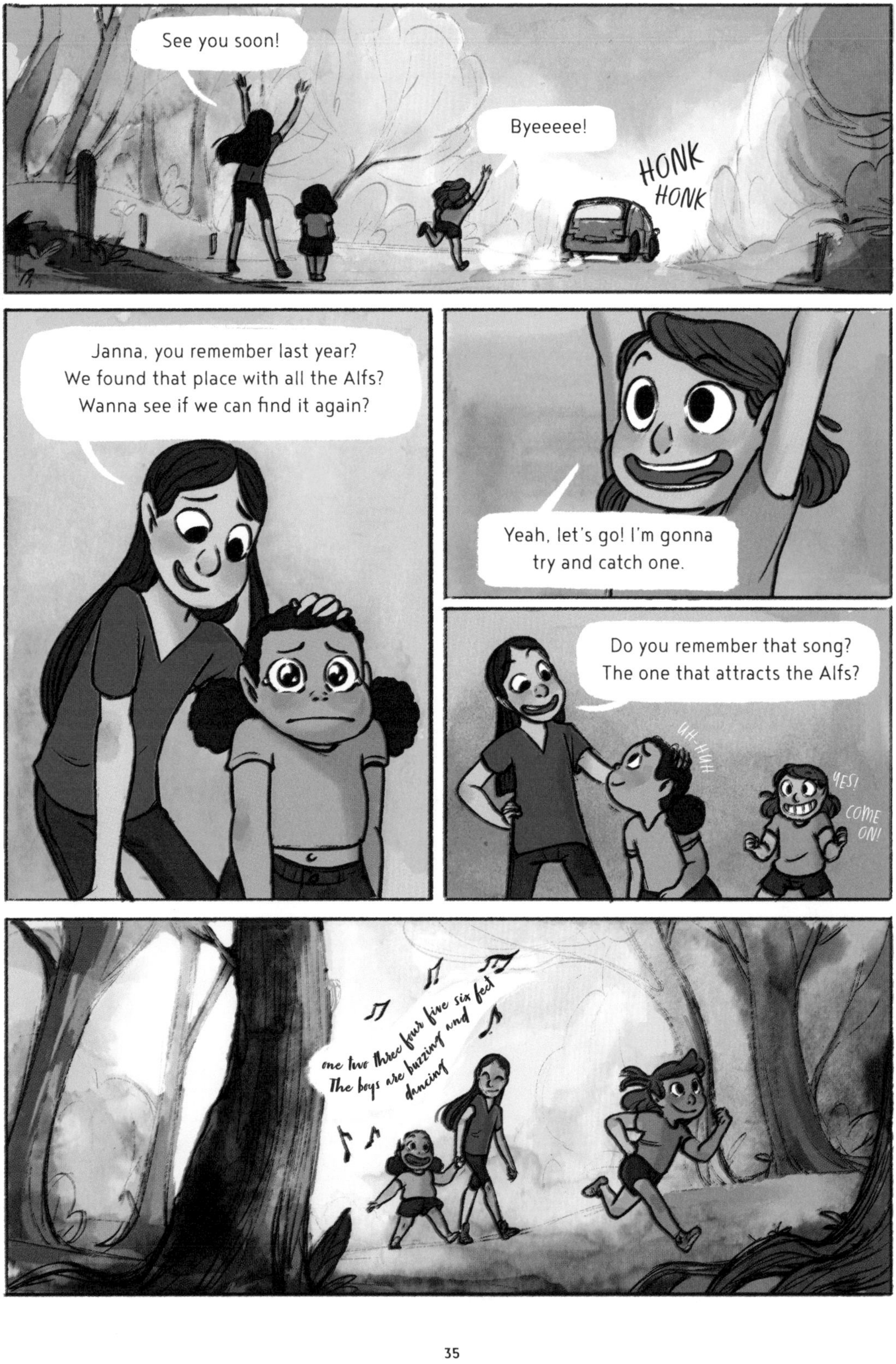
See you soon!
Byeeeee!
HONK
HONK
Janna, you remember last year? We found that place with all the Alfs? Wanna see if we can find it again?
Yeah, let's go! I'm gonna try and catch one.
Do you remember that song? The one that attracts the Alfs?
UH-HUH
YES!
COME ON!
one two three four five six feet
The boys are buzzing and dancing

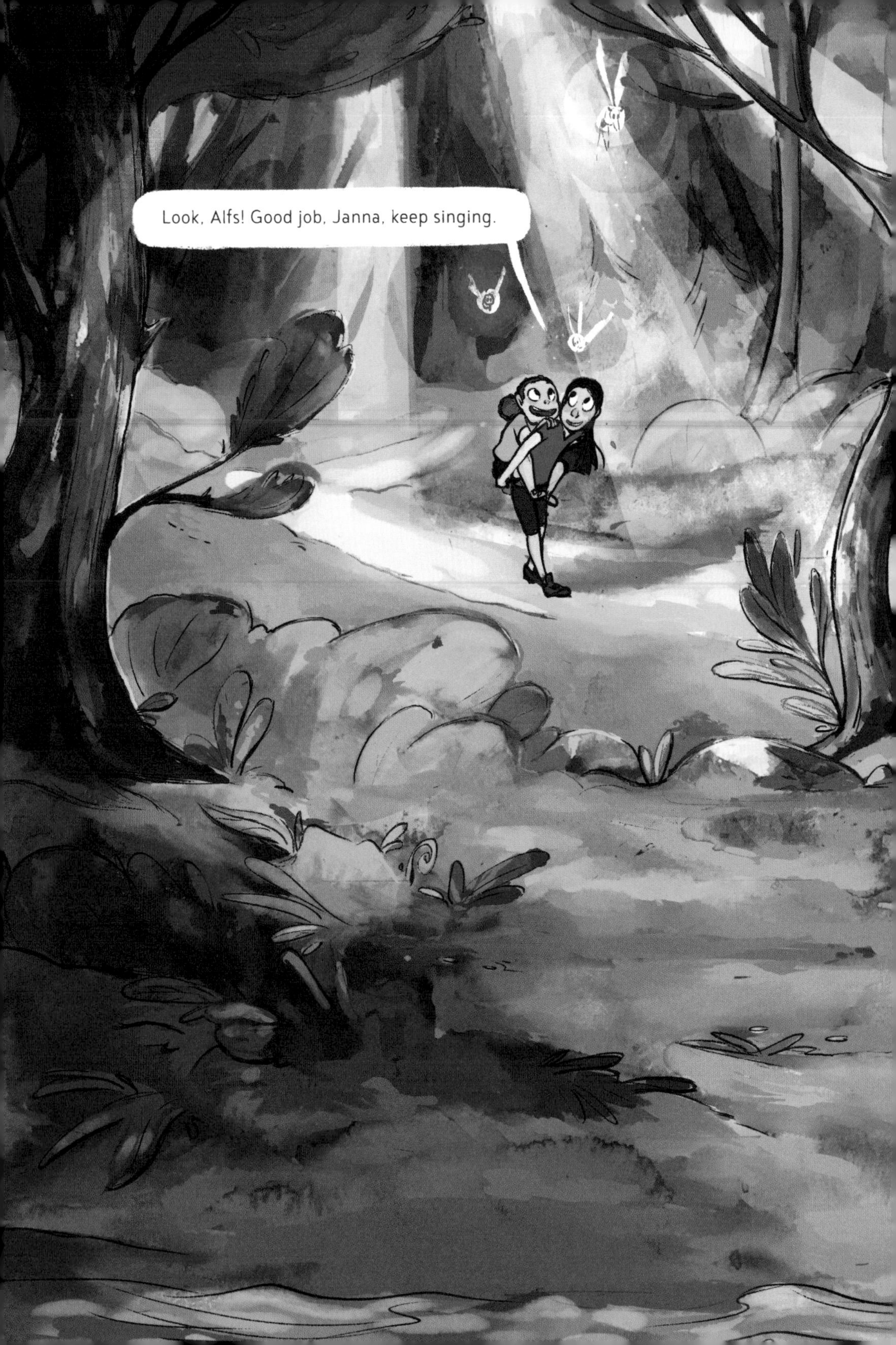
Look, Alfs! Good job, Janna, keep singing.

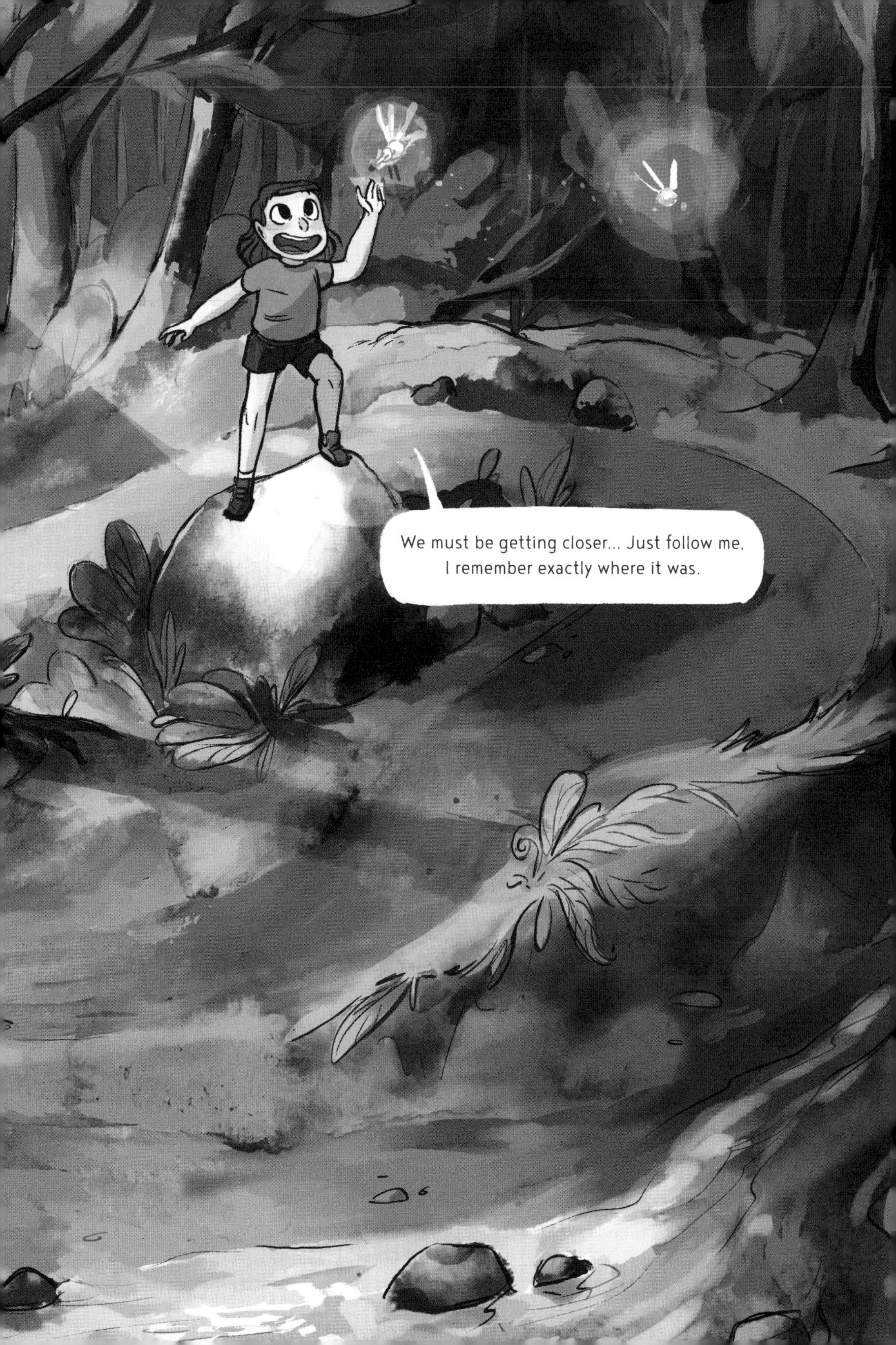
We must be getting closer... Just follow me, I remember exactly where it was.

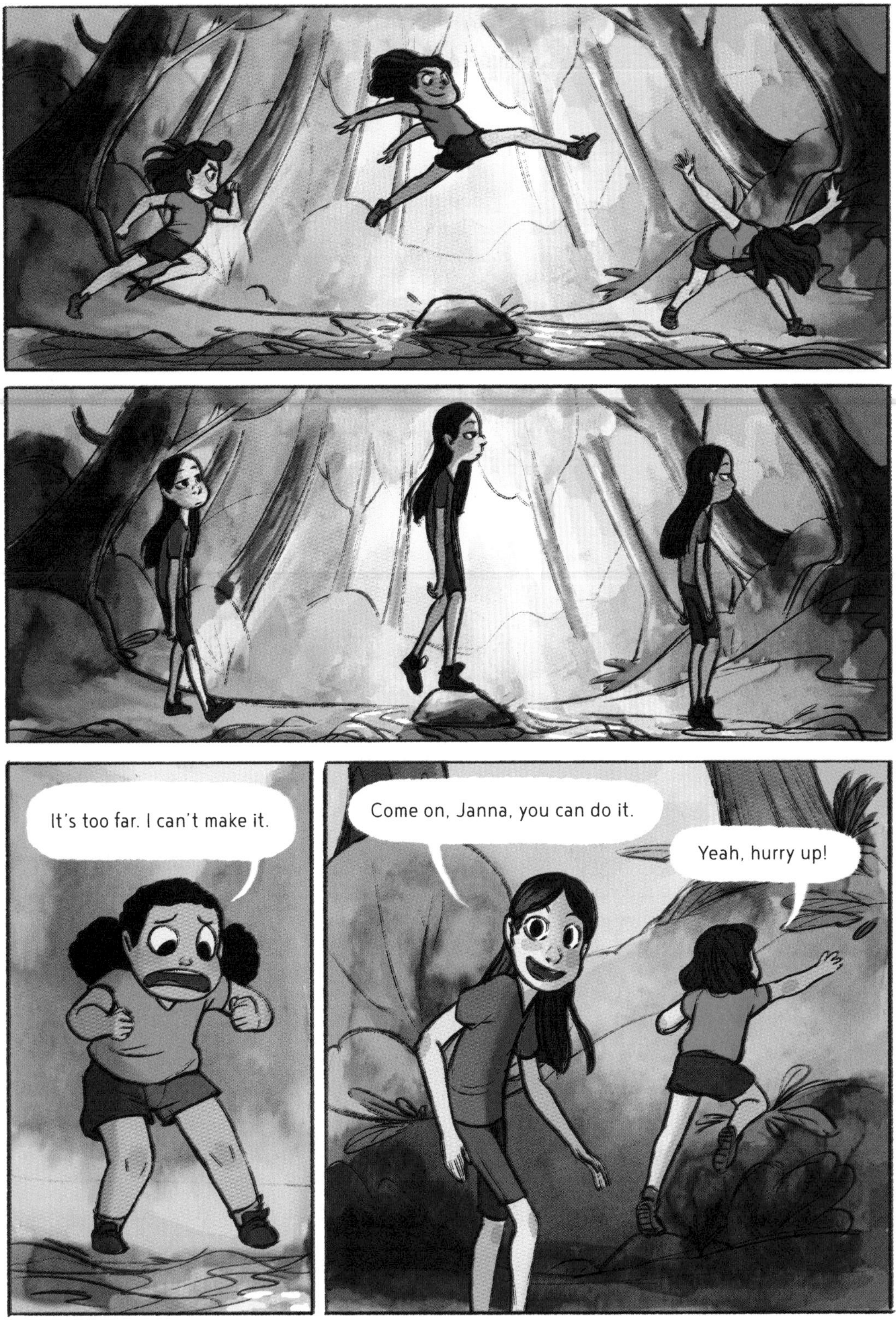
It's too far. I can't make it.
Come on, Janna, you can do it.
Yeah, hurry up!

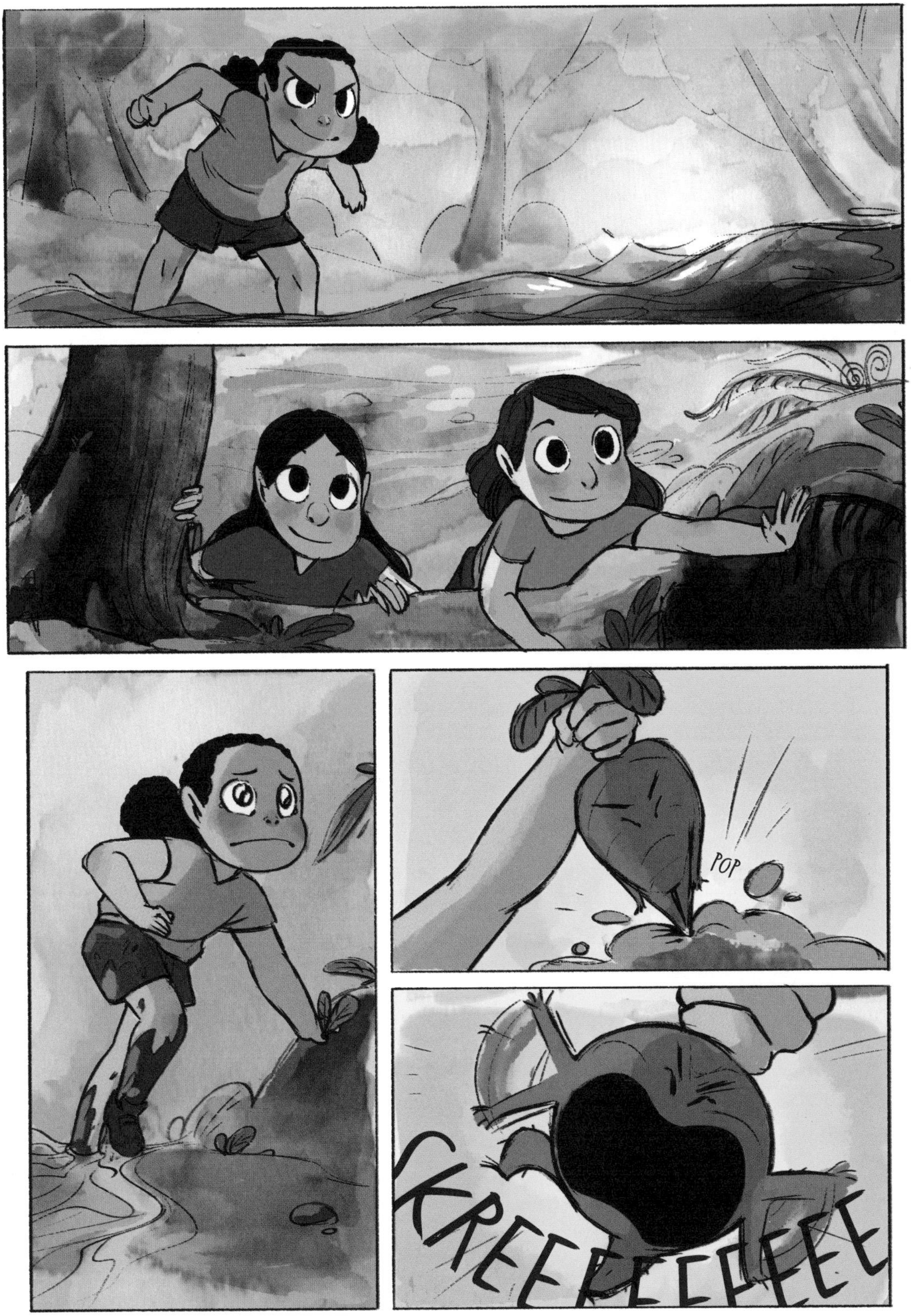
POP
SKREEEEEEEEE

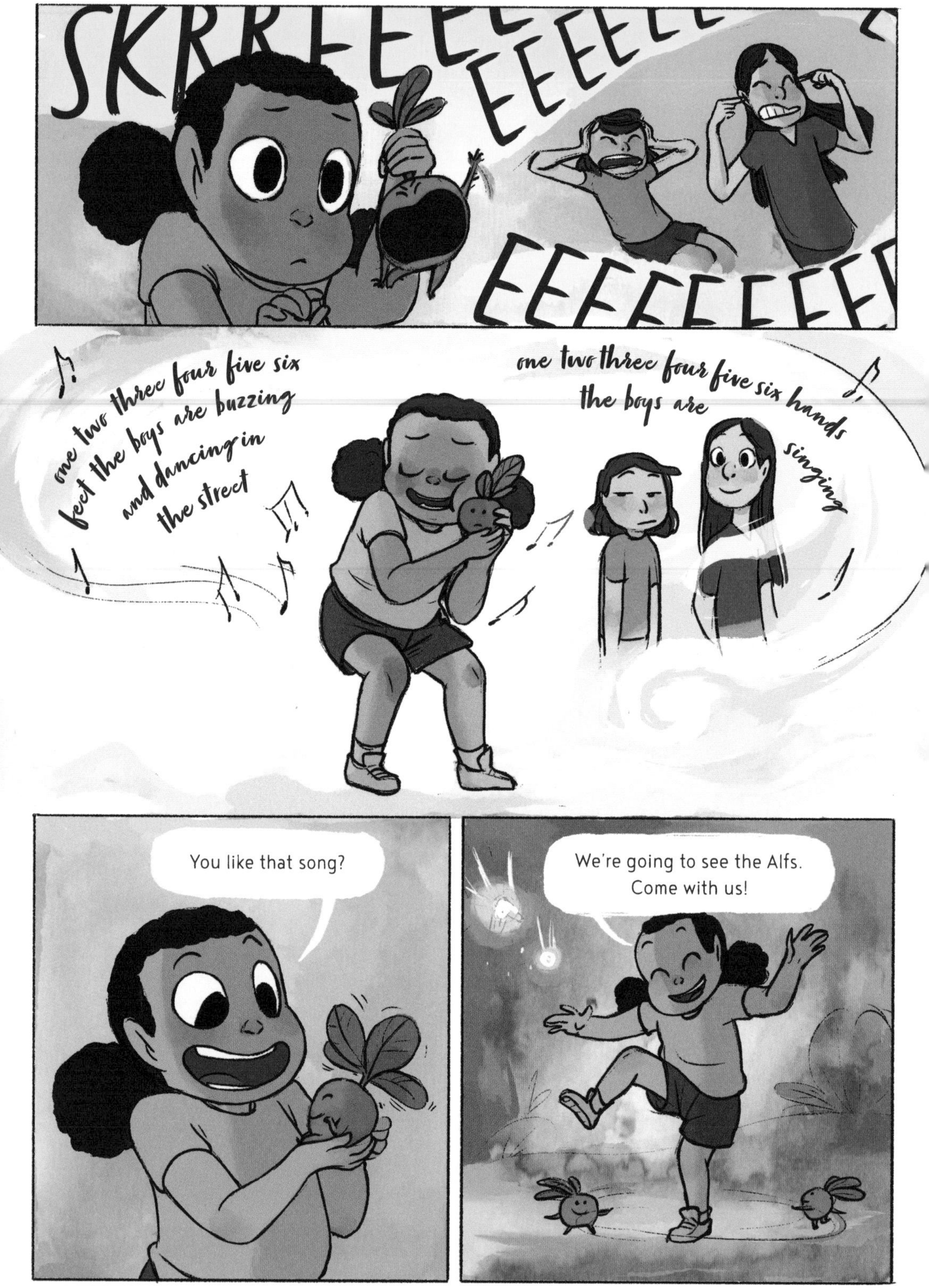
SKRREEEEEEEEEEEEEEEEEEE
one two three four five six feet the boys are buzzing and dancing in the street
one two three four five six hands the boys are singing
You like that song?
We're going to see the Alfs. Come with us!

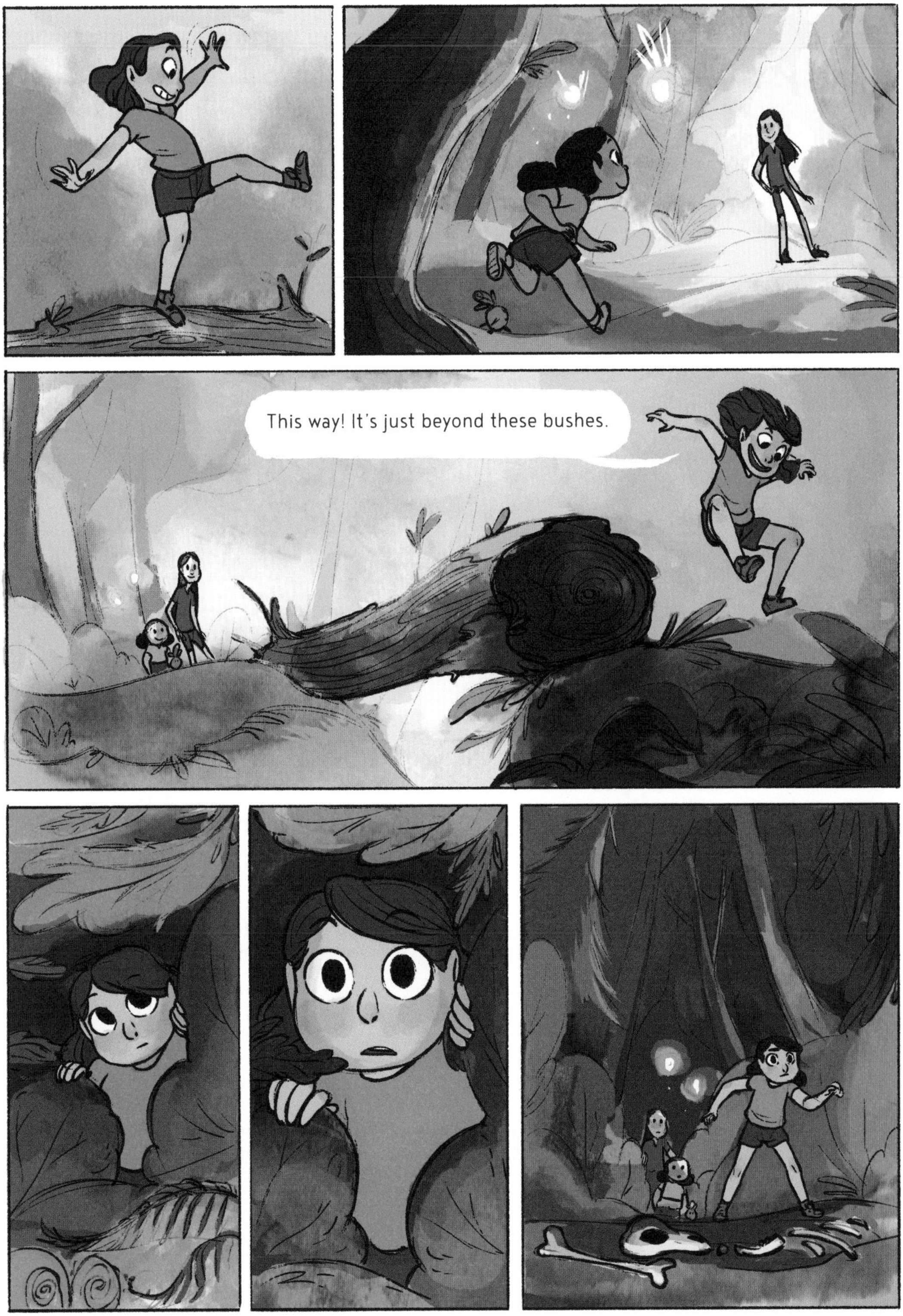
This way! It's just beyond these bushes.

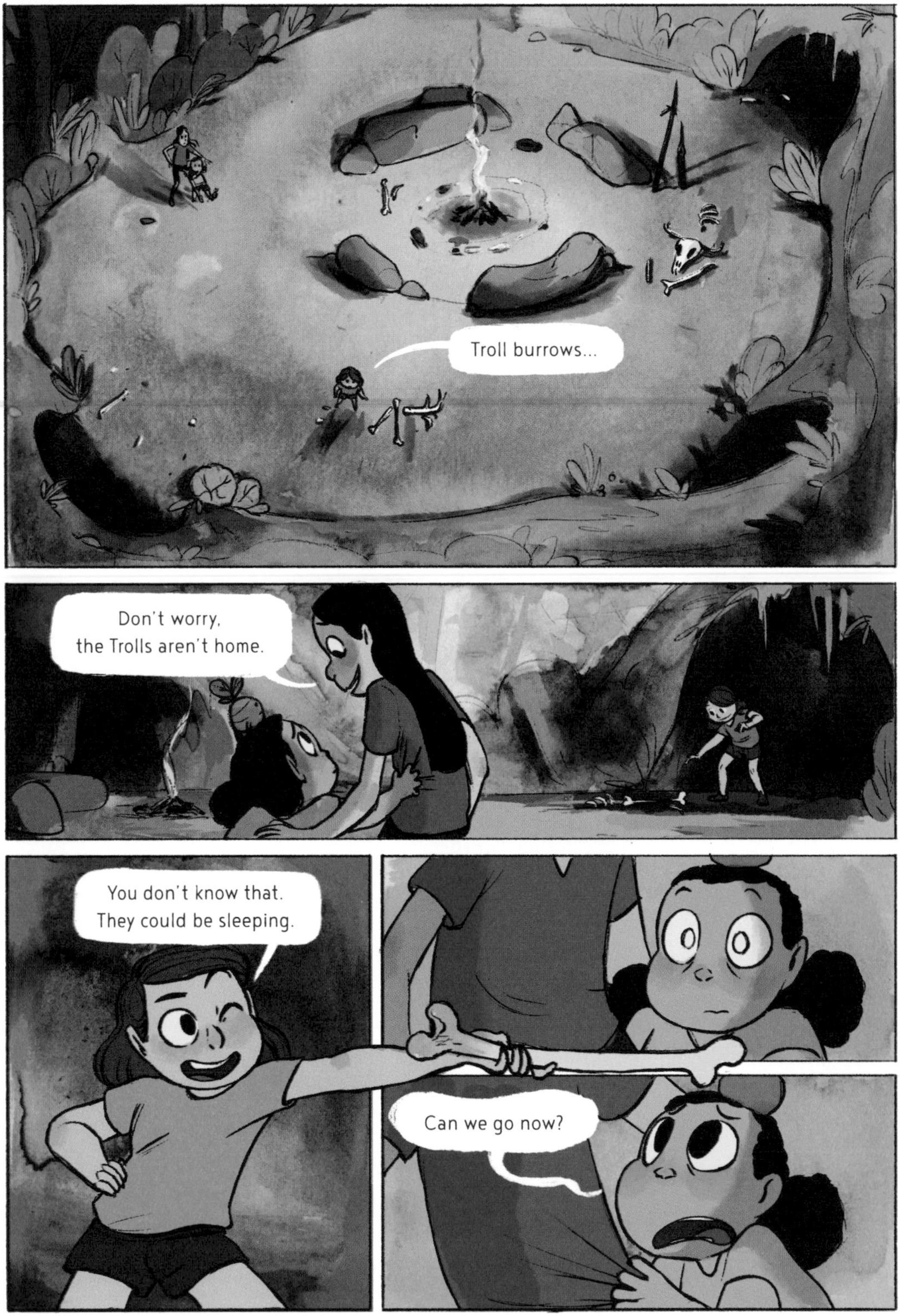
Troll burrows...
Don't worry, the Trolls aren't home.
You don't know that. They could be sleeping.
Can we go now?

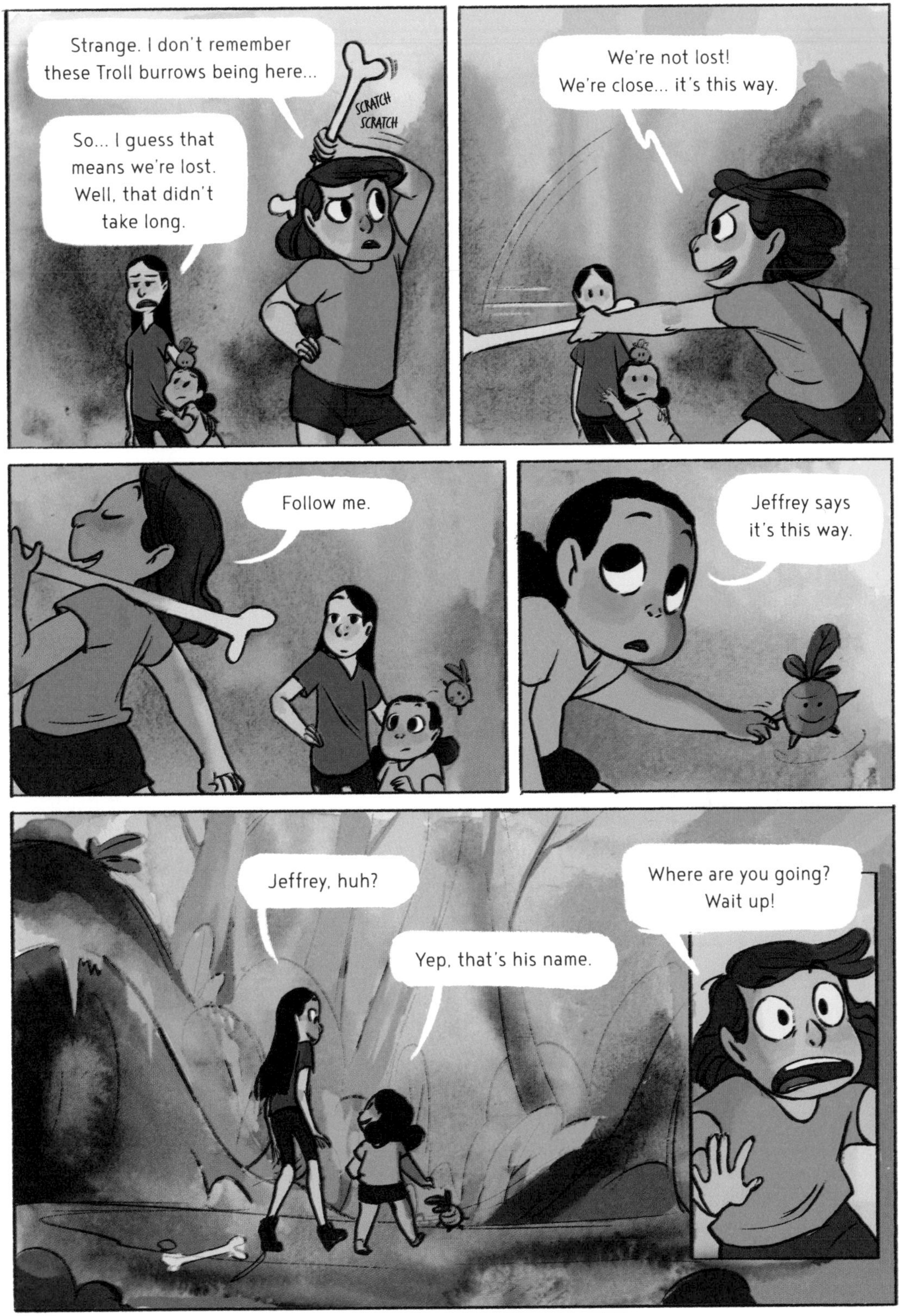
Strange. I don't remember these Troll burrows being here...
SCRATCH SCRATCH
So... I guess that means we're lost. Well, that didn't take long.
We're not lost! We're close... it's this way.
Follow me.
Jeffrey says it's this way.
Jeffrey, huh?
Yep, that's his name.
Where are you going? Wait up!

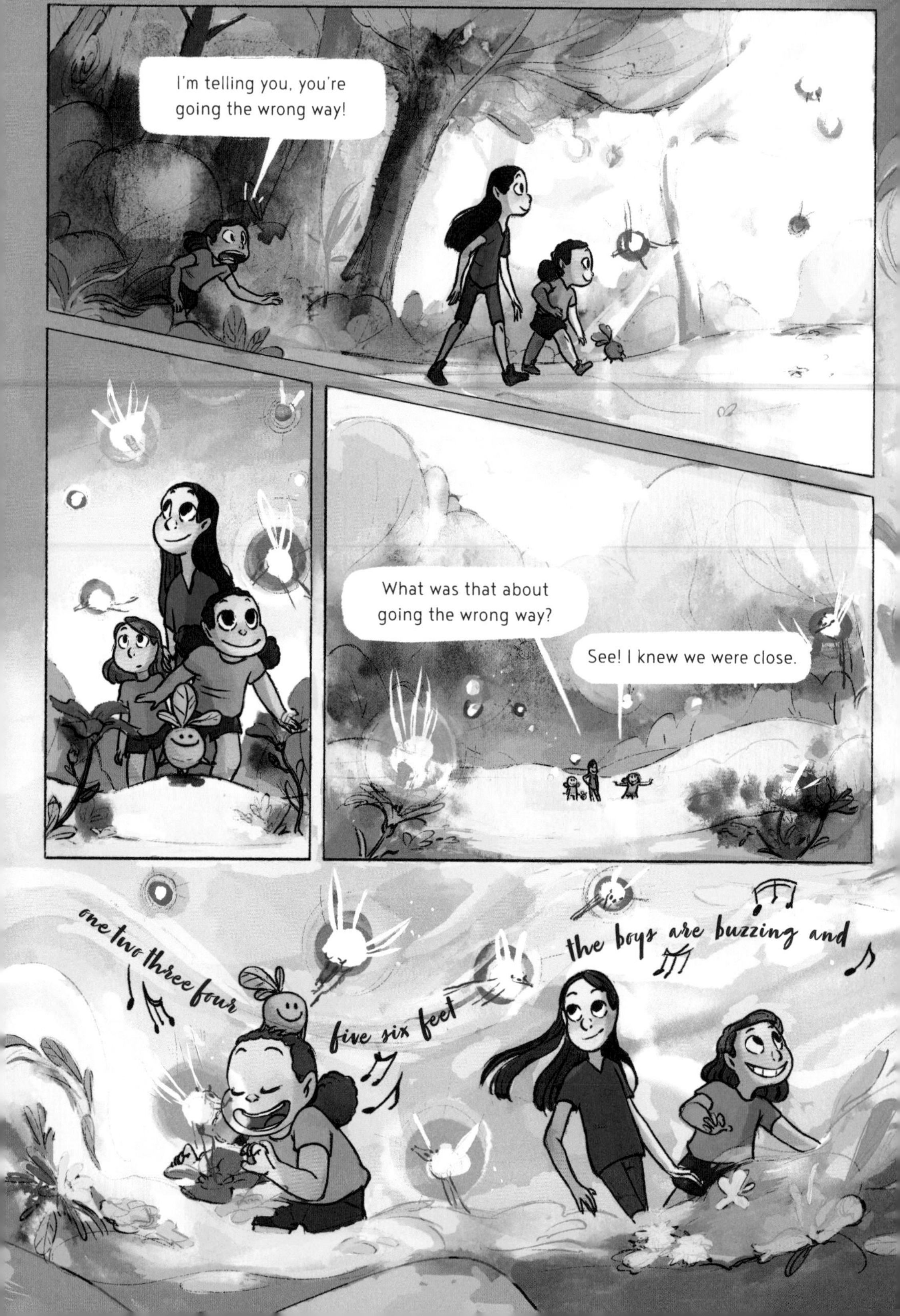
I'm telling you, you're going the wrong way!
What was that about going the wrong way?
See! I knew we were close.
one two three four
five six feet
the boys are buzzing and

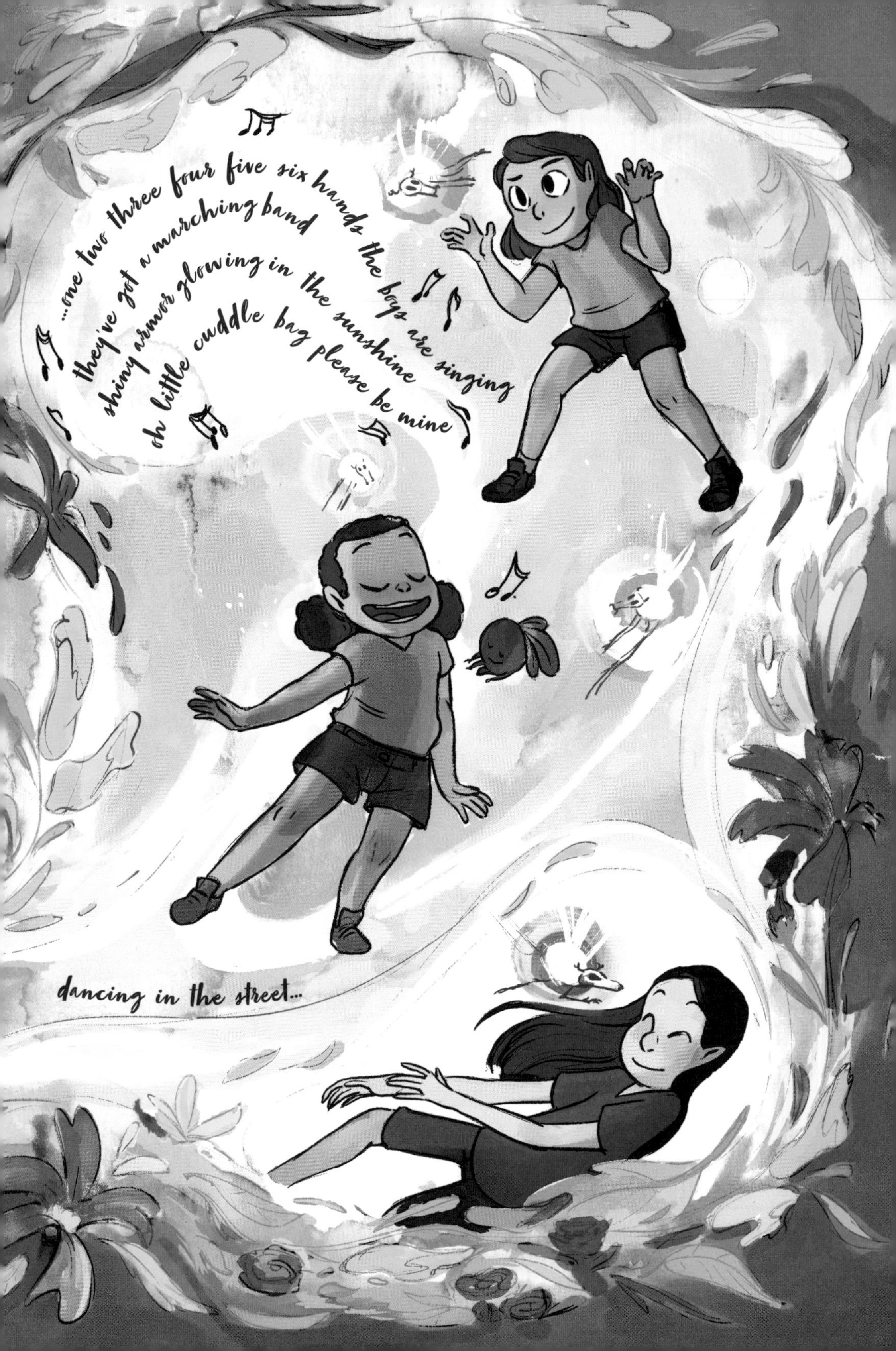
...one two three four five six hands the boys are singing
they've got a marching band
shiny armor glowing in the sunshine
oh little cuddle bag please be mine
dancing in the street...

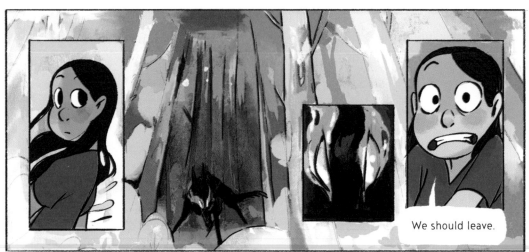

We should leave.

Right NOW.

Already? We only just got here.

Well, I'm staying.

GRRRR
RRRR
RRRR

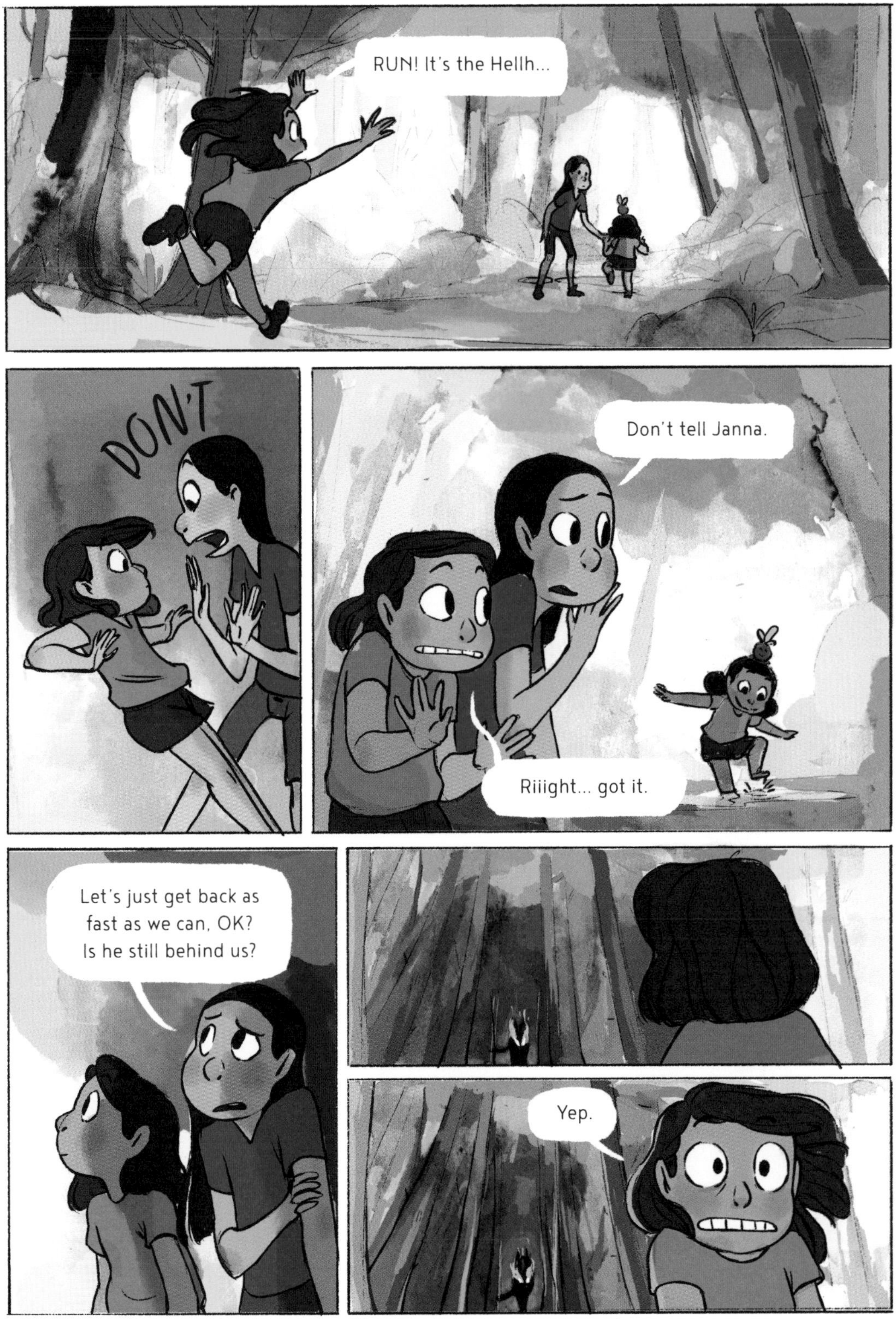
RUN! It's the Hellh...
DON'T
Don't tell Janna.
Riiight... got it.
Let's just get back as fast as we can, OK? Is he still behind us?
Yep.

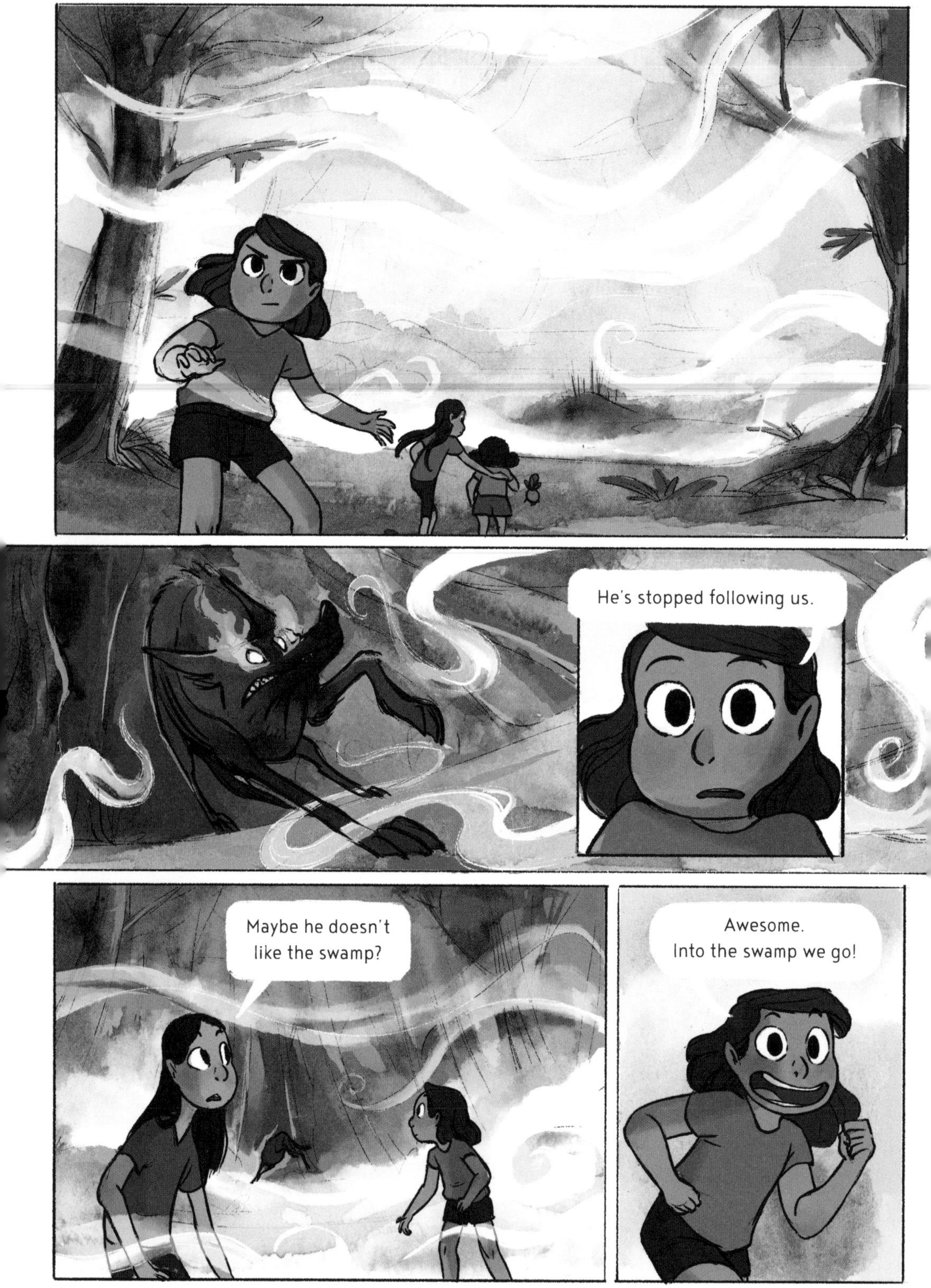
He's stopped following us.
Maybe he doesn't like the swamp?
Awesome. Into the swamp we go!

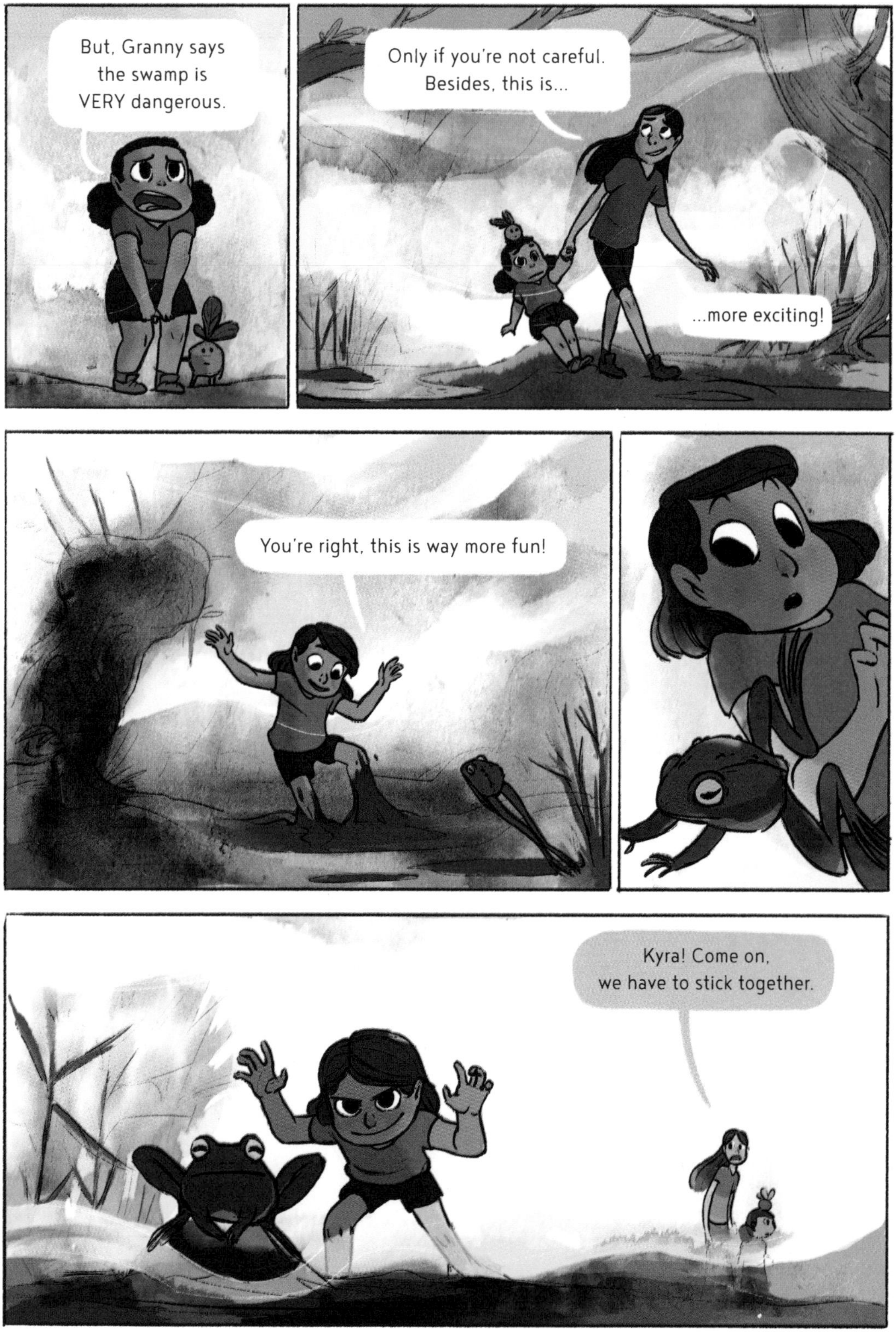
But, Granny says the swamp is VERY dangerous.
Only if you're not careful. Besides, this is...
...more exciting!
You're right, this is way more fun!
Kyra! Come on, we have to stick together.

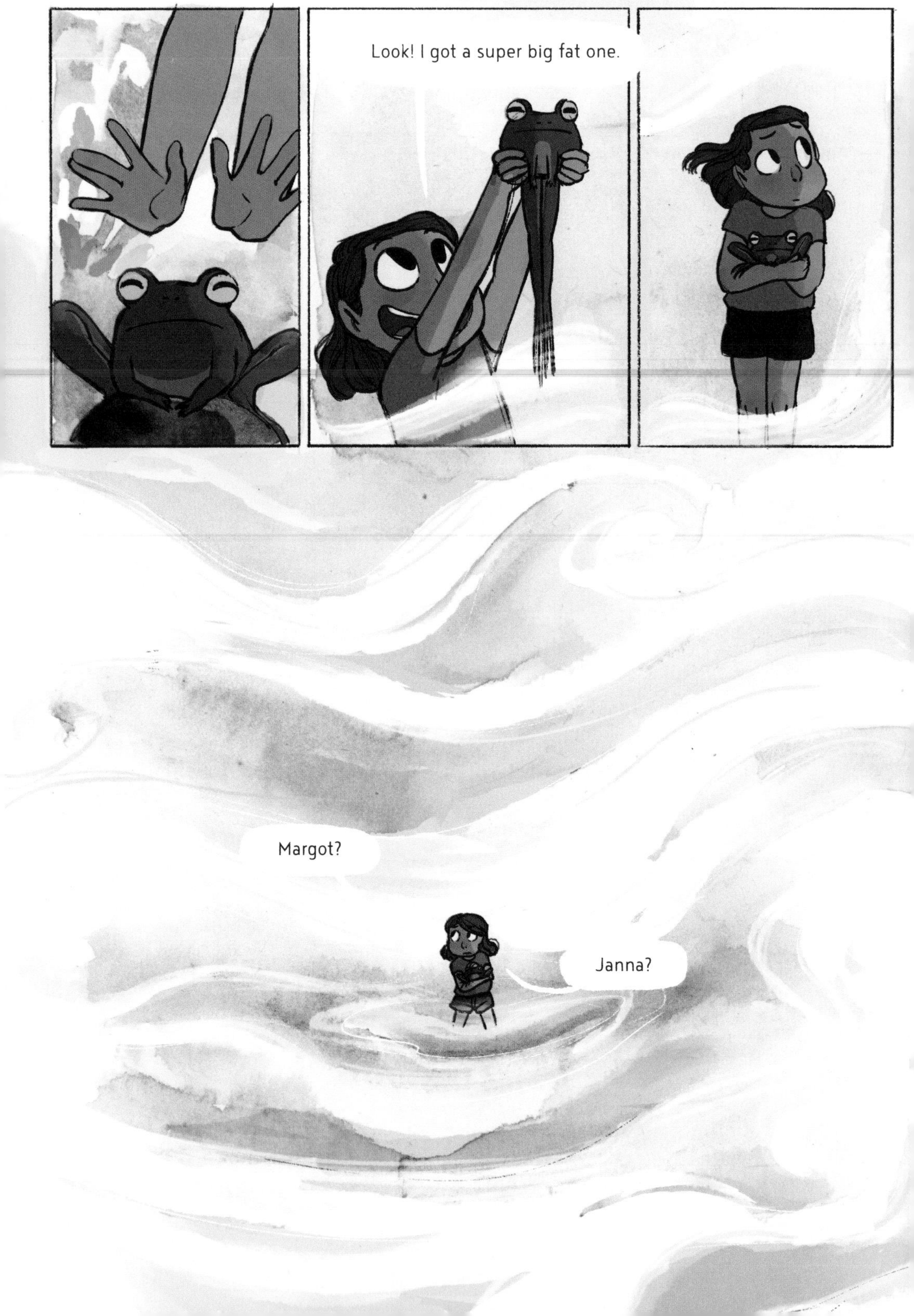
Look! I got a super big fat one.
Margot?
Janna?

MARGOT!

JANNA!

Come out, you guys...
This isn't funny!

KYRAAAAAAA

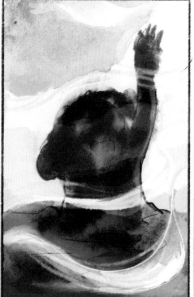

Janna!

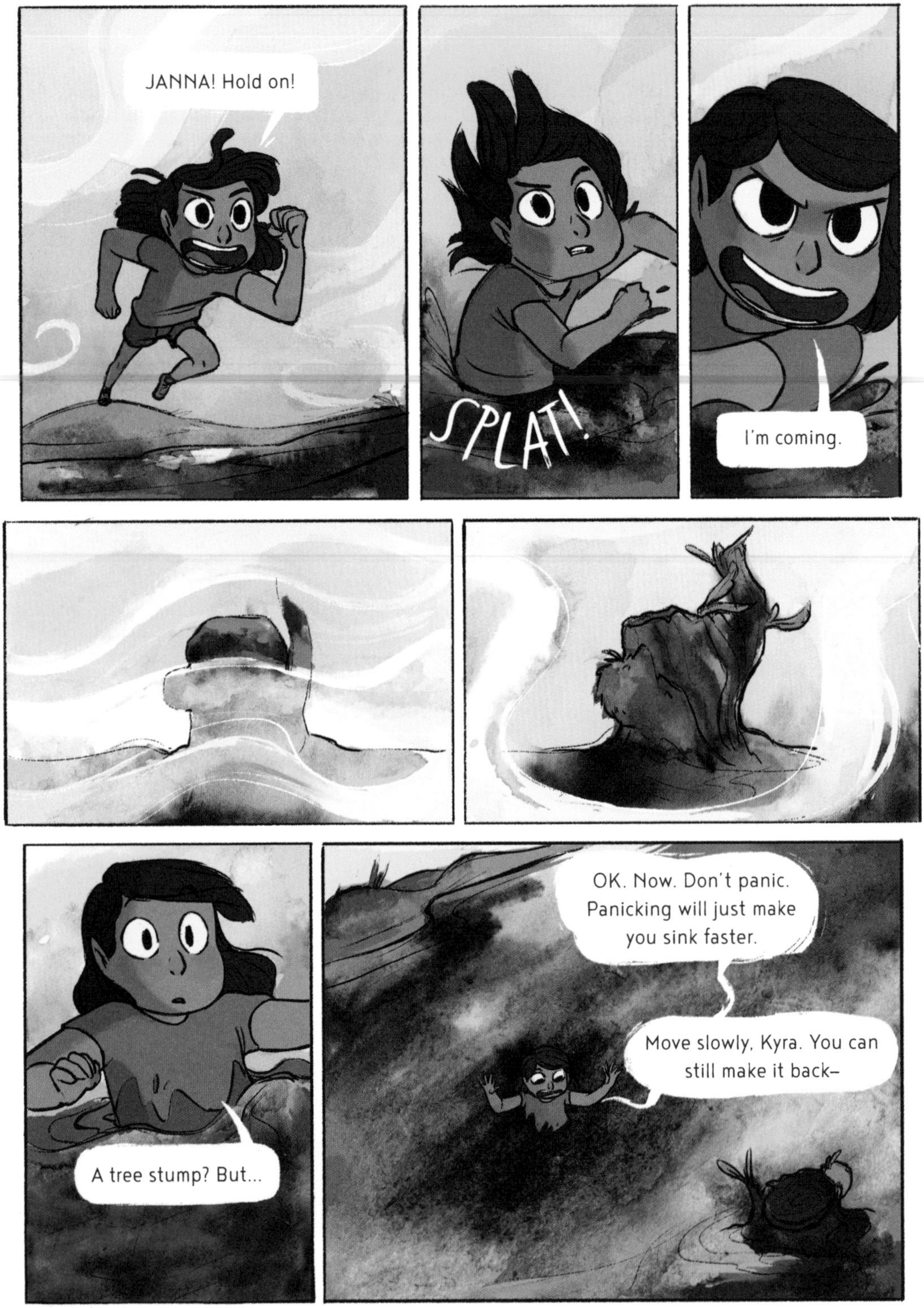

JANNA! Hold on!
SPLAT!
I'm coming.
A tree stump? But...
OK. Now. Don't panic. Panicking will just make you sink faster.
Move slowly, Kyra. You can still make it back–

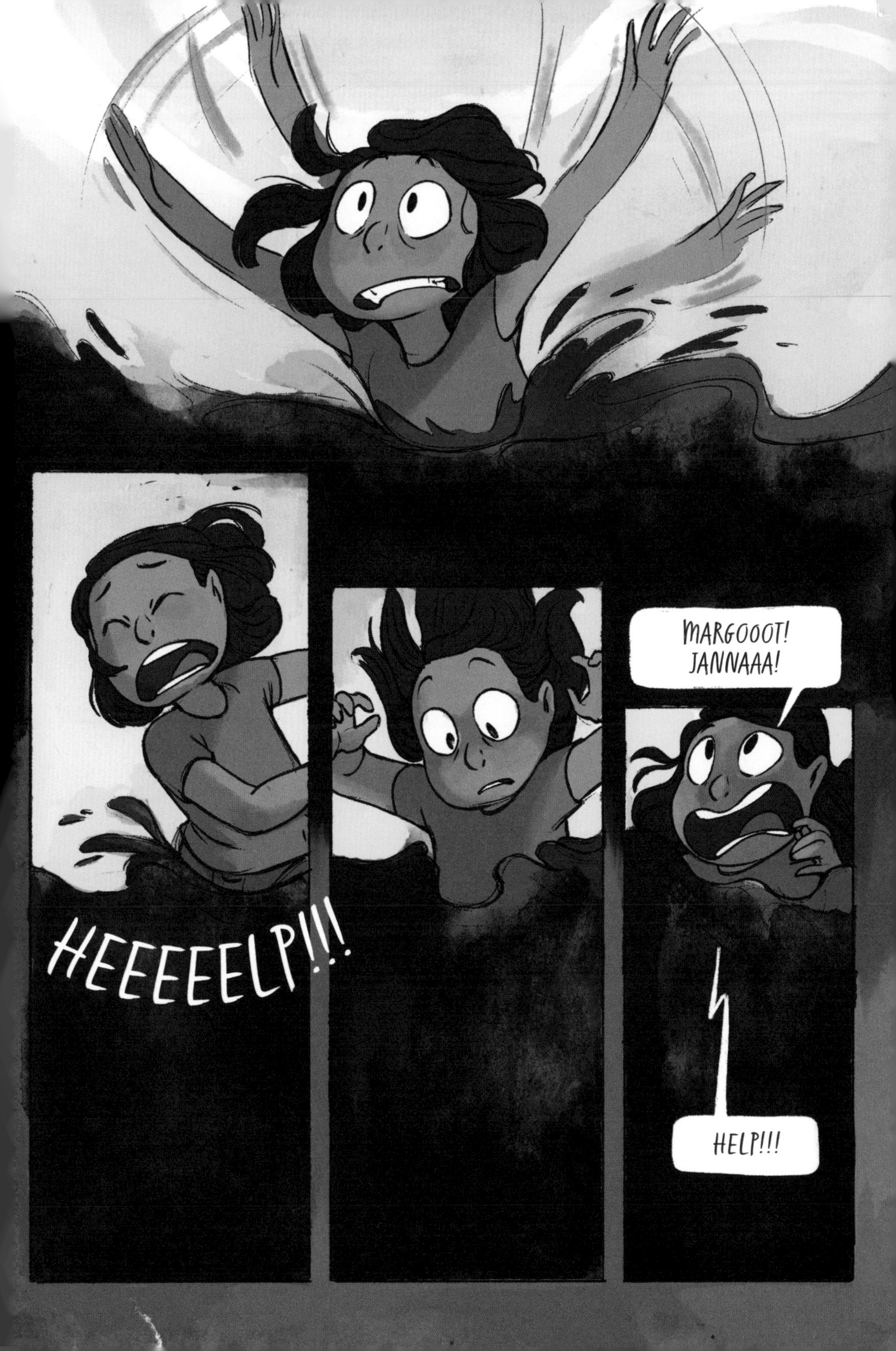
HEEEEELP!!!
MARGOOOT! JANNAAA!
HELP!!!

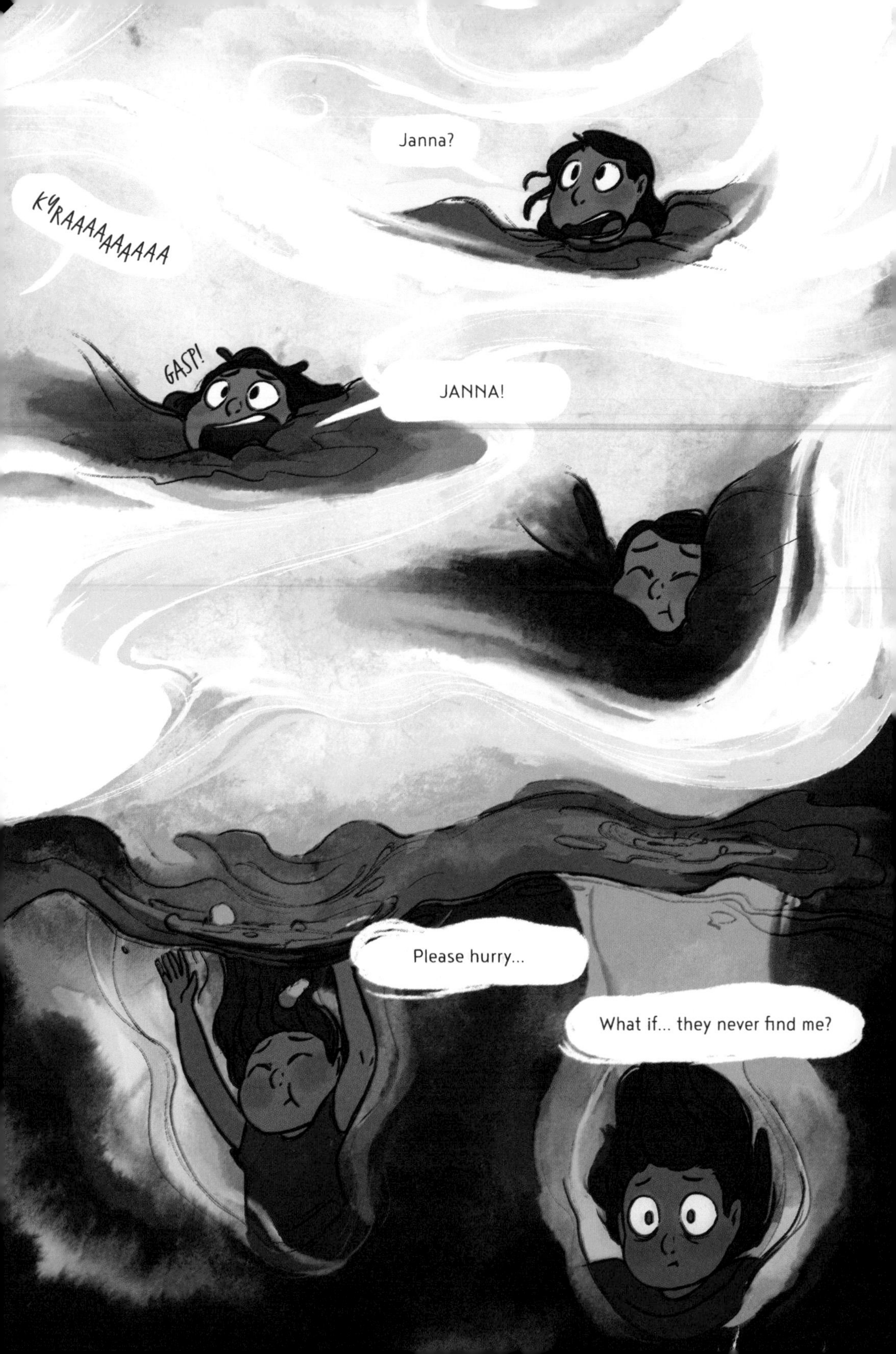
Janna?
KYRAAAAAAAAAA
GASP!
JANNA!
Please hurry...
What if... they never find me?

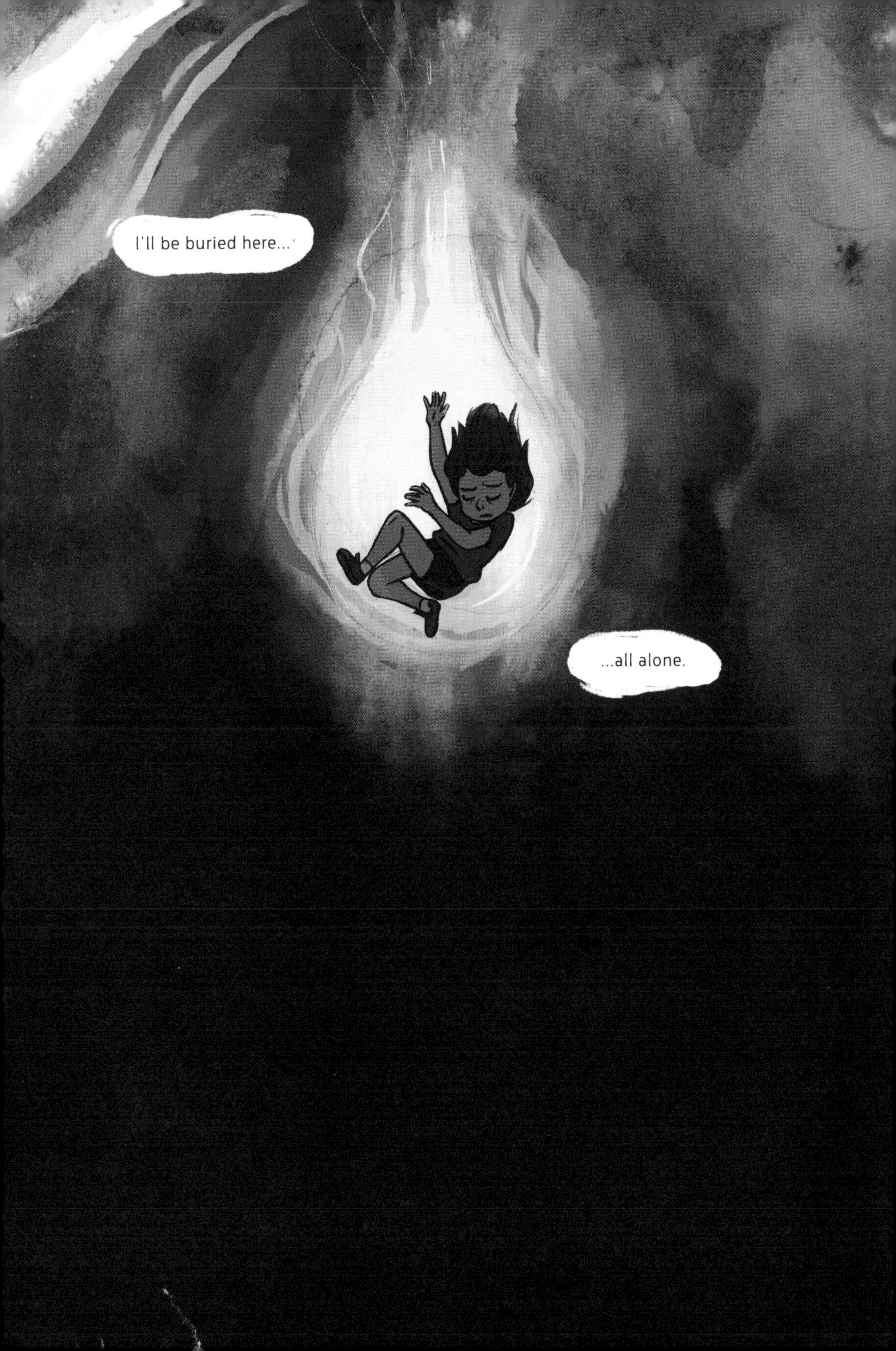
I'll be buried here...
...all alone.

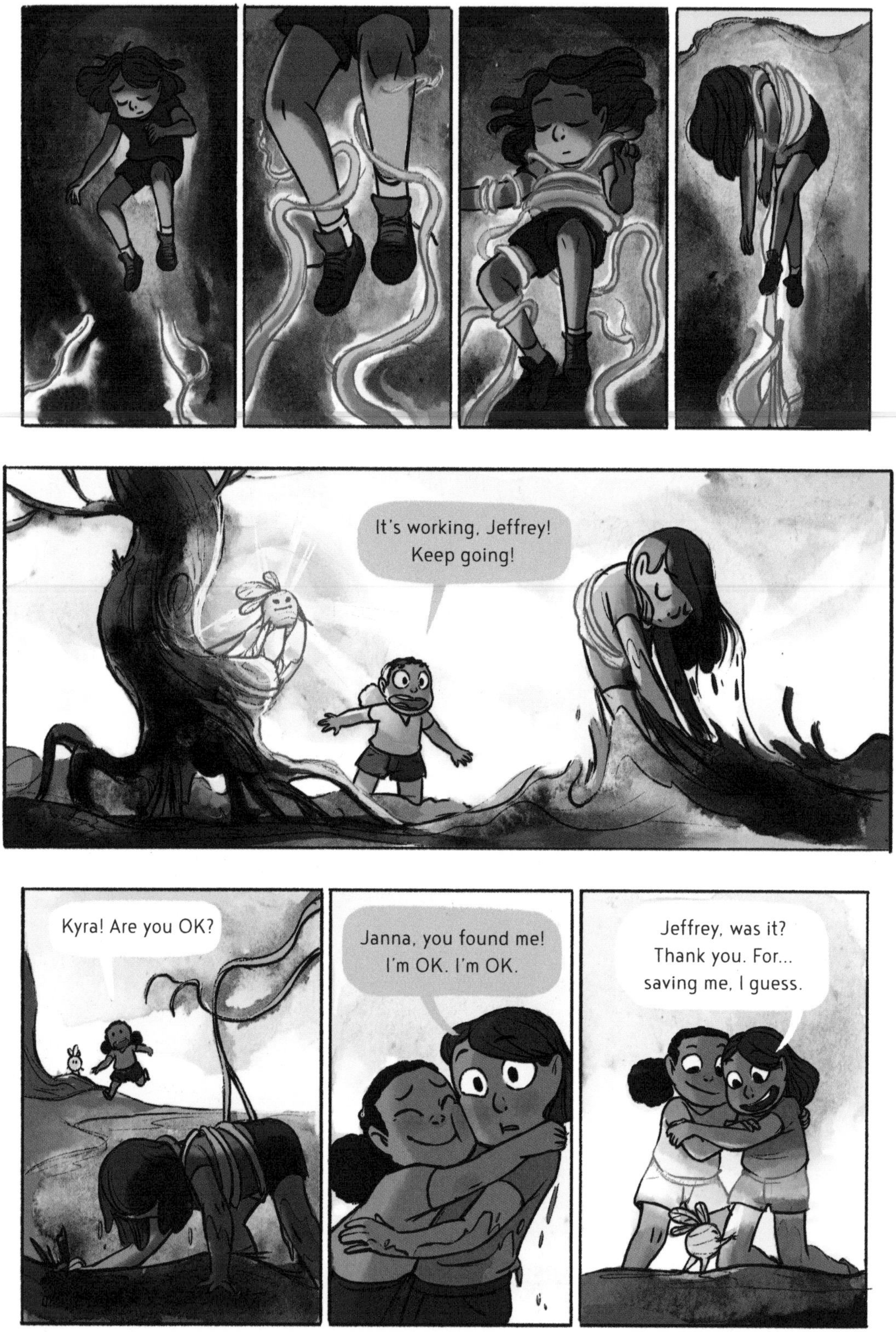
It's working, Jeffrey!
Keep going!
Kyra! Are you OK?
Janna, you found me!
I'm OK. I'm OK.
Jeffrey, was it?
Thank you. For...
saving me, I guess.

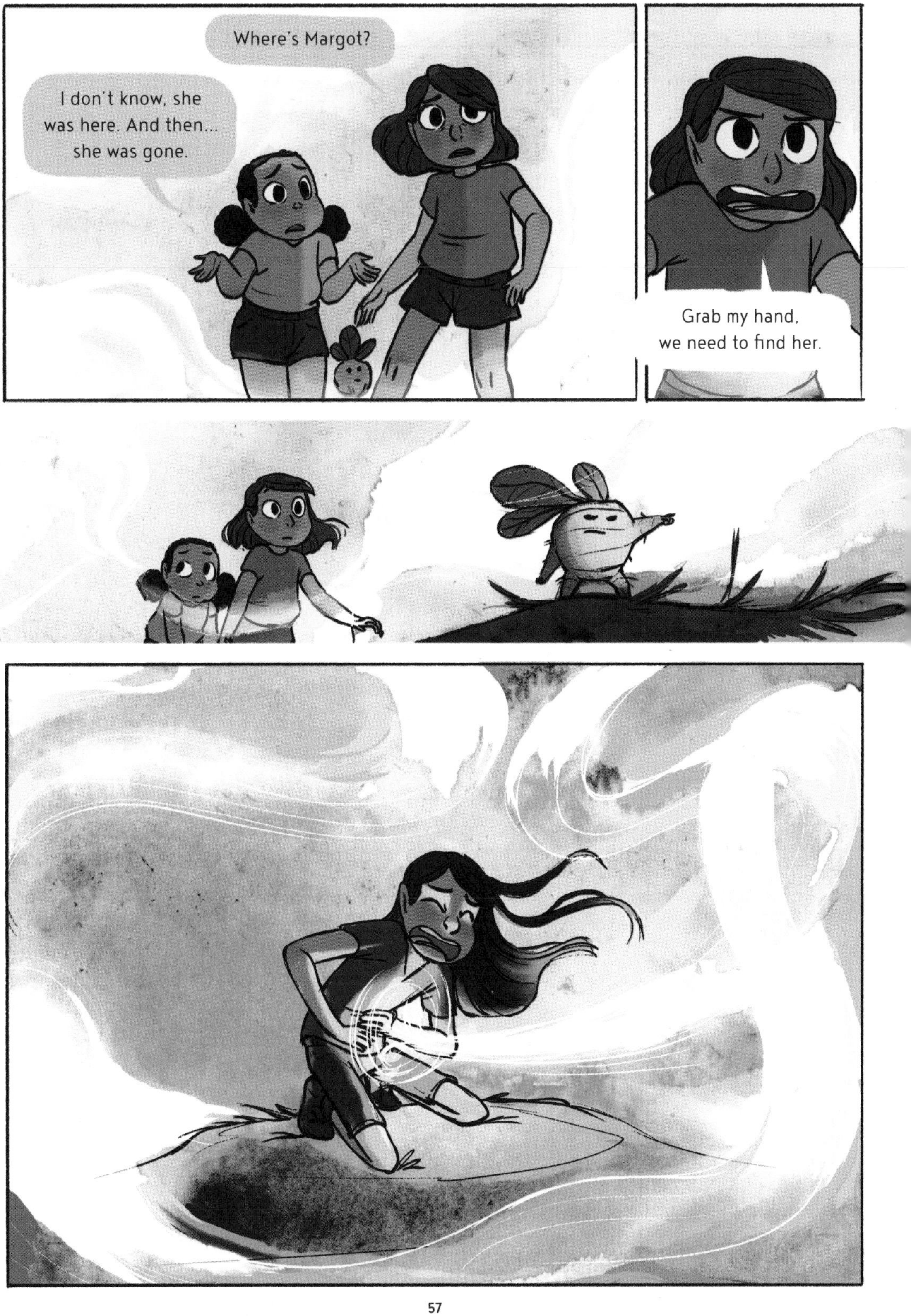
Where's Margot?
I don't know, she was here. And then... she was gone.
Grab my hand, we need to find her.

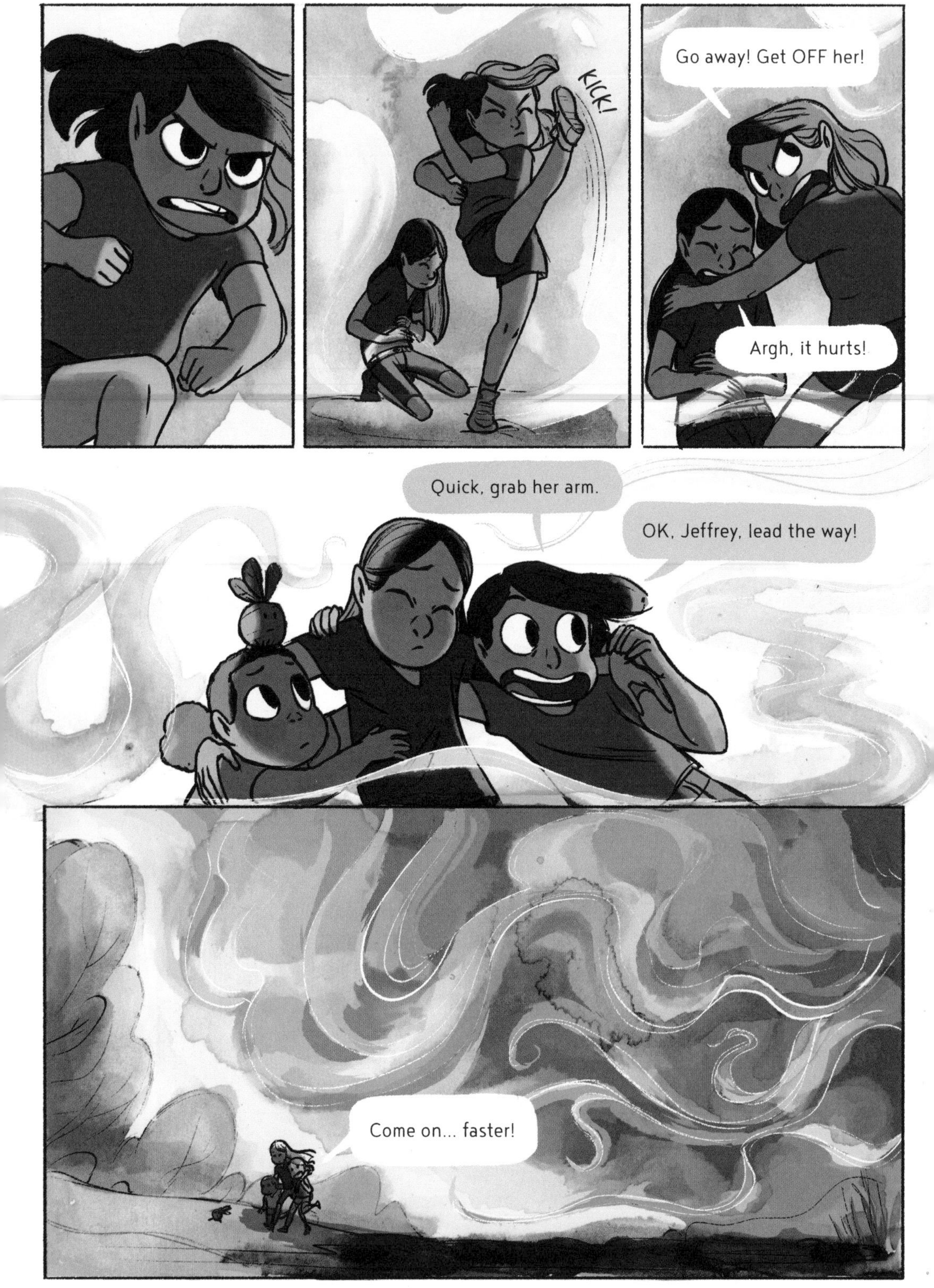
KICK!
Go away! Get OFF her!
Argh, it hurts!
Quick, grab her arm.
OK, Jeffrey, lead the way!
Come on... faster!

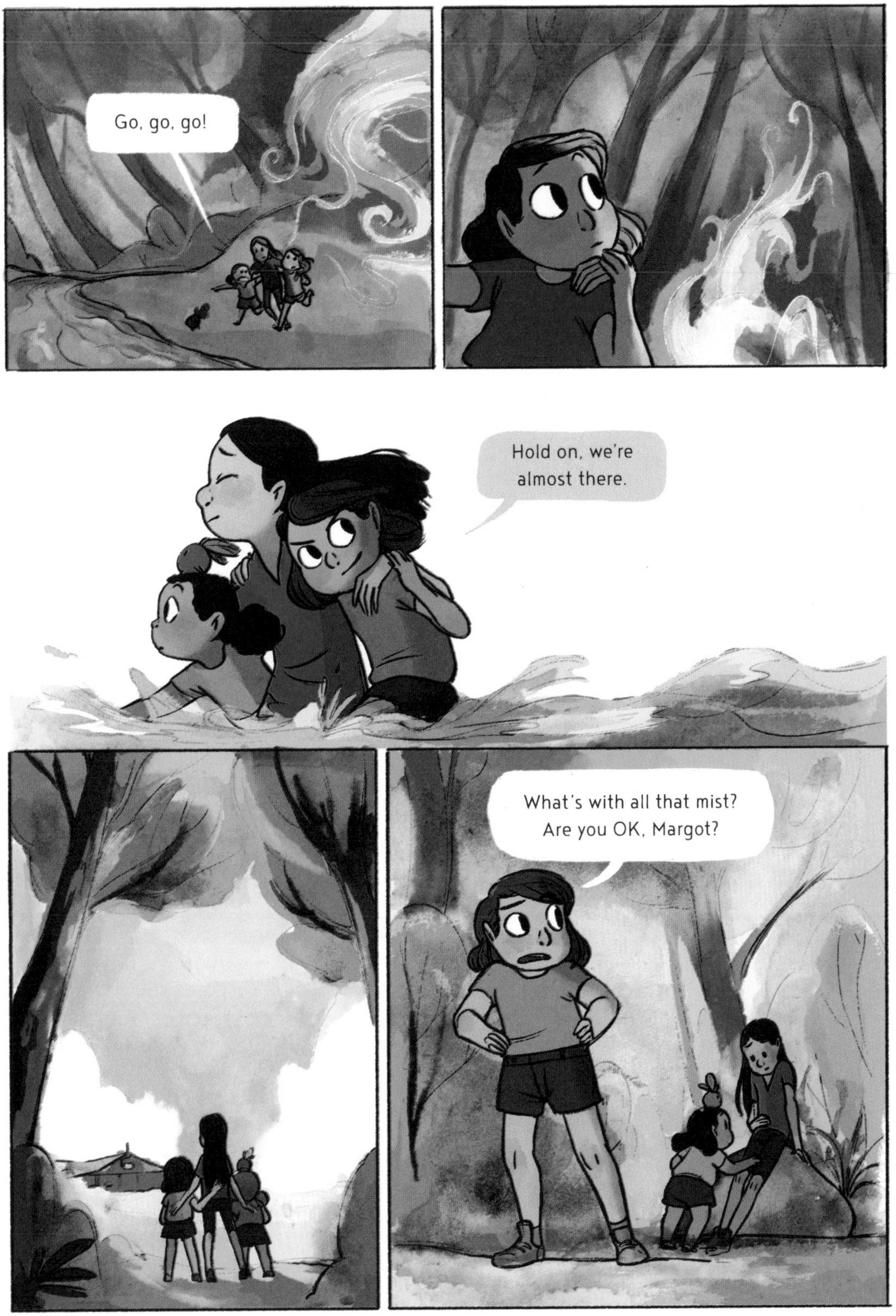
Go, go, go!
Hold on, we're almost there.
What's with all that mist? Are you OK, Margot?

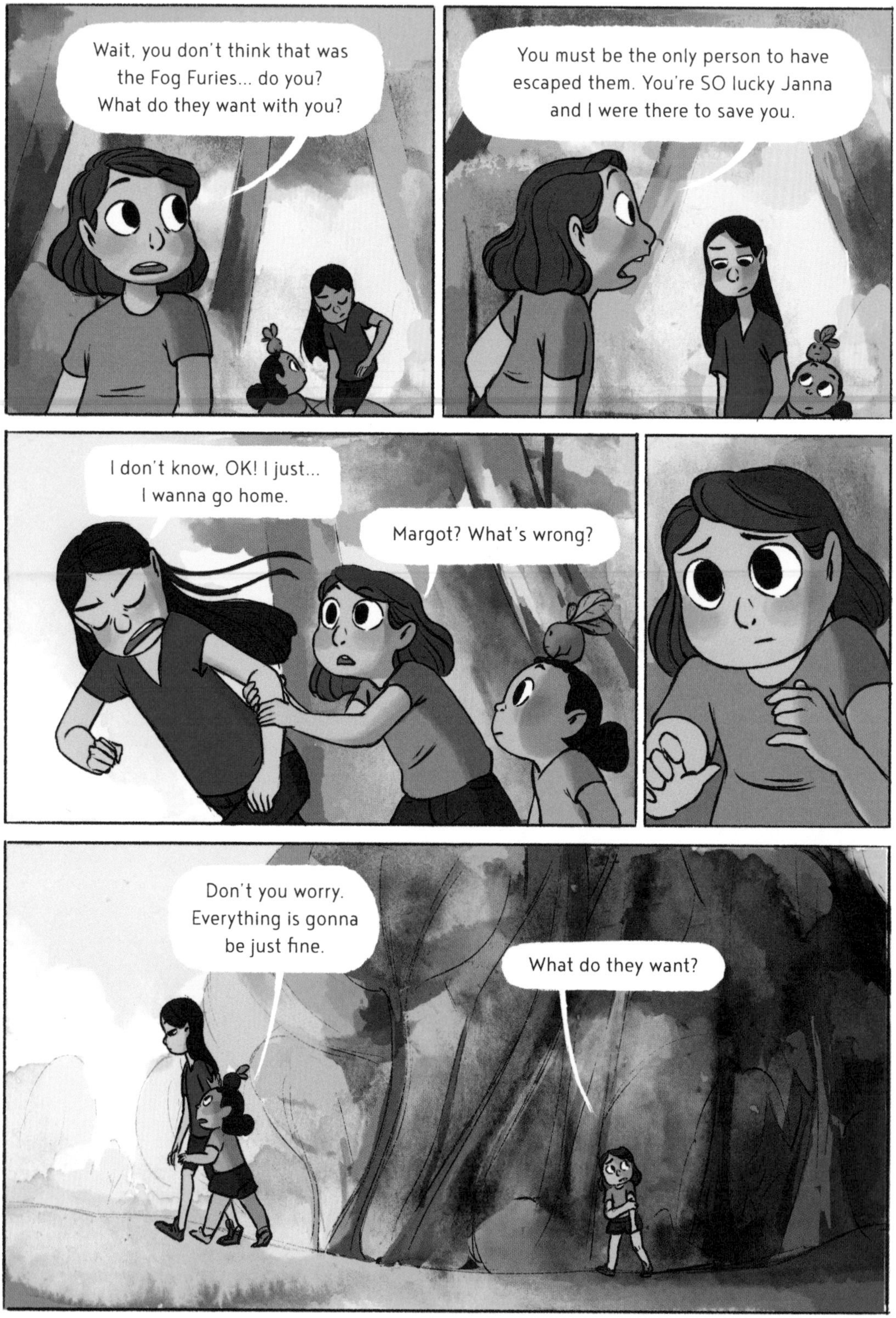

Wait, you don't think that was the Fog Furies... do you? What do they want with you?
You must be the only person to have escaped them. You're SO lucky Janna and I were there to save you.
I don't know, OK! I just... I wanna go home.
Margot? What's wrong?
Don't you worry. Everything is gonna be just fine.
What do they want?

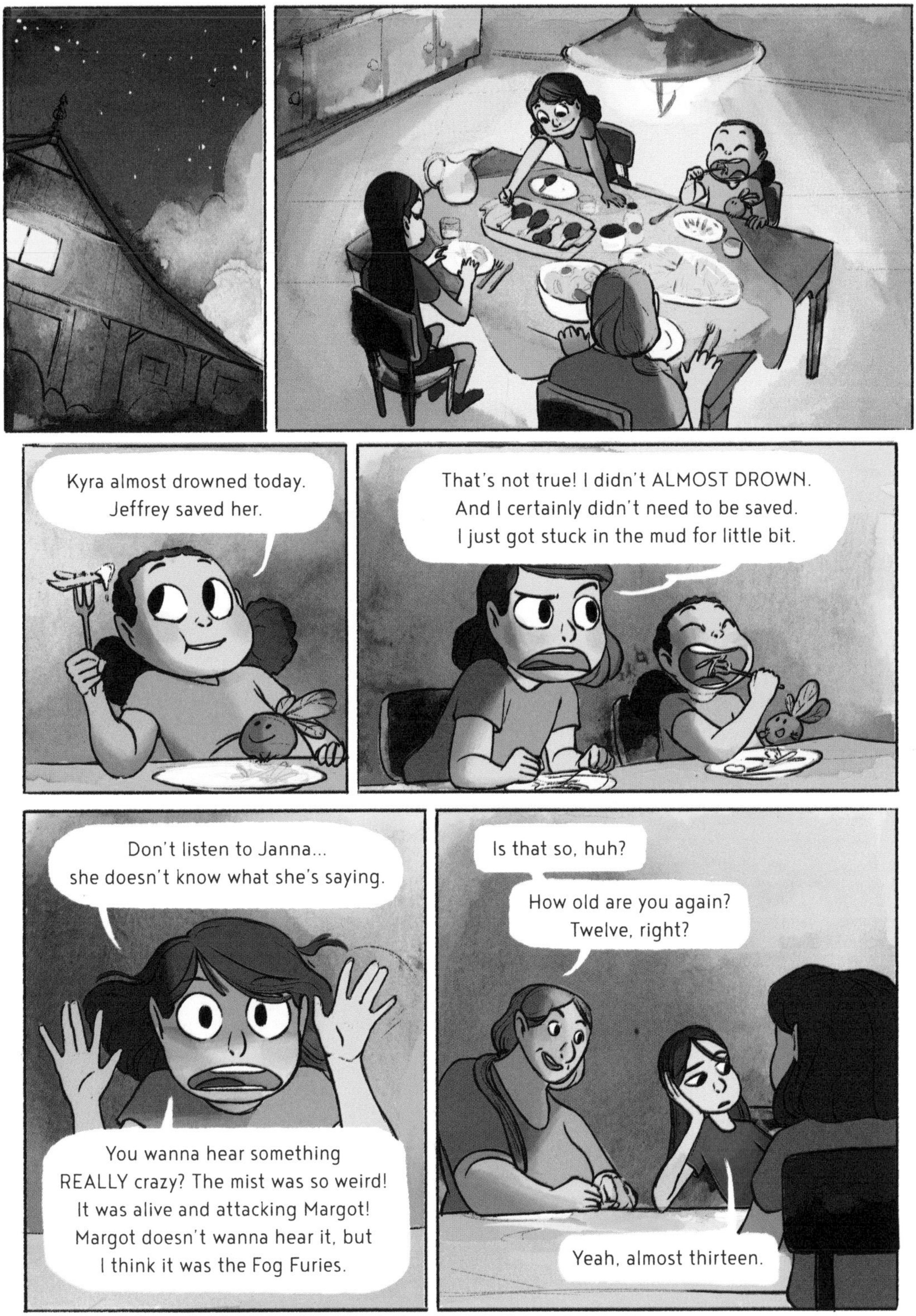

Kyra almost drowned today. Jeffrey saved her.
That's not true! I didn't ALMOST DROWN. And I certainly didn't need to be saved. I just got stuck in the mud for little bit.
Don't listen to Janna... she doesn't know what she's saying.
You wanna hear something REALLY crazy? The mist was so weird! It was alive and attacking Margot! Margot doesn't wanna hear it, but I think it was the Fog Furies.
Is that so, huh?
How old are you again? Twelve, right?
Yeah, almost thirteen.

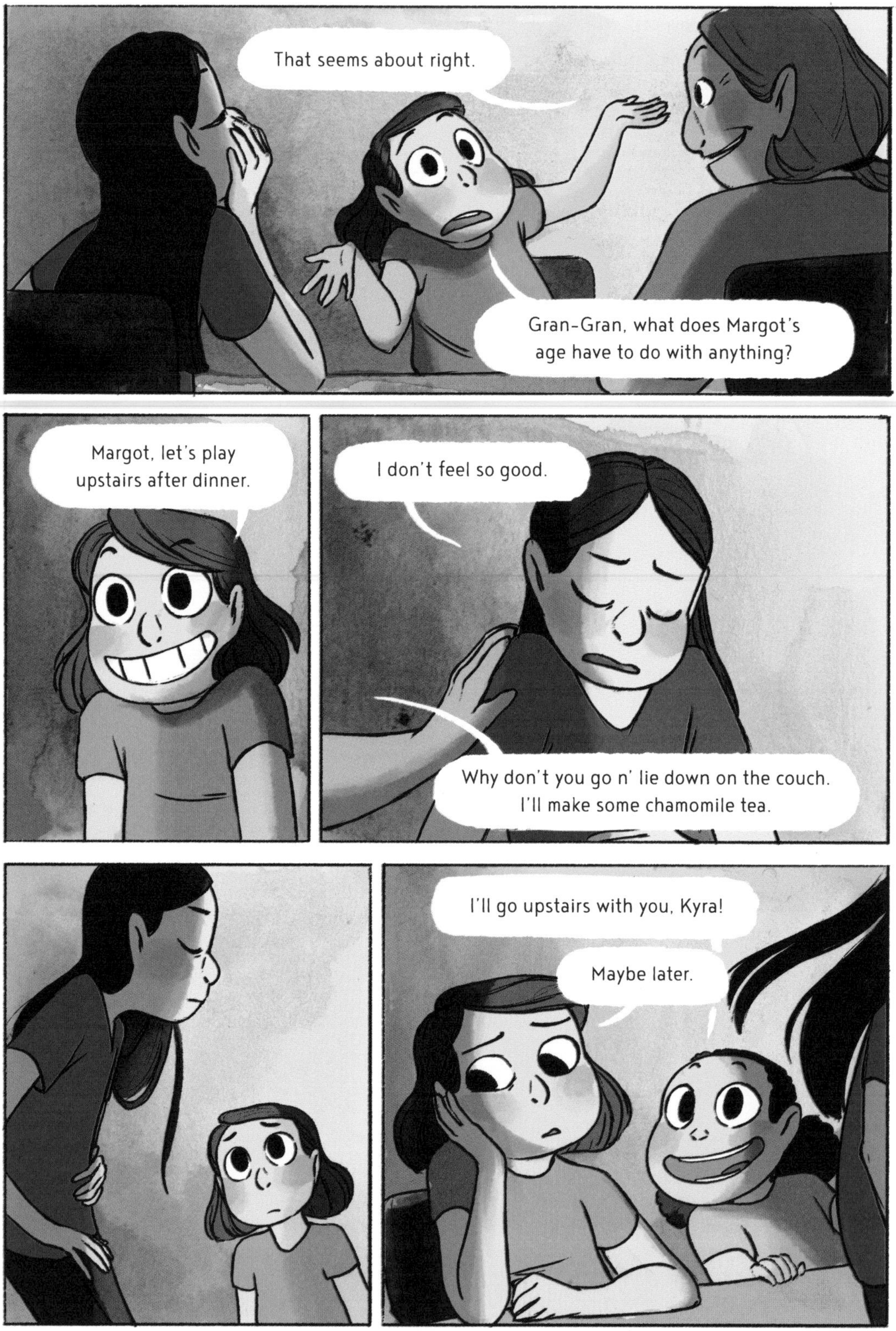
That seems about right.
Gran-Gran, what does Margot's age have to do with anything?
Margot, let's play upstairs after dinner.
I don't feel so good.
Why don't you go n' lie down on the couch. I'll make some chamomile tea.
I'll go upstairs with you, Kyra!
Maybe later.

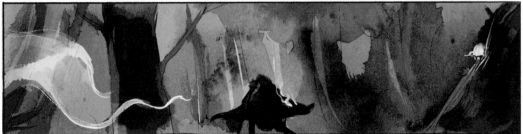

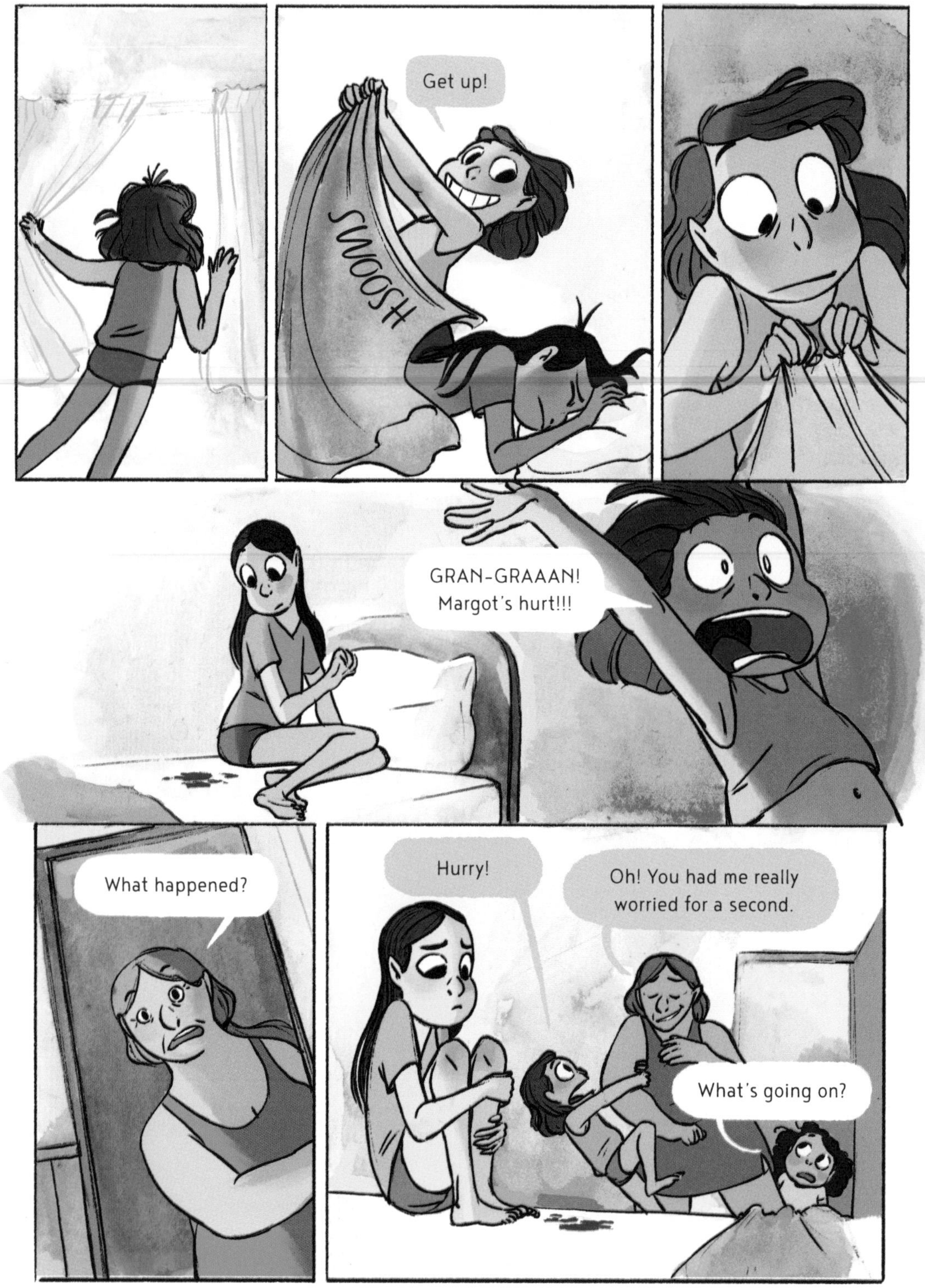
Get up!
SWOOSH
GRAN-GRAAAN!
Margot's hurt!!!
What happened?
Hurry!
Oh! You had me really worried for a second.
What's going on?

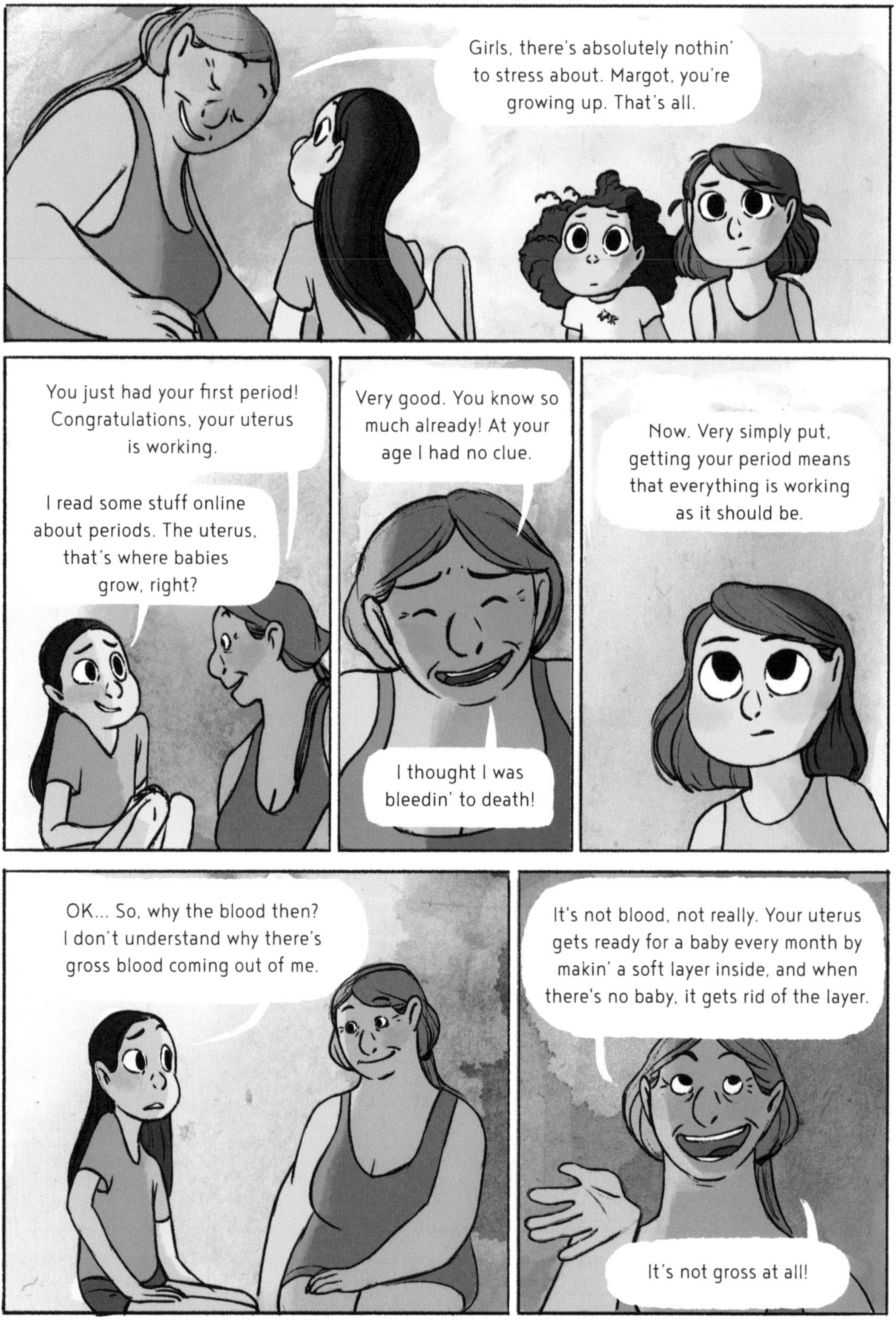
Girls, there's absolutely nothin' to stress about. Margot, you're growing up. That's all.
You just had your first period! Congratulations, your uterus is working.
I read some stuff online about periods. The uterus, that's where babies grow, right?
Very good. You know so much already! At your age I had no clue.
I thought I was bleedin' to death!
Now. Very simply put, getting your period means that everything is working as it should be.
OK... So, why the blood then? I don't understand why there's gross blood coming out of me.
It's not blood, not really. Your uterus gets ready for a baby every month by makin' a soft layer inside, and when there's no baby, it gets rid of the layer.
It's not gross at all!

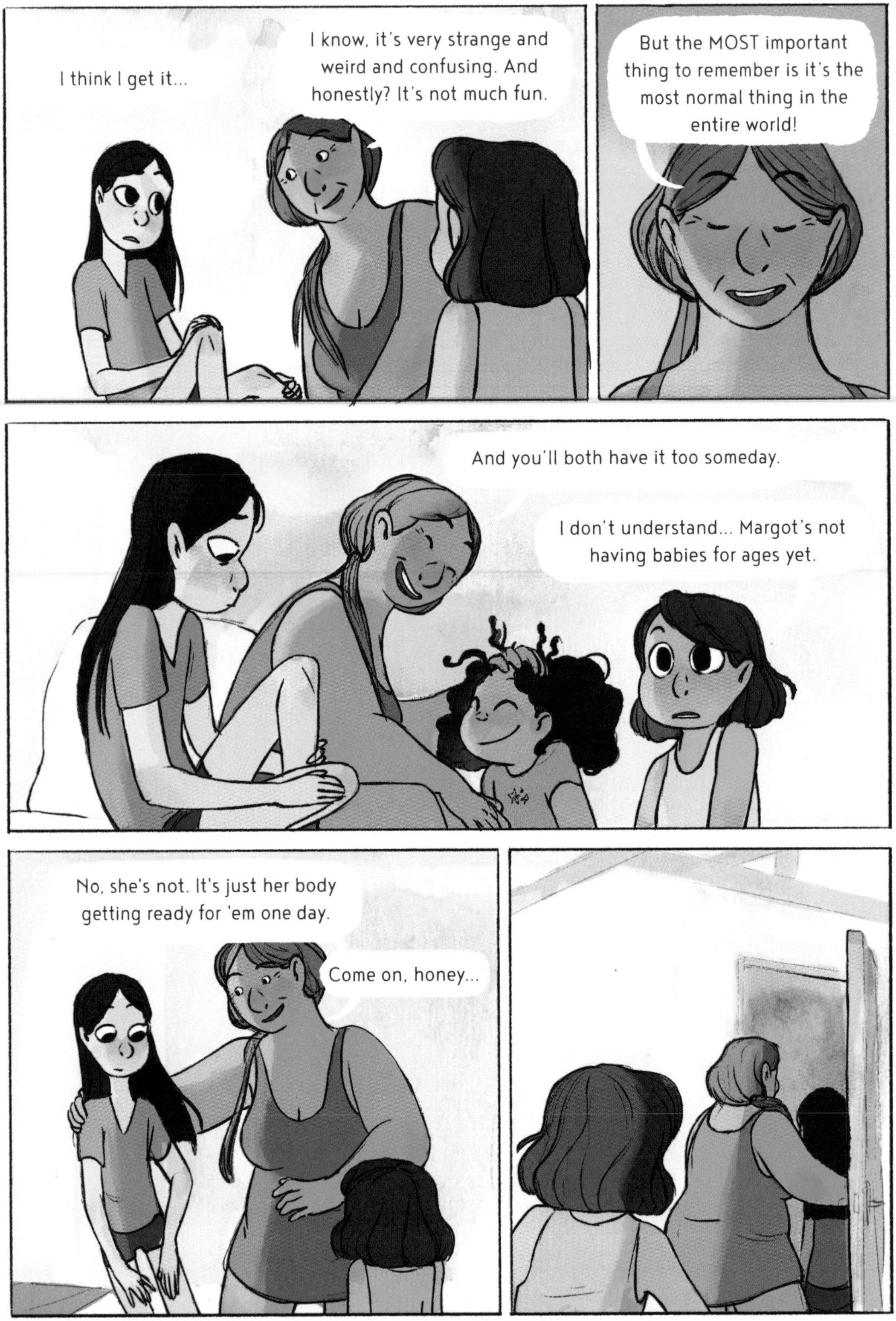
I think I get it...
I know, it's very strange and weird and confusing. And honestly? It's not much fun.
But the MOST important thing to remember is it's the most normal thing in the entire world!
And you'll both have it too someday.
I don't understand... Margot's not having babies for ages yet.
No, she's not. It's just her body getting ready for 'em one day.
Come on, honey...

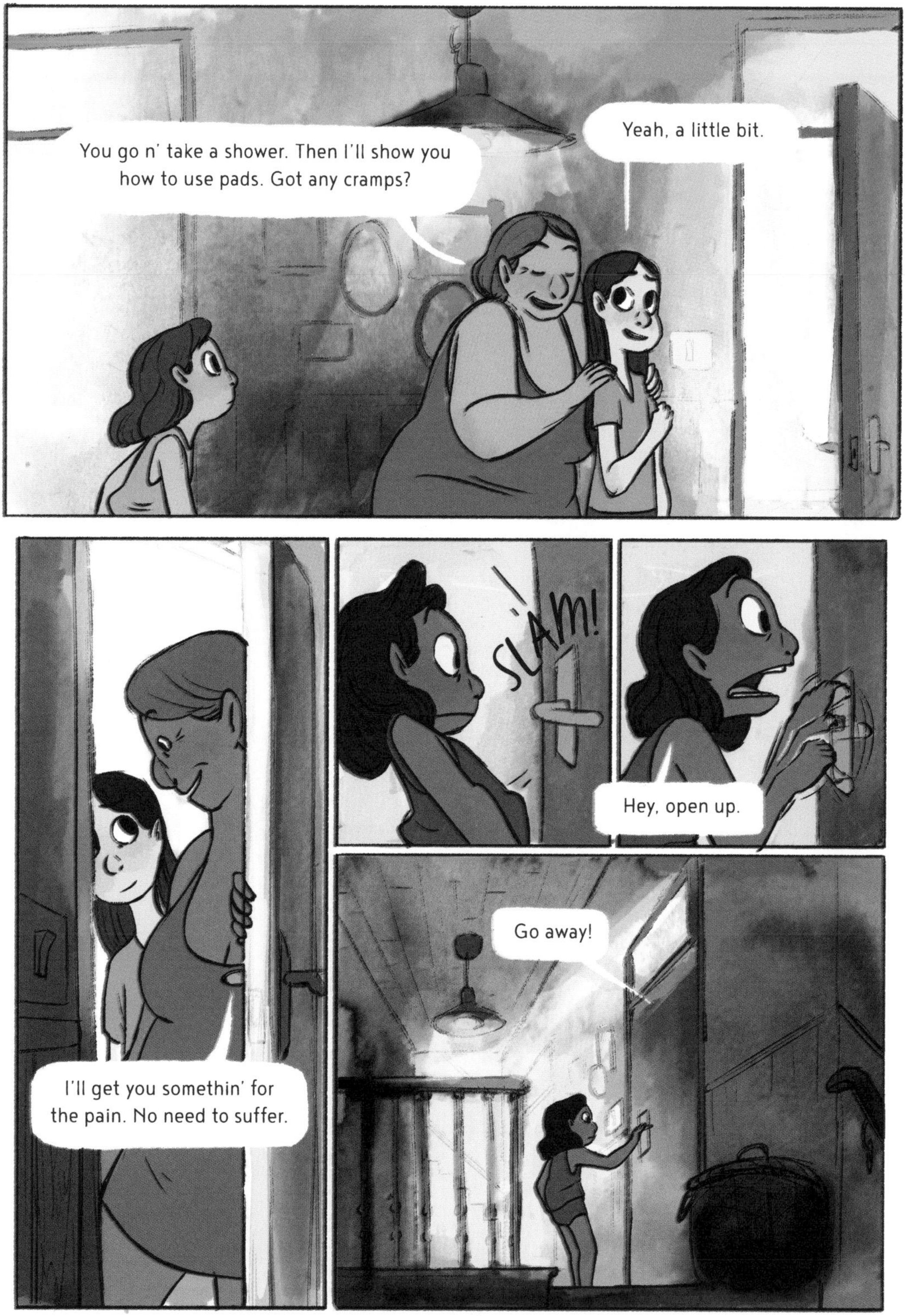
You go n' take a shower. Then I'll show you how to use pads. Got any cramps?
Yeah, a little bit.
I'll get you somethin' for the pain. No need to suffer.
SLAM!
Hey, open up.
Go away!

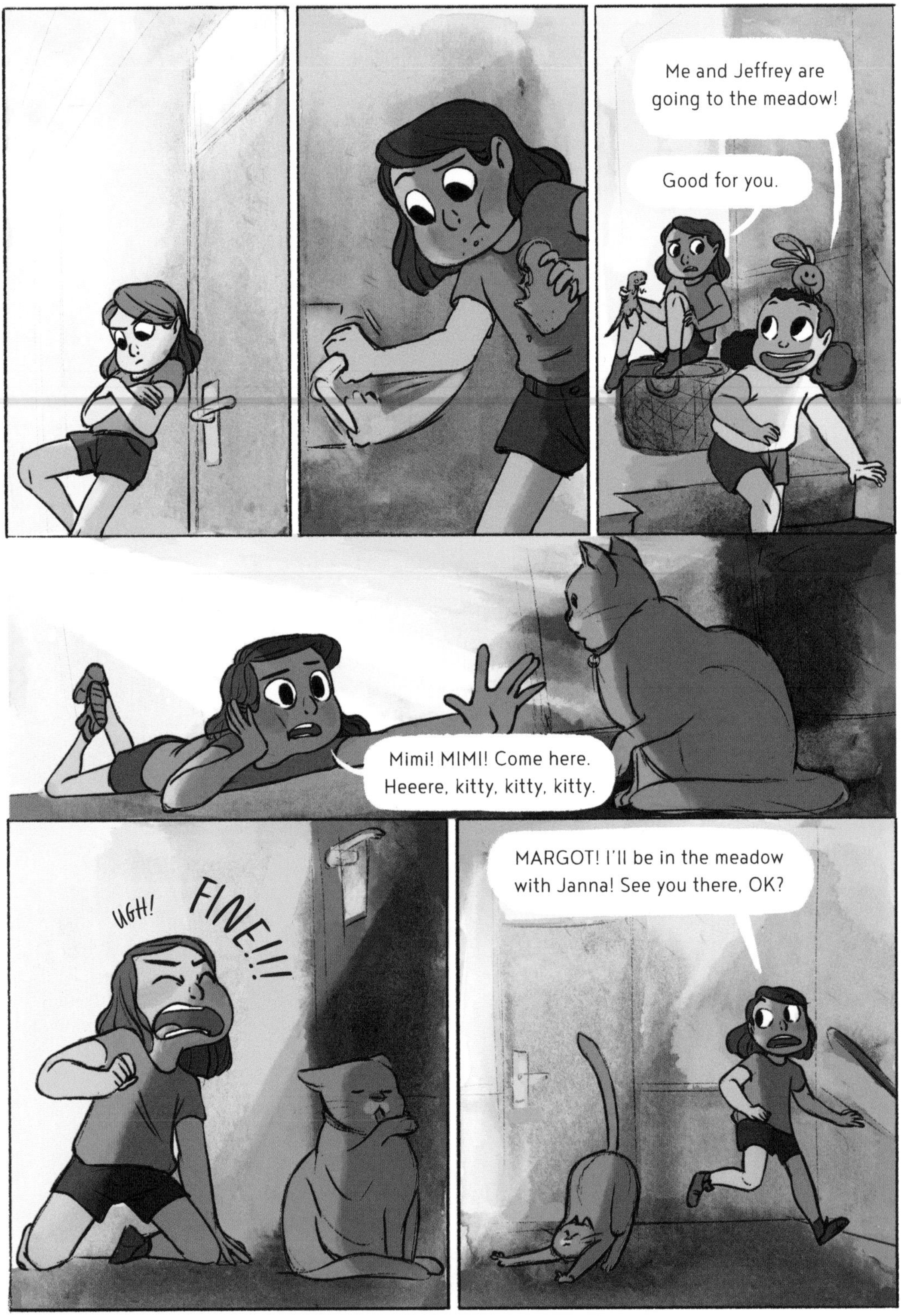
Me and Jeffrey are going to the meadow!
Good for you.
Mimi! MIMI! Come here. Heeere, kitty, kitty, kitty.
UGH!
FINE!!!
MARGOT! I'll be in the meadow with Janna! See you there, OK?

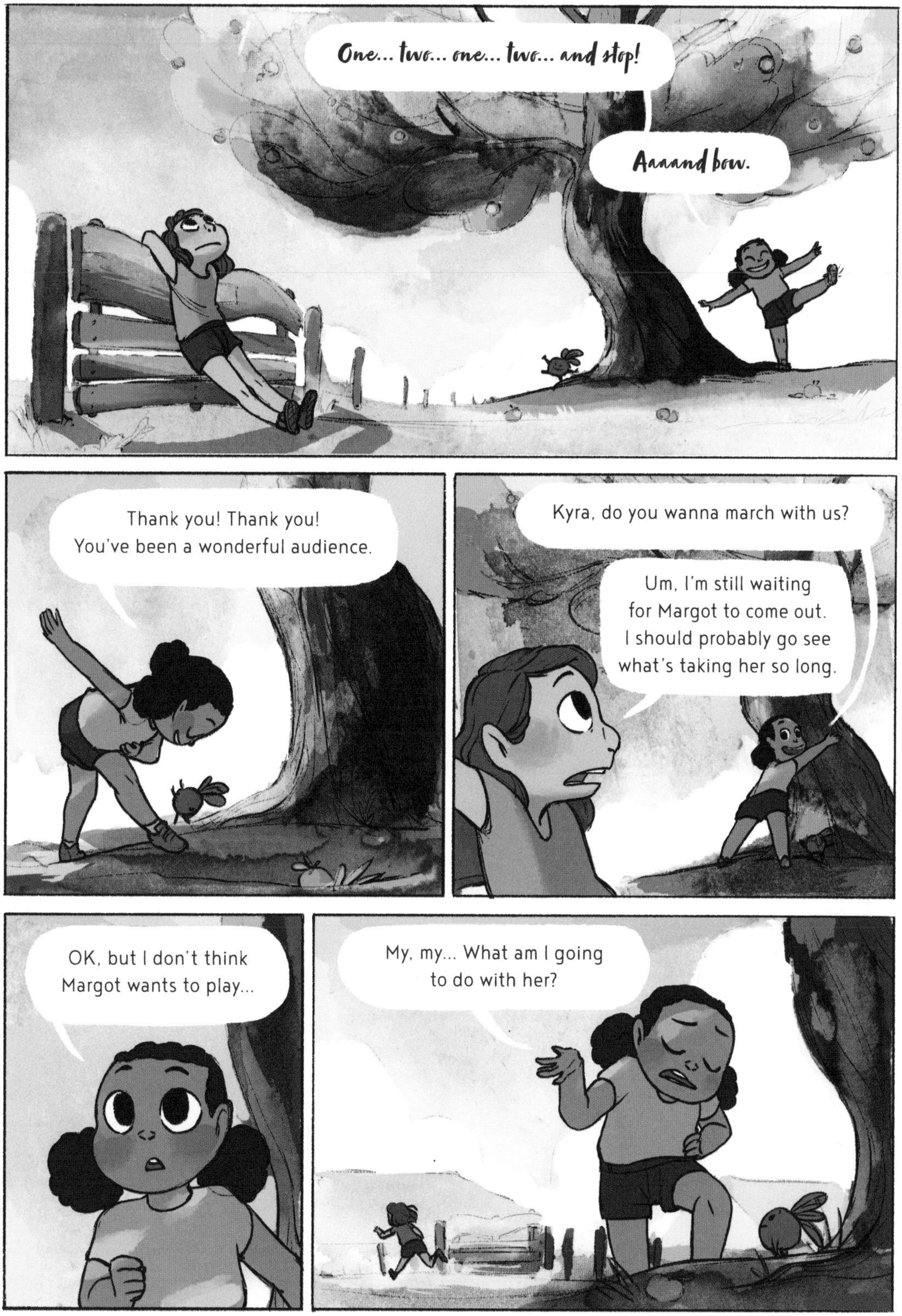
One... two... one... two... and stop!
Aaaand bow.
Thank you! Thank you! You've been a wonderful audience.
Kyra, do you wanna march with us?
Um, I'm still waiting for Margot to come out. I should probably go see what's taking her so long.
OK, but I don't think Margot wants to play...
My, my... What am I going to do with her?

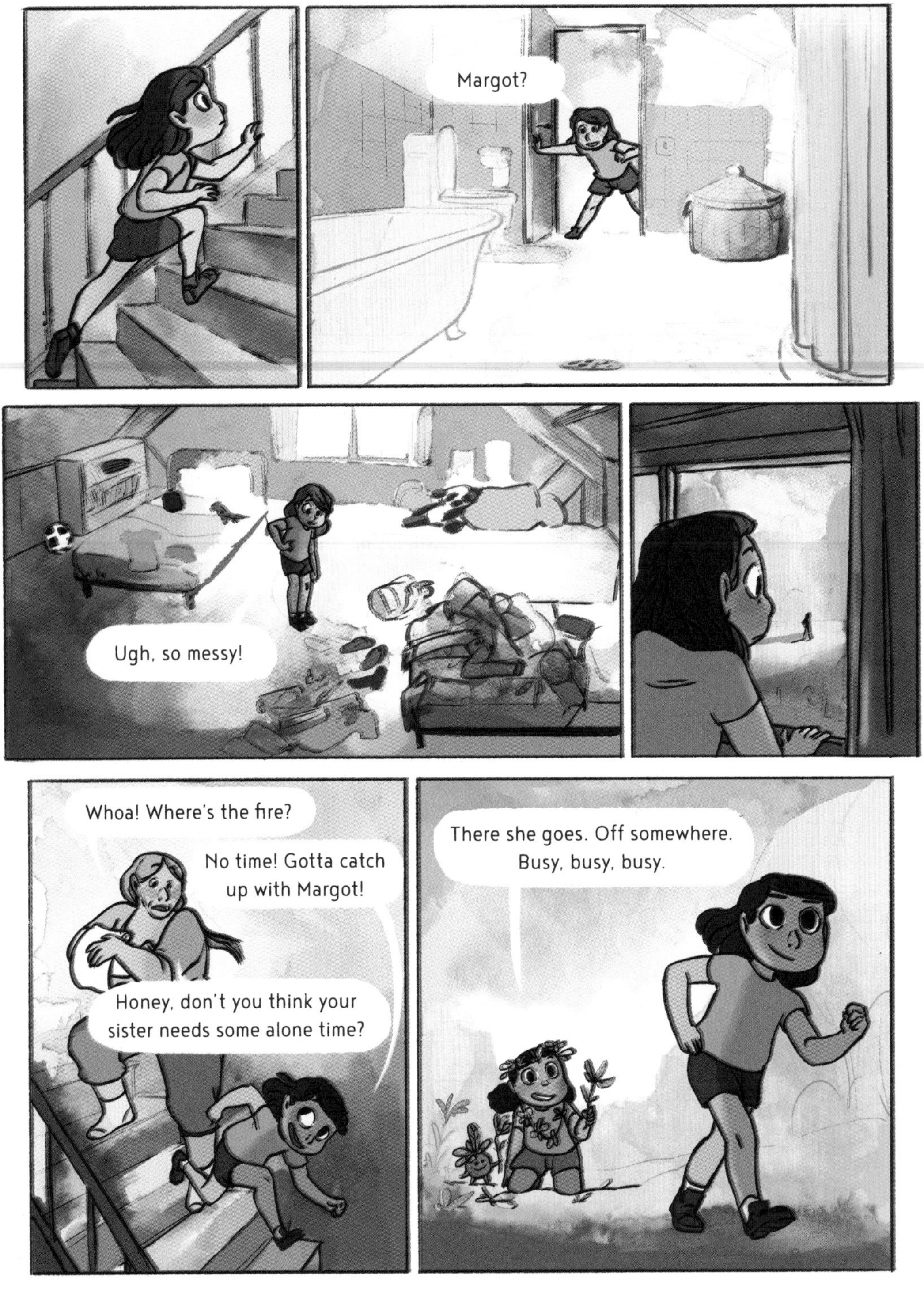
Margot?
Ugh, so messy!
Whoa! Where's the fire?
No time! Gotta catch up with Margot!
Honey, don't you think your sister needs some alone time?
There she goes. Off somewhere. Busy, busy, busy.

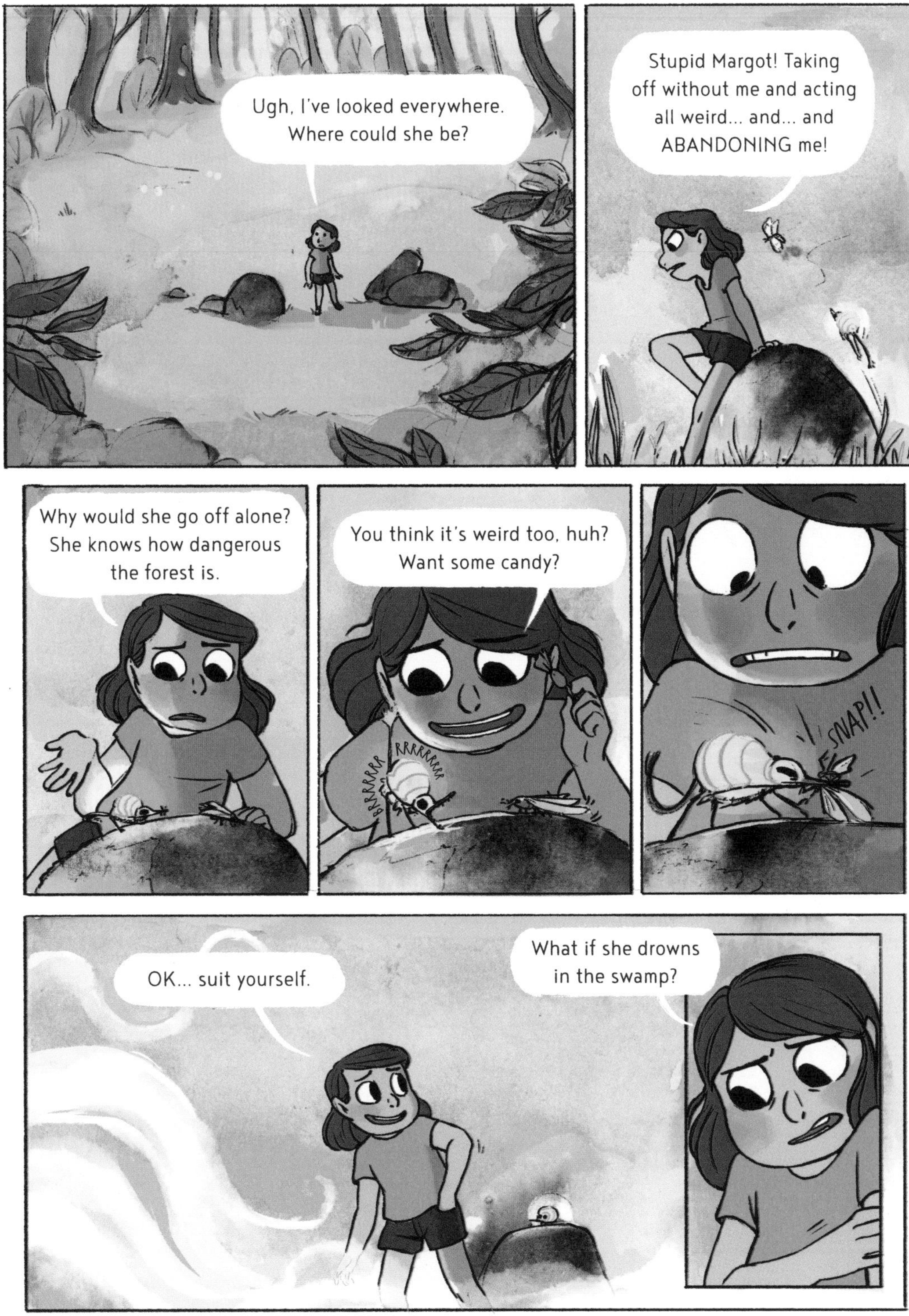
Ugh, I've looked everywhere. Where could she be?
Stupid Margot! Taking off without me and acting all weird... and... and ABANDONING me!
Why would she go off alone? She knows how dangerous the forest is.
You think it's weird too, huh? Want some candy?
SNAP!!
OK... suit yourself.
What if she drowns in the swamp?

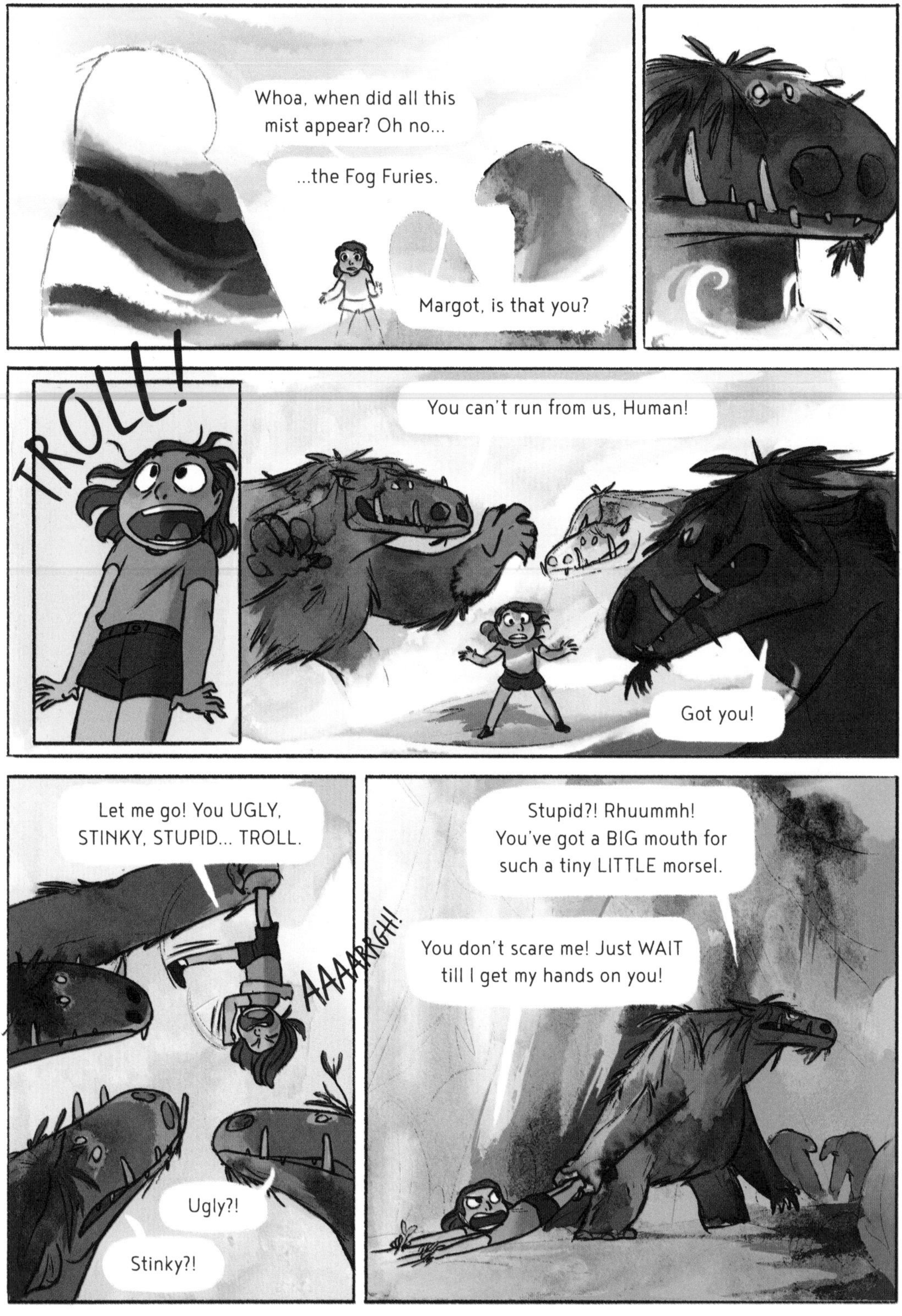
Whoa, when did all this mist appear? Oh no...
...the Fog Furies.
Margot, is that you?
TROLL!
You can't run from us, Human!
Got you!
Let me go! You UGLY, STINKY, STUPID... TROLL.
AAAARRGH!
Ugly?!
Stinky?!
Stupid?! Rhuummh! You've got a BIG mouth for such a tiny LITTLE morsel.
You don't scare me! Just WAIT till I get my hands on you!

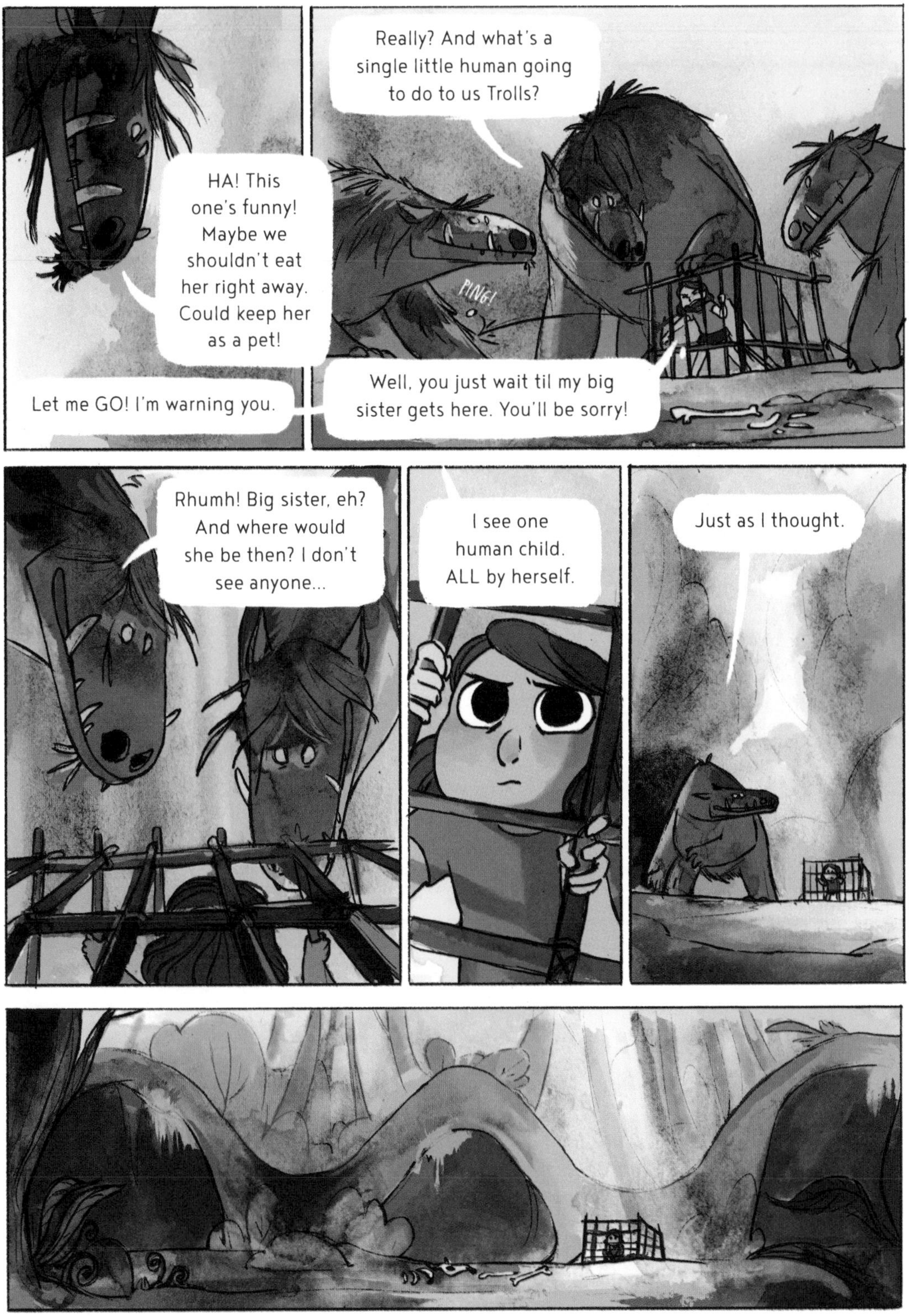
HA! This one's funny! Maybe we shouldn't eat her right away. Could keep her as a pet!
Let me GO! I'm warning you.
Really? And what's a single little human going to do to us Trolls?
PING!
Well, you just wait til my big sister gets here. You'll be sorry!
Rhumh! Big sister, eh? And where would she be then? I don't see anyone...
I see one human child. ALL by herself.
Just as I thought.

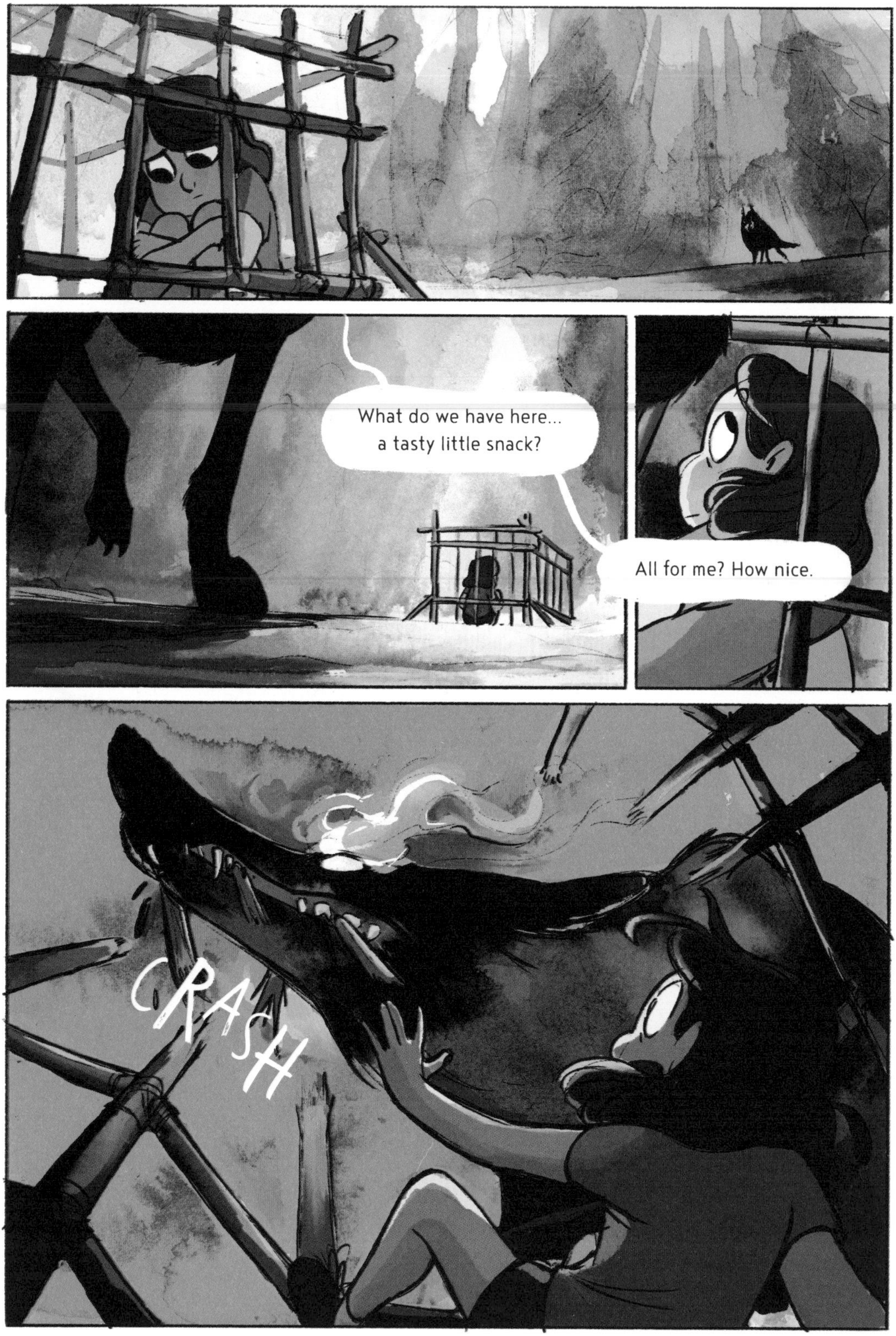
What do we have here...
a tasty little snack?
All for me? How nice.
CRASH

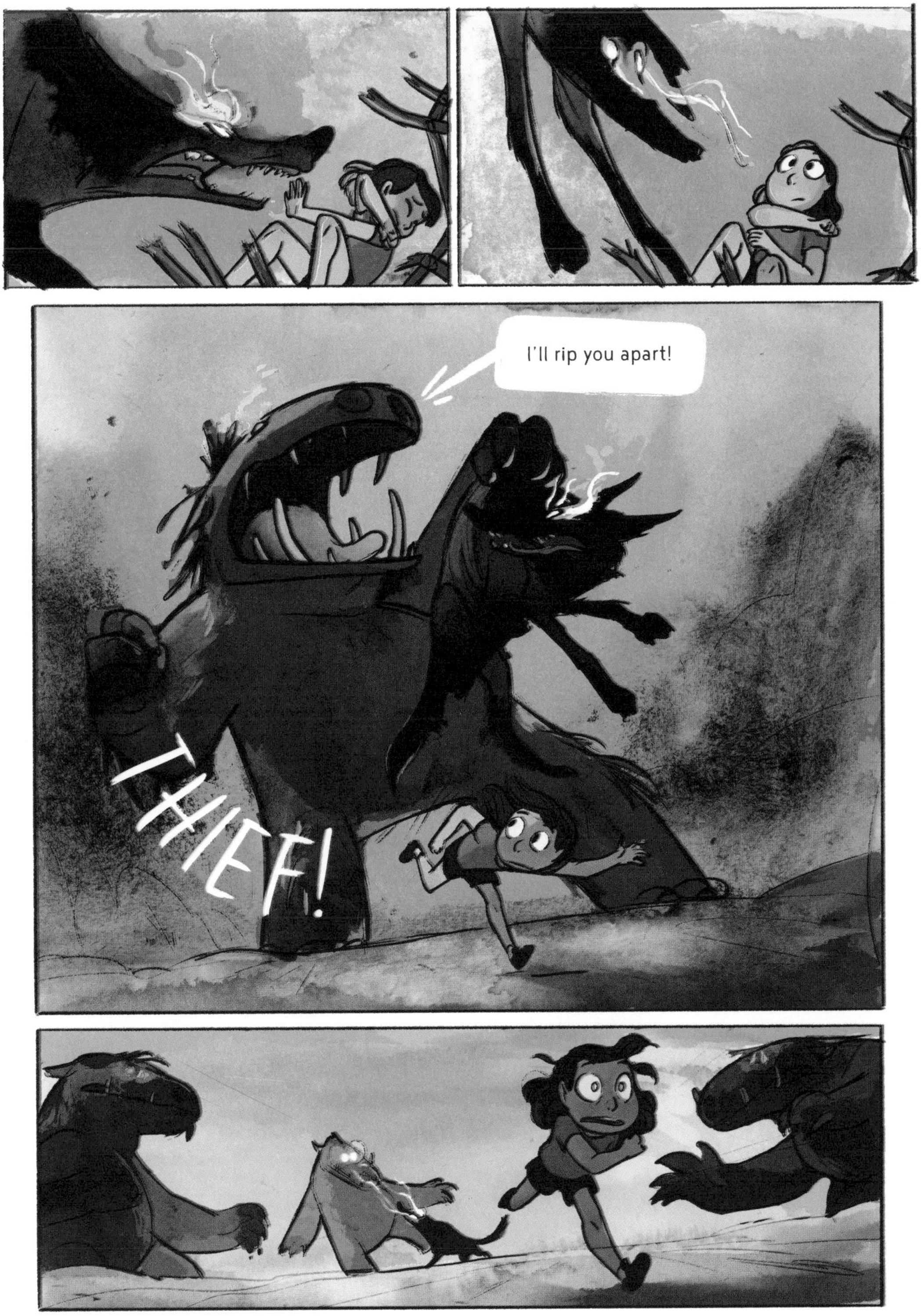
I'll rip you apart!
THIEF!

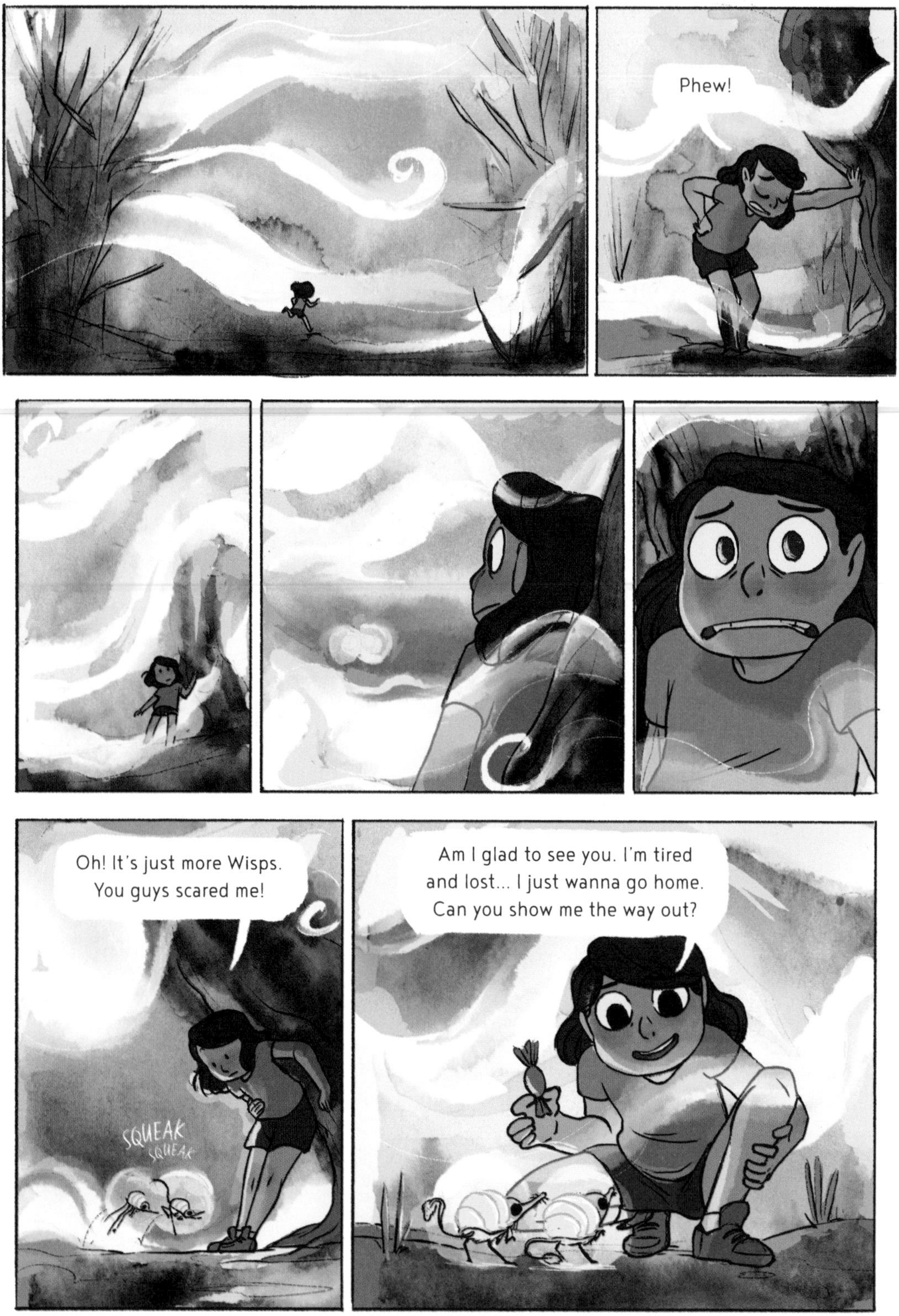
Phew!
Oh! It's just more Wisps.
You guys scared me!
SQUEAK
SQUEAK
Am I glad to see you. I'm tired
and lost... I just wanna go home.
Can you show me the way out?

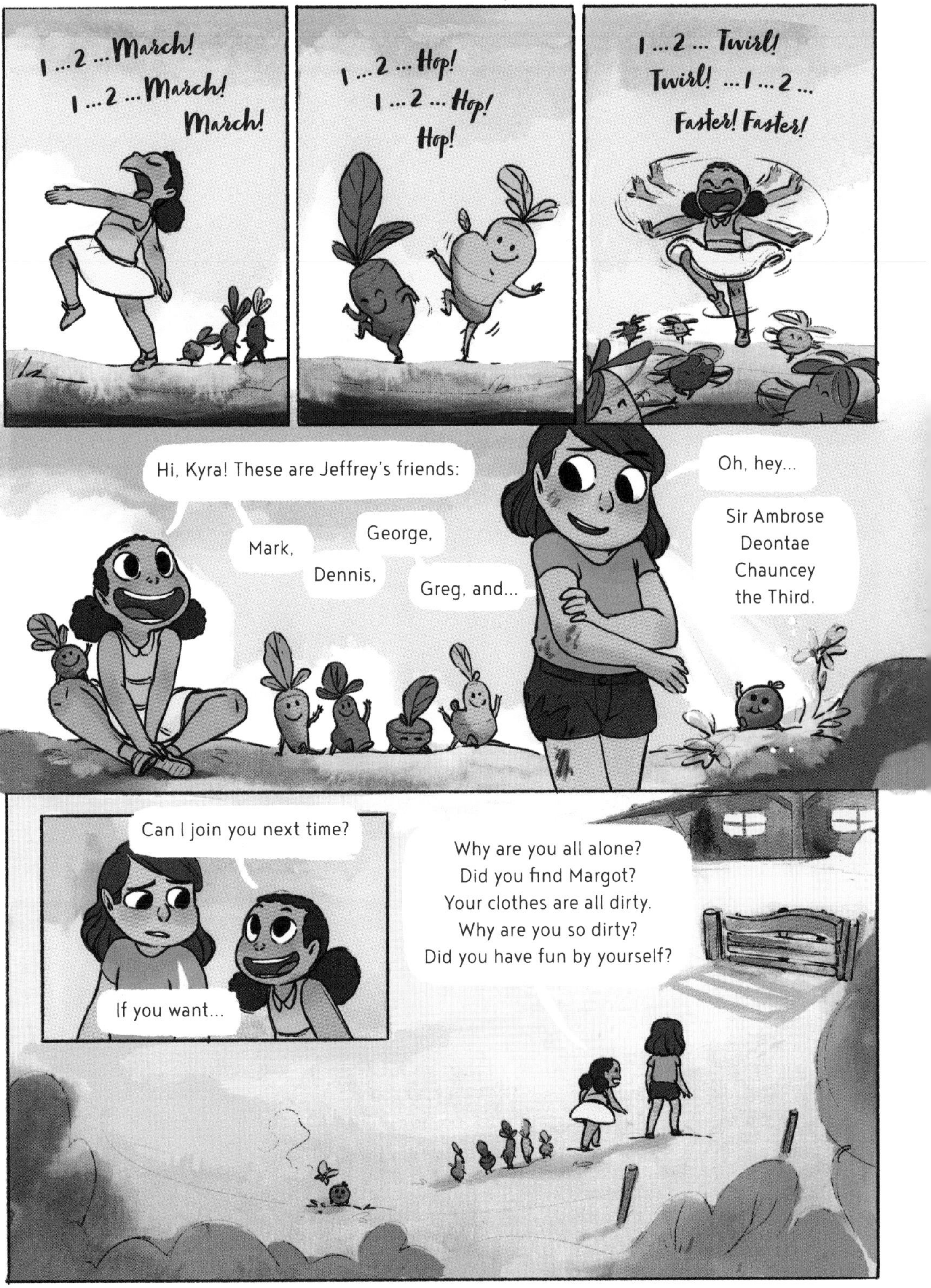
1 ... 2 ... March!
1 ... 2 ... March!
March!
1 ... 2 ... Hop!
1 ... 2 ... Hop!
Hop!
1 ... 2 ... Twirl!
Twirl! ... 1 ... 2 ...
Faster! Faster!
Hi, Kyra! These are Jeffrey's friends:
Mark,
Dennis,
George,
Greg, and...
Oh, hey...
Sir Ambrose Deontae Chauncey the Third.
Can I join you next time?
If you want...
Why are you all alone?
Did you find Margot?
Your clothes are all dirty.
Why are you so dirty?
Did you have fun by yourself?

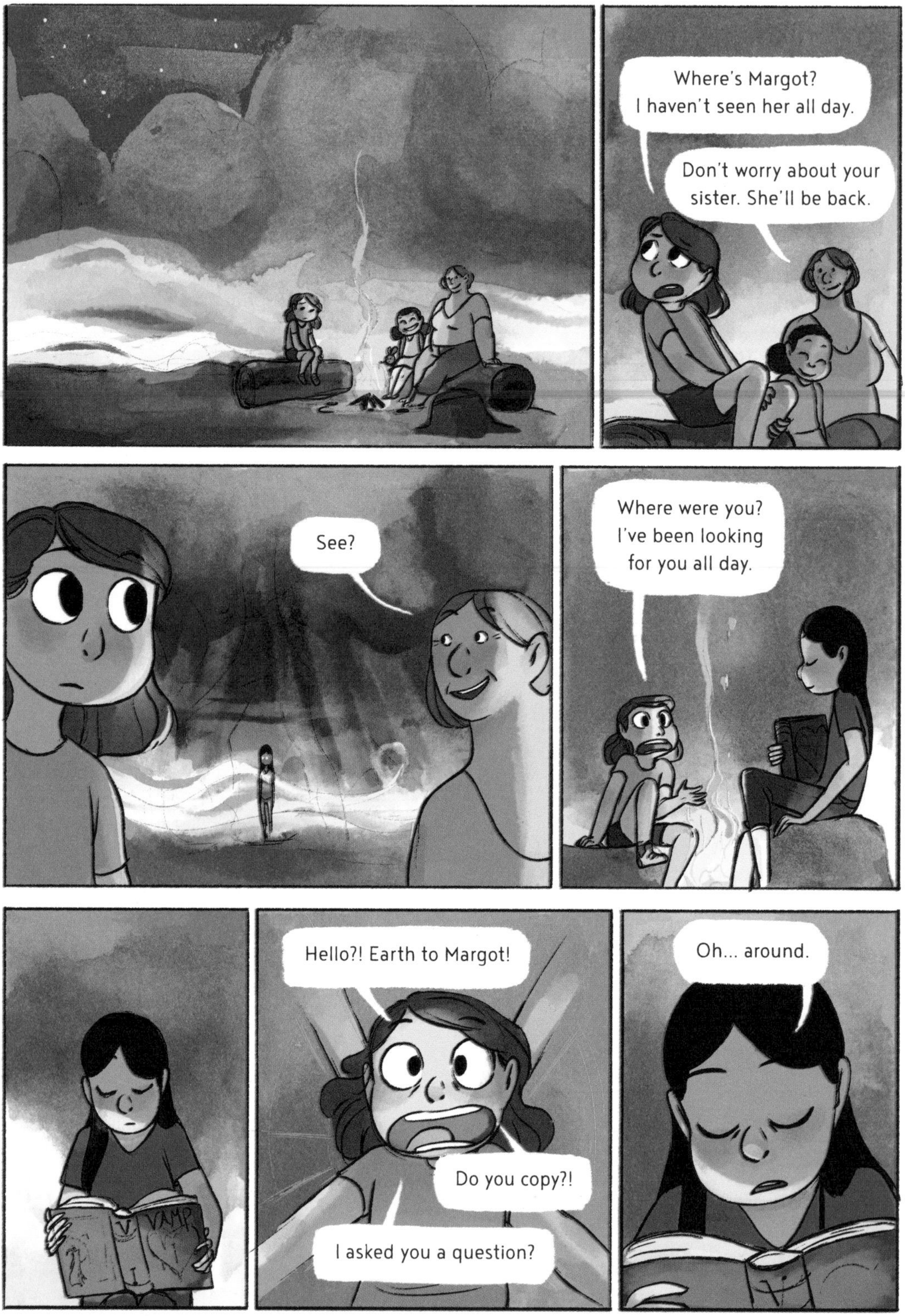
Where's Margot?
I haven't seen her all day.
Don't worry about your sister. She'll be back.
See?
Where were you? I've been looking for you all day.
Hello?! Earth to Margot!
Do you copy?!
I asked you a question?
Oh... around.

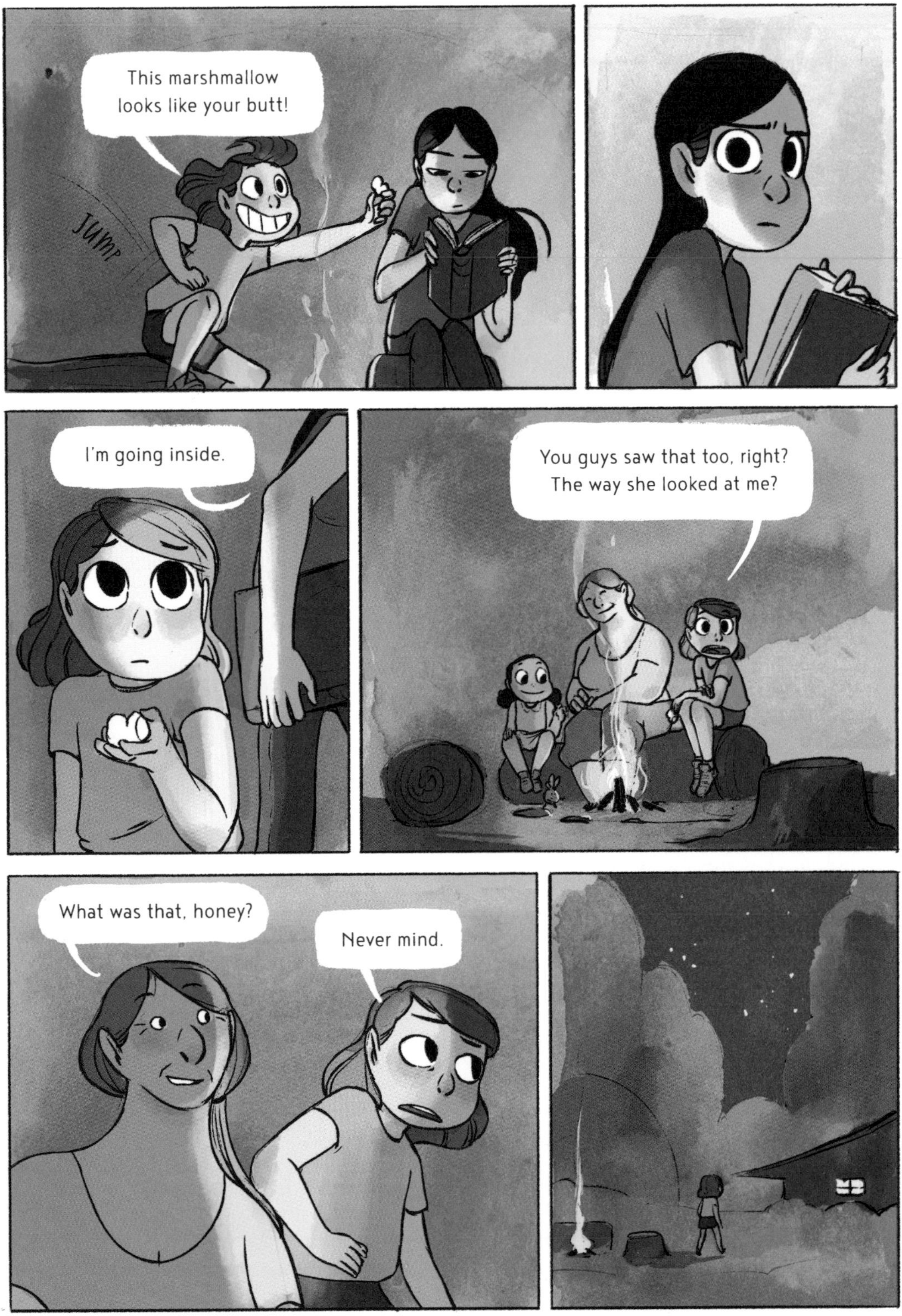
This marshmallow looks like your butt!
JUMP
I'm going inside.
You guys saw that too, right? The way she looked at me?
What was that, honey?
Never mind.

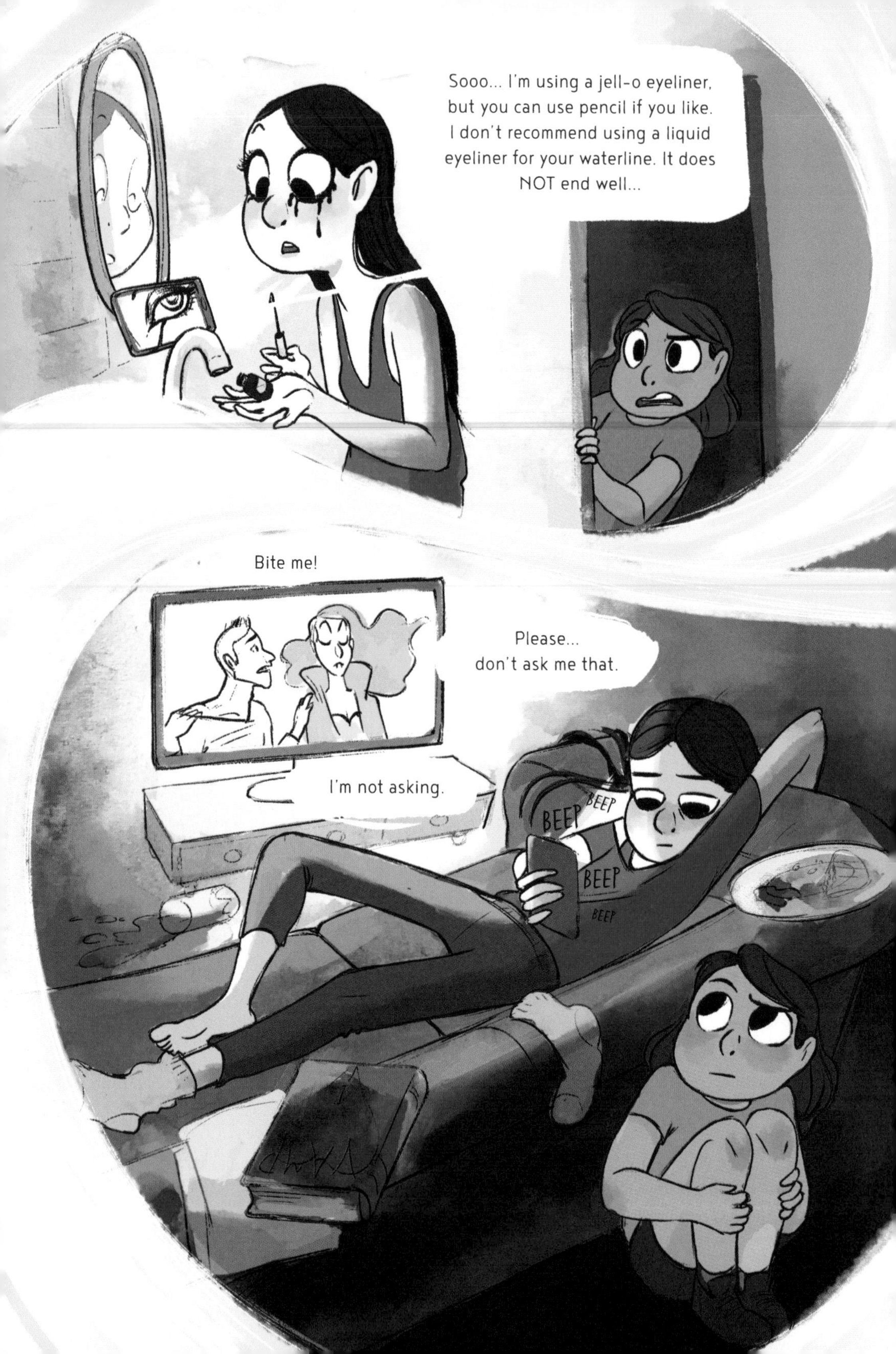
Sooo... I'm using a jell-o eyeliner, but you can use pencil if you like. I don't recommend using a liquid eyeliner for your waterline. It does NOT end well...
Bite me!
Please... don't ask me that.
I'm not asking.
BEEP
BEEP
BEEP
BEEP

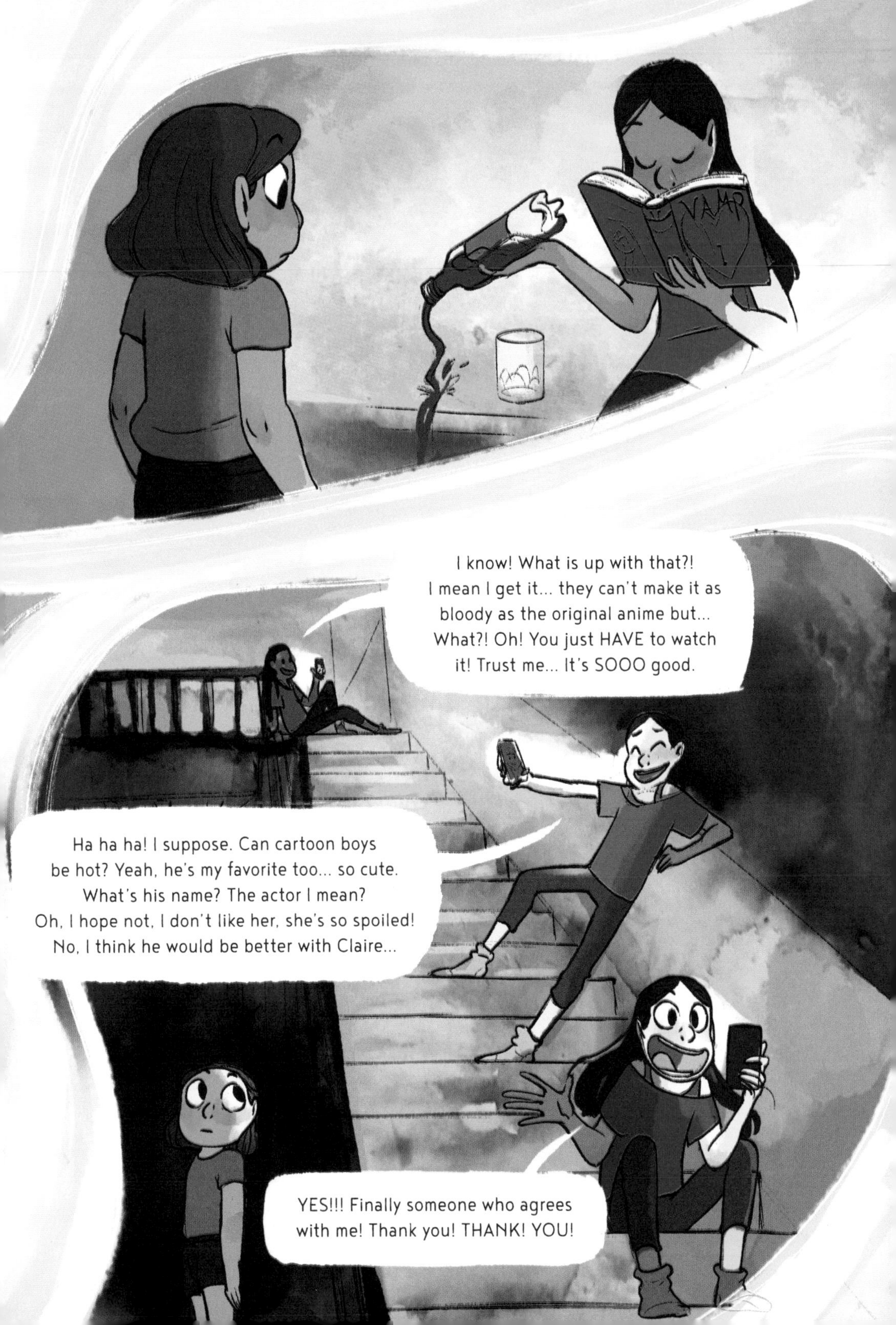
VAMP
I know! What is up with that?! I mean I get it... they can't make it as bloody as the original anime but... What?! Oh! You just HAVE to watch it! Trust me... It's SOOO good.
Ha ha ha! I suppose. Can cartoon boys be hot? Yeah, he's my favorite too... so cute. What's his name? The actor I mean? Oh, I hope not, I don't like her, she's so spoiled! No, I think he would be better with Claire...
YES!!! Finally someone who agrees with me! Thank you! THANK! YOU!

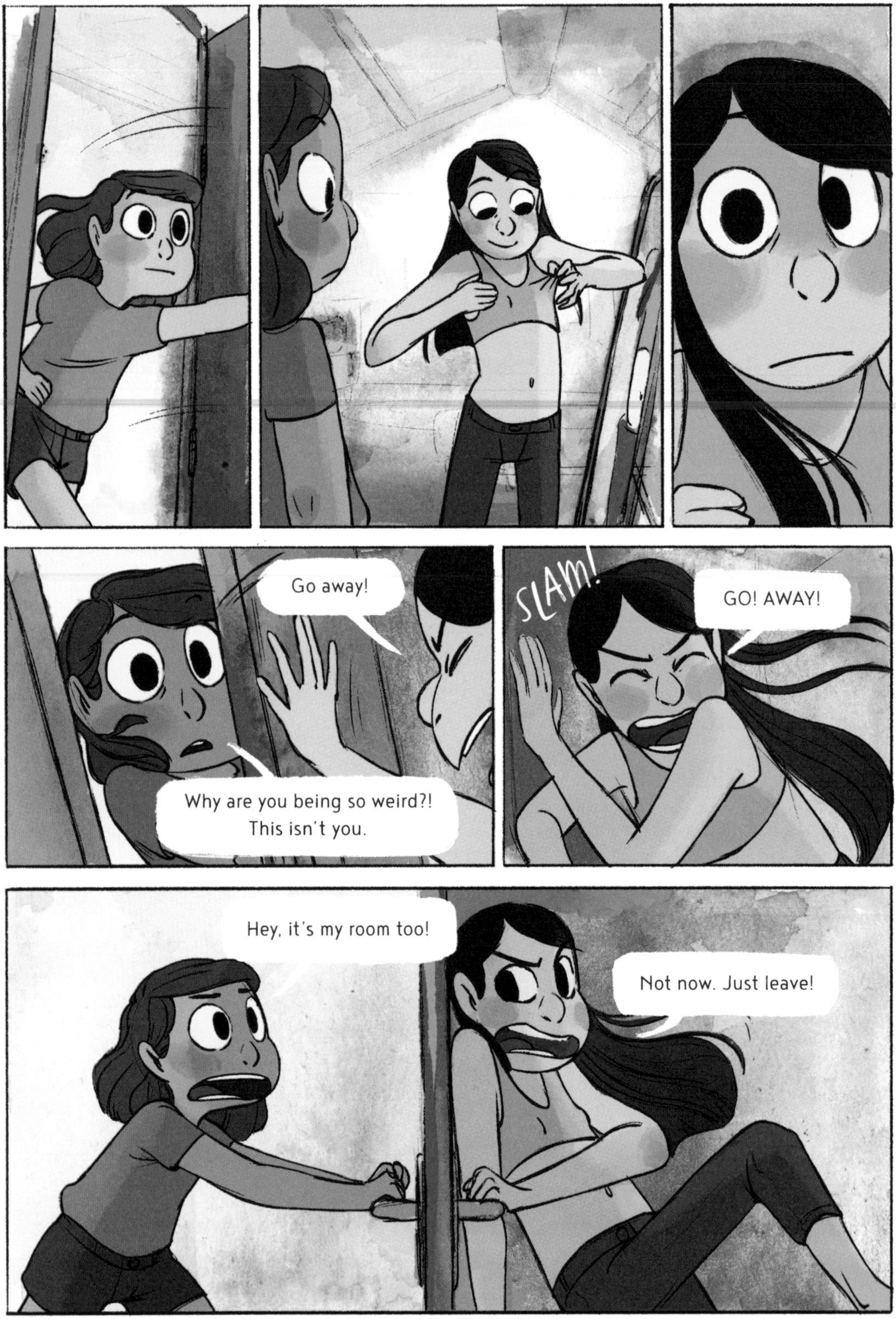
Go away!
Why are you being so weird?! This isn't you.
SLAM!
GO! AWAY!
Hey, it's my room too!
Not now. Just leave!

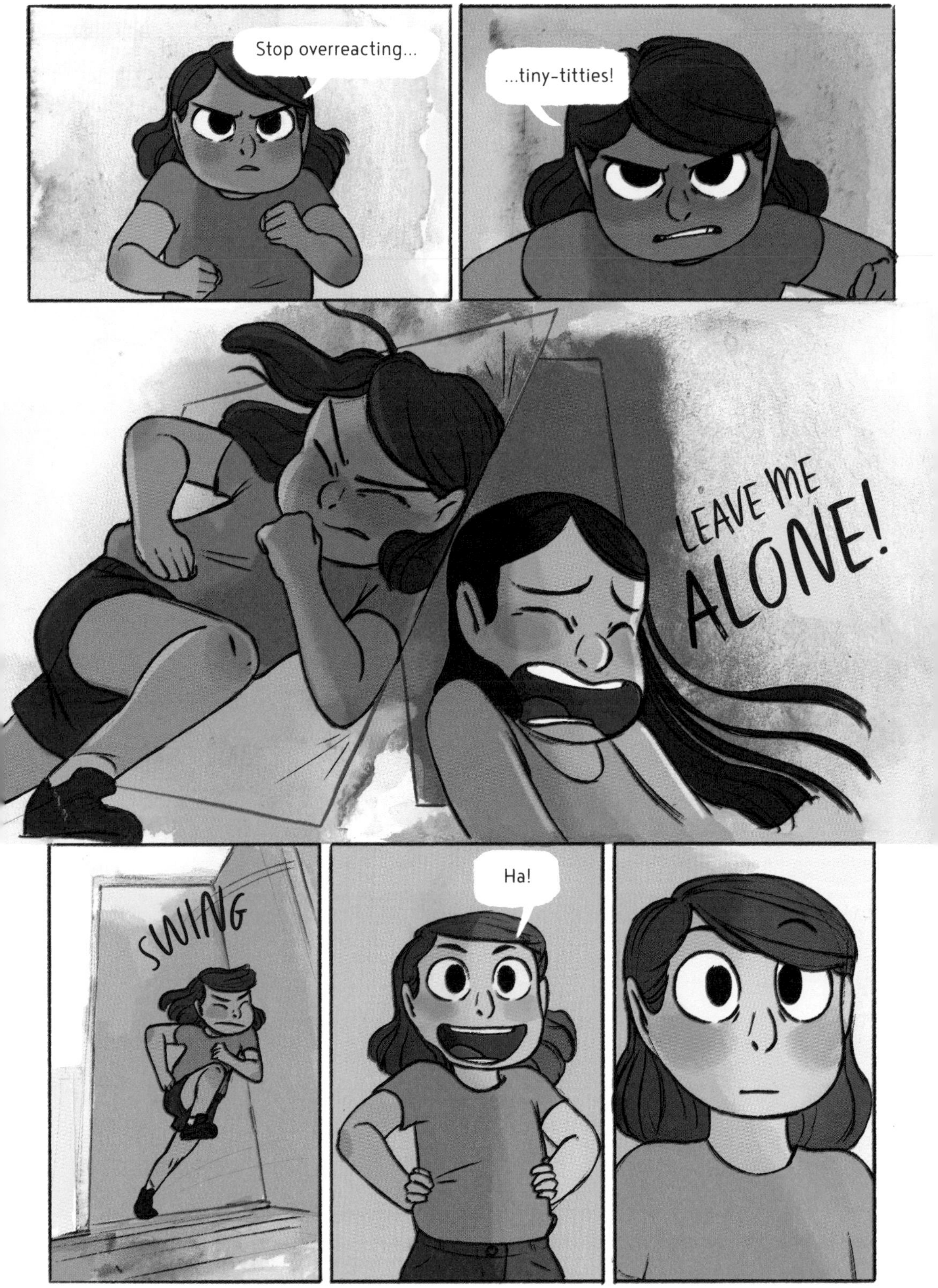
Stop overreacting...
...tiny-titties!
LEAVE ME ALONE!
SWING
Ha!

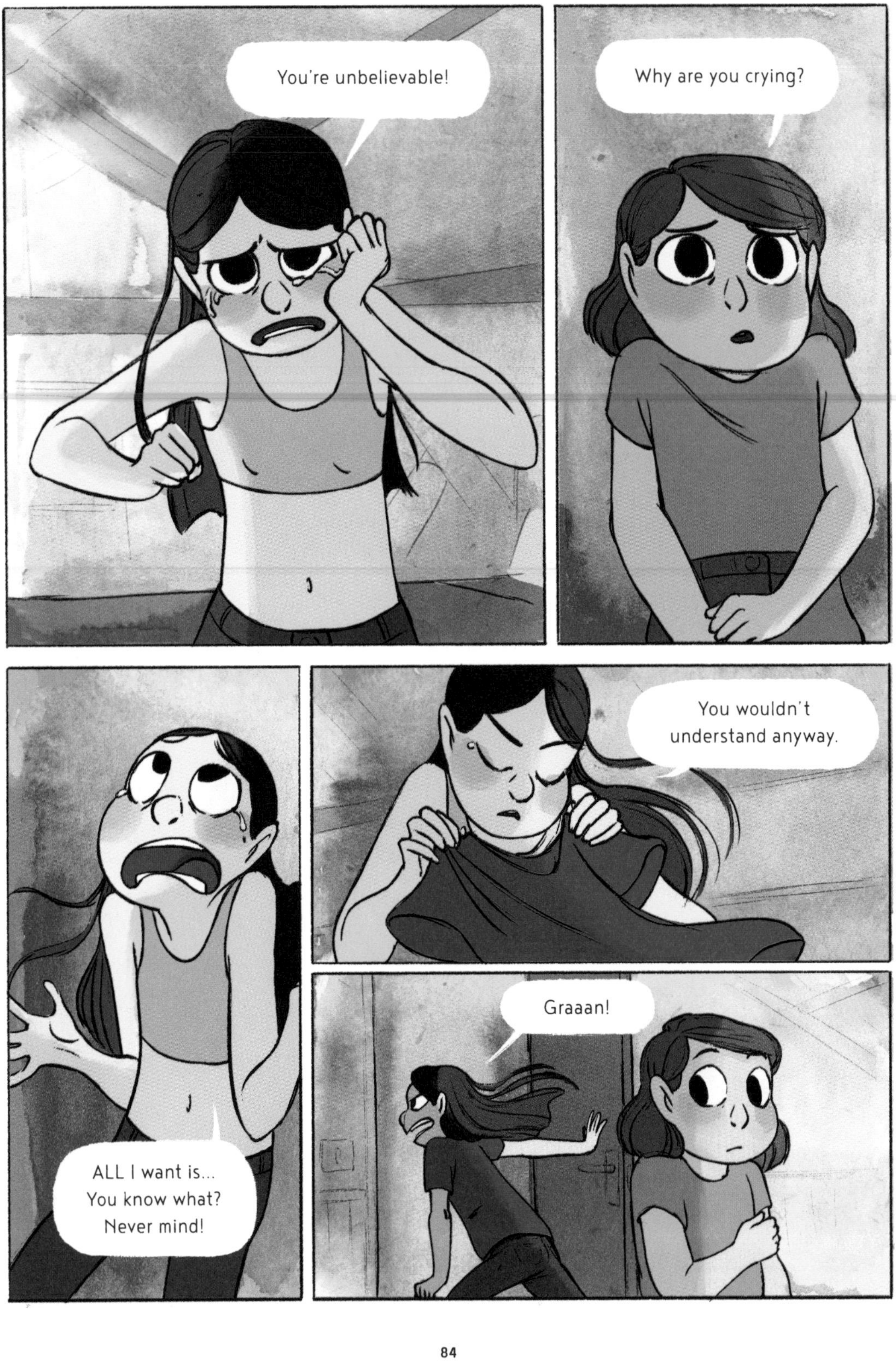

You're unbelievable!
Why are you crying?
ALL I want is... You know what? Never mind!
You wouldn't understand anyway.
Graaan!

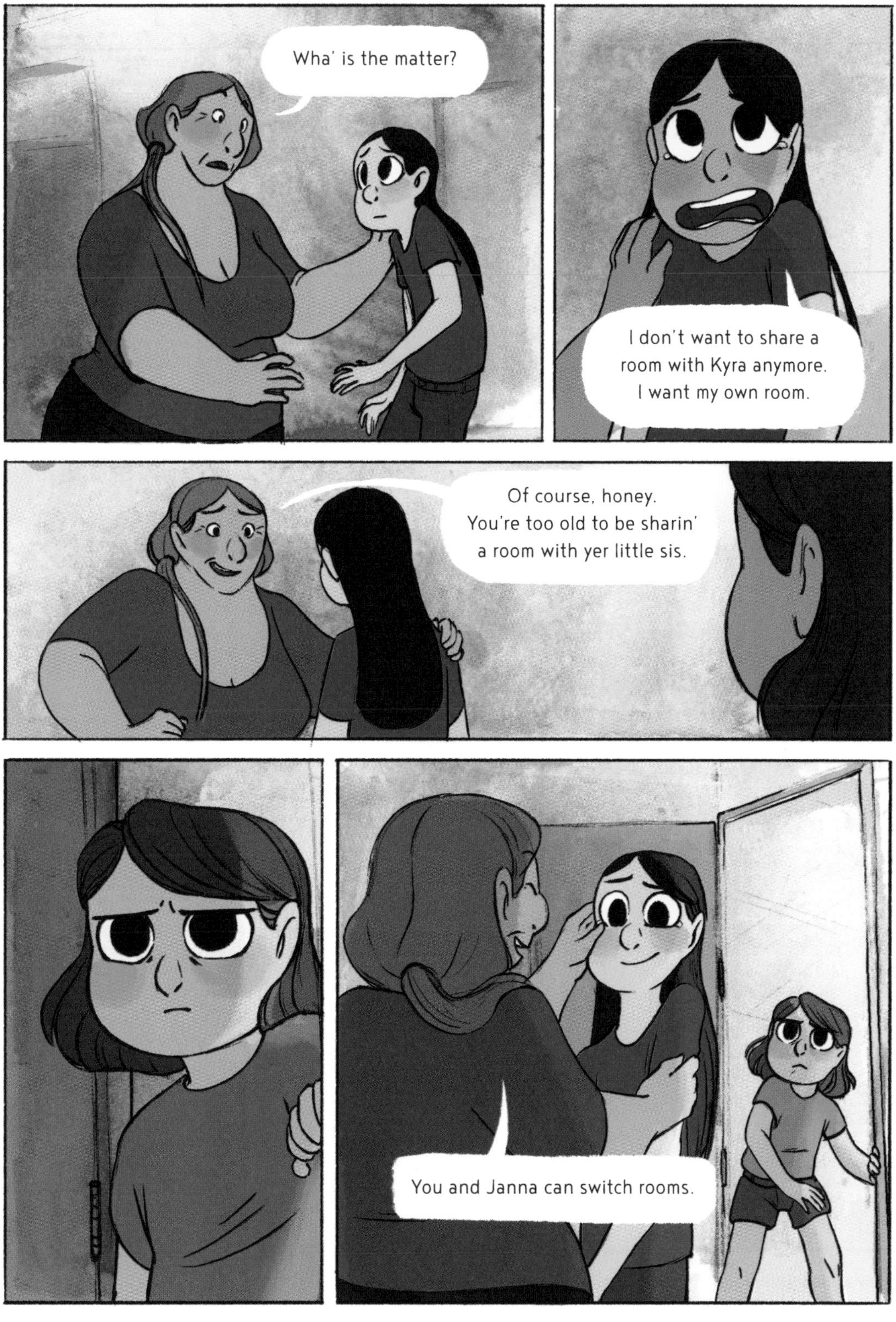
Wha' is the matter?
I don't want to share a room with Kyra anymore. I want my own room.
Of course, honey. You're too old to be sharin' a room with yer little sis.
You and Janna can switch rooms.

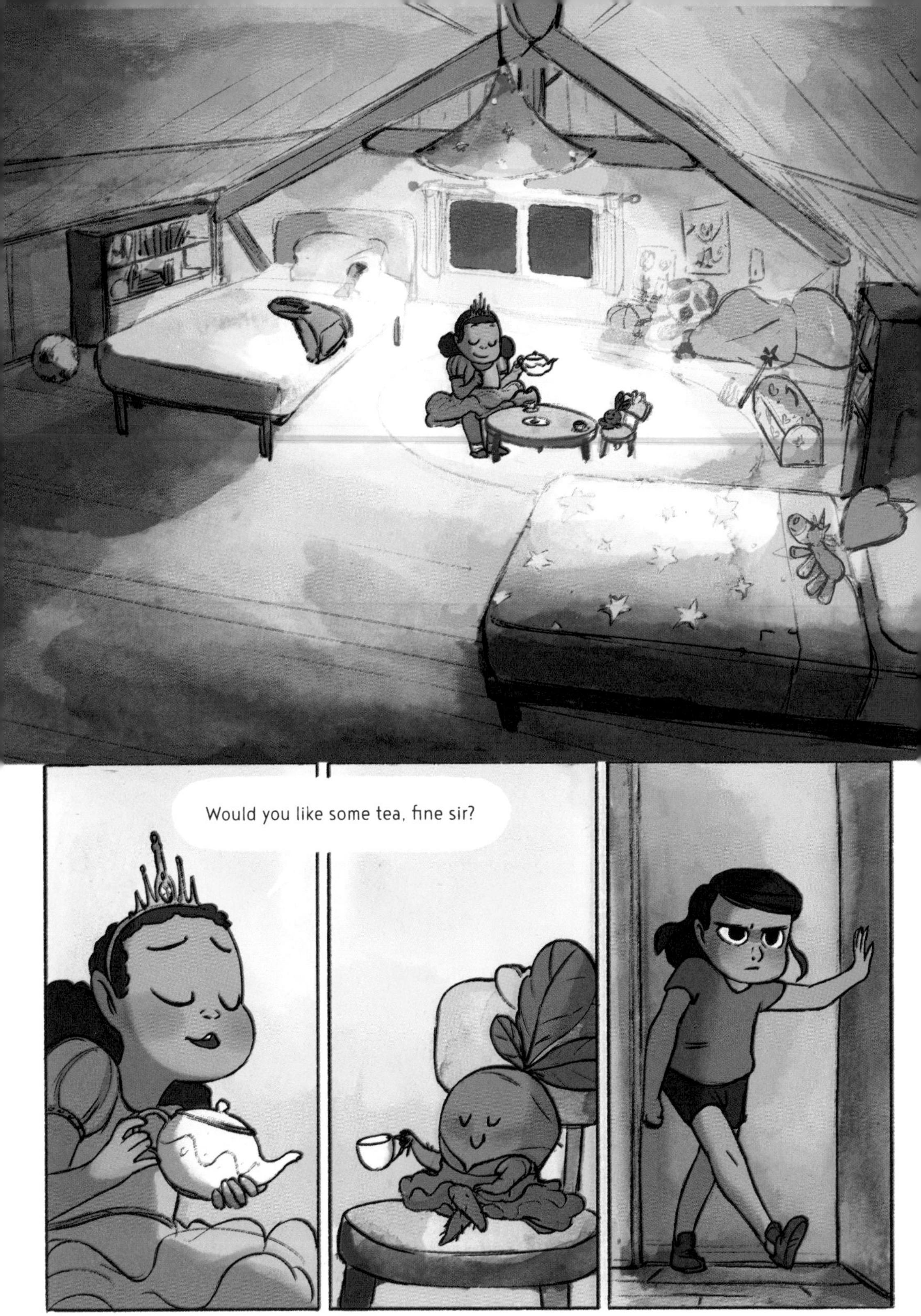
Would you like some tea, fine sir?

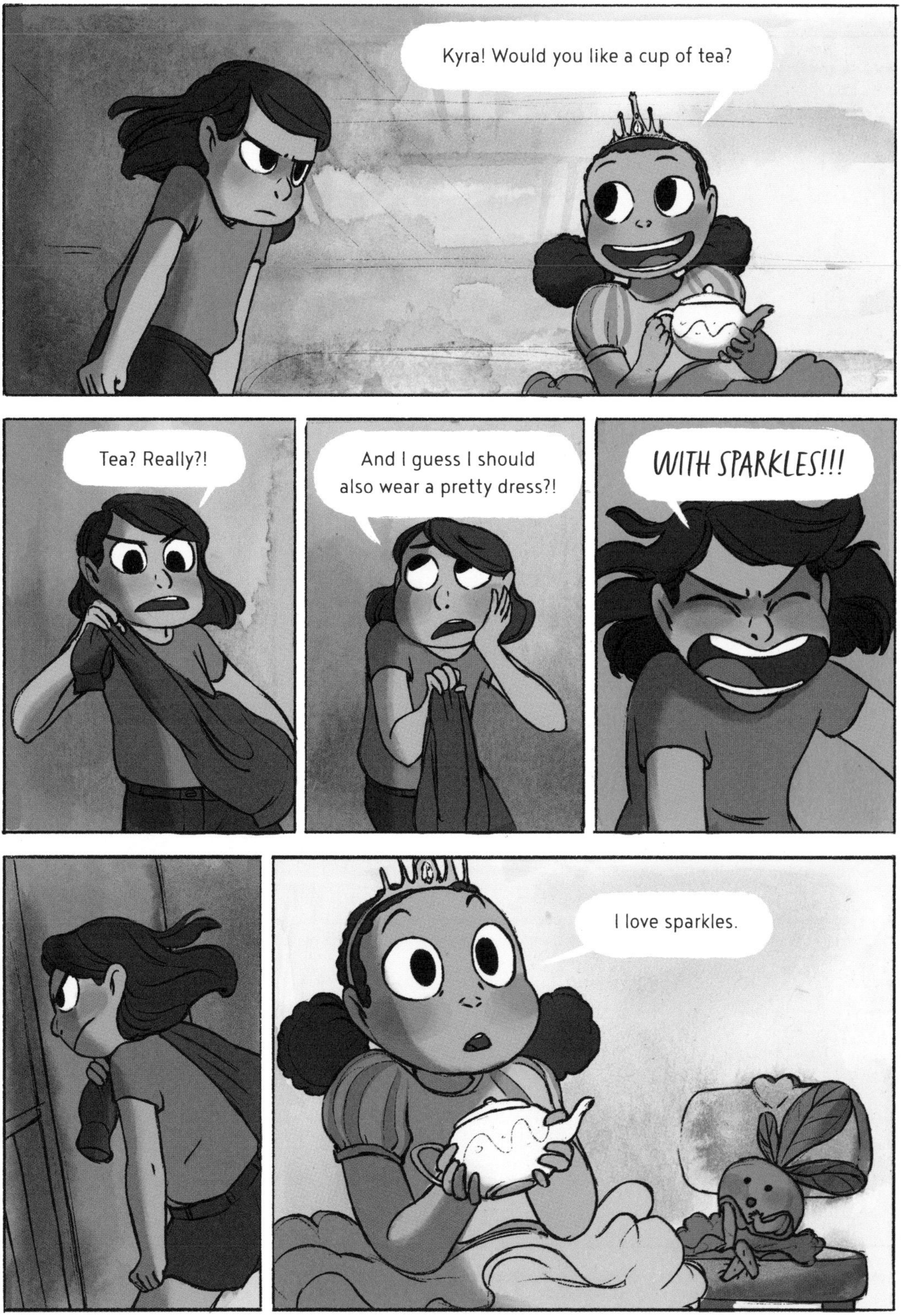

Kyra! Would you like a cup of tea?
Tea? Really?!
And I guess I should also wear a pretty dress?!
WITH SPARKLES!!!
I love sparkles.

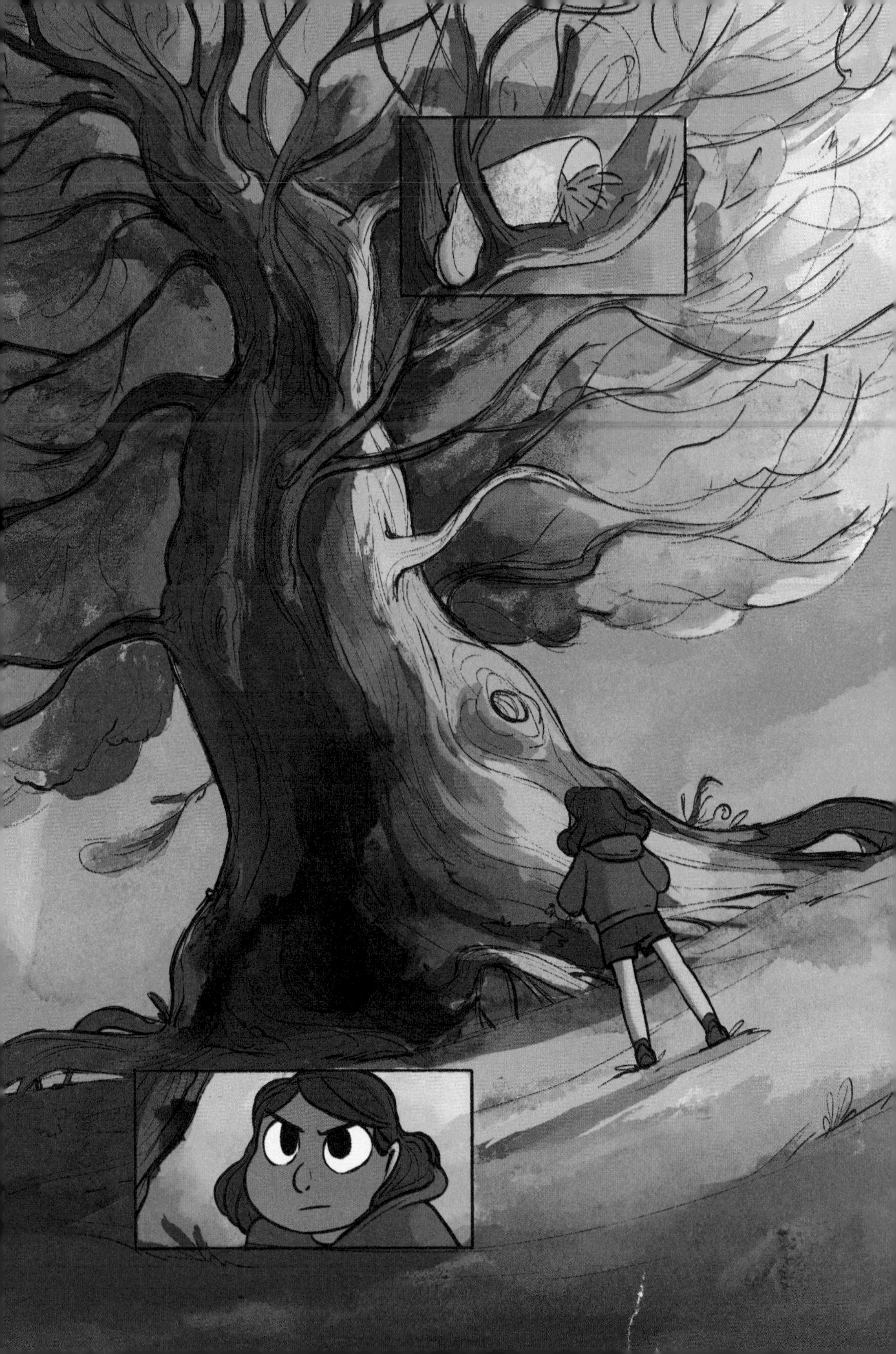

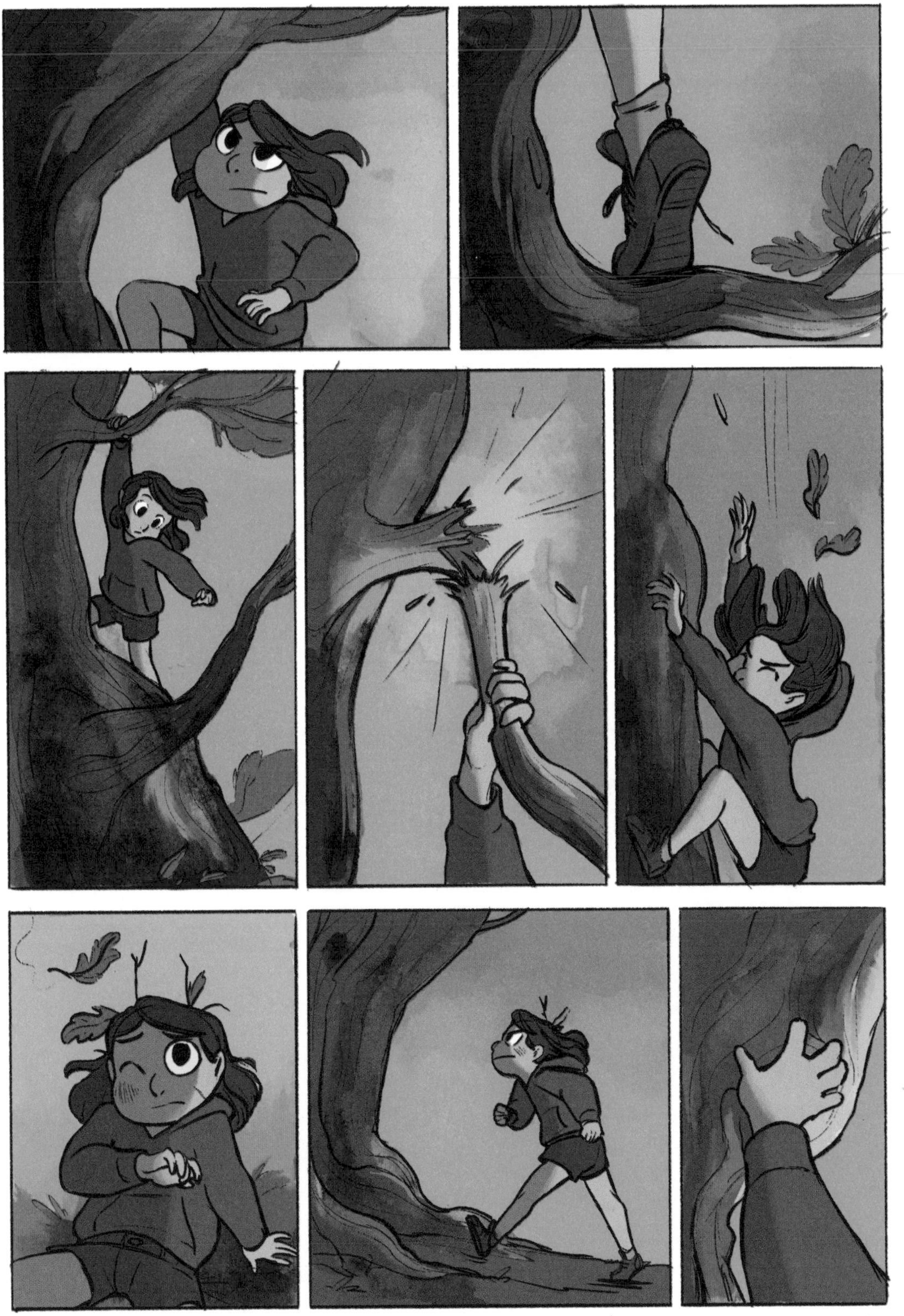

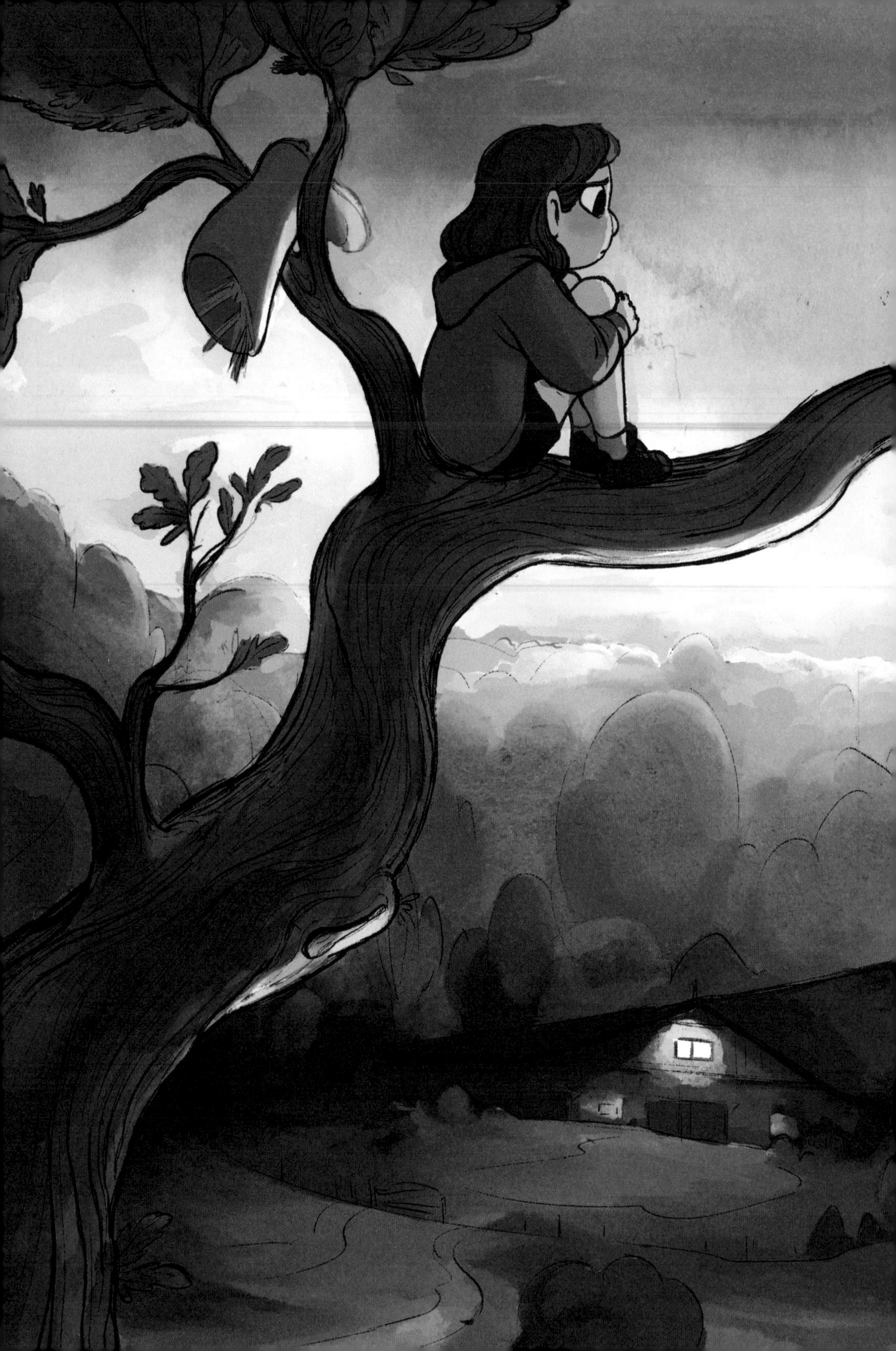

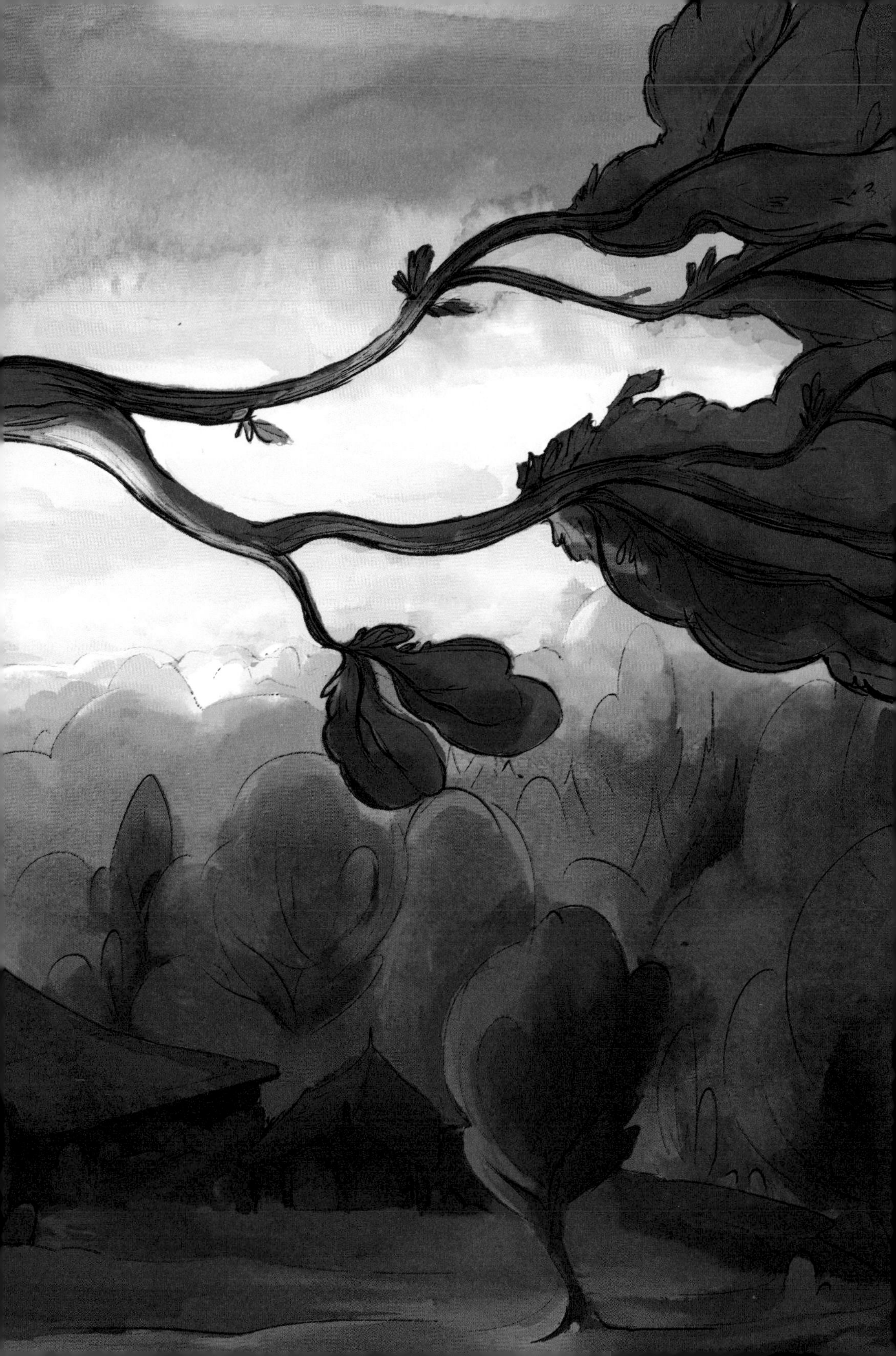

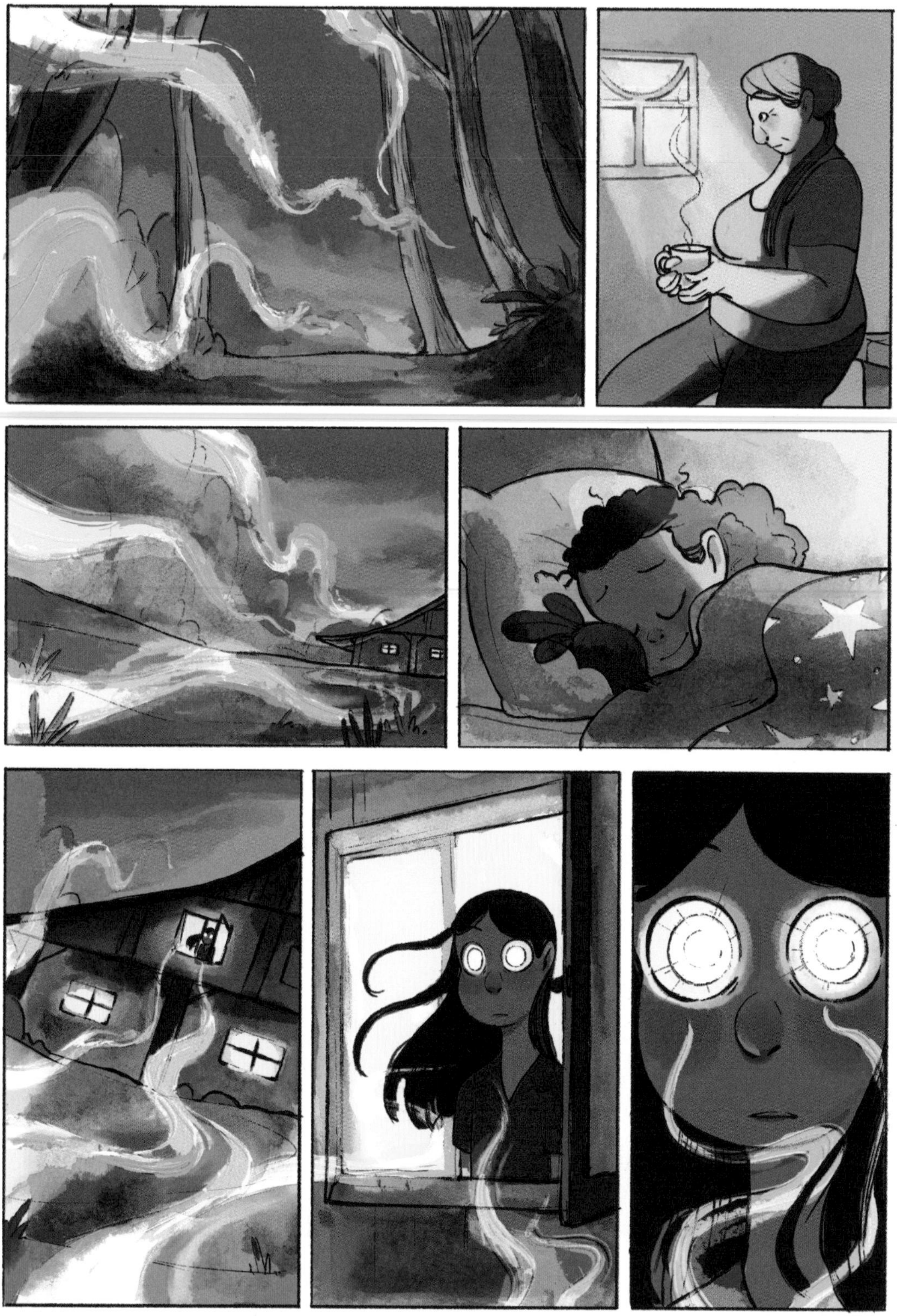

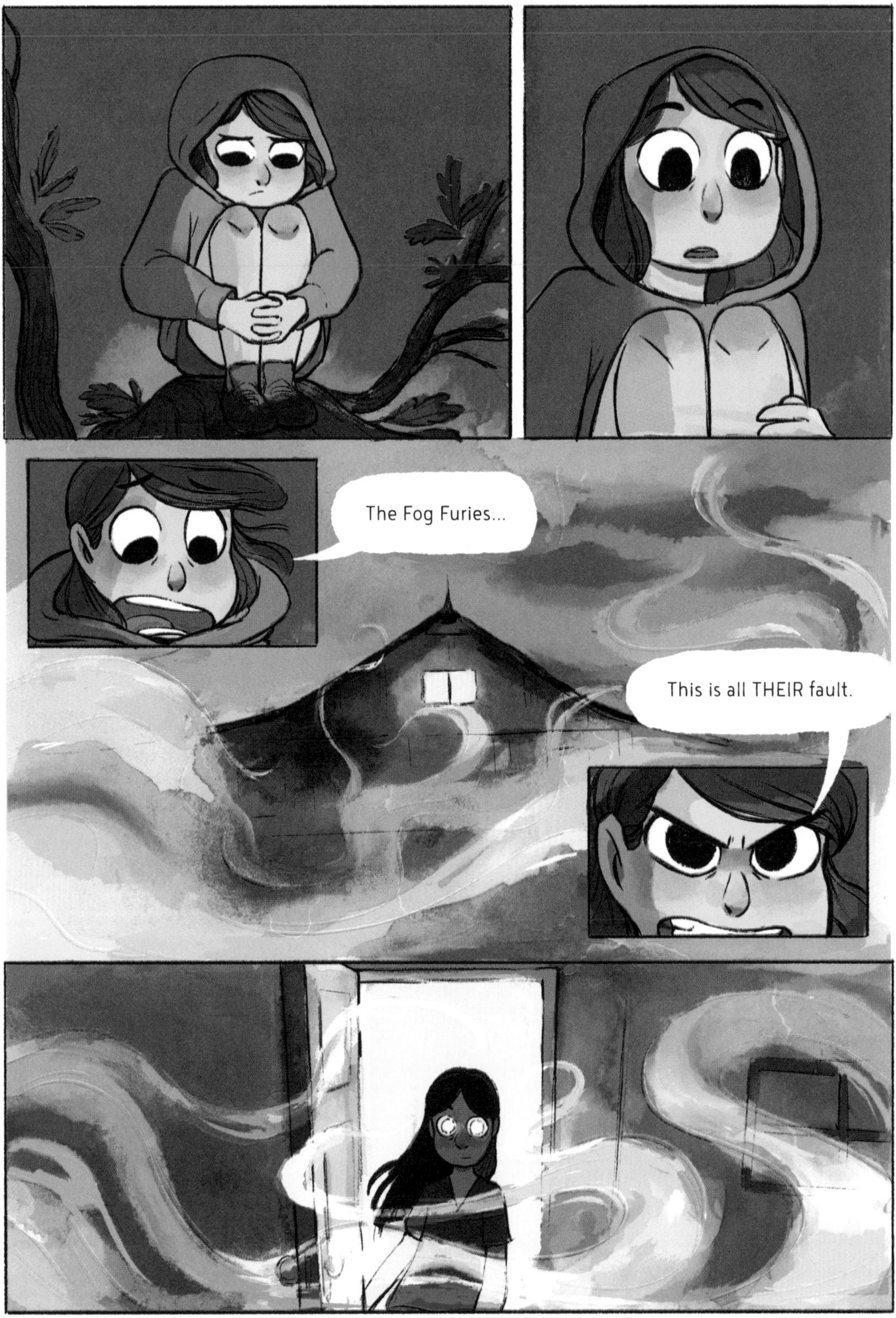
The Fog Furies...
This is all THEIR fault.

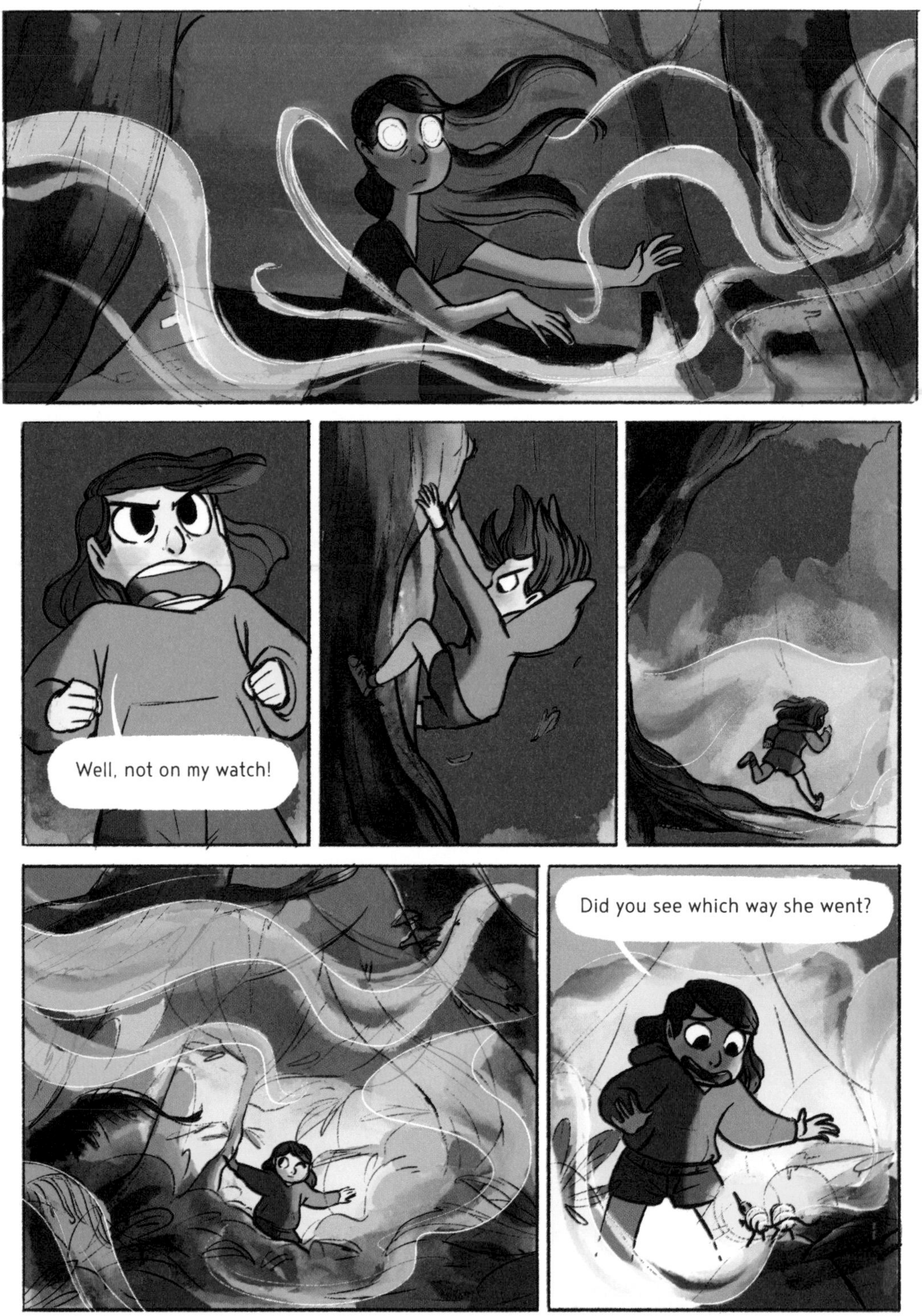
Well, not on my watch!
Did you see which way she went?

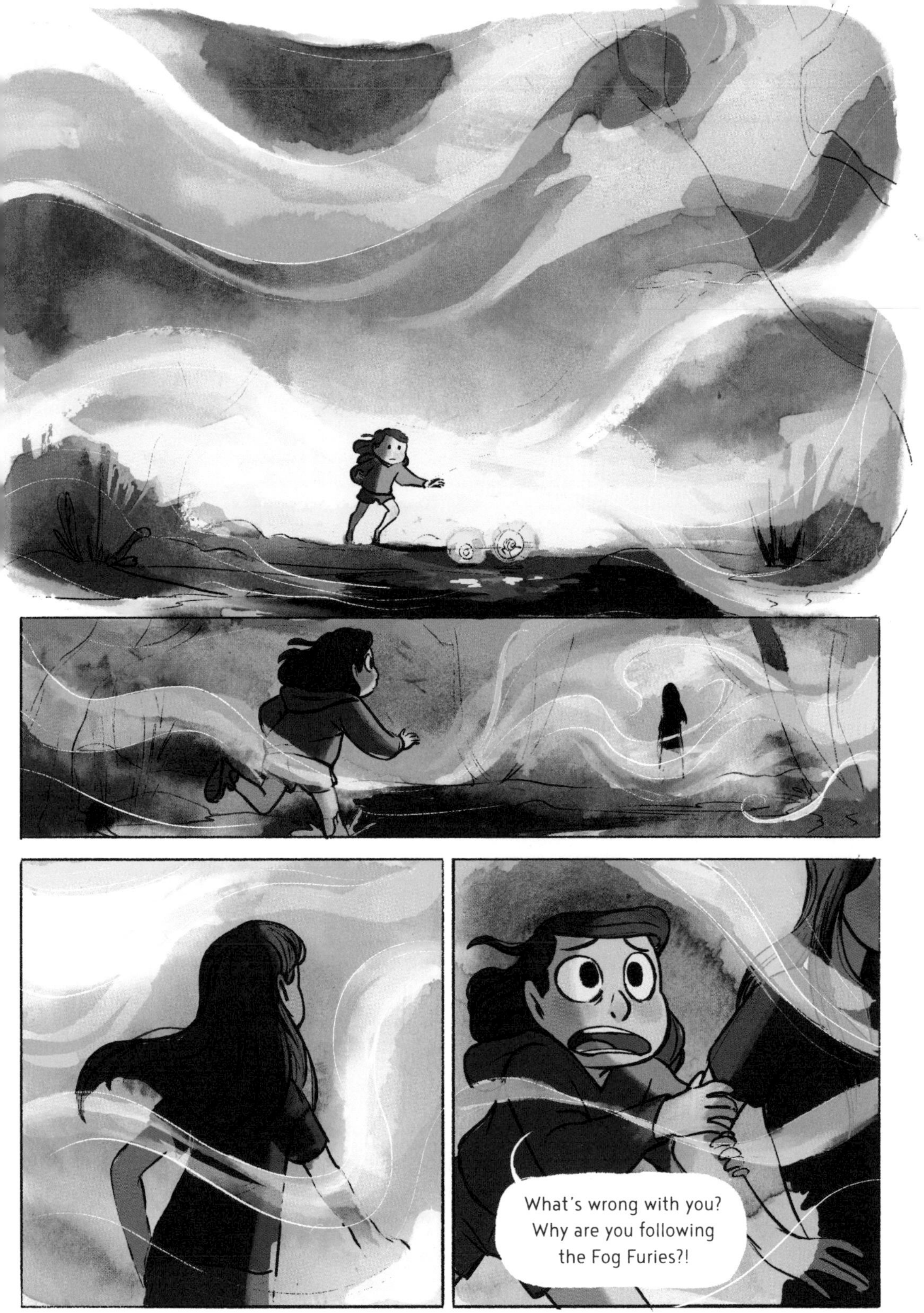
What's wrong with you? Why are you following the Fog Furies?!

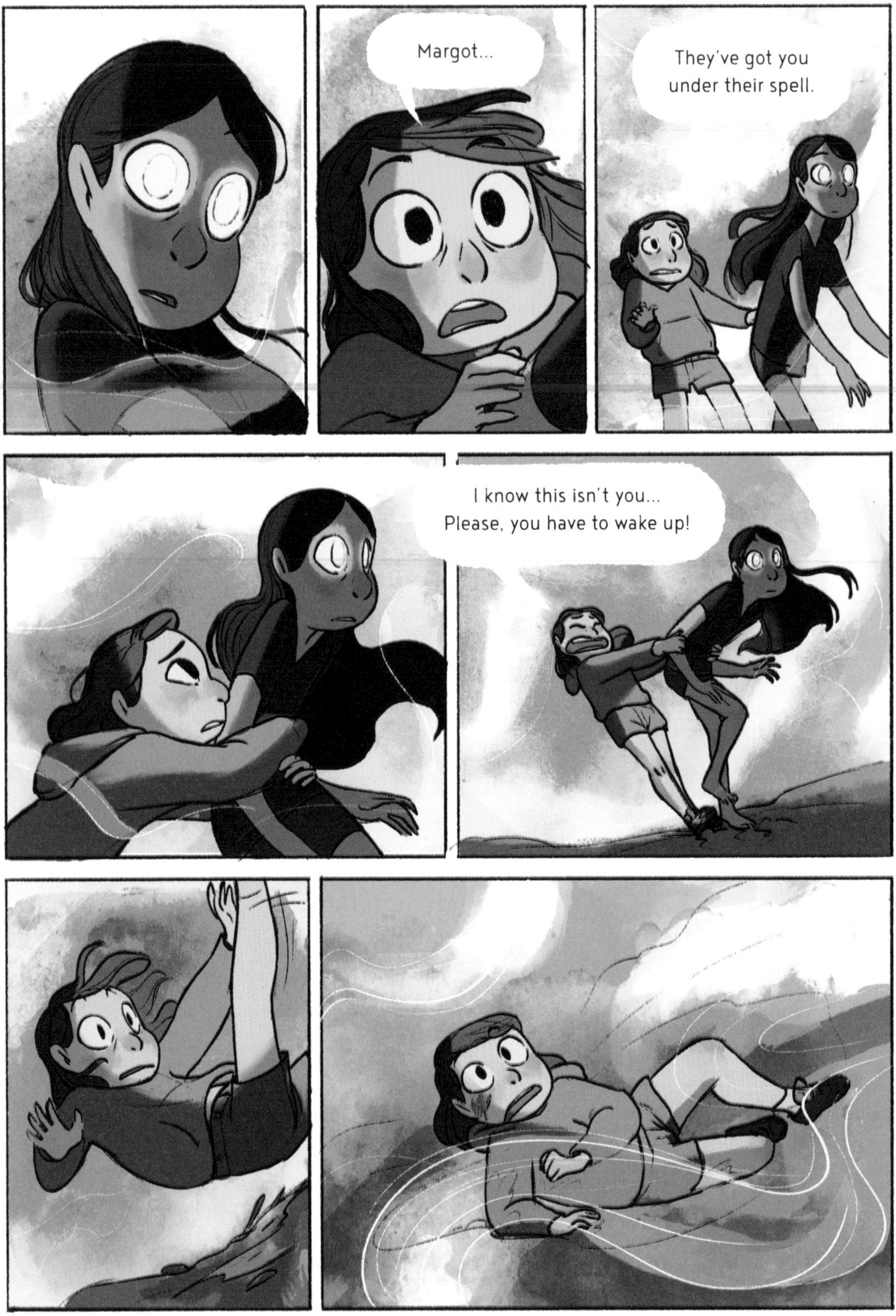
Margot...
They've got you under their spell.
I know this isn't you... Please, you have to wake up!

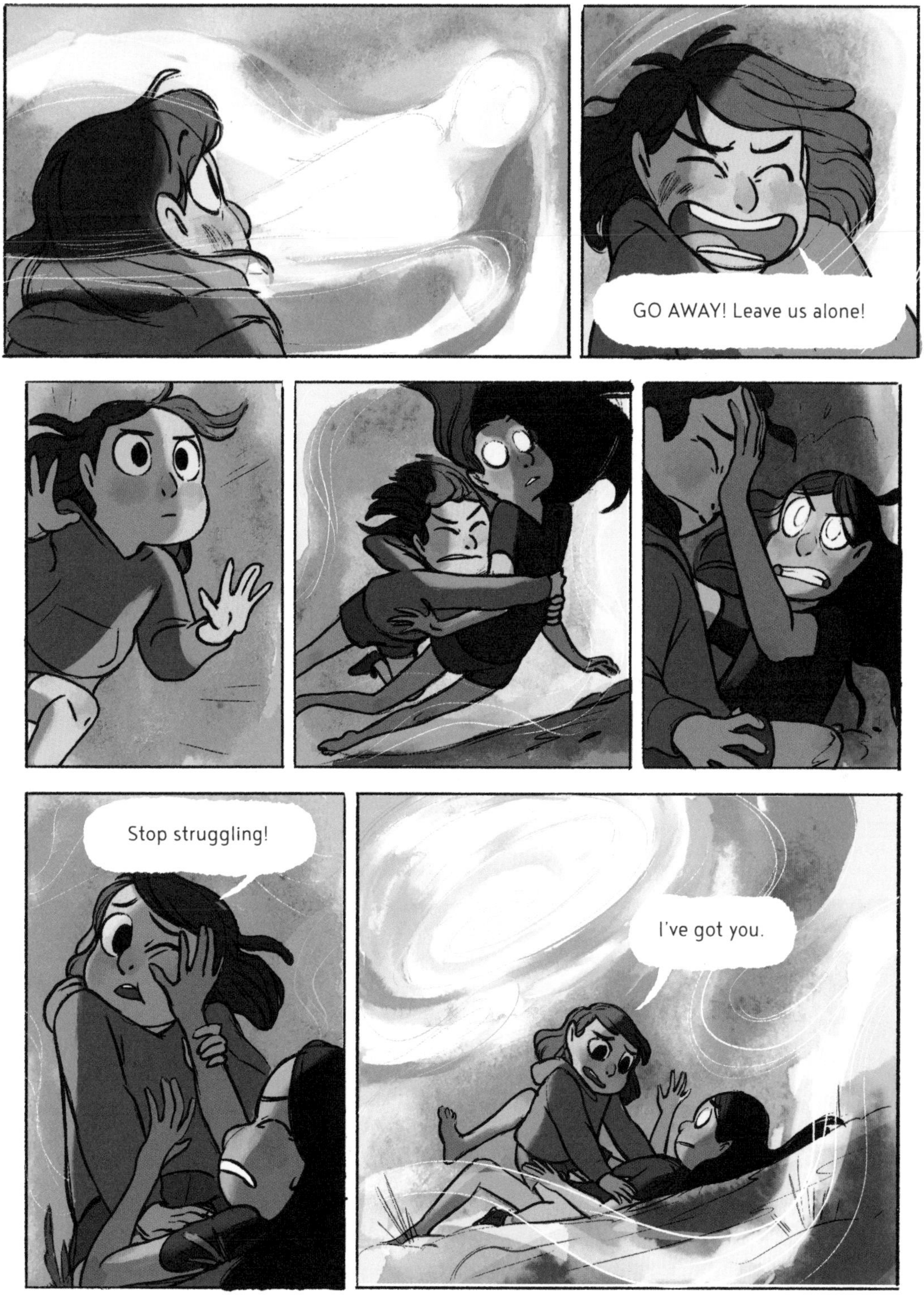
GO AWAY! Leave us alone!
Stop struggling!
I've got you.

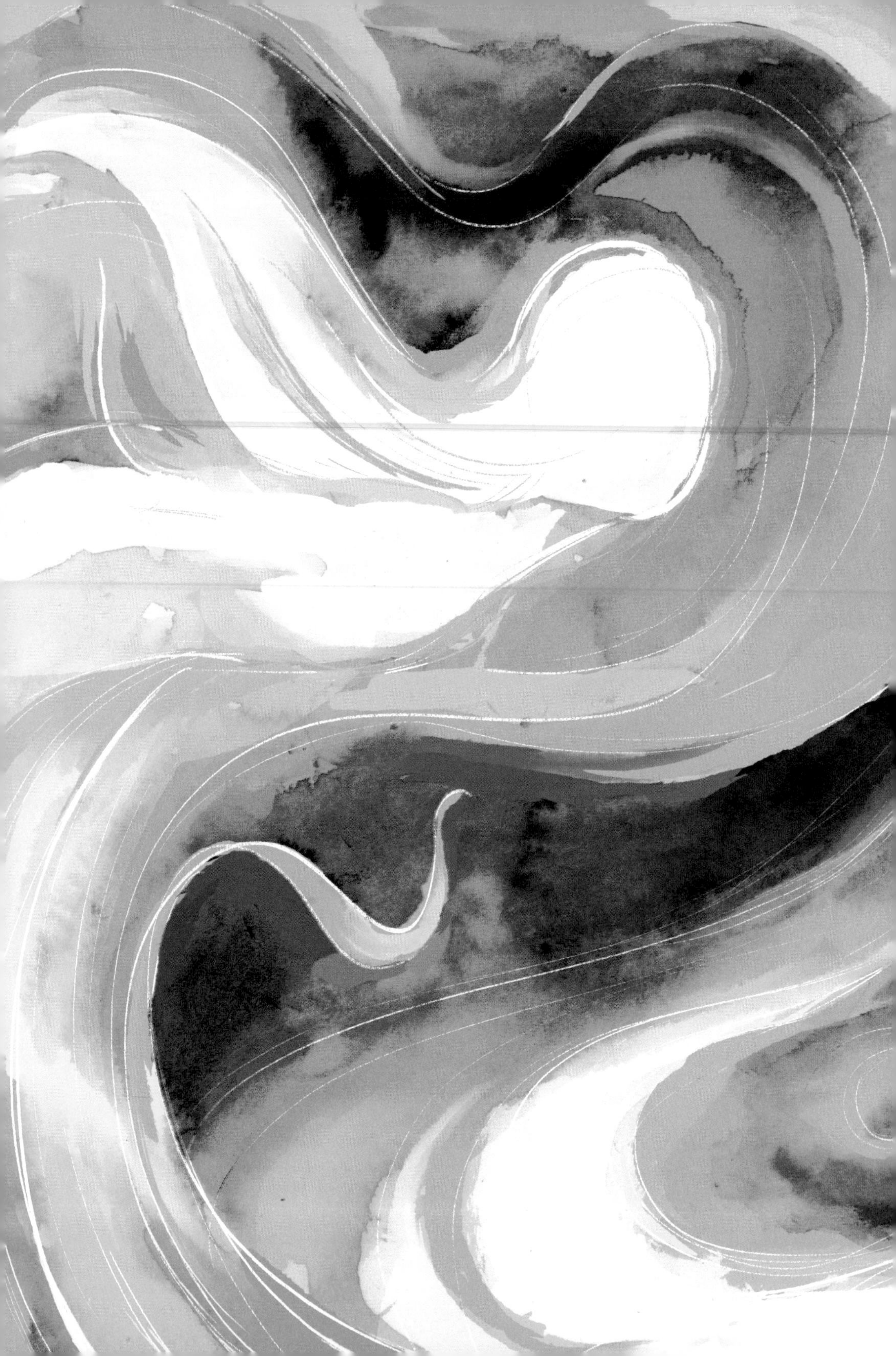

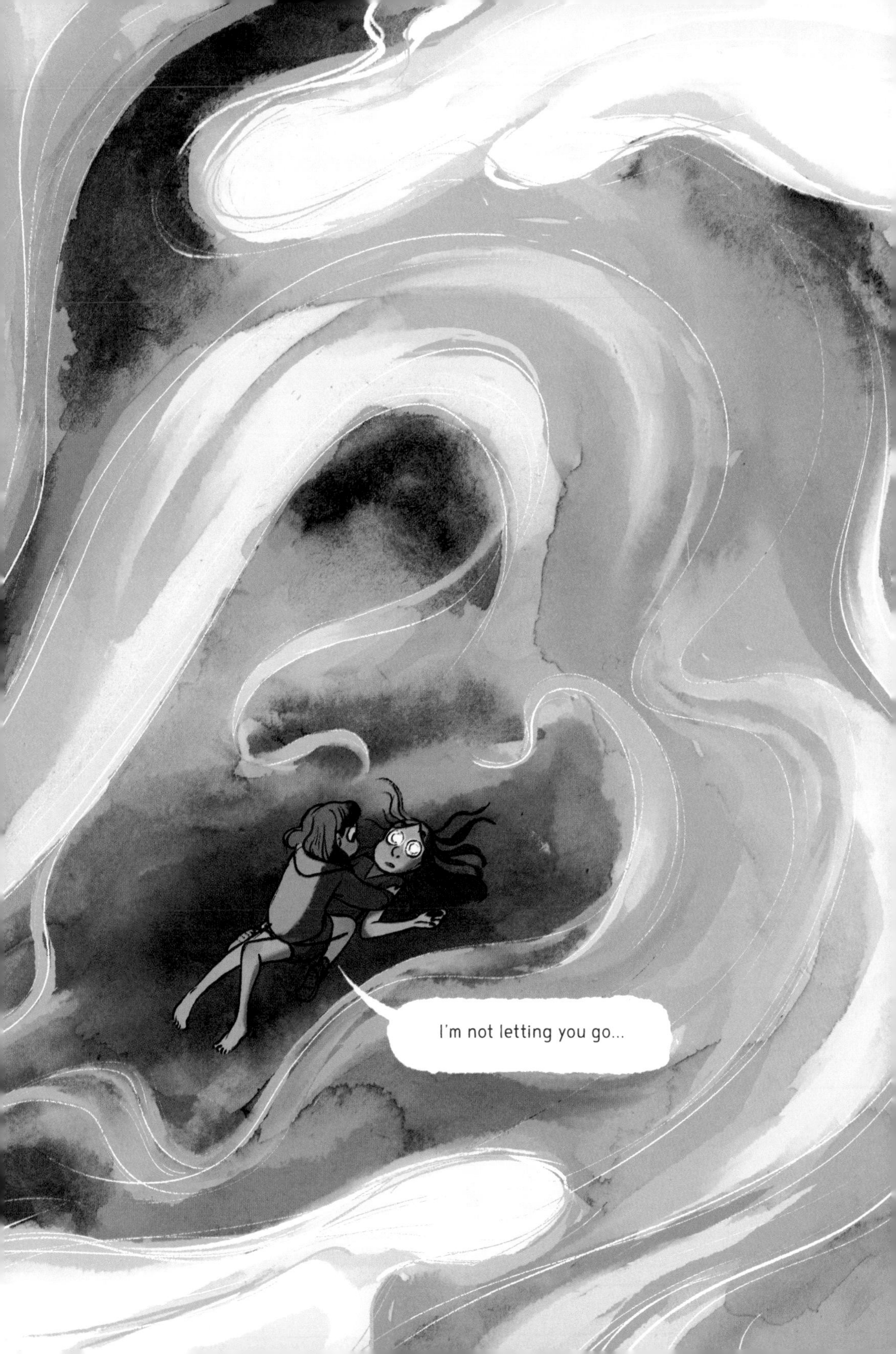
I'm not letting you go...

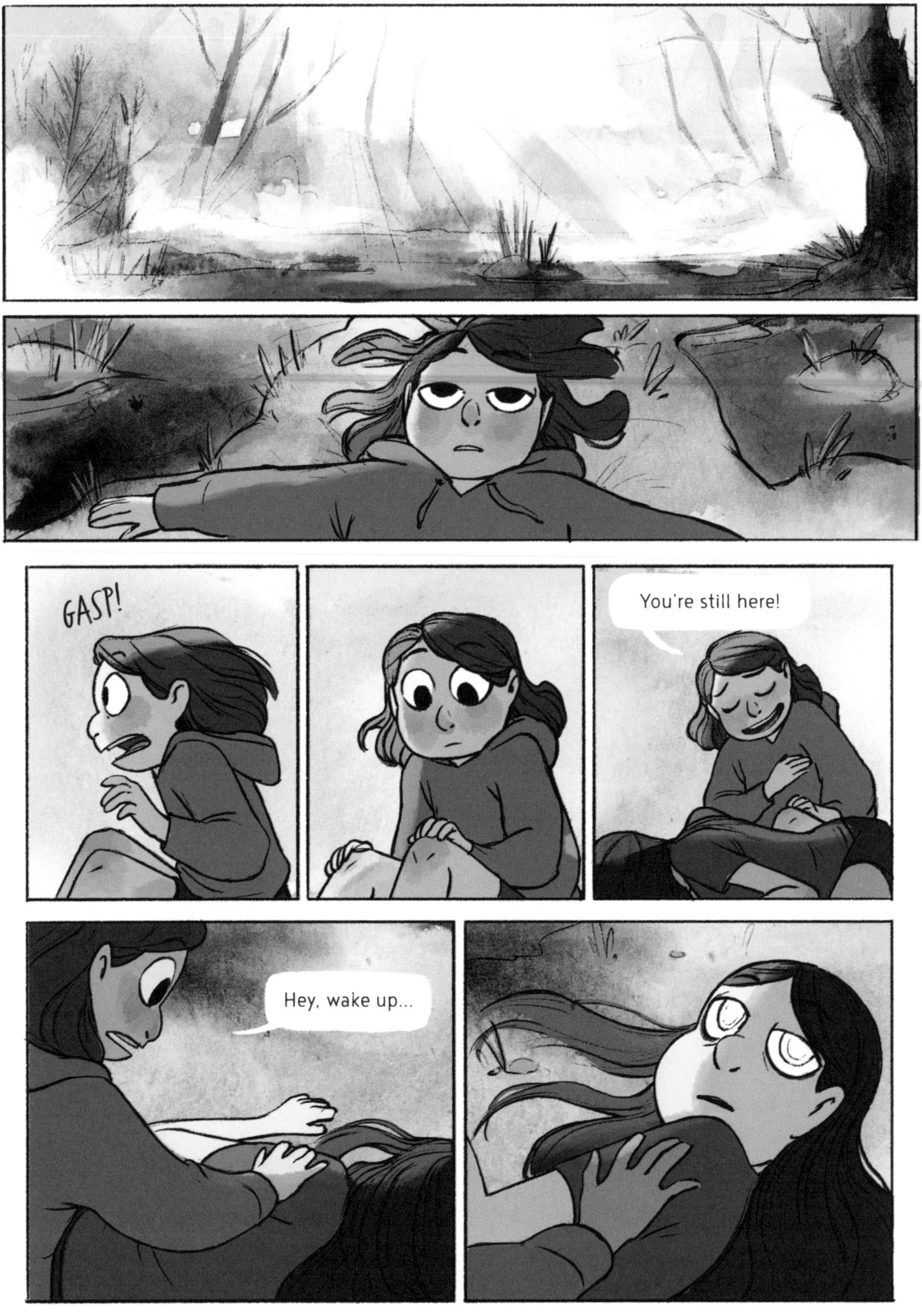
GASP!
You're still here!
Hey, wake up...

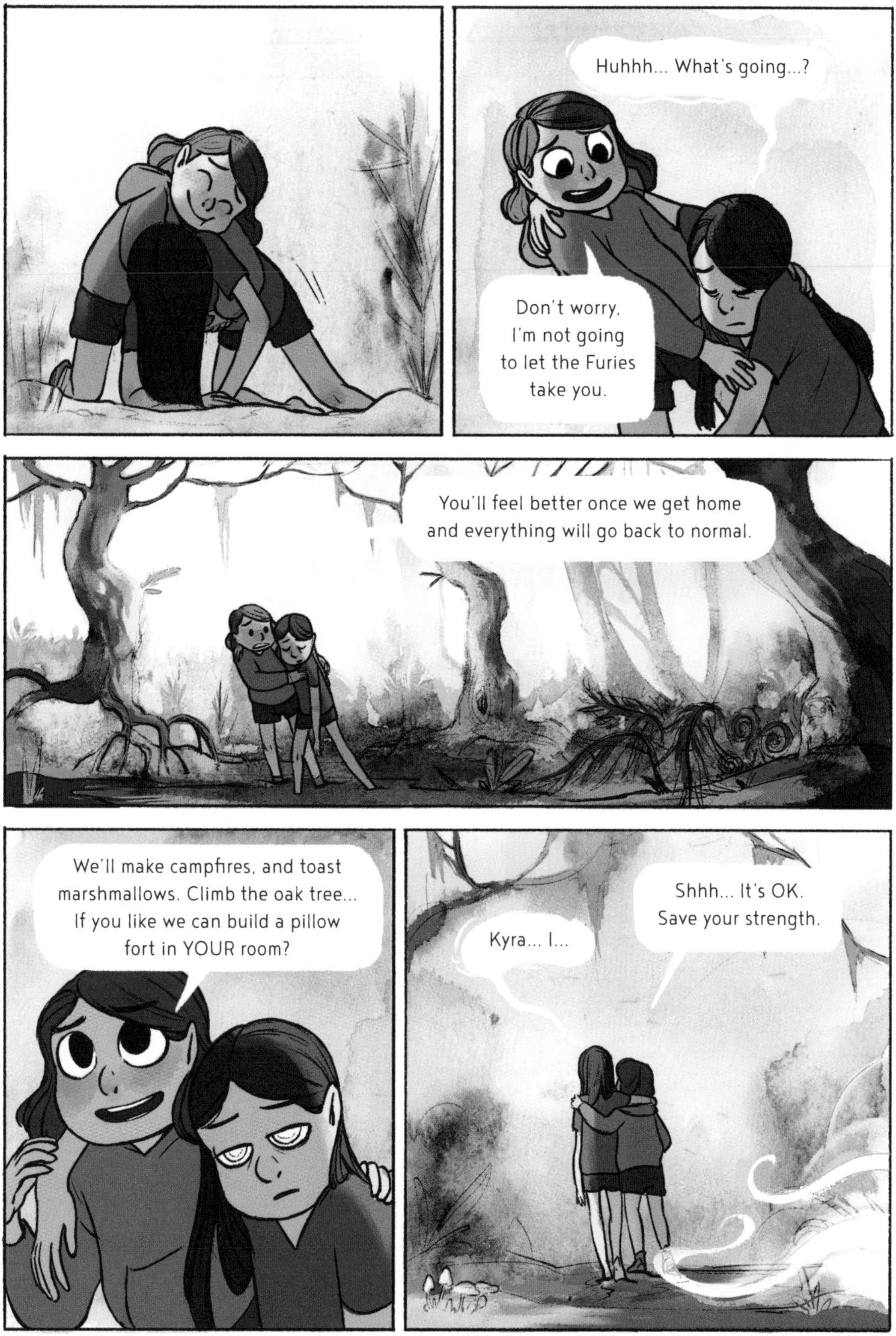
Huhhh... What's going...?
Don't worry, I'm not going to let the Furies take you.
You'll feel better once we get home and everything will go back to normal.
We'll make campfires, and toast marshmallows. Climb the oak tree... If you like we can build a pillow fort in YOUR room?
Kyra... I...
Shhh... It's OK. Save your strength.

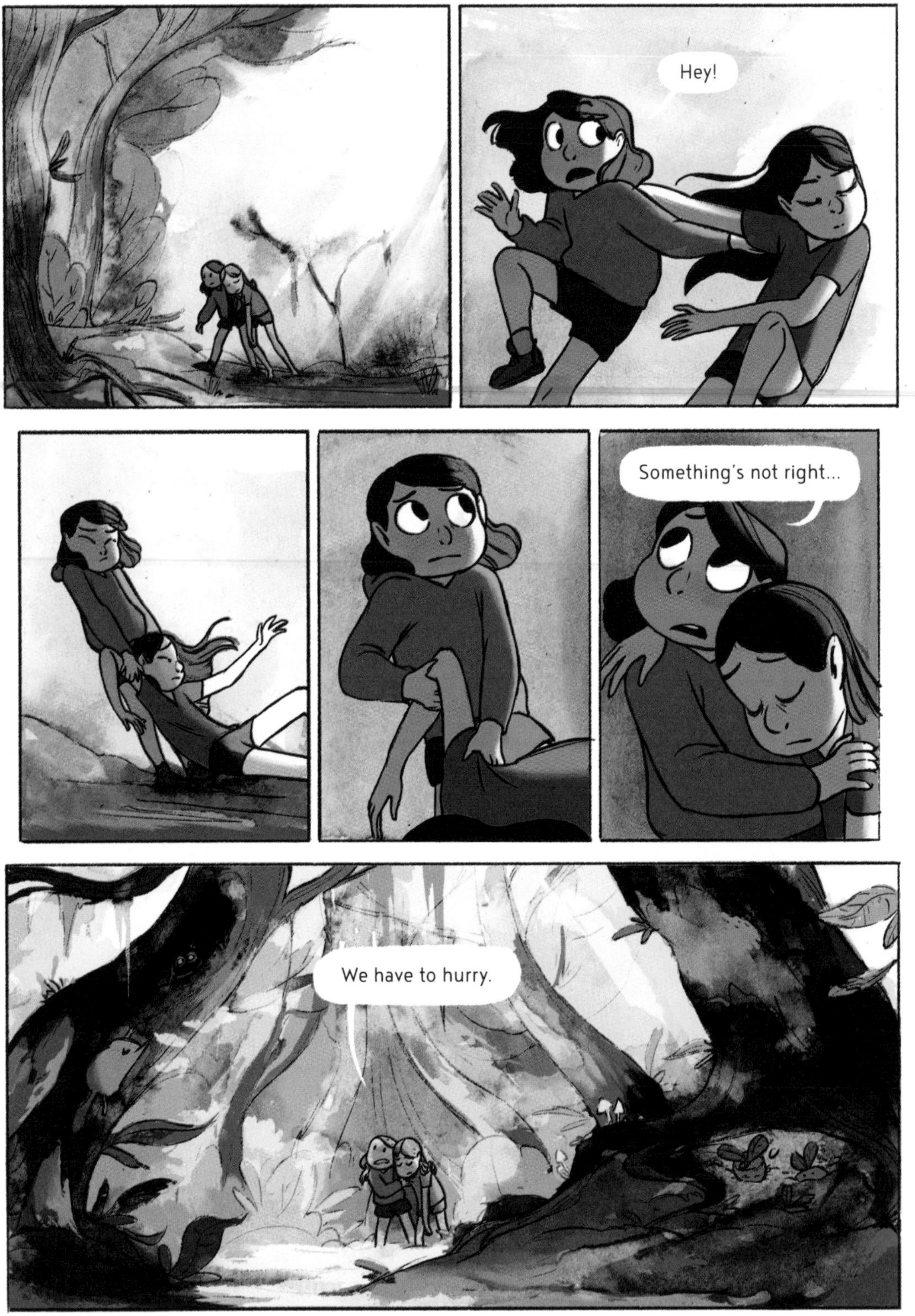
Hey!
Something's not right...
We have to hurry.

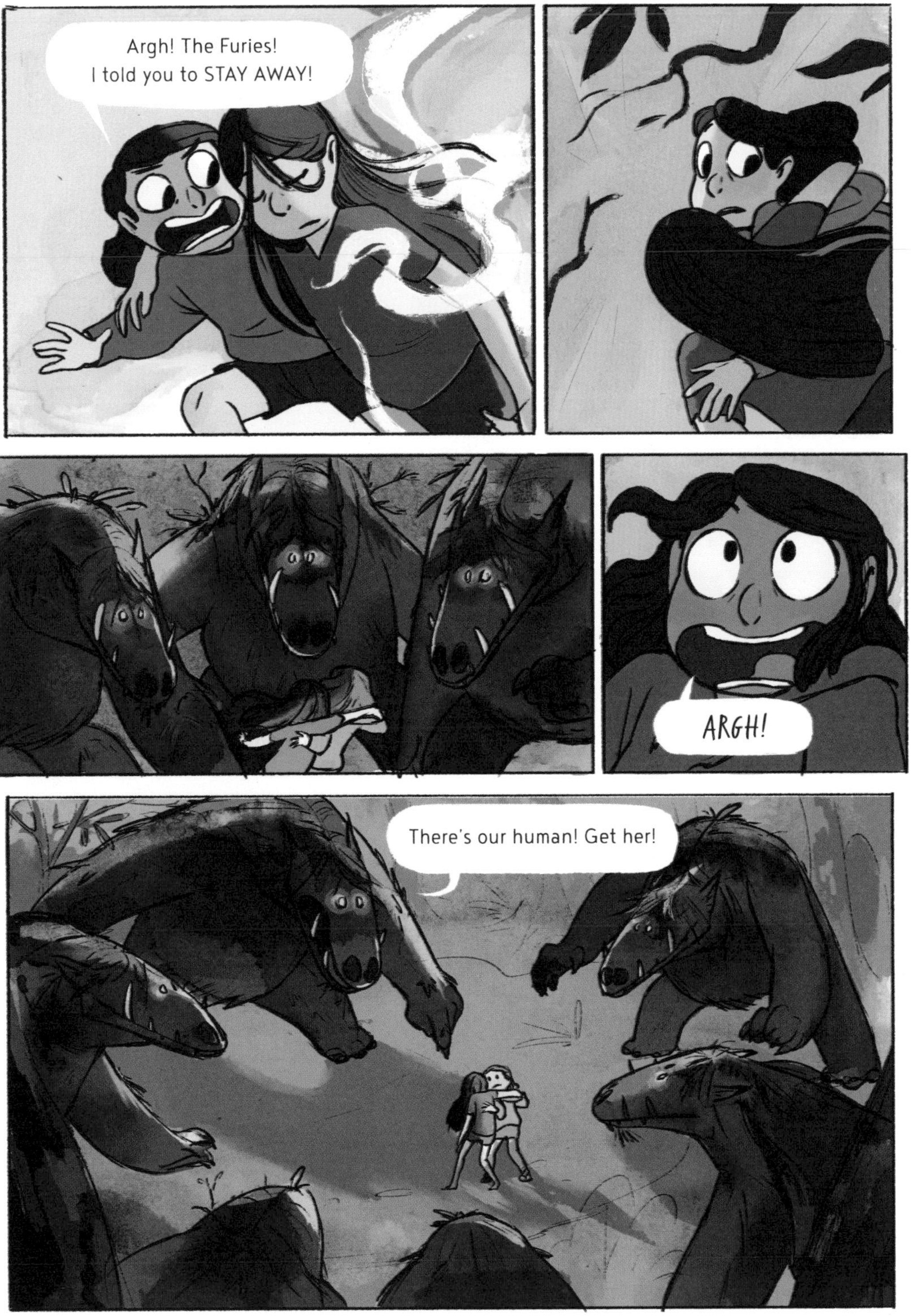
Argh! The Furies!
I told you to STAY AWAY!
ARGH!
There's our human! Get her!

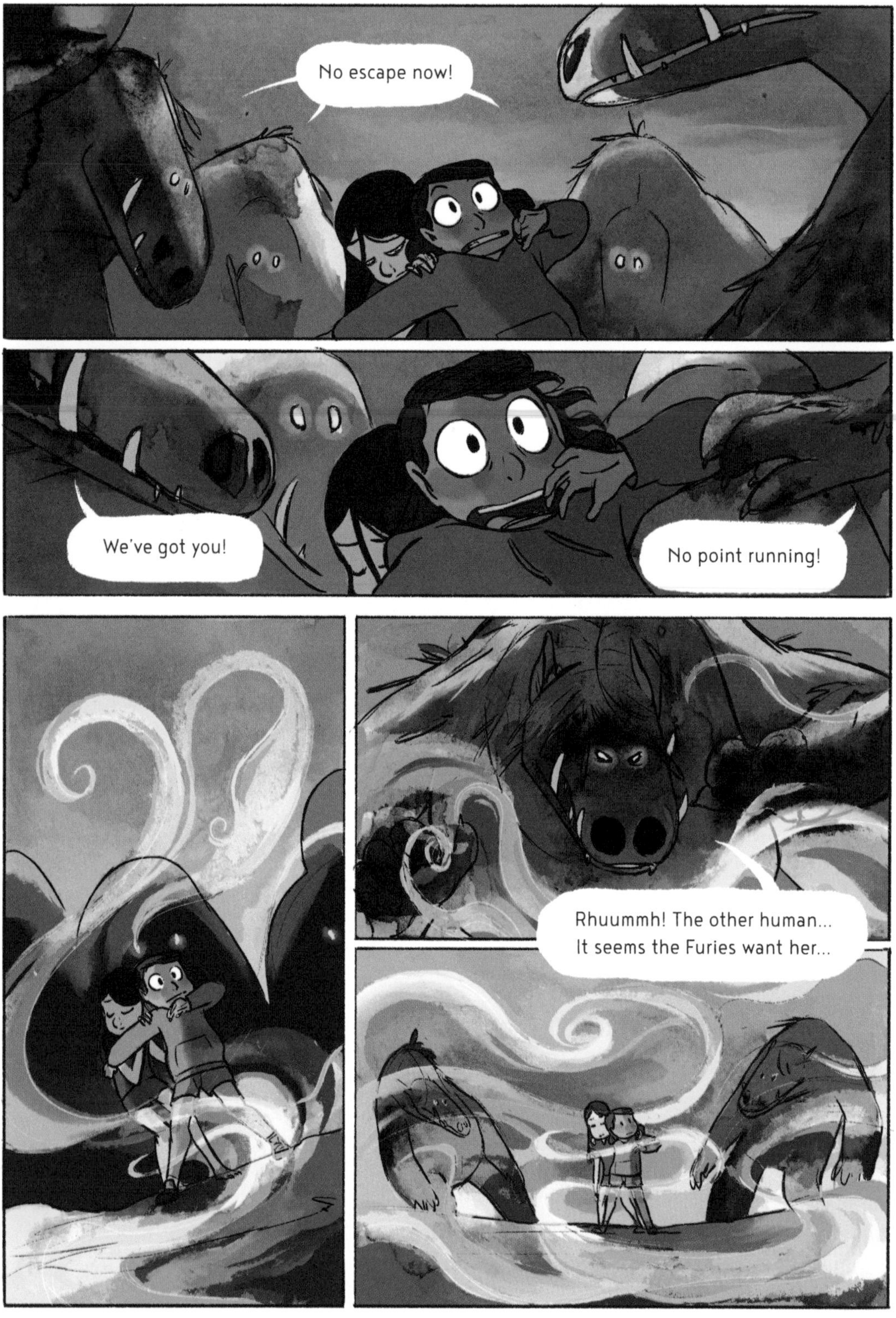
No escape now!
We've got you!
No point running!
Rhuummh! The other human... It seems the Furies want her...

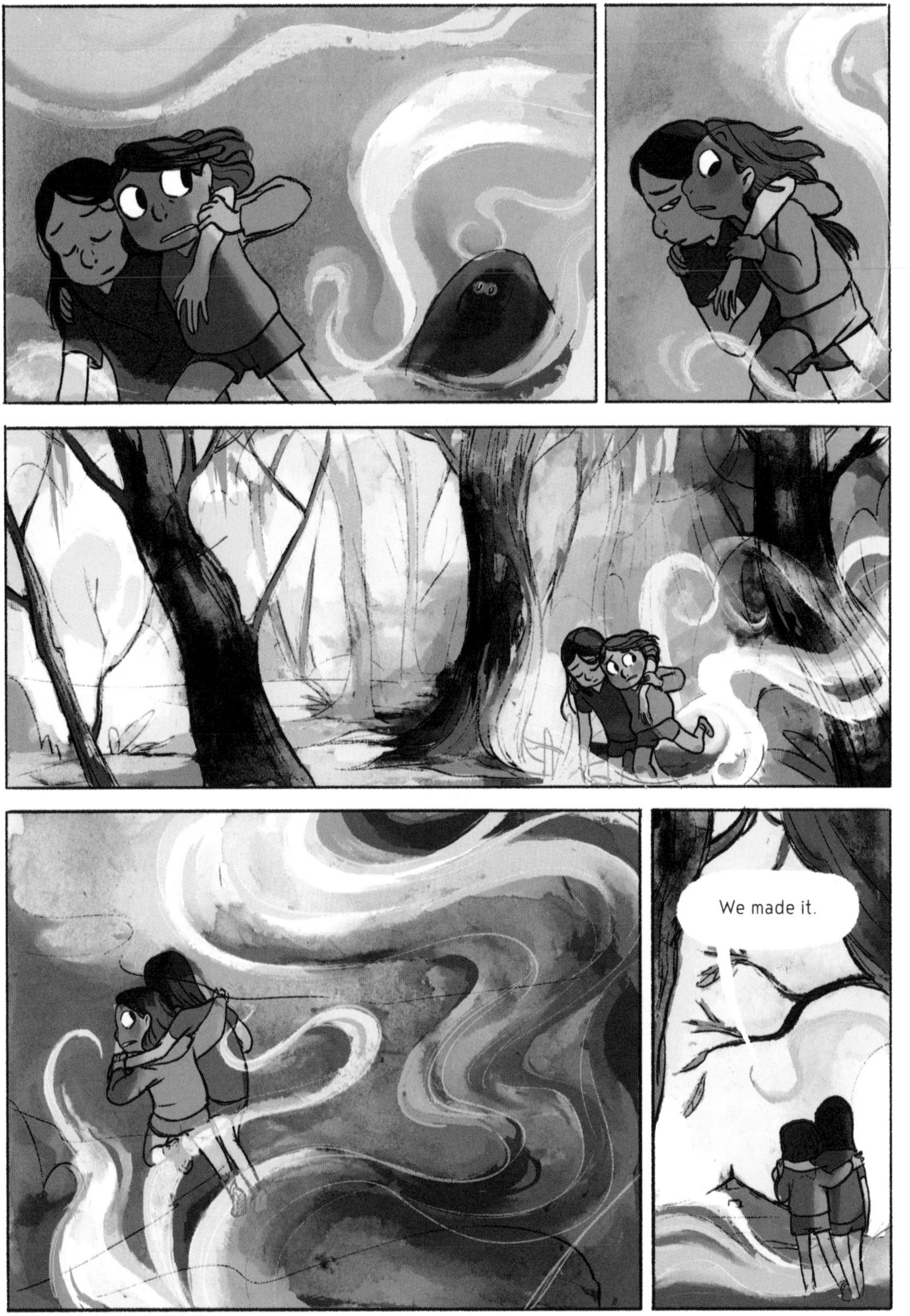
We made it.

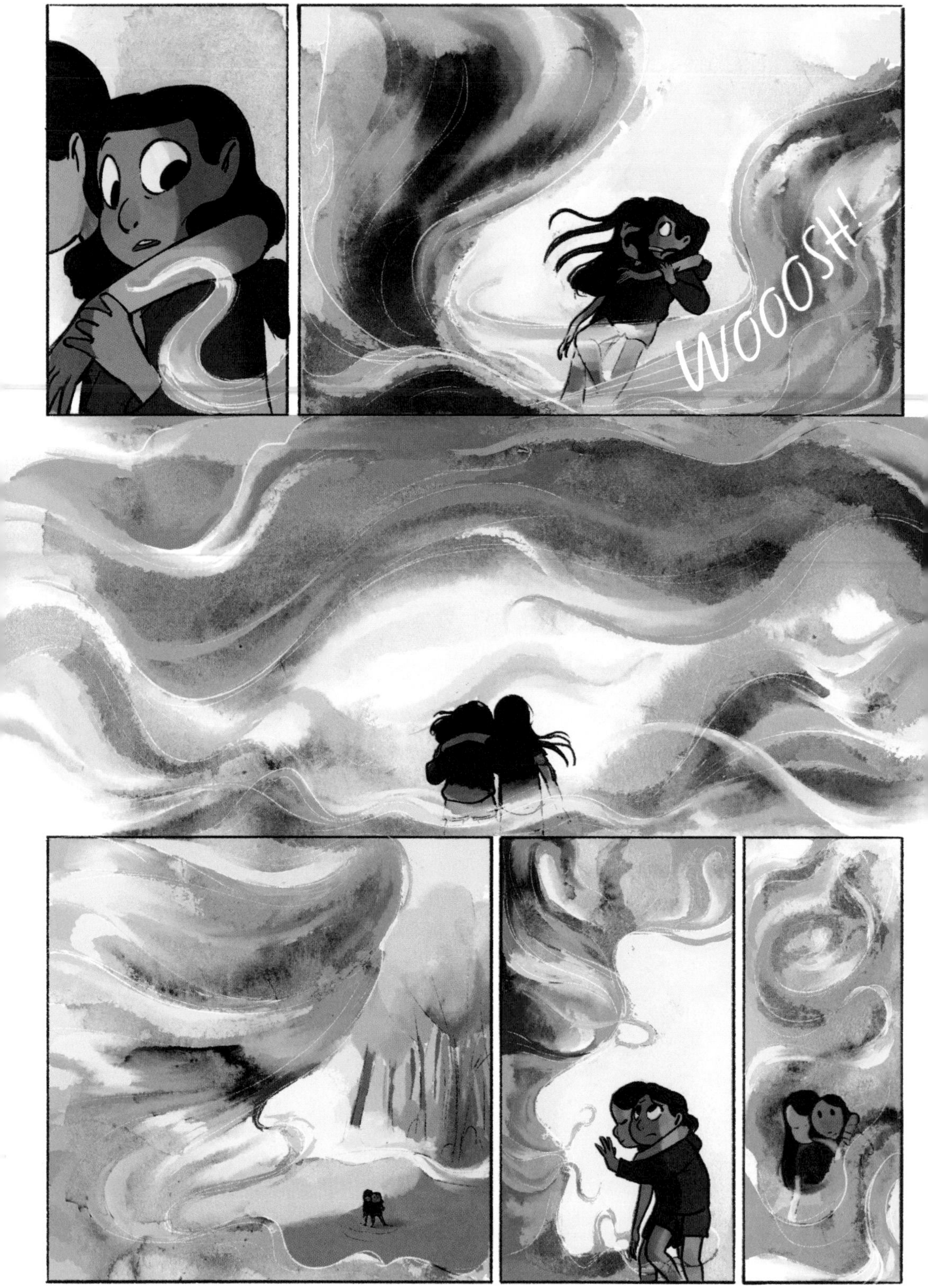
WOOOSH!

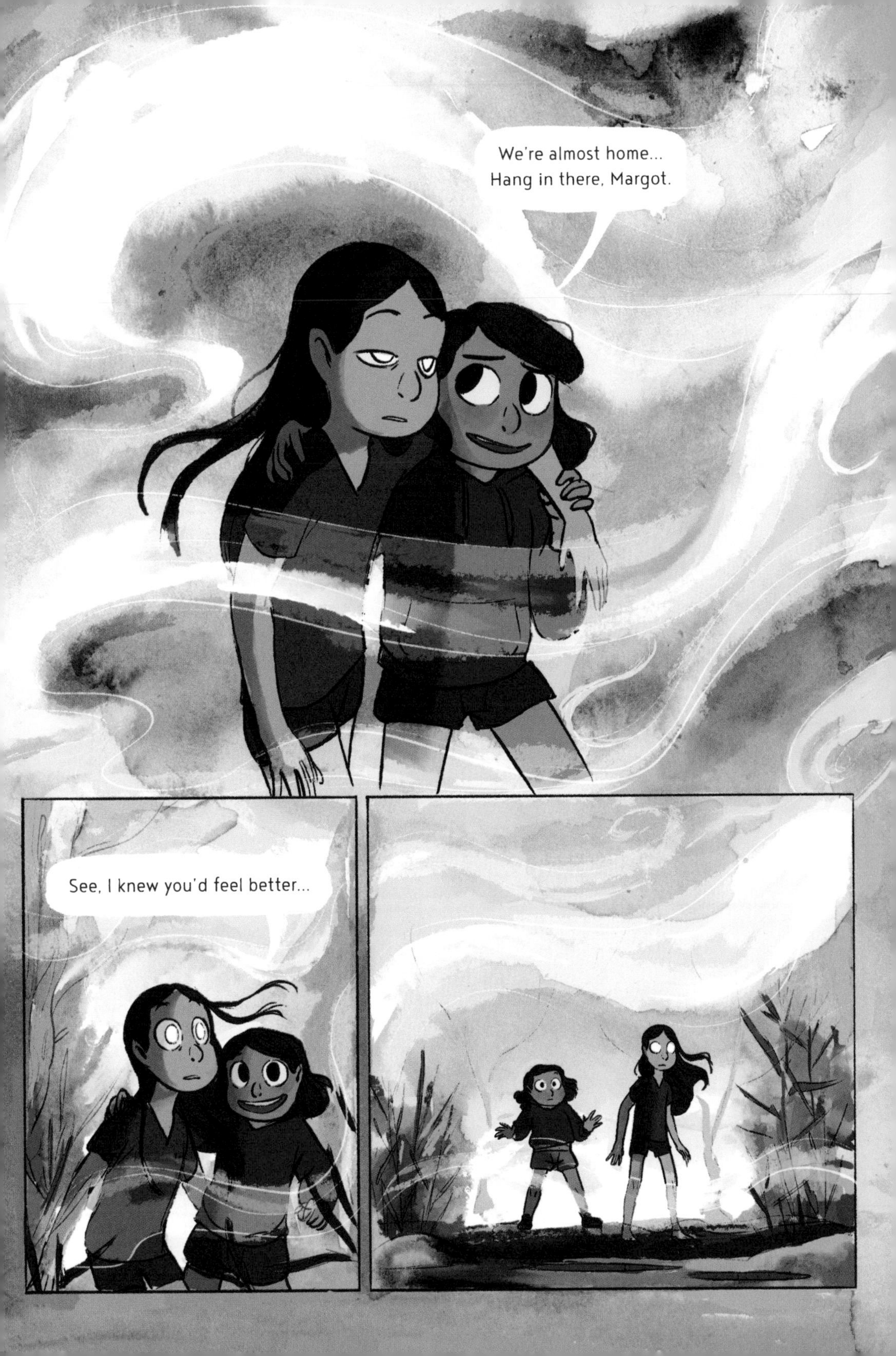
We're almost home...
Hang in there, Margot.
See, I knew you'd feel better...

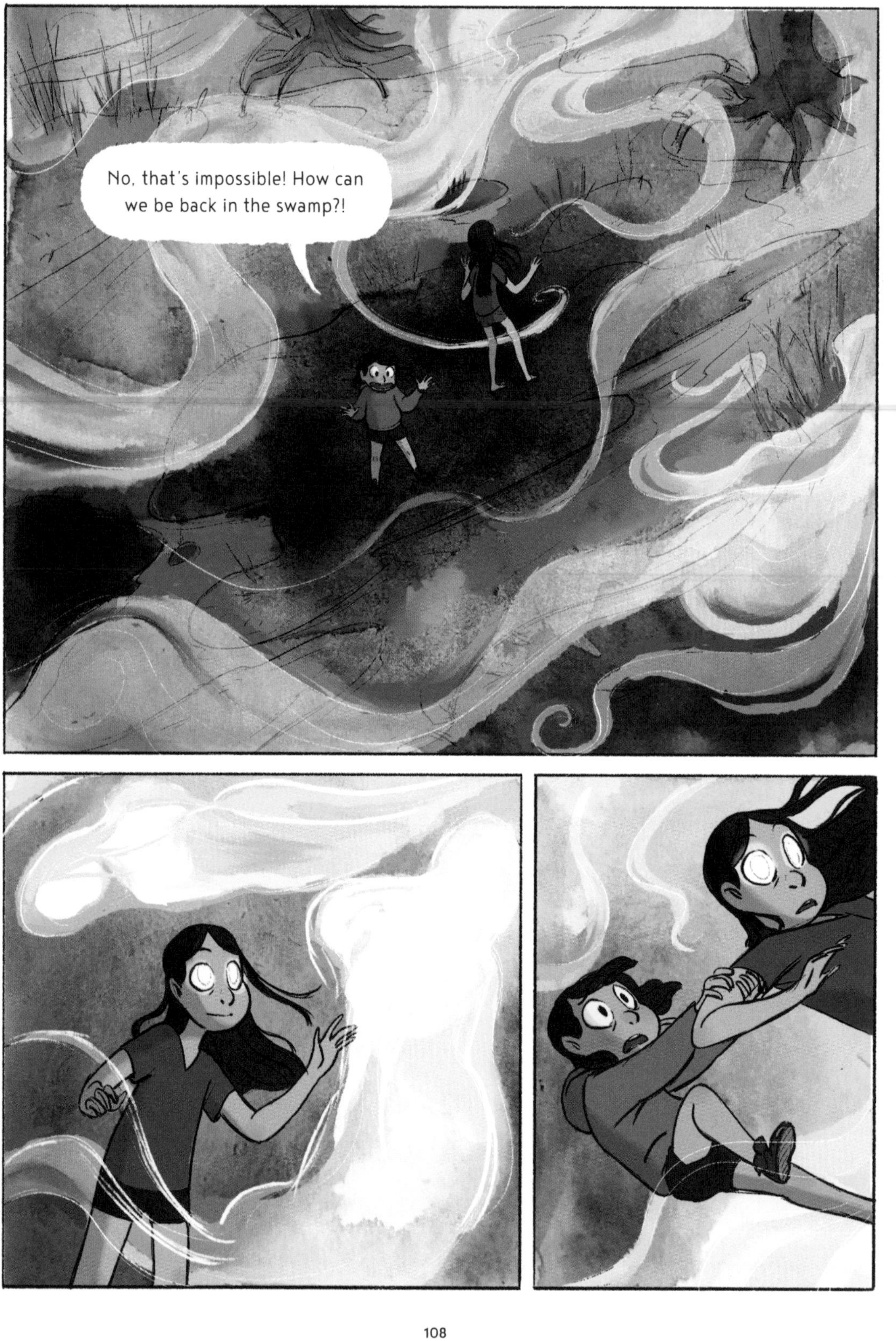
No, that's impossible! How can we be back in the swamp?!

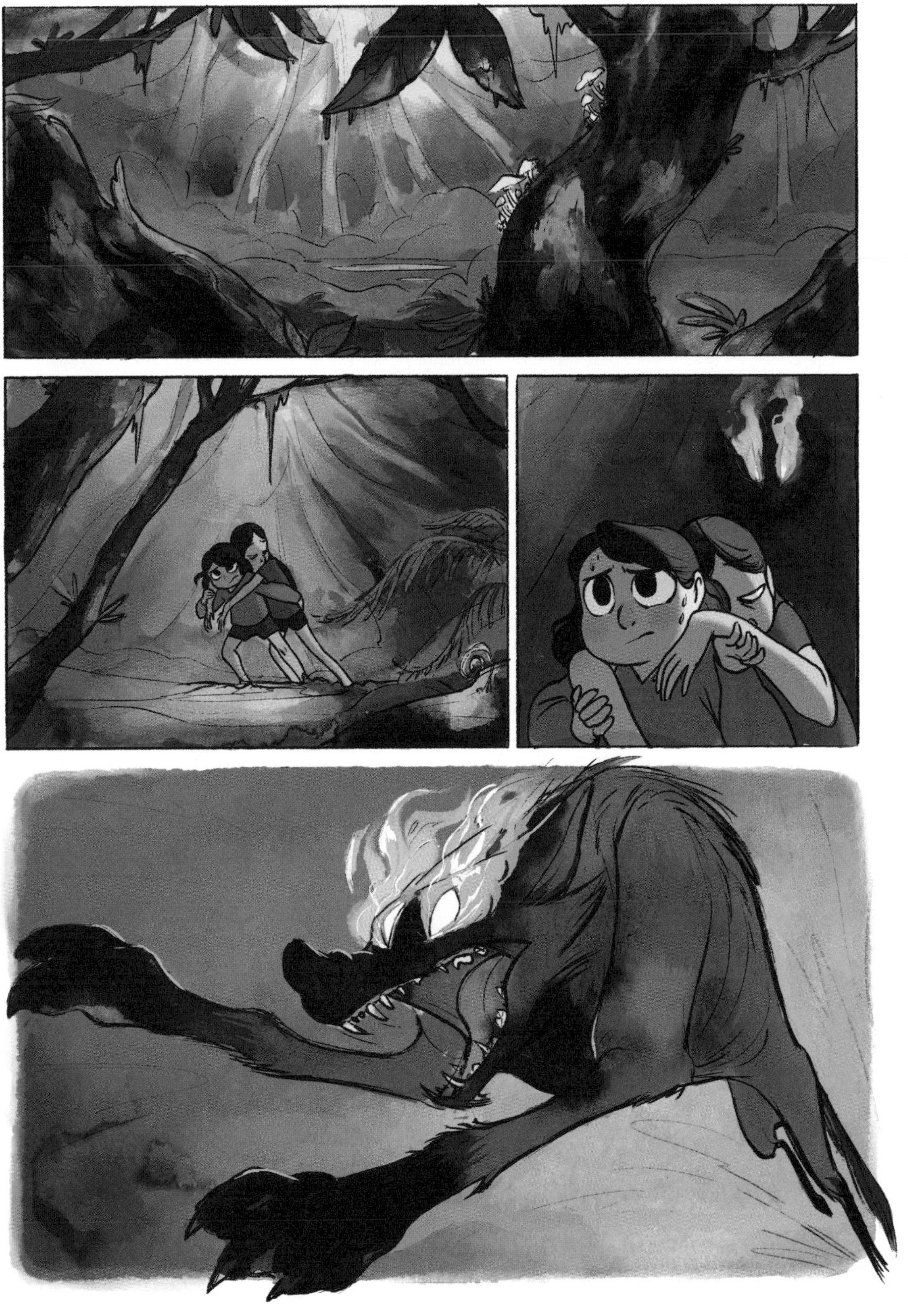

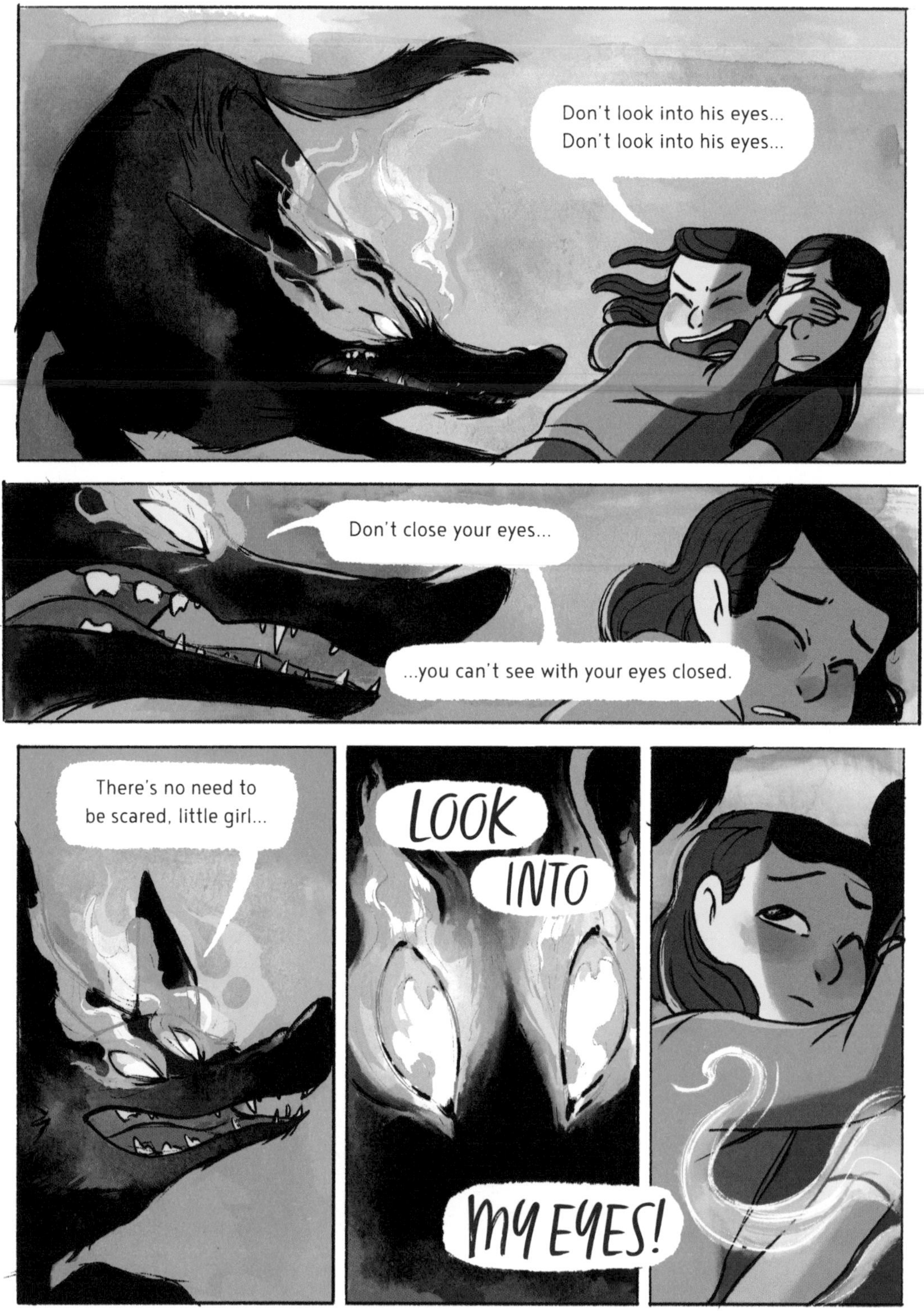
Don't look into his eyes...
Don't look into his eyes...
Don't close your eyes...
...you can't see with your eyes closed.
There's no need to be scared, little girl...
LOOK
INTO
MY EYES!

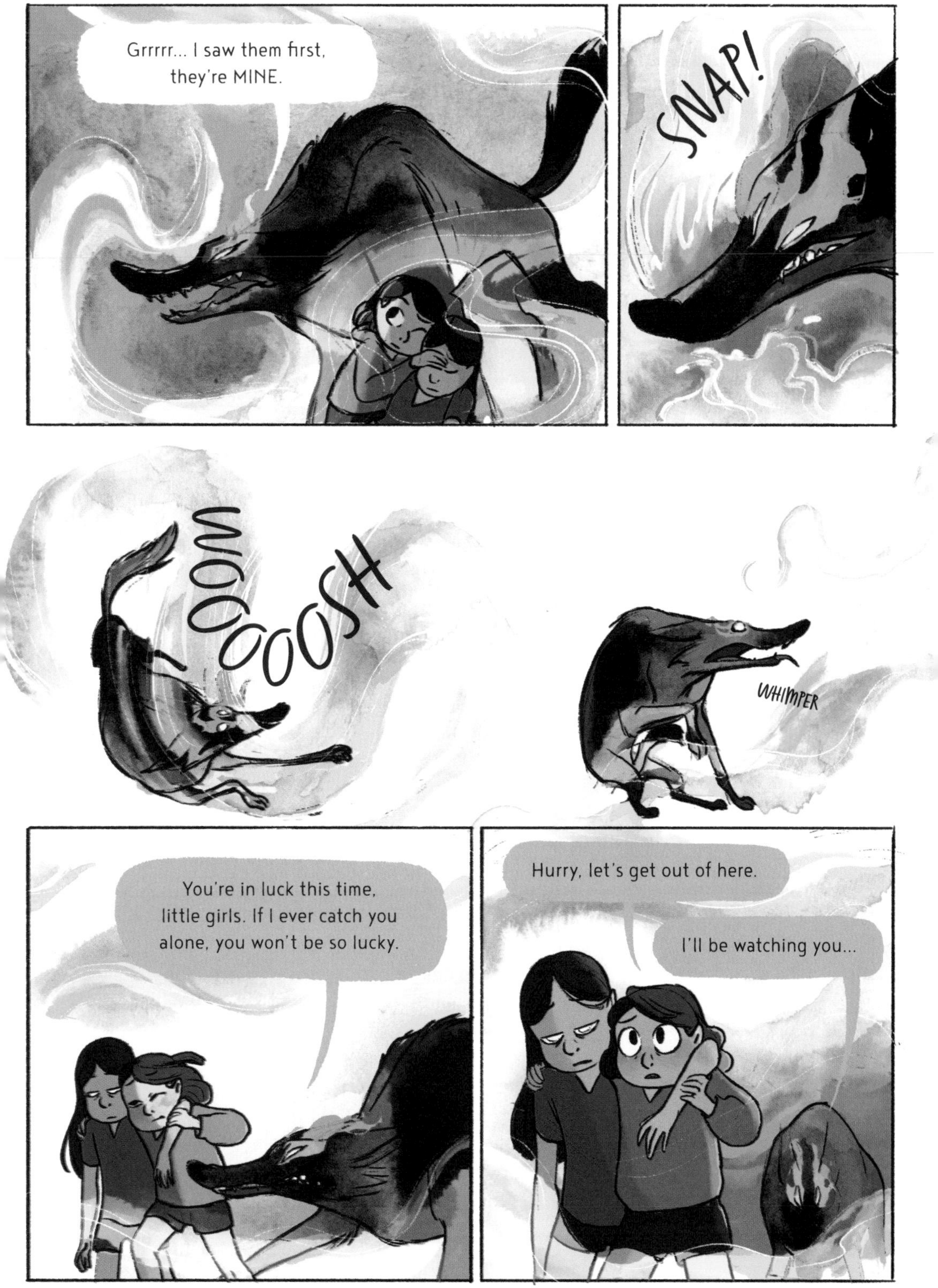
Grrrrr... I saw them first, they're MINE.
SNAP!
WOOOOOSH
WHIMPER
You're in luck this time, little girls. If I ever catch you alone, you won't be so lucky.
Hurry, let's get out of here.
I'll be watching you...

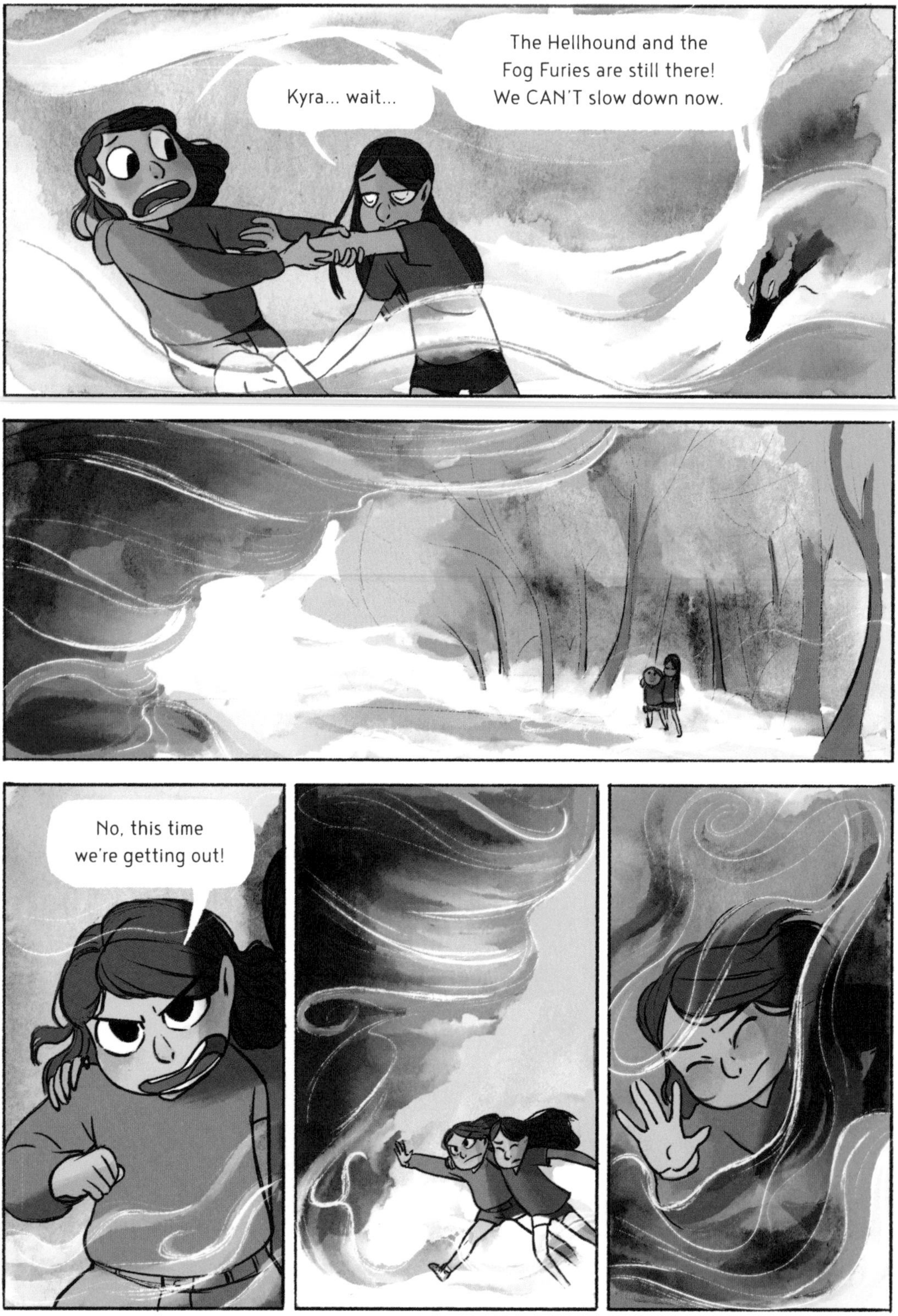
Kyra... wait...
The Hellhound and the Fog Furies are still there! We CAN'T slow down now.
No, this time we're getting out!

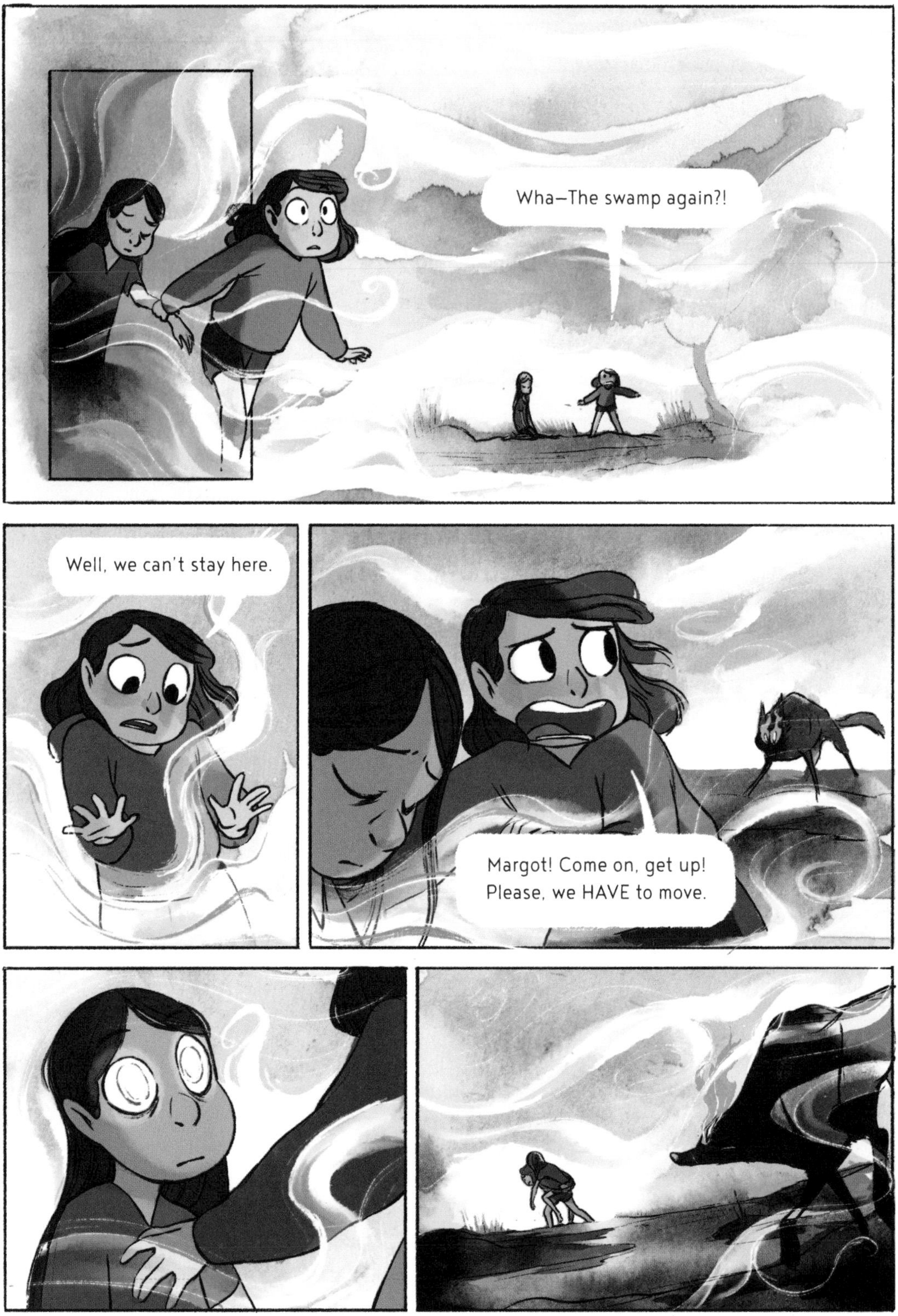
Wha—The swamp again?!
Well, we can't stay here.
Margot! Come on, get up! Please, we HAVE to move.

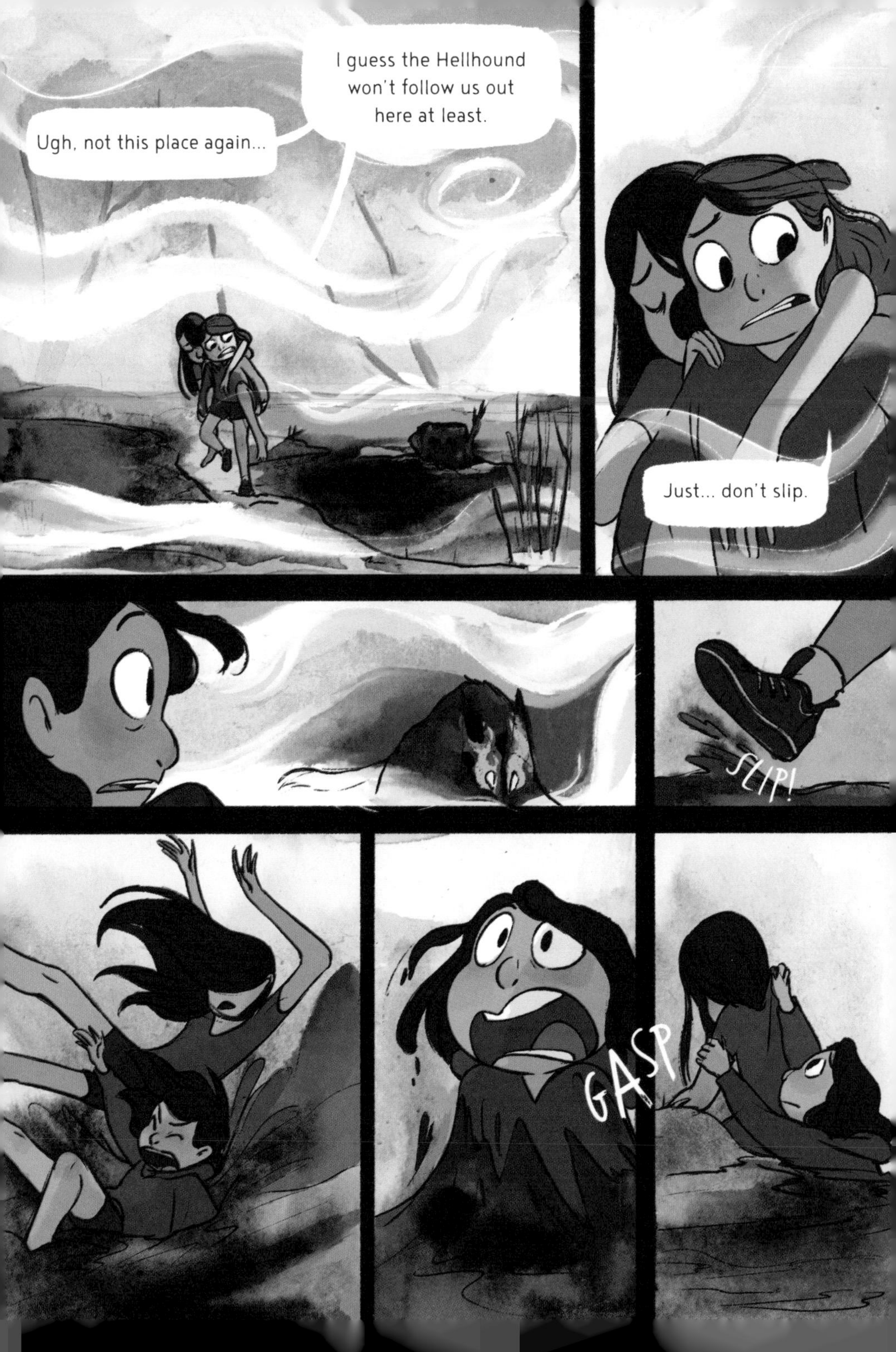
Ugh, not this place again...
I guess the Hellhound won't follow us out here at least.
Just... don't slip.
SLIP!
GASP

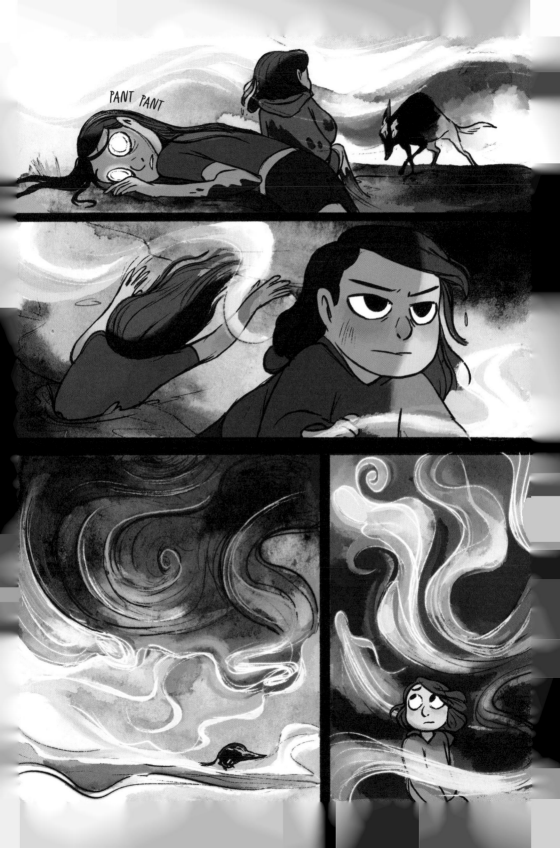

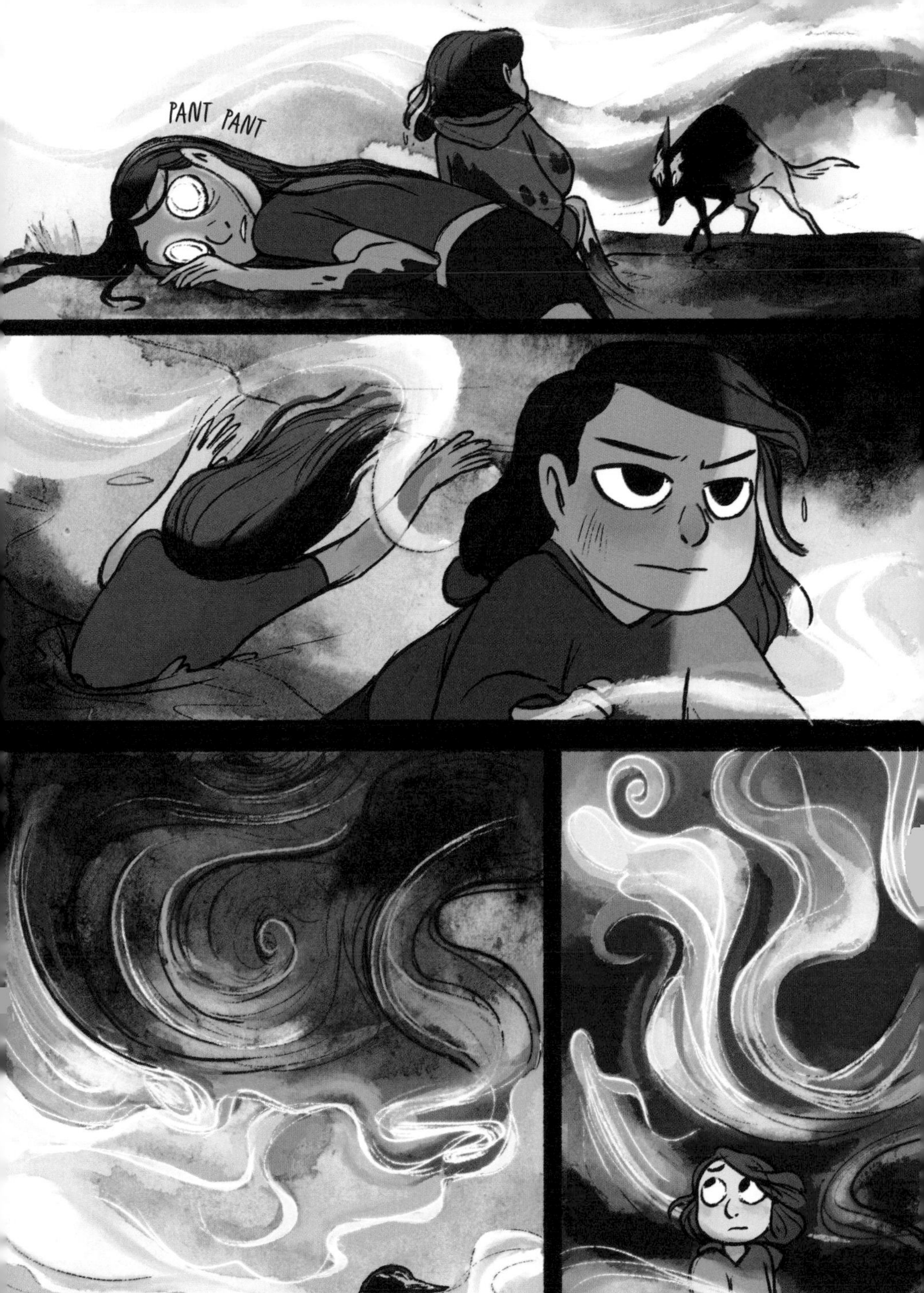
PANT PANT

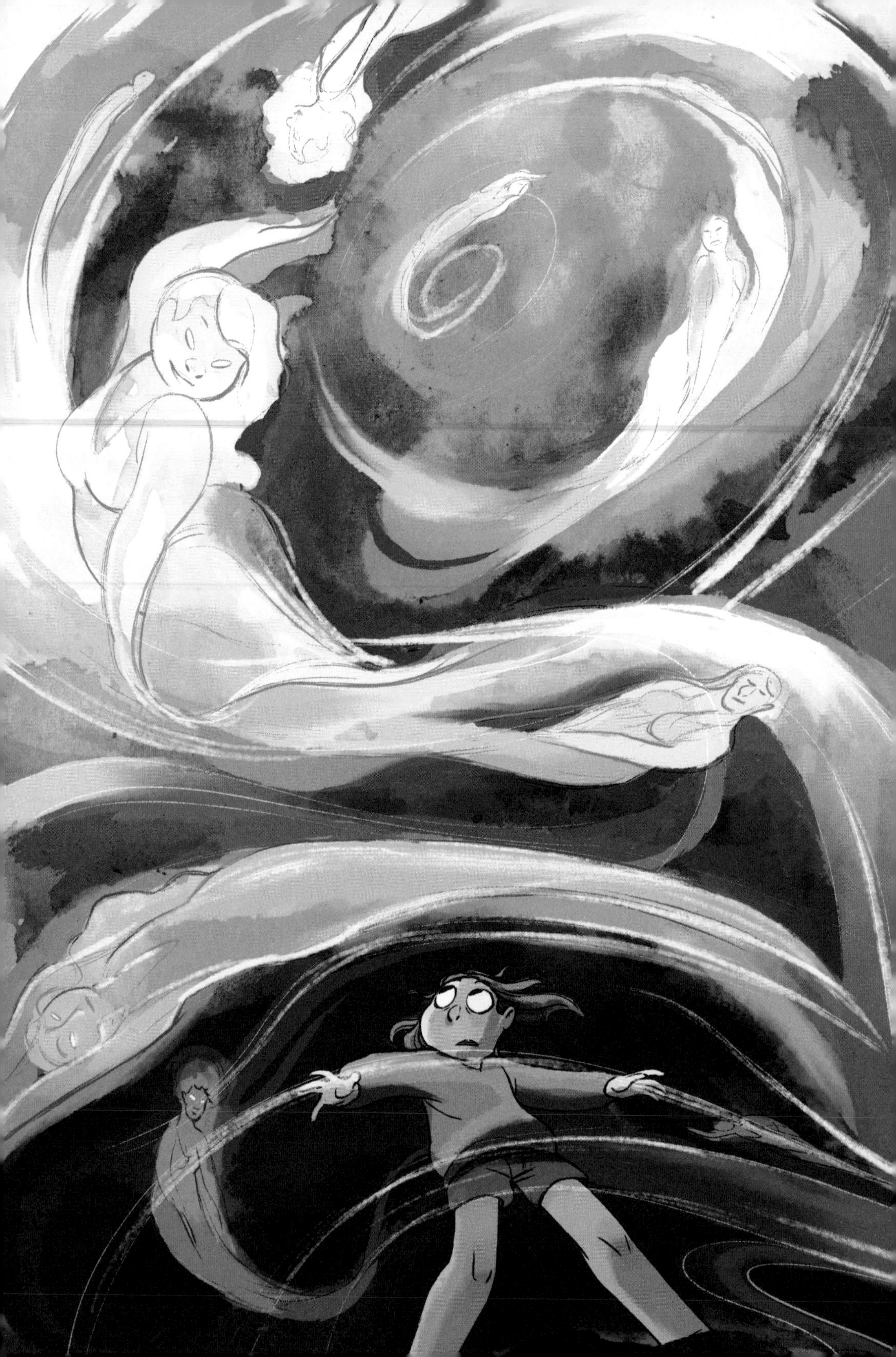

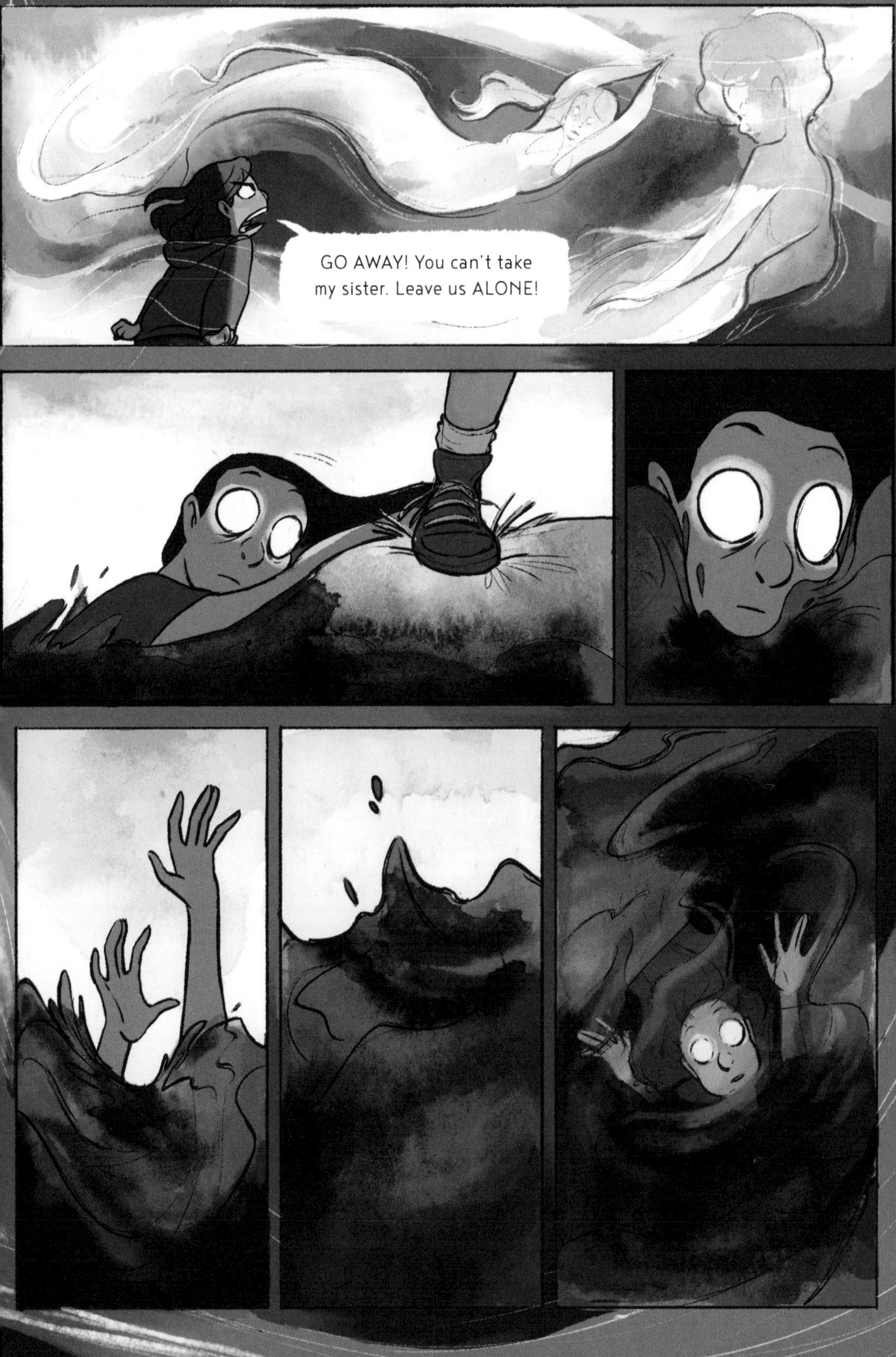
GO AWAY! You can't take my sister. Leave us ALONE!

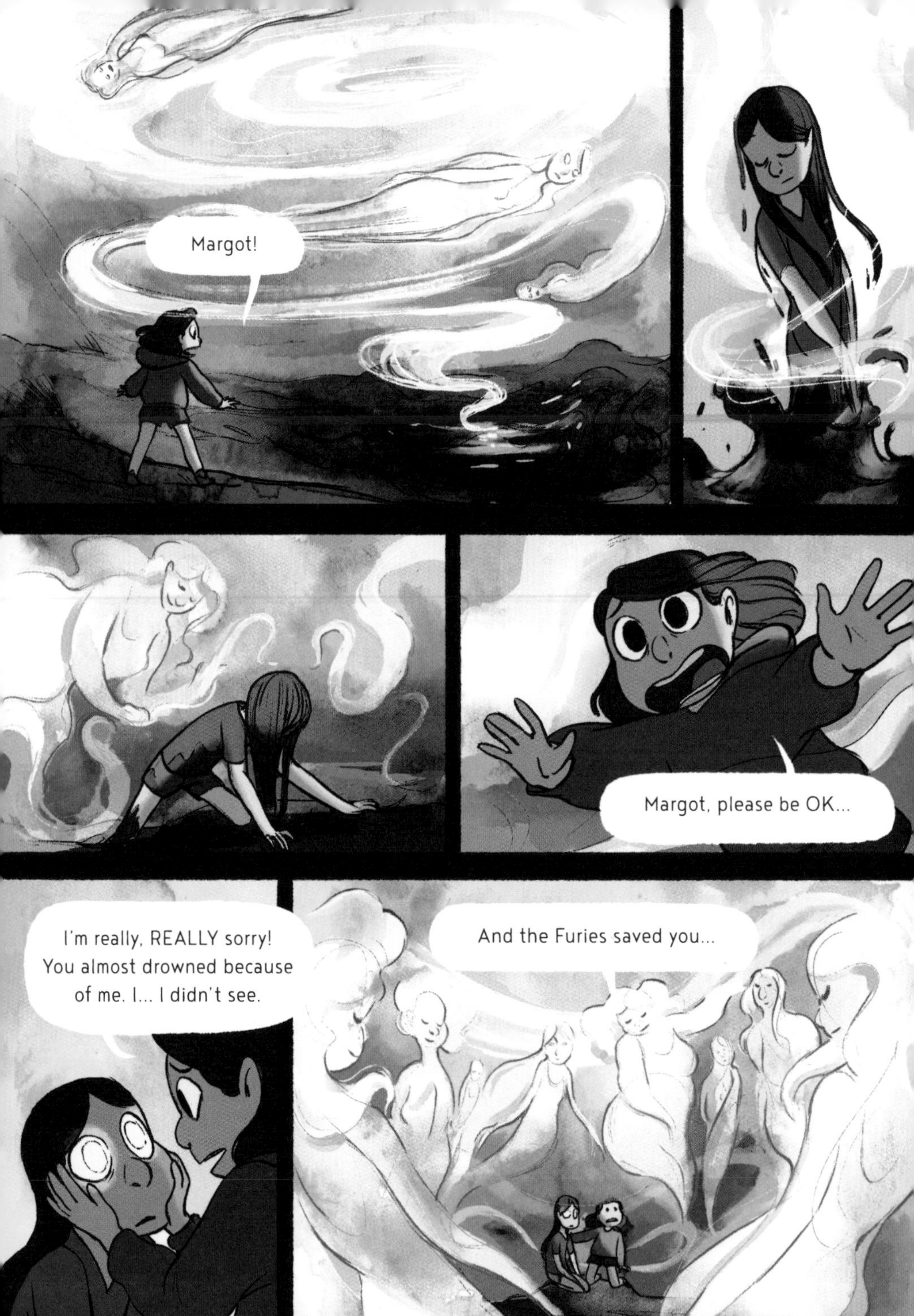
Margot!
Margot, please be OK...
I'm really, REALLY sorry! You almost drowned because of me. I... I didn't see.
And the Furies saved you...

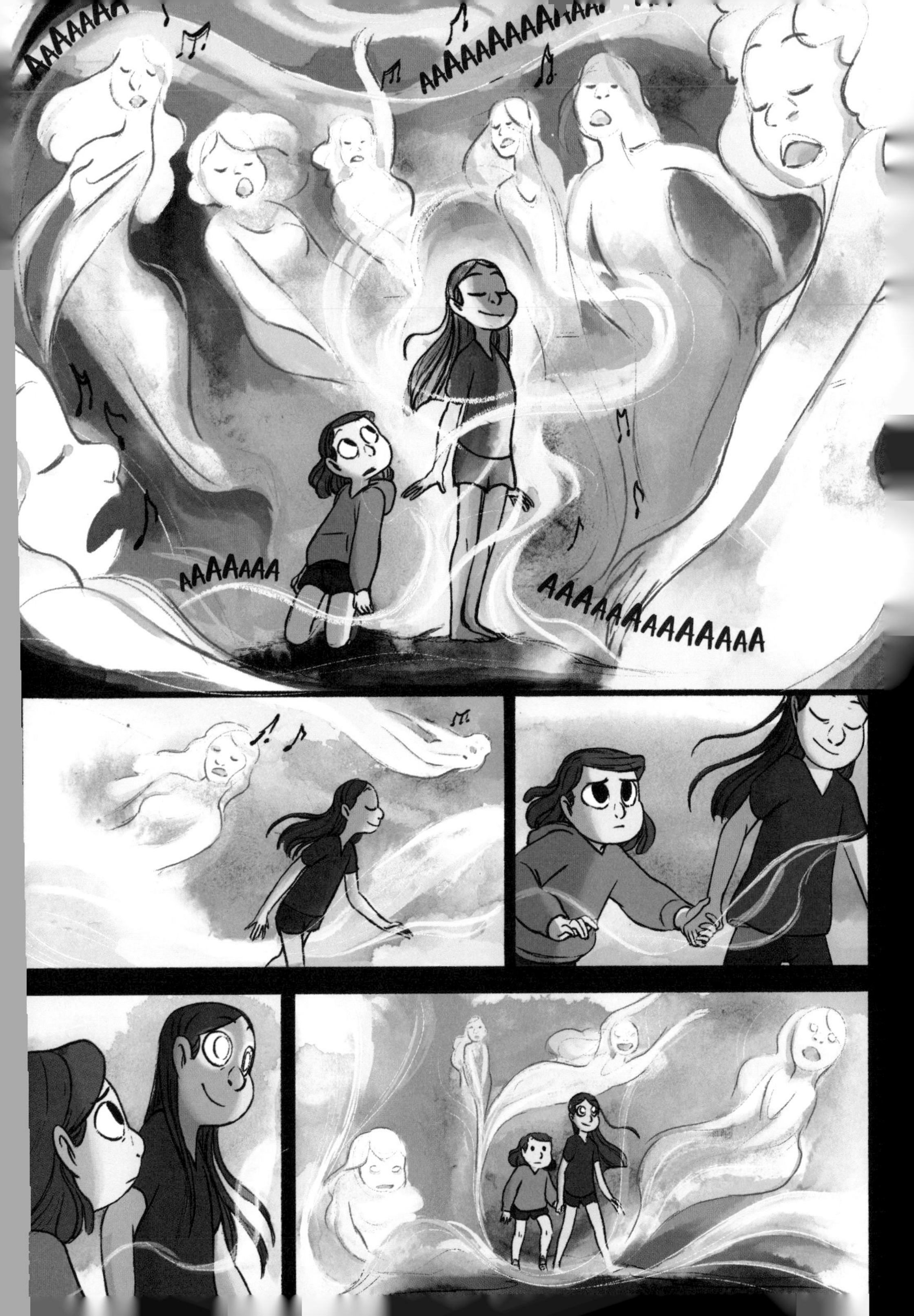
AAAAAAA
AAAAAAAAAAAAA
AAAAAAA
AAAAAAAAAAAAAA

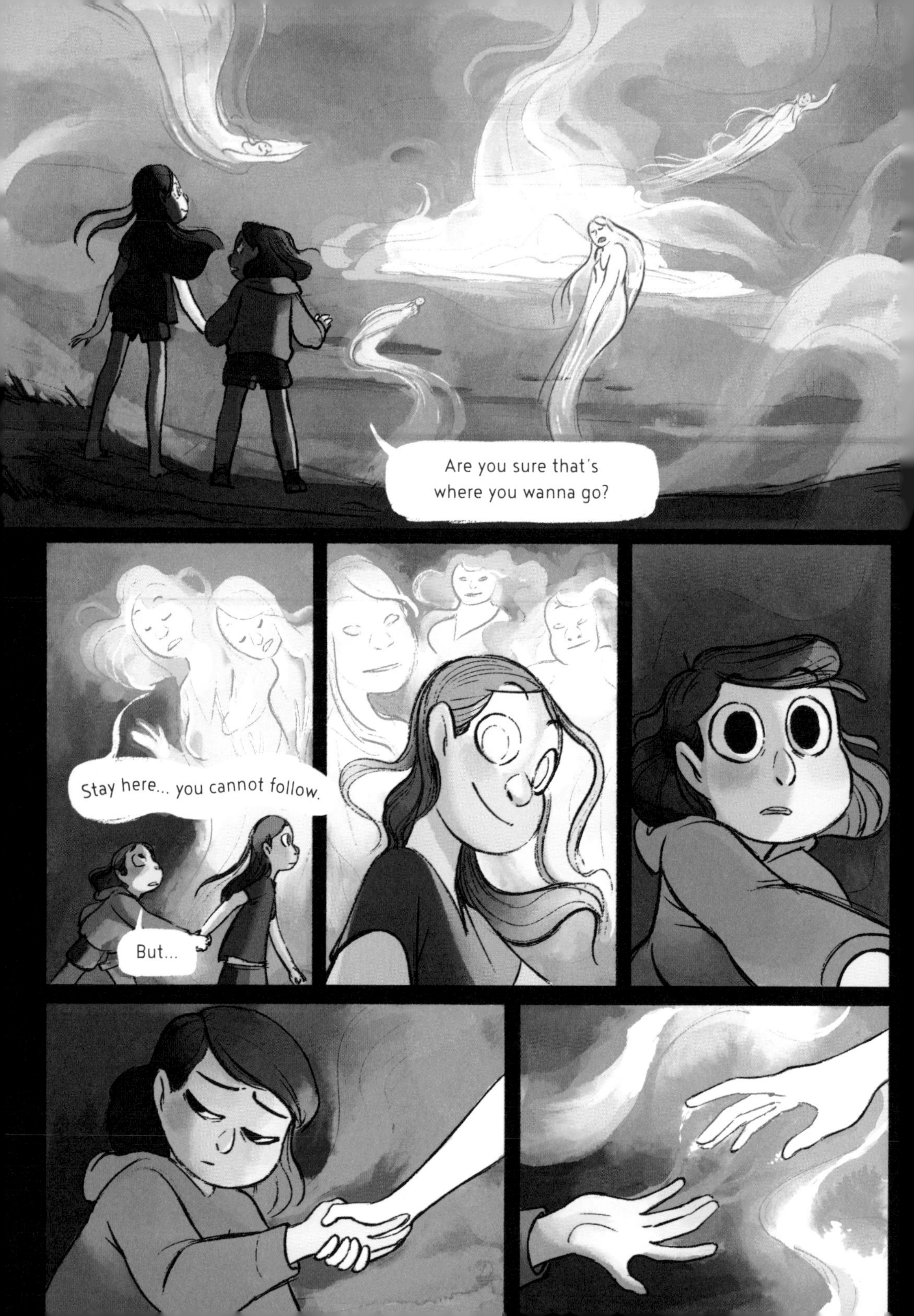
Are you sure that's where you wanna go?
Stay here... you cannot follow.
But...

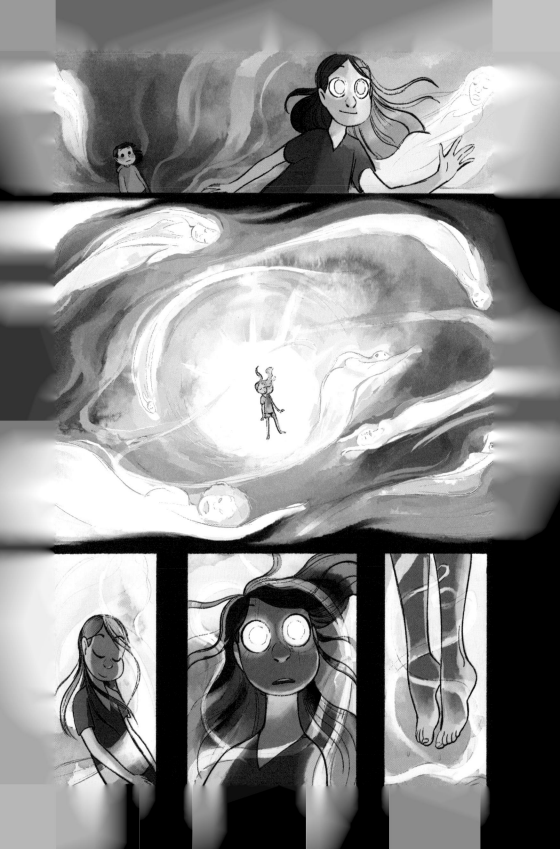

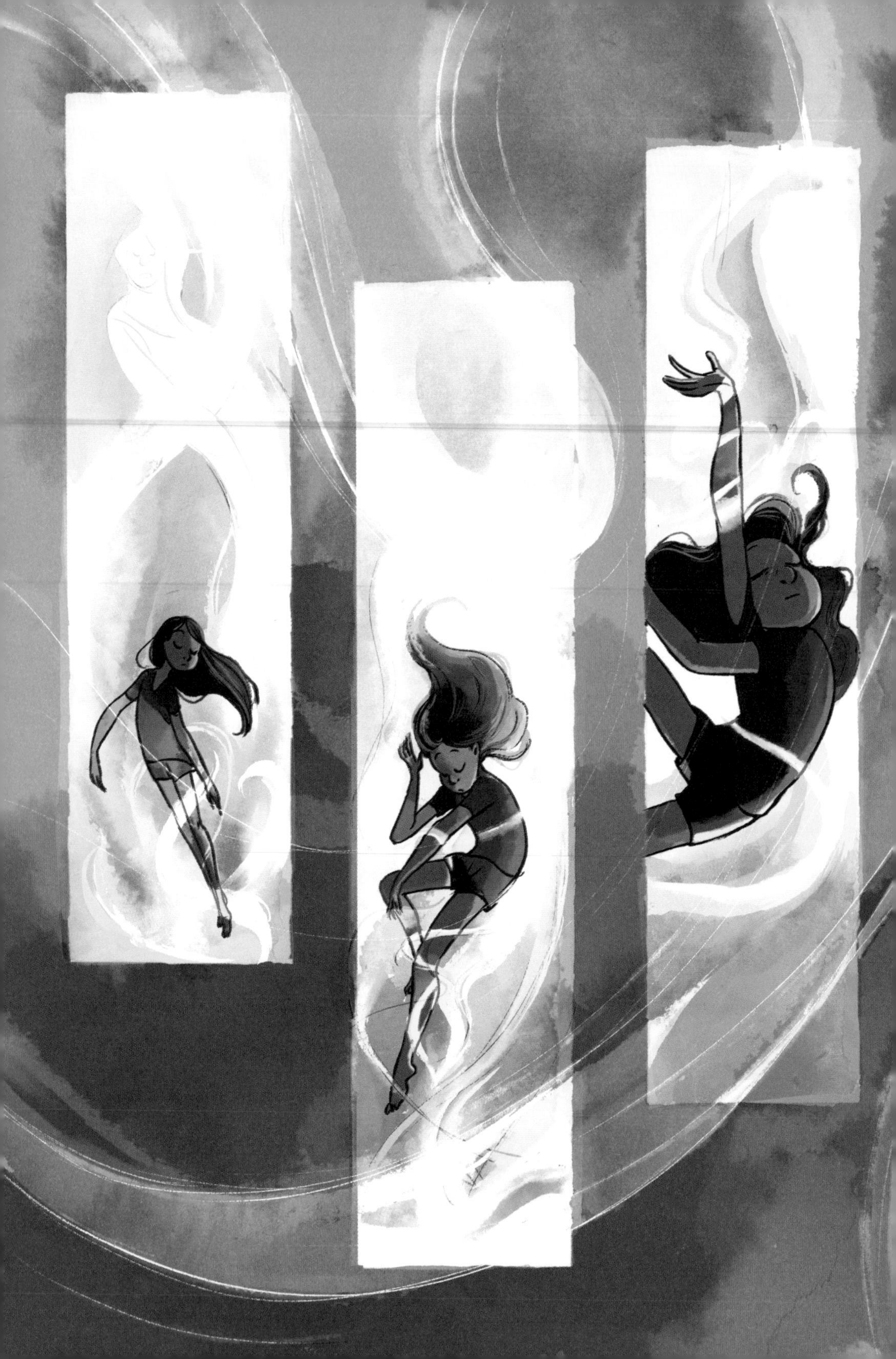

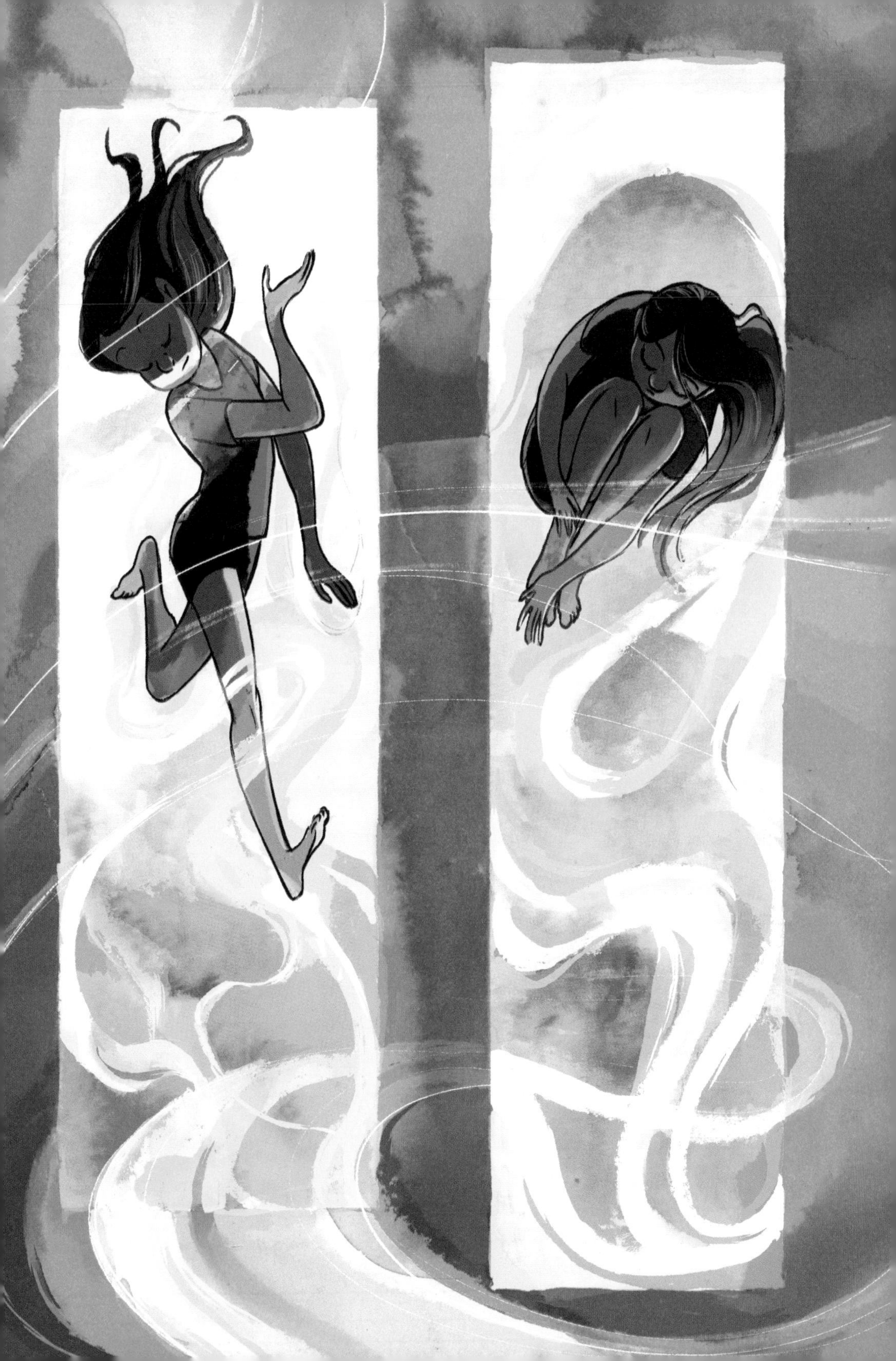

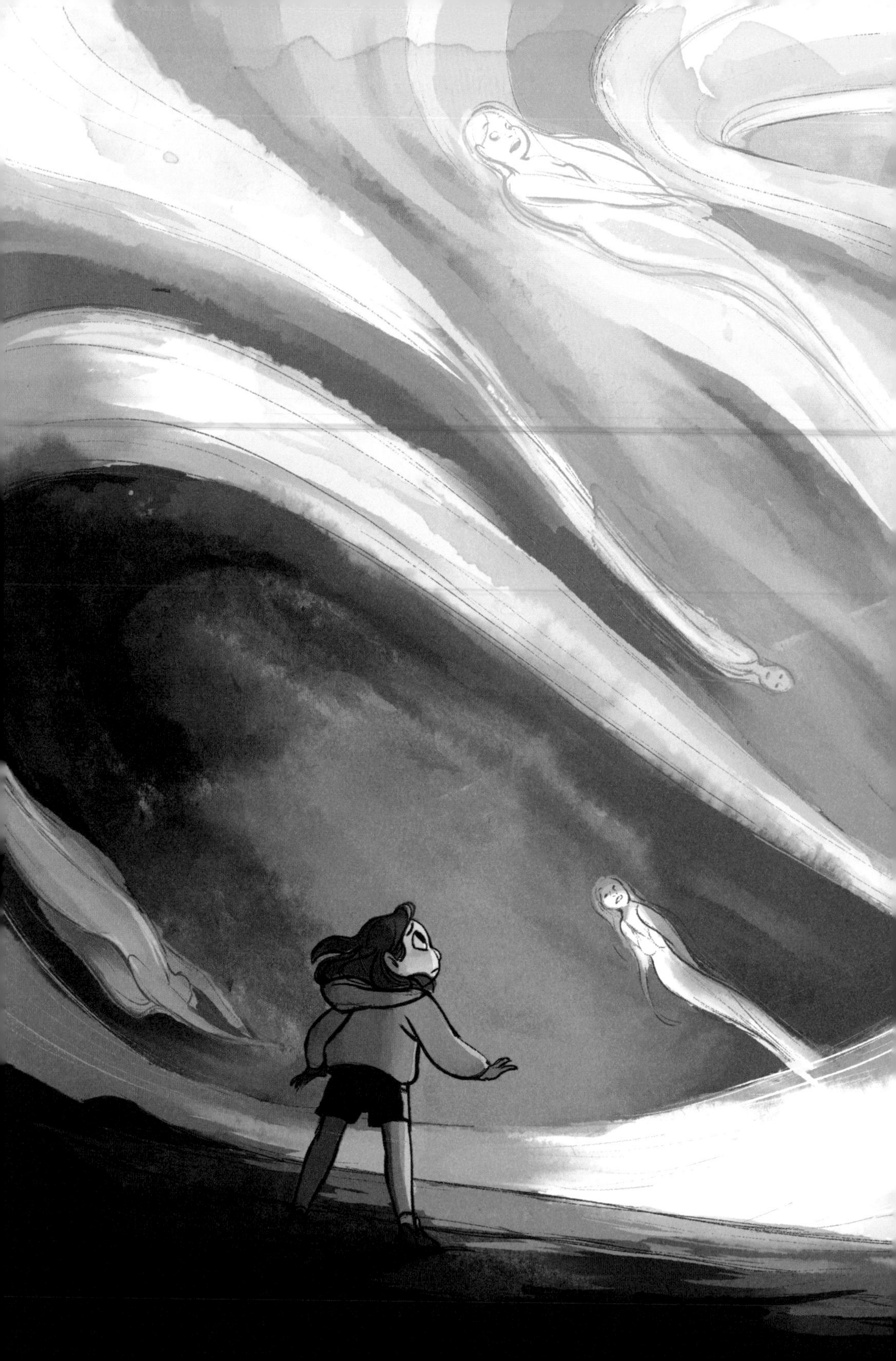

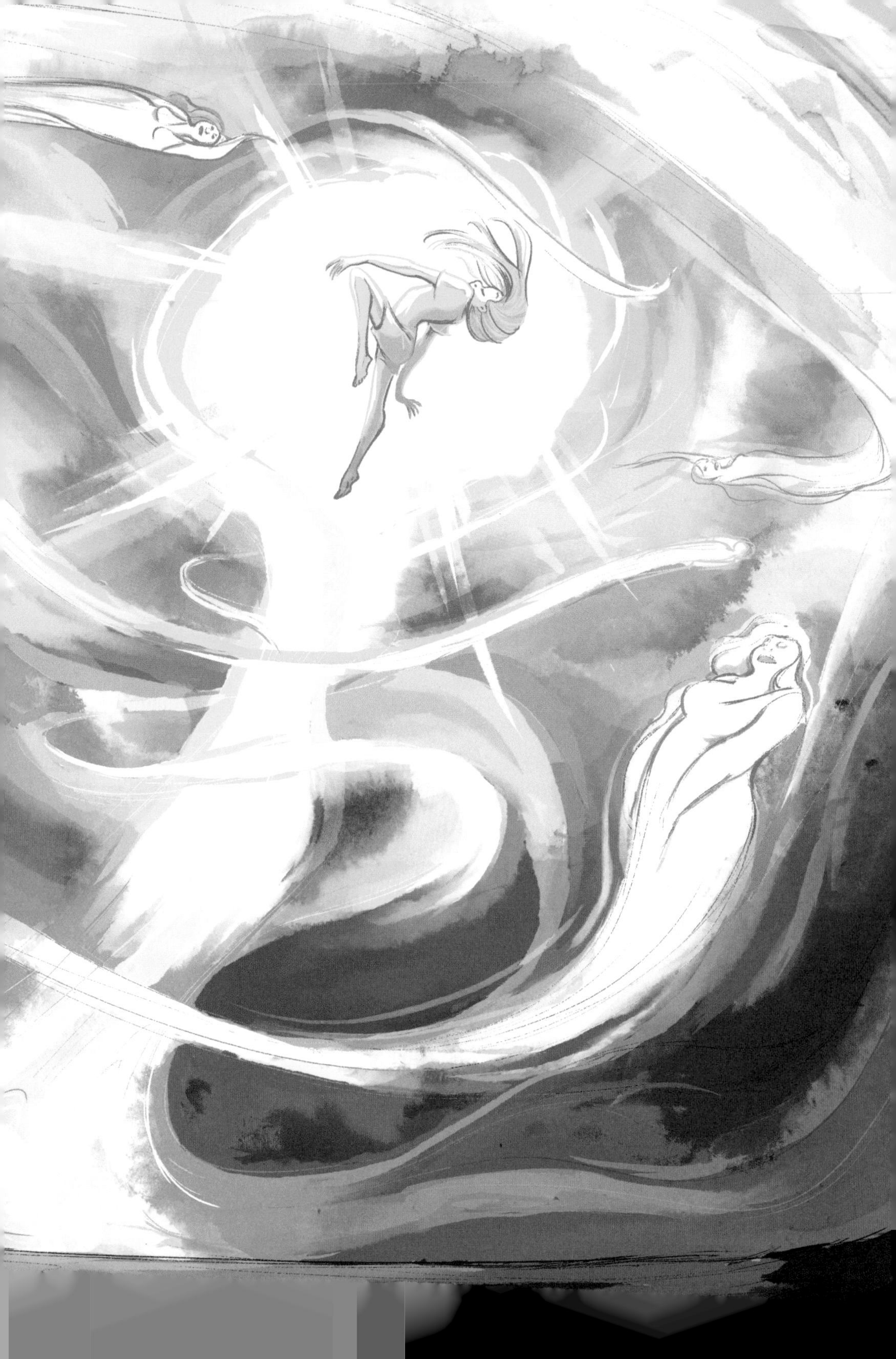

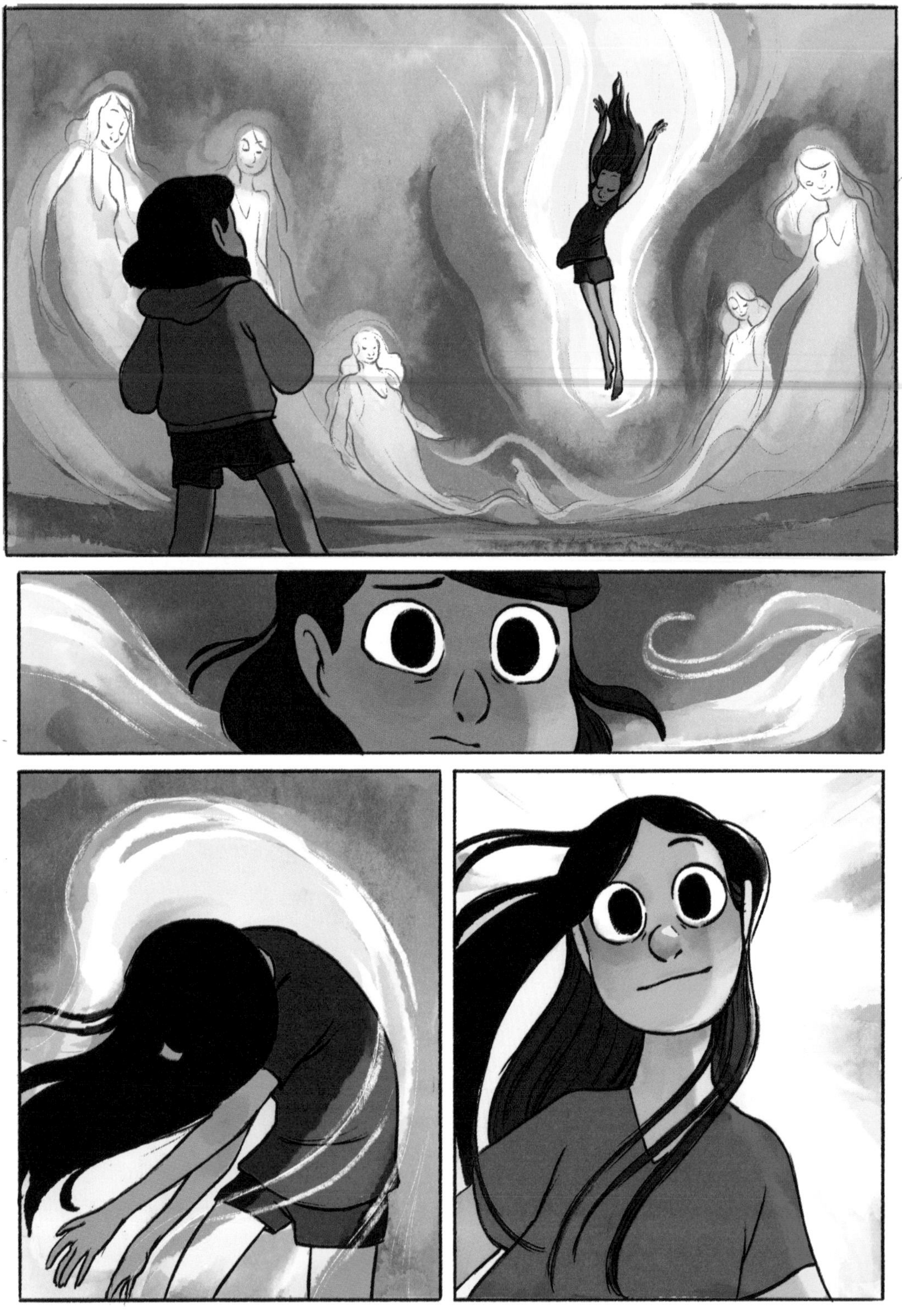

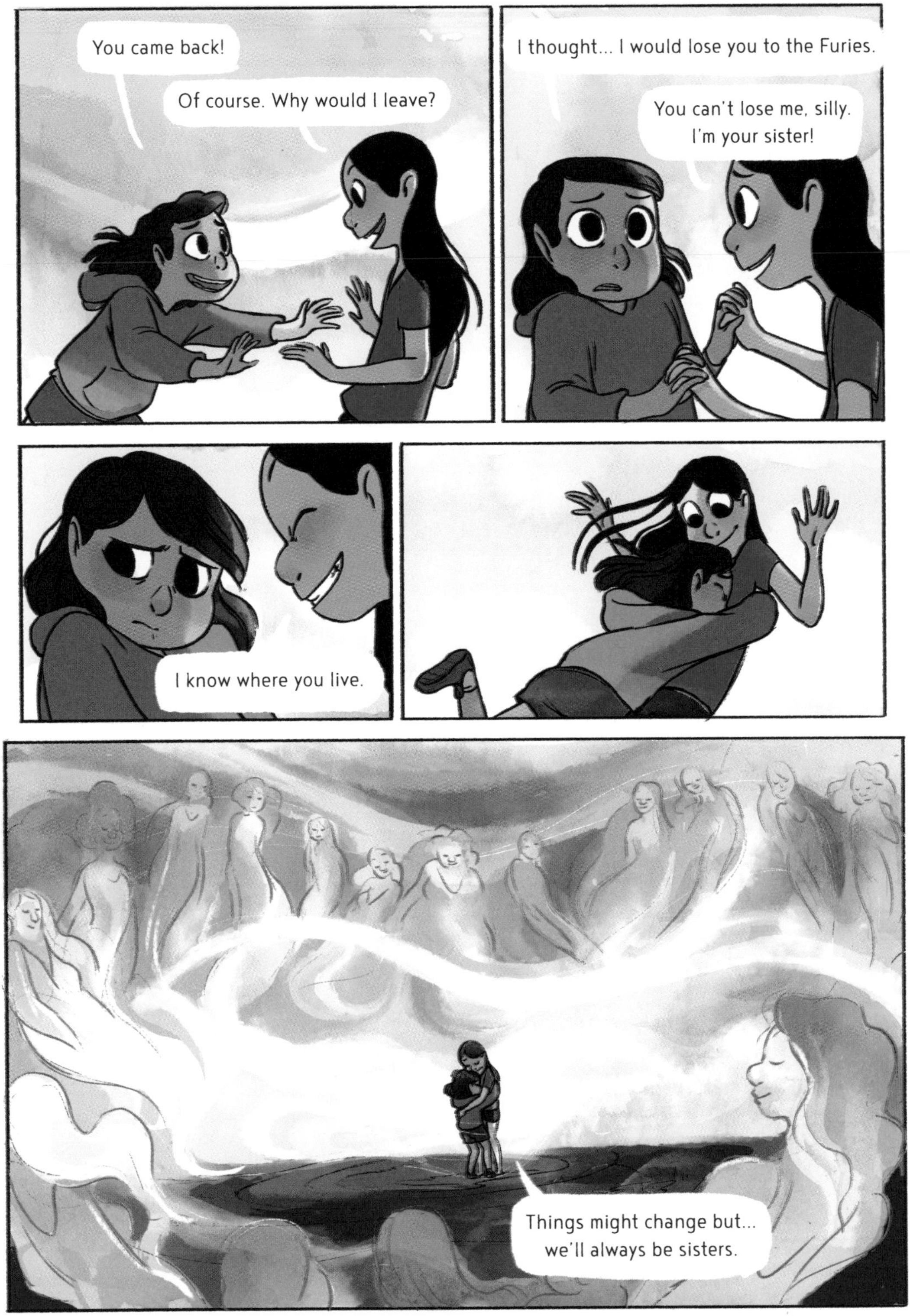
You came back!
Of course. Why would I leave?
I thought... I would lose you to the Furies.
You can't lose me, silly. I'm your sister!
I know where you live.
Things might change but... we'll always be sisters.

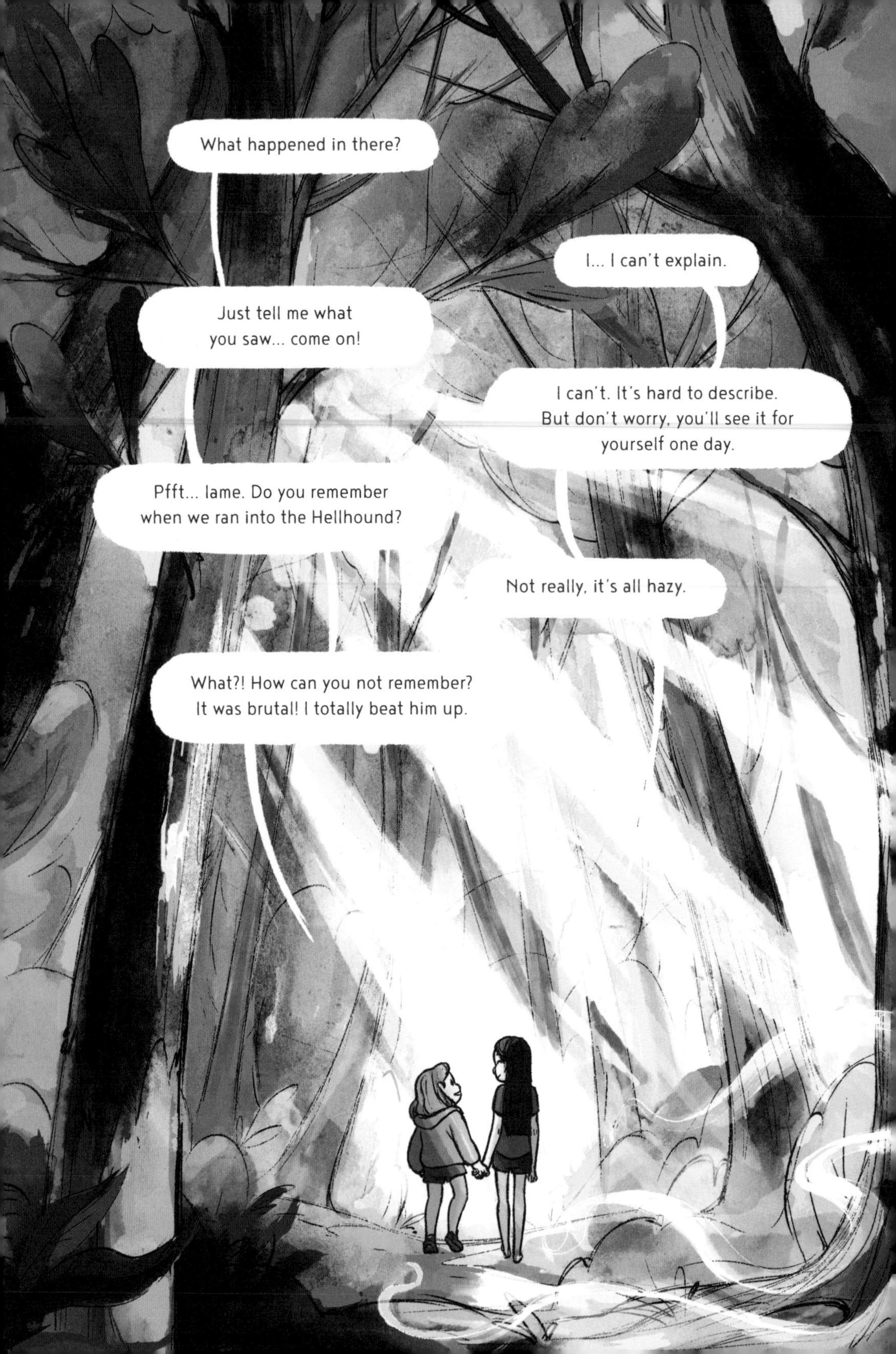
What happened in there?
I... I can't explain.
Just tell me what you saw... come on!
I can't. It's hard to describe. But don't worry, you'll see it for yourself one day.
Pfft... lame. Do you remember when we ran into the Hellhound?
Not really, it's all hazy.
What?! How can you not remember? It was brutal! I totally beat him up.

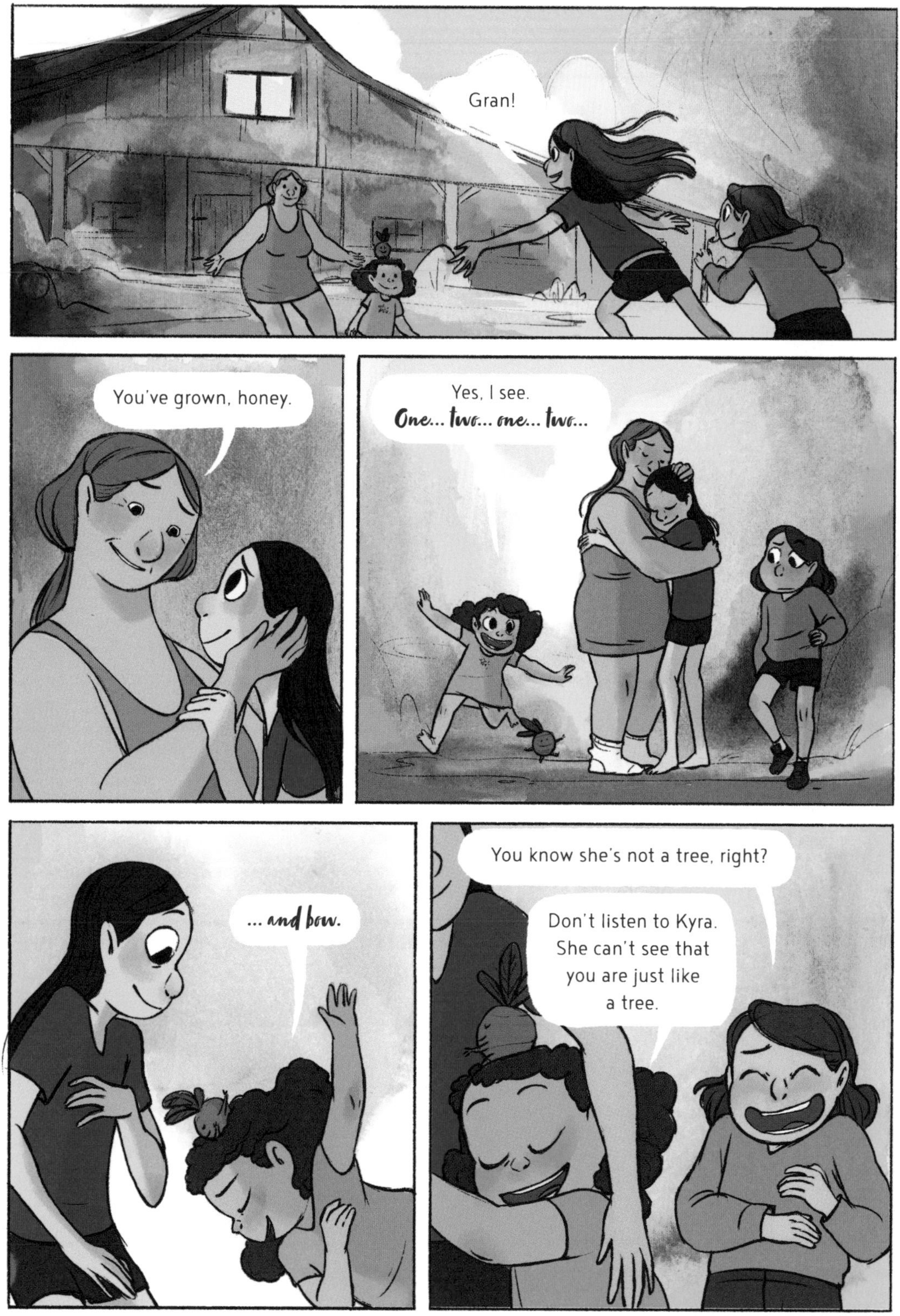
Gran!
You've grown, honey.
Yes, I see.
One... two... one... two...
... and bow.
You know she's not a tree, right?
Don't listen to Kyra. She can't see that you are just like a tree.

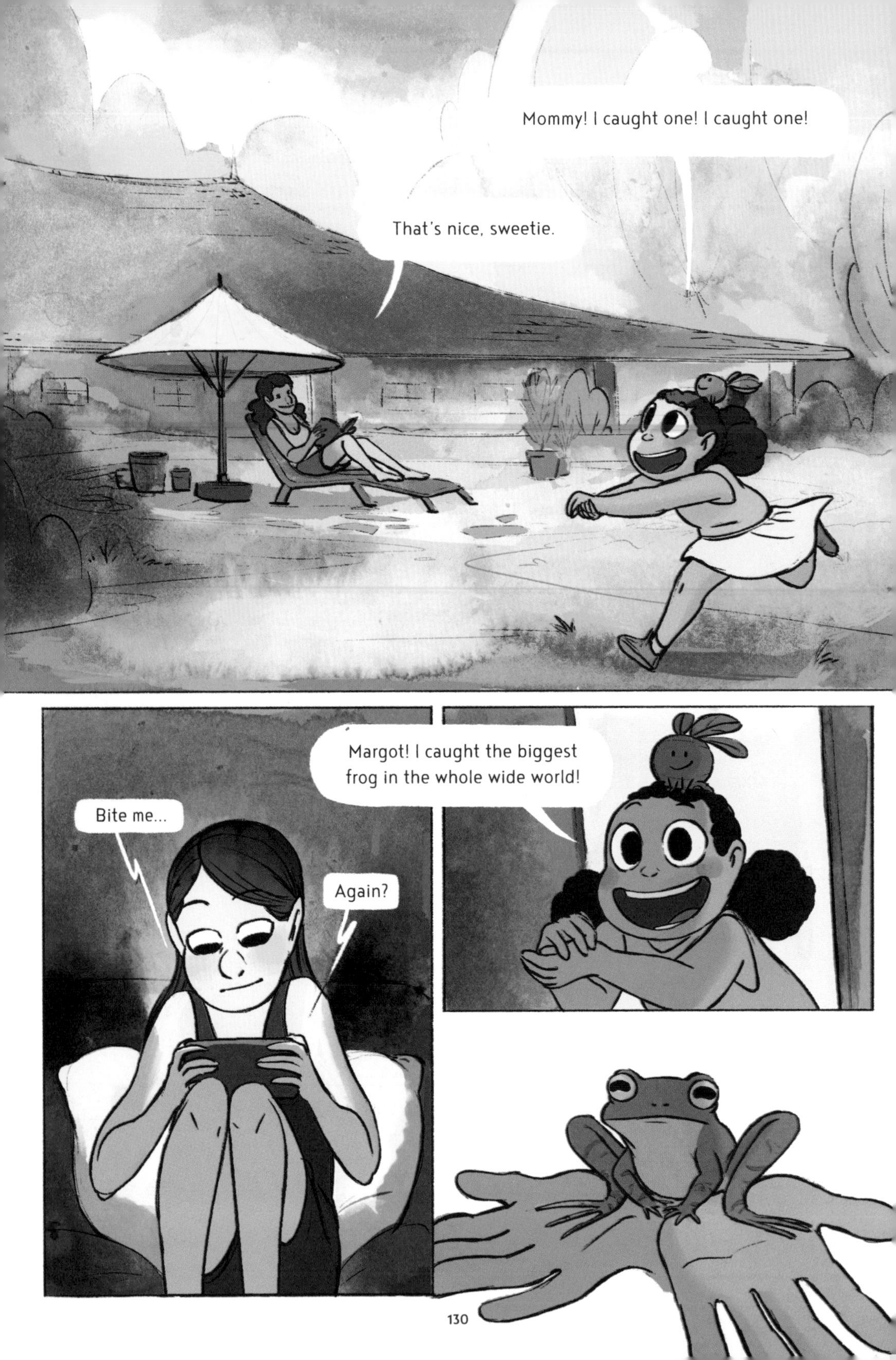
Mommy! I caught one! I caught one!
That's nice, sweetie.
Margot! I caught the biggest frog in the whole wide world!
Bite me...
Again?

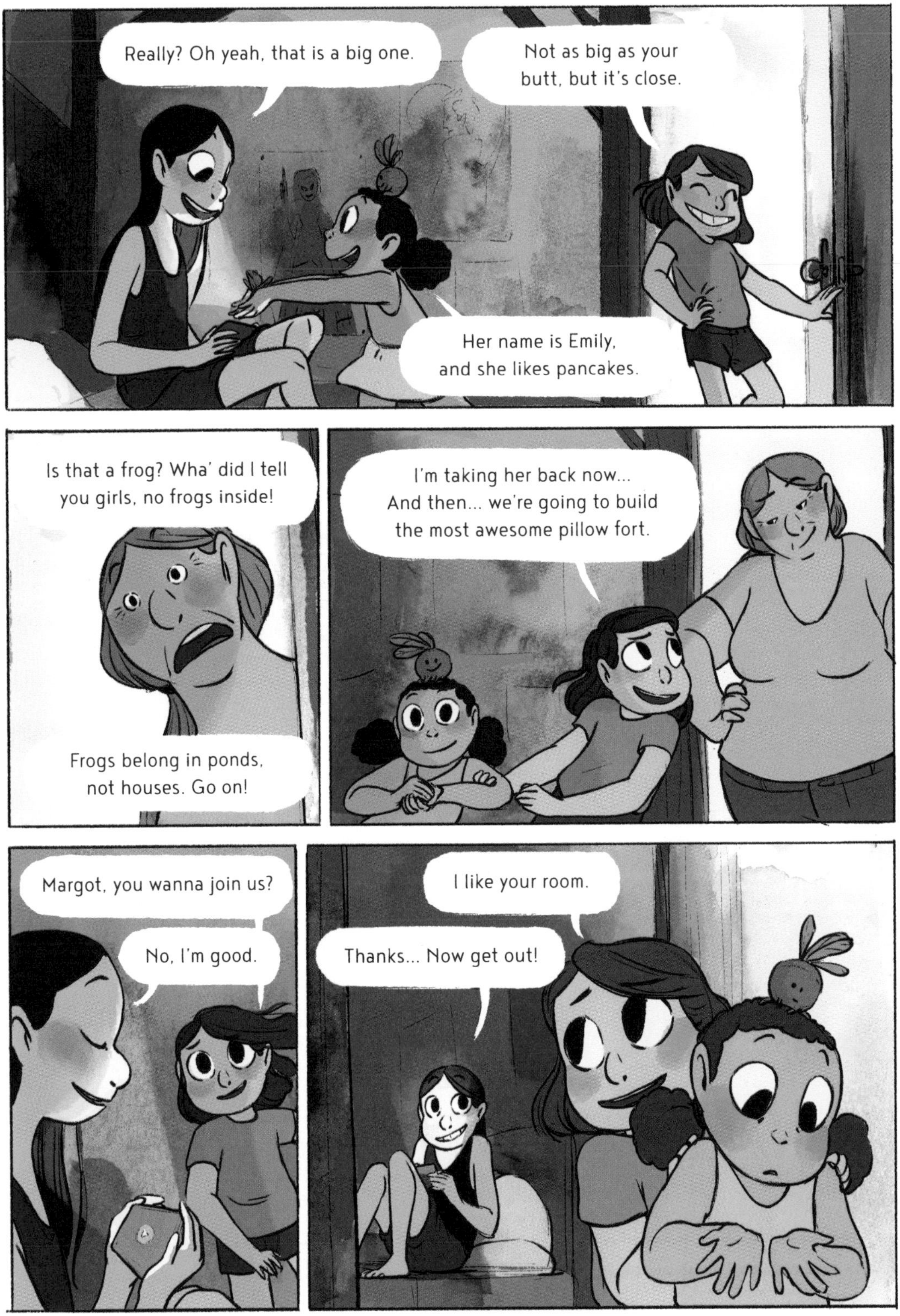
Really? Oh yeah, that is a big one.
Not as big as your butt, but it's close.
Her name is Emily, and she likes pancakes.
Is that a frog? Wha' did I tell you girls, no frogs inside!
Frogs belong in ponds, not houses. Go on!
I'm taking her back now... And then... we're going to build the most awesome pillow fort.
Margot, you wanna join us?
No, I'm good.
I like your room.
Thanks... Now get out!

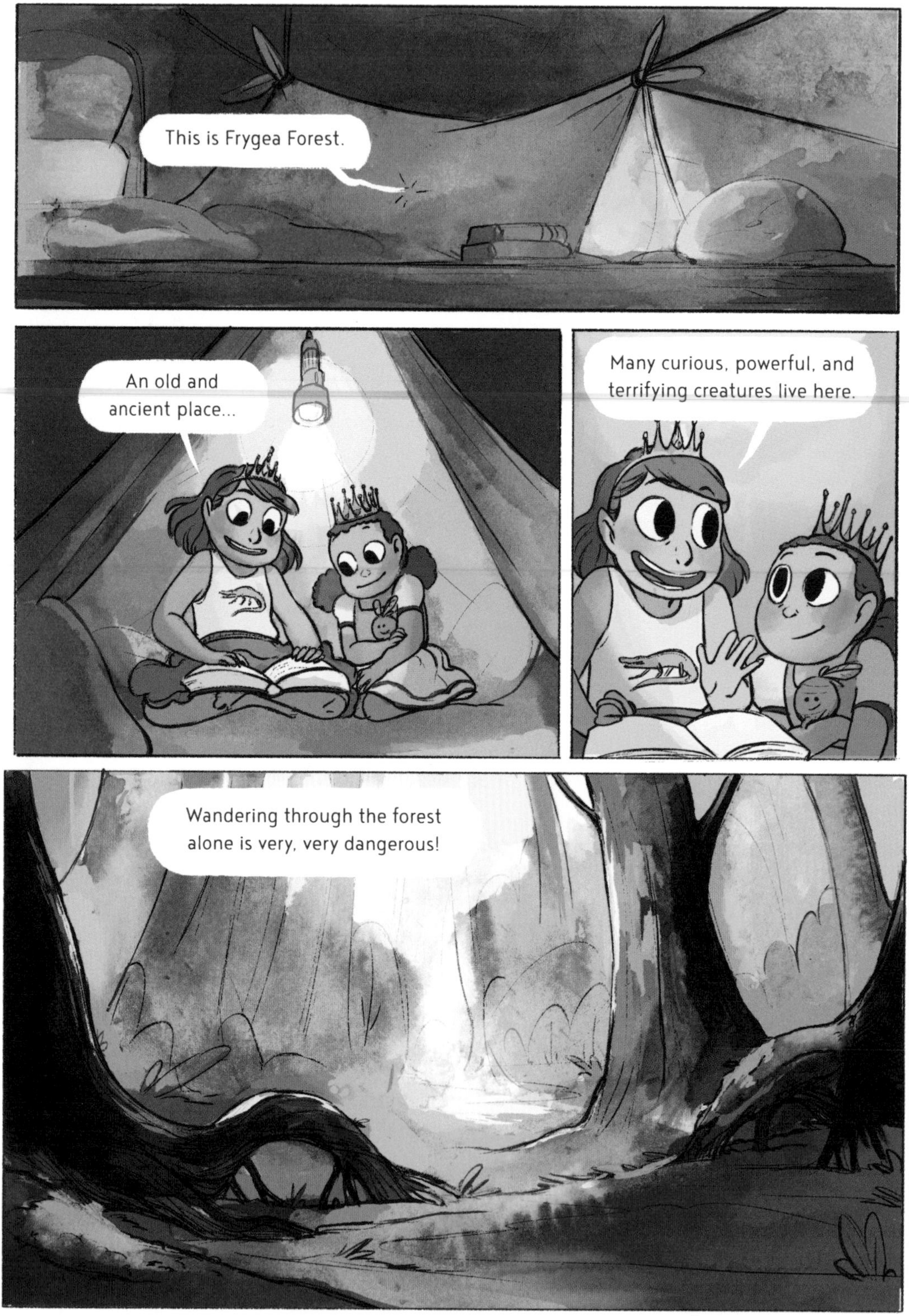

This is Frygea Forest.
An old and ancient place...
Many curious, powerful, and terrifying creatures live here.
Wandering through the forest alone is very, very dangerous!

You can get lost in the treacherous swamp.

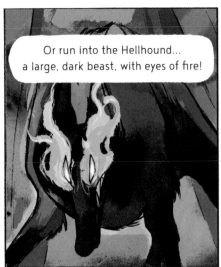

Or run into the Hellhound... a large, dark beast, with eyes of fire!

The Fog Furies are the most powerful creatures to inhabit this place.

They guide girls into the mist, transforming them into young women.

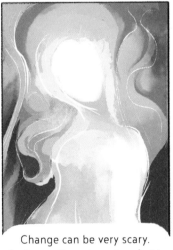

Change can be very scary. And even though you're afraid, sometimes...

... you have to let your biggest fears come true.

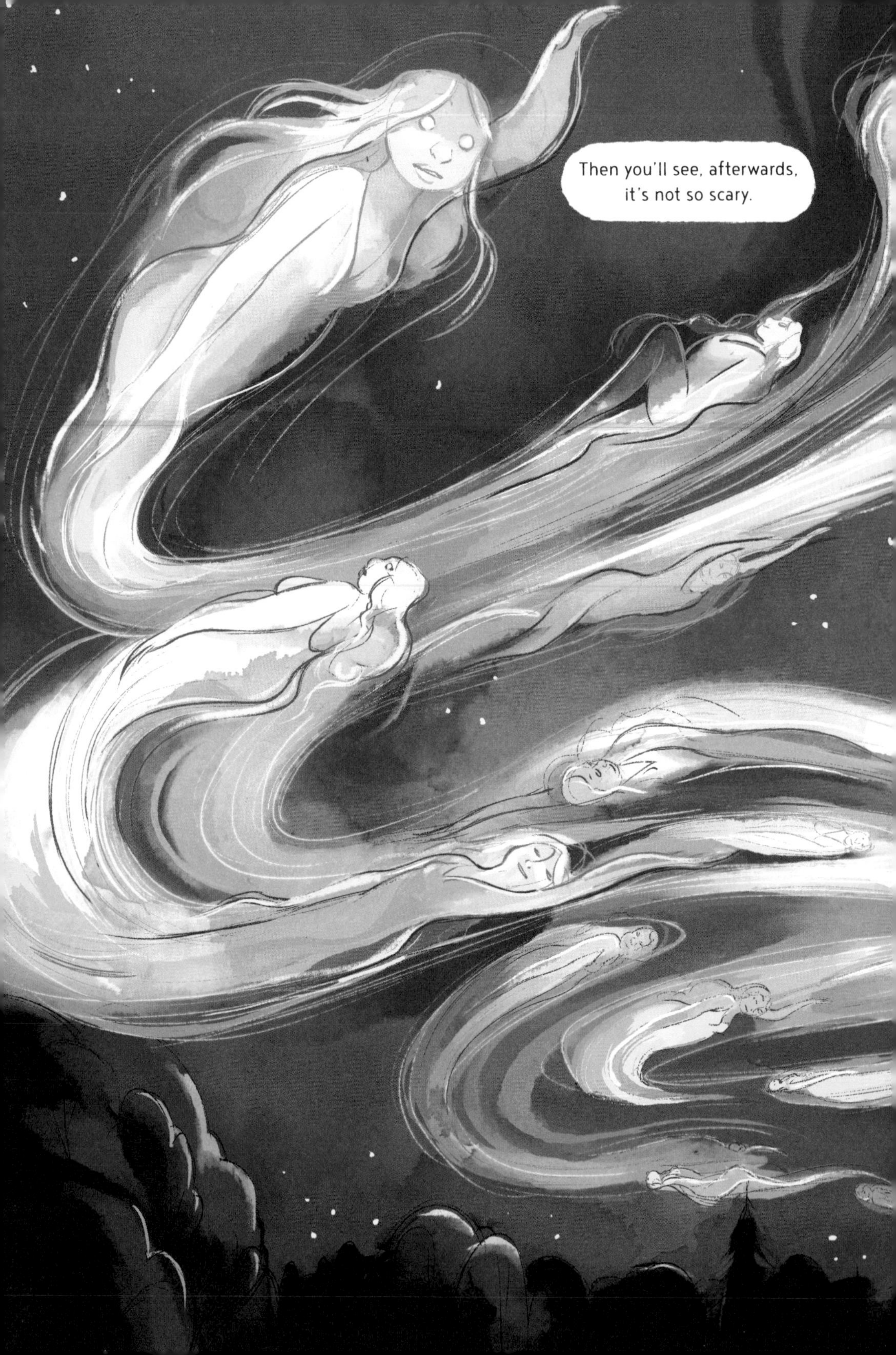
Then you'll see, afterwards, it's not so scary.

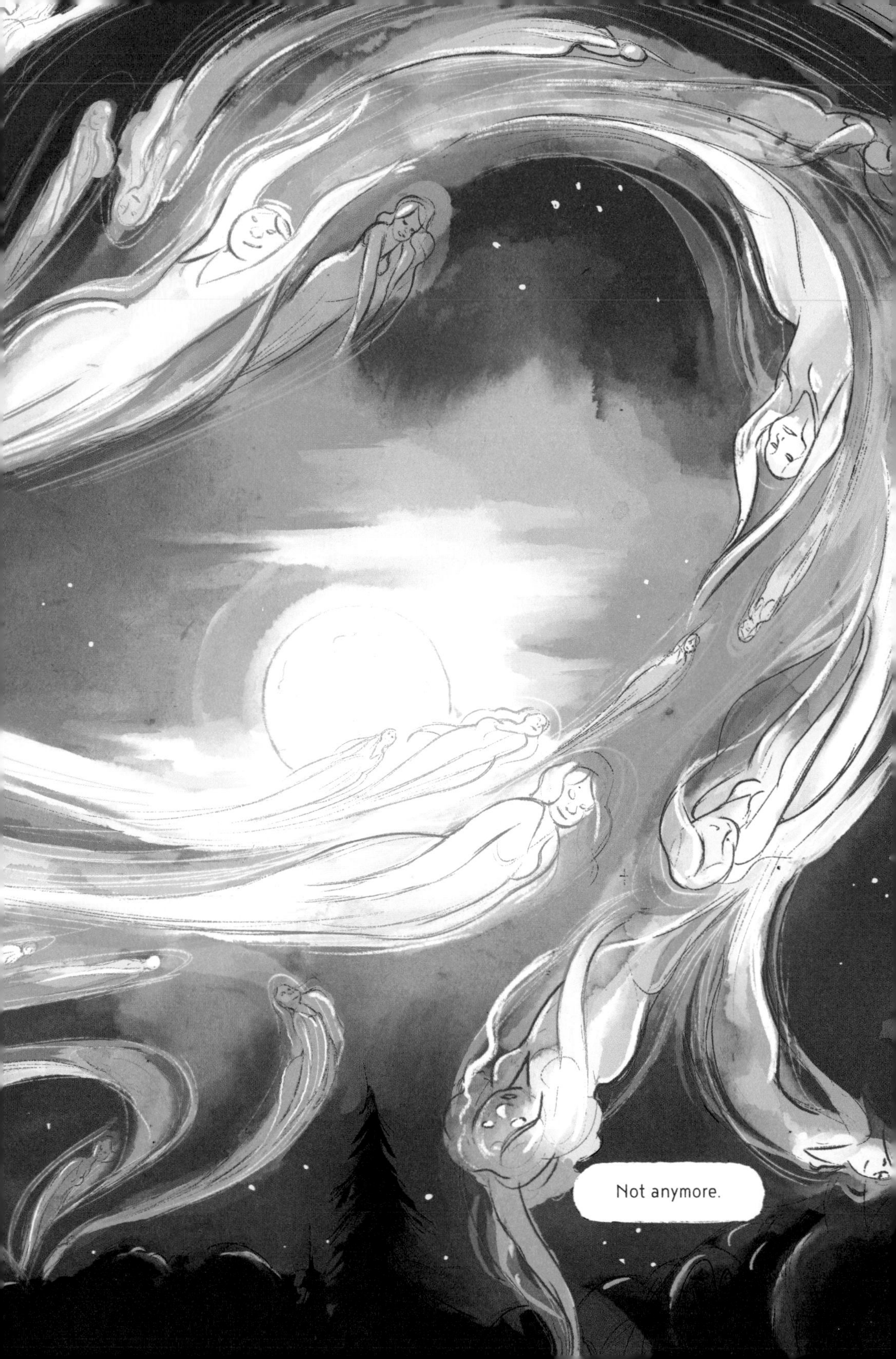
Not anymore.